D0977016

THE ALPINE VENGEANCE

THE
ALPINE
VENGEANCE

AN EMMA LORD MYSTERY

MARY DAHEIM

BALLANTINE BOOKS NEW YORK

The Alpine Vengeance is a work of fiction. Names, characters, places, and incidents are the products of the author's imagination or are used fictitiously. Any resemblance to actual events, locales, or persons, living or dead, is entirely coincidental.

Copyright © 2011 by Mary Daheim

Published in the United States by Ballantine Books, an imprint of The Random House Publishing Group, a division of Random House, Inc., New York.

BALLANTINE and colophon are registered trademarks of Random House, Inc.

Library of Congress Cataloging-in-Publication Data
Daheim, Mary.
The Alpine vengeance: an Emma Lord mystery/Mary Daheim.
p. cm.
ISBN 978-0-345-50257-5
eBook ISBN 978-0-345-51909-2
1. Lord, Emma (Fictitious character)—Fiction. 2. Women publishers—Fiction. 3. Washington (State)—Fiction. I. Title.
PS3554.A264A85 2011
813'.54—dc22
2010042095

Printed in the United States of America on acid-free paper

www.ballantinebooks.com

2 4 6 8 9 7 5 3 1

First Edition

To the real Dustin, who is not only a dear family friend but such a good photographer that Emma Lord would hire him if he could only move to Alpine.

AUTHOR'S NOTE

The narrative takes place in late November
and early December of 2004.

THE ALPINE VENGEANCE

ONE

Y TEENAGE DAUGHTER IS PREGNUNT BY A MARRED MAN who used to be my husband but isn't her father (far as I know) and she wants to keep the baby, but I got four other kids (besides her) so we'll be too crowded with only two bedrooms and one bathroom (outside) and the roof leeks'—that's L-E-E-K-S. 'I told my daughter to get a job and move out, but she don't feel good and can't work. I can't ether because my back hurts too bad and my boyfriend was layed off last week. My mama can't help out, because she's got the emfasima and my dad left town ten years ago with my second husband. What should I do? Oh—I need your recipe for how to pickel'—that's P-I-C-K-E-L—'a herring. Xmas is coming.' "

My House & Home editor whipped off her glasses and began rubbing her eyes until they squeaked. "Oooh! Why did I ever think it was a good idea to write an advice column? Why don't people have sense? Why didn't I do cooking hints instead?"

"You do that already with syndicated filler," I reminded Vida Runkel, tactfully omitting that she knew far more about human behavior than she did about cooking. "I think you've handled the first two weeks of letters very well. How about telling whoever this is that they should talk to their clergyman? If they have one."

Vida put her glasses back on and cradled her chin in her hands. "That's so pat, Emma."

"Do you know who it is?"

"It's signed, 'Stumpied,'" Vida replied, fingering the two sheets of lined notebook paper. "I don't know if she meant 'stumped' or 'stupid,' but the latter word is more apt." She studied the handwritten letter and the envelope. "The postmark is Alpine, but offhand, I'm not sure who wrote this." She scowled and tossed the missive onto her desk. "Almost everyone in town has indoor plumbing, so I assume it's someone in the county. It's aggravating not to know the sender. I usually do."

Vida wasn't bragging. As a native, she is the resident Source of All Things Alpine, including the rest of Skykomish County. Vida can practically count all the hairs on each head in our mountainous part of the world. Upon rare occasion, she doesn't recognize a newcomer or—God forbid—someone else who has slipped under her radar.

My ad manager, Leo Walsh, wasn't in, so I sat on the edge of his desk, which is next to Vida's. "What are you going to tell Ms. Pickled?" I asked, expecting a typical no-nonsense, no-holds-barred response.

But Vida looked uncomfortable, one hand fiddling with the big bow on her green-and-white-striped blouse. She didn't reply immediately, and when she did, the words came in a whisper: "Where's Amanda? I can't see her behind the desk in the reception area."

"She's probably in the back shop, delivering Kip's mail and the first batch of classifieds for this week's edition."

Vida nodded once. "After Amanda finally settled down, she's done a good job filling in for Ginny. I hate to see her go, but of course the post office needs her."

The mention of Amanda Hanson's temporary stint as our office manager touched upon the matter at hand. It also rubbed at a raw wound in Vida's heart. "Okay," I said quietly, in case Amanda suddenly reappeared, "I assume you're alluding .to a suggestion that Ms. Pickled Herring's grandchild should be put up for adoption?"

"Yes." Vida straightened her wide shoulders. "This nitwit who wrote the letter doesn't mention how far along her daughter is. If Amanda and Walt's plan to take in Holly Gross's children drags on through all the red tape involved with a mother who is in prison, it might be better for the Hansons to step in and pay for this silly teenager's medical care."

"Good point," I agreed, but was loath to say more since the youngest of Holly's three kids had been fathered by Vida's grandson Roger. In the past six weeks since their drug-dealing mother had been arrested for shooting her partner in crime, any discussion of the baby's fate was off-limits. But a day never went by that I didn't want to ask Vida if her daughter Amy and son-in-law Ted had made any decisions regarding their grandson. I didn't dare, for fear of embarrassing Vida any further. While my House & Home editor might divulge the most intimate secrets of anyone within her purview, Vida's own problems were tucked securely under her innumerable and often outlandish hats. "One of us could talk to Amanda. I know she and Walt are getting frustrated."

"I'll do it," Vida volunteered. "We don't have much time in terms of publishing this letter in my column for Wednesday's edition."

"Right," I said, glancing at Leo's desk calendar. It was

Monday, November 29. Thanksgiving was past, Christmas was less than a month away, and we'd had a few snow flurries at Alpine's almost three-thousand-foot level. I scooted off the desk as our sole reporter, Mitch Laskey, entered the office.

"You should've warned me," Mitch said, though I wasn't sure if he was addressing Vida or me—or both. "Never interview Fuzzy Baugh on a Monday morning. He kept dozing off in his mayoral chair."

"Fuzzy is no spring chicken," Vida declared. "He dozes off frequently, including at city council meetings. Surely you heard he literally put himself to sleep yesterday morning when he gave witness at the Baptist church."

Mitch grinned. "Is that why he has a bandage on his forehead?"

"Yes," Vida said in disapproval. "He hit his head on the pulpit. I haven't figured out if it's a two-inch news story or an item for my 'Scene Around Town' column. It's time for Fuzzy to retire."

"Hunh," Mitch said, settling his lanky frame behind his desk across from Leo's. "I thought he was elected for life."

"It's an item for 'Scene,'" I said, in one of my gentle reminders that I was *The Alpine Advocate*'s editor and publisher. Vida wasn't the only one who needed an occasional refresher course in the paper's pecking order. Her tenure went back some forty years, and many an Alpiner assumed she *was* the *Advocate*.

"Perhaps so," she allowed. "I need four more items. Put on your thinking caps, please."

As often happens, my grasp on power shifted once again. Smiling wryly, I headed for the cubbyhole that was my office. The phone rang just as I sat down.

"Emma?" a wan voice said at the other end.

"Yes, Ginny?"

"I've been thinking," my longtime office manager said, "and

after talking it over with Rick, I don't think I should come back to work so soon. I mean, I know my maternity leave ends as of Friday, and Amanda is supposed to fill in at the post office for the holiday rush, but with the new baby and Christmas and everything else, I'm way too tired. After New Year's, I should feel stronger. Is that okay?"

I told myself I should've seen this coming. Ginny had stopped in at the office only a couple of times since the Erlandsons had their third son in October. Looking back, I realized I hadn't seen her since we'd run into each other at the Grocery Basket the first week of November.

"Amanda plans to quit tomorrow," I said. "The post office needs her starting December first. In fact, they need her now. We figured we could cope on our own for three days, but it's a little late in the game to find somebody to fill in for the whole month of December."

"Oh—you're mad at me," Ginny said in that glum, put-upon voice I knew so well. "I don't blame you, but I'm really tapped. You've no idea what it's like to cope with three boys when you're not feeling good. Rick's great, but now that he's the bank manager, he can't take over as much, especially this time of year."

Although I'd had only one boy, his father had been absent for the first couple of decades, and I'd managed to soldier on. There was, however, the daunting prospect of insisting that Ginny come back to work ASAP, and then having her bitch, pout, and sulk all the way through December. Even during the other eleven months of the year, *merry* was not a word I'd think of in connection with our efficient but often cheerless office manager.

I tossed the ball back to her. "Who would you suggest as a replacement?"

"I've already thought about it," Ginny said, sounding almost cheerful—or at least not morose. "Denise Petersen. I mean, Denise *Jensen*. She kept her married name after the divorce."

"I thought she'd gone back to work at the bank," I said.

"She did," Ginny replied, "but she never liked her teller's job, and because her grandfather owns the Bank of Alpine, she felt she had to work there. Denise isn't all that great with numbers and she can't stand on her feet all day. She has really bad arches. She only went back because she needs the money after splitting up with Greg."

I held my head with the hand that wasn't holding the phone. "I don't want to sound unsympathetic, Ginny, but you should've given me more notice. You're putting us in a real bind."

There was a pause before she spoke again. "I thought you always told me family came first. Was I so wrong?"

"That's not fair," I said, wondering why I felt defensive. "Look," I said, seeing Sheriff Milo Dodge lope into the newsroom, "please give this a little more thought. Maybe we can work out something part-time."

"Ohhh . . . that's complicated." Ginny sounded as if the concept overwhelmed her. "Before, it was all I could do to get Rick's sister to take the kids full-time at the day care. I don't think Donna would go for anything else. She's already giving us a family discount."

"At least," I said, watching Milo loom over Vida's desk, "think about it overnight. As for Denise, I honestly don't know how she'd fit in. I hate to sound uncharitable, but she's never struck me as . . ." I paused, noting that Mitch had joined Vida and the sheriff. "Sorry. I got distracted. Does Rick really think Denise could handle your job? He's worked closely with her," I went on, realizing that Milo's usually laconic demeanor seemed to have succumbed to aggravation. "If Rick has any doubts, maybe he can suggest someone else."

"If he had," Ginny huffed, "he'd have mentioned it. Denise has matured in the past few years. She's been through a lot. Greg hung out most of the time with his buddies and their stupid band. He was totally selfish about . . ."

Leo Walsh had entered the newsroom, greeting the sheriff with an amiable "Good morning." Milo turned abruptly and glared at Leo. My ad manager stopped midway between the door and Vida's desk. "Guess it's not so good," I heard Leo say.

I hadn't, however, heard what Ginny was saying about Denise or Greg or anyone else. In fact, I cut her off. "I've got to go, Ginny. There's a crisis brewing. It's Monday—as you may recall, the day before deadline. Talk to you later." I hung up and hurried into the newsroom.

"Whoa!" I shouted, interrupting whatever Milo was saying to the rest of my staff. "What's up with you?"

The sheriff towered over me by more than his usual thirteen-inch advantage—not including his regulation trooper's hat. His chilly hazel eyes veered in Vida's direction before he answered the question. "I don't want to hear about anybody else's problems with letters. I've got my own, goddamnit, and I'm not in the mood for bullshit."

"I can see that," I said with a straight face. "Do you want to grab a cup of coffee and tell me about it, or would you rather stand here and implode?"

Milo looked in the direction of the coffeemaker and the pastry tray. "Are those the cinnamon rolls with pecans?"

Leo, who had made the morning run to the Upper Crust Bakery, made a little bow. "Half with, half without. Better hurry. Mitch already ate two of them."

Mitch chuckled. "I thought I put my name on all six."

"You could scarf those down and it'd never show," Leo said. "What's your secret, Laskey?"

"Born skinny," Mitch replied, waiting for the sheriff to make a move on our goodies stash. "Just plain dumb luck."

"Luck's luck," Leo said, pressing a hand against his slight paunch. "Too wide, too short. Bad combination."

The sheriff ignored the banter, but he went to the table, grabbed a pecan roll, and poured himself a mug of coffee. I returned to my office. "What now?" I asked as Milo settled into one of my two visitors' chairs.

"Here." He reached inside his jacket and took out three letter-sized envelopes. "See for yourself. Don't worry about fingerprints. There are too damned many to ID any one person."

The three white envelopes were all addressed by hand to Milo at his office. The postmarks were from Alpine, dated November 22, 23, and 26. There was no return address. The stamps were from the U.S. Postal Service's Cloudscape series. "Interesting," I murmured, carefully taking out the first single sheet of paper.

"What?" Milo asked impatiently.

"Most people use the plain stamps. Adam used to collect . . ." I stopped. The plain white sheet of paper had a brief printed message that had been applied with Scotch tape: "HISTORY RE-PEATS ITSELF. DIDN'T YOU LEARN FROM YOUR LAST MISTAKE?"

Milo had lighted a cigarette. "Well?"

"That's cryptic," I said. "What mistake?"

"Who knows?" He shrugged. "Where's the damned ashtray?"

"Oh." I opened the drawer where I kept the ashtray for smokers like Milo and Leo. "Here."

The sheriff put the cigarette down and took a big bite from his pecan roll. I read the second message, also typed and affixed to the page with Scotch tape. "WELL? HAVE I GOT YOUR ATTEN-TION?"

I grimaced. "This is weird, but it doesn't say much."

Milo wiped a crumb off his long chin. "Keep going."

The third message jolted me. "LARRY PETERSEN IS INNOCENT. SHOULDN'T YOU BE LOOKING FOR LINDA'S KILLER?"

I stared at the sheriff. "This is about the murder of Linda Petersen Lindahl ten years ago?"

"That what it says." Milo looked grim. "What makes it really weird is that Sam Heppner got an FYI call this morning from the state penitentiary in Walla Walla. Larry died of a heart attack Saturday around seven A.M."

I was stunned. "Are you sure the information was genuine?"

"Oh, yeah. I called the warden to confirm Larry's death."

"Does the family know?"

"What family?" Milo looked disgusted. "Larry's wife, JoAnne, moved away after he got arrested for killing his sister, Linda. Marv and Cathleen Petersen retired to Arizona, and the last I heard from Aunt Thelma, Marv had Alzheimer's."

I'd almost forgotten the family connection between the sheriff and the Petersens. Milo's aunt had married Elmer Petersen. Unlike his older brother, Marv, Elmer hadn't followed their late father and Bank of Alpine founder into the business. Instead, Elmer and Thelma had owned a modest farm until they sold the property and moved into the local retirement home.

"But," I said, "you must've talked to your aunt and uncle about Larry. Weren't there a couple of other Petersen aunts who moved away?"

"I haven't told Uncle Elmer and Aunt Thelma about Larry," Milo replied, relighting his cigarette, which had gone out while he was eating his roll. "I don't know if Elmer and Marv's sisters are still alive. They broke off whatever connection they had with the rest of the Petersens after Linda was murdered." Milo took a drag on his cigarette. "All I had time to do this morning was verify Larry's death. Now I'm wondering who the hell is sending this crap—and why." He took the letters from me. "You know what's going to happen next."

"I do?"

Milo regarded me as if I were the dimmest suspect in a police lineup. "Legal problems. Threats. Dealing with a nut-job. I don't need more grief right now. Hell, it's only been a little over a month since the shootout at the trailer park."

"It's a crackpot," I said. "Larry never denied killing Linda. I'll admit I didn't attend the entire trial, but that was because the defense wanted a change of venue and the case was tried in Everett."

"I know, I know." He waved away the plume of smoke from his cigarette. "I got so damned tired of having to be there that I spent two nights in a motel. The commute was killing me."

"And Larry tried to kill *me*," I reminded the sheriff. "Thank God you came along or I wouldn't be here listening to you bitch about some stupid letters."

Milo was silent for a long moment. "Did you ever wonder if Larry wanted to tell you something instead of turning you into his next victim?"

I thought back to what had been one of the most frightening moments in my life. "To be honest, no. In fact, that's how the whole situation began. It was snowing that night. I was in front of the bank, waiting for Vida and Rick to come out after we inveigled him into letting her inside. Larry drove up and realized something odd was happening. He did say he wanted to talk to me, but I was suspicious of him by then, so I suggested we go over to the *Advocate*. Then everything went downhill. He got very agitated and dragged me inside the car. You know the rest."

Milo sighed. "What if Larry did just want to talk?"

It was my turn to pause before speaking again, trying to force myself back in time to my emotional, as well as intellectual, reactions. "I was on guard from the get-go. I sensed his desperation. It scared the hell out of me. I already figured him for the killer. So did you."

The sheriff nodded. "Everything fit. If it hadn't, I'd never have made the arrest."

"Of course you wouldn't." I smiled softly. "That's the way you always work."

"Right." He shook his head, obviously unhappy. "It's a hell of a way to spend a Monday morning. The first two letters were so vague that I almost chucked them. The timing bothers me, now that Larry's dead."

"The letters were sent before Larry died," I pointed out.

"I know. But still . . ." He shrugged. "Coincidences happen."

I waited while he finished the roll before I posed a question. "Are you here because you want us to run a story about these letters?"

The sheriff stuffed the letters inside his jacket. "God, no!" He frowned, his eyes fixed on my wall map of Skykomish County. "Maybe I just wanted to blow off steam. It must be a crank. The woods are full of them. All this Internet stuff—somebody reads something that sets them off, and even if it has nothing to do with them, they get their rocks off by jumping into whatever. It's just one step away from the crazies who confess to a murder they didn't commit or claim to have information about a terrorist plot to blow up Grand Coulee Dam."

"Exactly," I said. "Go solve some real cases. If you have any." I looked inquiringly at Milo. "Do you? I haven't talked to Mitch about the police log from the weekend."

The sheriff put out his cigarette and stood up. "Mitch hasn't been in yet. Nothing much to report anyway, just the usual DUIs, traffic violations, and a couple of non-injury vehicular accidents on Highway 2."

I also stood up. "No break-ins? No domestic violence? No lost livestock?"

Milo shook his head. "Funny thing about the weekend after Thanksgiving. We never do get much real crime. I guess everybody's too stuffed and sleepy from eating big Thanksgiving dinners."

"That could be a story in itself," I said.

Milo looked amused. "You must be desperate for headlines."

"I am, actually," I admitted. "But we've had enough excitement around here already this year, and much of it hasn't been pleasant. I'd prefer a quiet holiday season."

"Me too." Milo awkwardly patted my shoulder. "I feel better. Maybe I'll concentrate on winter steelheading."

"Good plan," I said. "Don't ask for trouble."

"I won't." He ambled into the newsroom, pausing just long enough to exchange a few words with Leo, Mitch, and Vida. *Peacemaking,* I thought. *Nice. Especially with Christmas around the corner.*

As I turned to go behind my desk and sit down, I bumped into the drawer I'd left open. I banged my knee, winced, and swore under my breath. It occurred to me that there was a problem with corners, even the ones on desks.

You can't see what's around them.

TWO

As soon as Milo left, Vida charged into my office. "What was that all about?" she demanded, leaning on my desk. "I merely mentioned that the letters I receive asking for advice are a perfect example of how foolishly people can behave—even in Alpine—and suddenly he went off on a tangent."

"He's gotten some weird letters lately," I explained, emptying the ashtray. "I think he's in a bad mood because his ex forced him to spend Thanksgiving with her and their kids to prove they could behave like a real family when their daughter gets married. Milo's not too thrilled with Tanya's choice, but he's never liked any of the guys she's dated. He didn't go into mourning a couple of years ago when Tanya broke up with that live-in sculptor after her miscarriage."

Vida avoided my gaze. Her own family gathering had been tarnished by Roger's illegal and immoral behavior. "Yes, I understand. Awkward, sometimes."

Ordinarily, Vida would've changed the subject immediately, but her reticence amplified her shame and guilt for having spoiled Roger the past twenty-odd years. Thus, I reverted to the sheriff's problems. "Did you know Larry Petersen died over the weekend?"

Vida looked stunned. "No! How can that be?"

"Presumably a heart attack in the penitentiary at Walla Walla."

"My goodness," she murmured. "Larry couldn't have been more than early fifties. Has Milo talked to Elmer and Thelma?"

"Not yet," I replied. "Do you know where Larry's ex-wife lives?"

"In Seattle, but I don't have her address. I can find out, though," Vida said, her aplomb returning. "In fact, Rick Erlandson should know. He would've been involved in changing JoAnne's accounts after Larry was sent to prison. Besides Denise, there were two boys who were away at college when the tragedy occurred." She drummed her fingers on the back of the visitor's chair. "Frankie's the eldest and Cole's the youngest, with Denise in the middle. The boys must be in their late twenties or even early thirties. As for Marv and Cathleen, I doubt they have enough brains left to take this in. If it hadn't been for Andy Cederberg taking over at the bank, the rest of the Petersens might've sold out. I've always said moving to Arizona is a bad idea. So much sun! It must wither the brain cells."

The concept of any Alpiner moving away always baffled Vida. Why move to Hell when you could live in Heaven? "Marv had two sisters," I said. "Have you heard from them since the disaster?"

Vida straightened up and squared her wide shoulders. "Certainly not. Offhand, I don't recall the sisters' married names, but they were at Linda Petersen's funeral. Or should I say Linda Lindahl? She never changed her name back after divorcing Howard. I can call Driggers Funeral Home. There was a guest book. I wonder who has it?" She didn't wait for an answer.

"Marv, probably. He grieved deeply for his daughter. To realize that Linda was killed by her brother because Larry's dream of running the bank had been dashed would be enough to make any parent want to blot out reality. Alzheimer's, indeed! Every disease and condition has a ridiculous name these days for something that's been around since time began. In my opinion, Alzheimer's is a cliché diagnosis for shutting out the past, refusing to recognize the present, and fending off the future. I can't blame Marv for any of that."

Once again, I wondered if Vida was thinking of herself—and Roger. "Milo should know how a prison death is handled," I said. "Next of kin would be notified. Larry's kids, I suppose." I suddenly remembered Denise. "Oh, my God! Ginny was just talking to me about Denise Petersen Jensen. I wonder if she—Denise, I mean—knows."

"Ginny?" Vida scowled. "Why was she talking about Denise?"

A quick check of my watch told me it was going on ten. The morning was passing too quickly. I still hadn't written my editorial. In fact, I hadn't even decided on a topic. "Ginny's waffling about coming back to work. She wants to wait until after New Year's, and she suggested Denise as a fill-in."

"Oh, for goodness sakes!" Vida stopped just short of removing her glasses and attacking her eyes again. "Denise is a nitwit! And whatever is wrong with Ginny? I thought she had more gumption than to act as if she'd been paralyzed in a car accident instead of merely having a baby. If you tell me she's pleading postpartum whatever it's called, I'll lose all respect for her. Such nonsense! What's wrong with young women these days? That's what I've said all along about equality between the sexes. Why on earth did women ever want to lower themselves to the level of men? Ginny's a perfect example, what my dear mother would've called a 'weak sister.' She was, of course, referring to *men* who behaved like weak sisters."

I'd heard similar rants many times from Vida, and given the tales she'd told about the early female residents of Alpine, most of them could've given Paul Bunyan a run for his money. Or his ox or axe or . . .

But Vida wasn't finished. "Even Buck, who I must confess is sometimes rather old-fashioned in his views, thinks that women make excellent fighter pilots. He calls it their 'mother lioness nature,' in this case defending their country instead of their cubs."

Buck Bardeen was a retired air force colonel who had been Vida's longtime companion. His brother, Henry, managed the ski lodge, and although I didn't know Buck well, he was obviously a man who could put up with Vida while accepting whatever limits—physical and emotional—she might set. "Understandable," I agreed. "Most women can—"

I was interrupted by Mitch Laskey, who was standing in the doorway. "I'm off to interview the new prof at the college," he said. "I'll check the police log on my way back, okay?"

I nodded. "Sure. Good luck. He's science, right?"

Mitch, who is in his fifties and a veteran of the *Detroit Free Press,* grinned at me. "Whatever he teaches will have to be translated. Science is not my specialty. Give me race riots, drug busts, crooks in high places, and a UAW strike with blood on the picket line any day." With a casual wave, he headed back through the newsroom.

"Detroit," Vida murmured. "It's a wonder Mitch and his wife got out alive."

"They lived in Royal Oak, a suburb," I reminded Vida.

"It's still Detroit."

I didn't argue. The Laskeys had moved to Alpine because their son was serving a five-year term in the Monroe Correctional Complex for dealing drugs. Mitch and Brenda had thought he'd moved out west to find himself. Instead, he'd found a market and a supplier for doing business as usual. Troy Laskey might as well have stayed in Michigan.

Vida had gotten to her feet. "I'll call Al Driggers. As funeral director, he should know if Denise or her grandparents have been notified of Larry's death."

"Okay." I slumped in my chair as Vida walked out in her splay-footed manner. I was still pondering my various problems a few minutes later when Leo came into my office.

"You look like the last rose of summer," he remarked, sitting down in the chair Milo had vacated. "A pretty rose, but fading fast."

"Thanks," I said dryly. "If you've got a dilemma, can you keep it to yourself until noon?"

Leo chuckled. "I'm still sorting out my Thanksgiving interlude with Liza and the kids. It seemed almost like old times. Except," he added wistfully, "it wasn't."

Leo had finally been invited back into the family fold after ten years of divorce from his wife and estrangement from his children. "They must've been glad to see you sober and gainfully employed," I said.

"If that hadn't been the case, Liza would never have let me in the door." Leo's weathered face was like a map of the roads he'd traveled in the past twenty years or more. "It was tough at first for all of us, but what broke the ice was when the turkey caught fire. There's nothing like a threat to life, limb, and a paid-off mortgage to bring people together. I didn't even need to remind Liza that I was the one who made the last payment on the house in Santa Maria, the BBQ capital of the world. We must've violated a city ordinance by roasting the damned bird instead of firing up the grill. Which," Leo went on before I could do more than laugh, "brings up an idea I have for our advertisers. Why can't Alpiners call themselves the something-or-other capital of the world and make some money off of it?"

"My God," I said in mock horror, "have you turned into Ed Bronsky?"

Leo leaned his head back and stared at the low dappled ceiling panels that were beginning to show wear and tear after four years. As the print media increasingly became an endangered species, I wondered if the *Advocate* or my office would be the first to collapse. "We'll do okay during the Christmas season, but come January, we're always a little thin. I'm scheduled to be the chamber of commerce speaker right after the first of the year. I thought I might stir up the merchants by suggesting we find something unique about Alpine as a promotional theme. 'World Capital of Vida Runkel' would be fitting, but I'm not sure it'd sell ads or goods beyond SkyCo."

I grinned at Leo. "For a moment, I thought you might've been channeling your predecessor." Ed's ideas—on the rare occasions that he had them—were always borderline absurd. I sucked in my breath. "Speak of the devil," I murmured. "Here comes Ed."

Ed, however, had stopped by Vida's desk. Leo turned discreetly to look into the newsroom. "He's sitting down. That's not a good sign."

"Better Vida than me," I said. "Or you."

"True." I leaned to one side, trying to see what Ed was doing. Talking, of course, and gesturing with his pudgy hands. He obstructed my view of Vida—no surprise, since Ed was wide enough to block out a hippopotamus.

Leo and I looked helplessly at each other. "Should I rescue the Duchess?" he whispered, using his nickname for Vida that she claimed to despise.

"She may've already passed out from listening to him." But before I could say anything else, I heard her voice.

"That's a fine idea, Ed," she said in a calm manner. "Why shouldn't you run for county commissioner? The trio we have now are all senile. And you aren't deaf."

Leo shot me an incredulous look. "Didn't we just hold an election?" he murmured.

I nodded. The only commissioner who'd been up for re-election in early November was Alfred Cobb. He won because his opponent, Arnold Qvale, dropped dead on Halloween. There hadn't been time to remove Arnold's name from the ballot. Even though his opponent was deceased, Alfred had won by only a slim margin. Frankly, it had been hard to tell the difference between the two candidates. "You've heard talk about a special election in March, right? Alfred can barely sit up at the meetings, let alone participate."

Leo sighed. "As I recall, Ed was going to run for office a couple of years ago, but didn't make the filing date." He stopped, seeing my signal to shut up. Ed was chugging toward us.

"Hey, hey, hey!" Ed exclaimed, greeting Leo with a loud slap on the shoulder. "Bronsky's back and SkyCo's got him!"

"I'll be damned," Leo said, wincing. "What's up, Ed?"

My former ad manager pulled out the other visitor's chair and wedged himself between the armrests. "I've got it on good authority that Alfred Cobb's stepping down from the county troika. He's announcing it at the commissioners' meeting tomorrow night. You better tell Kip to stop those presses, Emma."

"We always hold a space open for their meetings since they changed the night to a Tuesday," I said blandly. "It's a nuisance, especially when the meetings drag and drone on for so long."

The chair creaked under Ed as he leaned forward, fists on my desk. "You got it! That's why I'm running. This county is stuck in the mud. You wouldn't believe the plans I've got to perk things up!"

"I'll bet I wouldn't," I said, trying to keep a straight face. "Will you be speaking at the meeting tomorrow night?"

Ed made a face. "I'm not sure. It depends on what happens. If Alf—I've always called him that, even when I was a working stiff—if he announces he's stepping down due to ill health, I might. You know—to show that I'm ready for action and rarin' to go."

Leo, who had shot Ed a sharp glance, scooted his chair a few inches from his predecessor and stood up. "Excuse me," he said, "but this working stiff has to work." He winked at me. "Later, Emma. Don't forget, we're going seventy/thirty this week."

"I can't forget that," I said with a grin for Leo. "Nicely done."

Ed's eyes widened. "Seventy/thirty? That's . . . good." He settled back in his chair. "It's holiday season, of course. That always pushes the ad ratio up. Way back before you took over, I usually ran about seventy-five/twenty-five or better. Marius Vandeventer used to give me a bad time because he didn't have enough room for news or photos. He was kidding, of course." Ed chuckled.

As far I was concerned, Ed was kidding, too. If he'd even gotten us a sixty percent amount of advertising on a regular basis, I wouldn't have had to scrimp and scrounge for revenue while he remained on the staff. "So, are you settled into your new house?" I asked, deciding to change the subject lest I say something rash.

Ed nodded, chins jiggling. "We got in for Thanksgiving. Really nice, cozy, too. That double-wide was cramped. And of course I quit the restaurant business. But you knew that—Vida put it in 'Scene.' "

Ed, who had squandered his sizable inheritance on the so-called villa he'd built above the golf course, had not only been forced to sell Casa de Bronska to developers, but had become so mired in debt that the family had to move to a mobile home. To keep the wolf from the door, he'd gone to work at the Burger Barn. I'd actually felt sorry for him. But the final payment from the house sale had come through in the past month, enabling the Bronsky brood to buy a small home near the fish hatchery. His wife, Shirley, had renewed her teaching certificate and was substituting for the Alpine school district.

"I understand ReHaven will open its doors not long after the first of the year," I said, noting that Vida had put on her new plum-colored winter coat and an almost-matching pillbox hat with swatches of long bright feathers.

Ed didn't look pleased at the mention of ReHaven. "I hate to think of all those drunks and druggies trashing our villa, but I suppose it's for the best." He grunted as he stood up. "Better get going. Don't forget—big news tomorrow night. Will Lashley be there?"

"It's Laskey," I told Ed for at least the third time. "Yes."

"Good." He stumbled a bit, apparently over his own feet. "Oof. New shoes. I need to break them in."

"Do that. Bye, Ed." I'd remained seated. Vida had already left the office. Ed took a detour, and though he was briefly out of sight, I knew he was probably stuffing his pockets with Upper Crust pastries.

Maybe Ed had inadvertently given me an idea for my editorial. Alfred Cobb, and his fellow county commissioners, George Engebretsen and Leonard Hollenberg, weren't the only public officials who'd outlived their usefulness, if not their ability to pork-barrel. The U.S. Senate and House had several members who couldn't function much more effectively than an oven mitt.

I'd also heard firsthand tales about certain Supreme Court justices who had trouble remaining conscious while hearing arguments on vital national issues. Then there was the judiciary on the state and local level, not to mention Mayor Fuzzy Baugh . . .

My mind wandered in and around these possibilities until I, too, began to feel drowsy. I might've nodded off if the phone hadn't rung to jolt me out of my lethargy.

"My computer died," my brother Ben announced. "I can't e-mail, so I'm calling to see if you survived Thanksgiving all by yourself."

"I had a wonderful time," I said with unbridled sarcasm. "It was such fun to *not* have my brother and my son with me as planned."

"Hey—we're priests. We have a higher calling. Besides, the Pilgrims were Protestants. Don't tell me that in your basic Scandinavian community you didn't celebrate Martin Luther's birthday on November tenth."

"We only do Martin Luther King's," I retorted. "Now that I think about it, he wasn't a Lutheran or a Scandinavian."

"You always were a little slow," Ben said with that familiar crackle of humor in his voice. "Seriously, were you too miserable?"

"Well . . ." I thought back to the previous Thursday, with the promise of sun in the morning, followed by heavy clouds, a brisk wind off the mountains, and stinging sleet before sunset. "Let's say it wasn't exactly festive. Even Father Den had taken off for the long weekend. It's not a holy day of obligation, so I didn't drag my lonely body to the communion service."

"Jeez," Ben said, though I couldn't tell if he was dismayed or mocking. "You really are a mess."

"I *was,* past tense. I've recovered. It just happened to be the first time that everybody around here had somewhere else to go for Thanksgiving and I didn't have you and Adam to keep me company. I'm over it, okay?"

"Okay." Ben paused. "It's possible that you may be seeing much more of me in the coming year."

The sudden heaviness in my brother's voice alarmed me. "Why?"

"Father Jim—the priest I'm filling in for—is giving up his religious vocation. He's fallen in love with a widow and they're getting married in June. I hope and pray he's doing the right thing, but meanwhile I'm stuck here in Cleveland until a replacement can be found. When that happens, I'm taking my long overdue six-month sabbatical to sit on my ass, drink beer, and watch sports on TV."

"Oh! You scared me. I thought you were the one in crisis."

Ben laughed. "Hell, no. I picked the right vocation. If I'd gotten married, I'd probably have about four ex-wives by now. You and I were never intended for domestic bliss."

I bristled at the remark. "I would've done just fine if I'd finally married Tom instead of having him buried."

"Death has a way of spoiling fairy tales," Ben said flatly.

"That's harsh," I snapped. "What are you going to say next—that it was all part of God's plan that I should stay single?"

"You know me better than that," my brother said with a touch of asperity. "Ever hear of free will? It's a basic Catholic concept. Hey—got to go. Lunch date with a couple of guys from the chancery to figure out all this mess. Maybe they'll ask me to give a wedding shower for the happy couple. Stay loose, Sluggly."

"Yeah. Right . . . Stench." I couldn't resist tossing back my childhood nickname for Ben. "Sluggly" was about as annoying to me as "Duchess" was to Vida.

My production manager, Kip MacDuff, swung into my office. "Any clue about page one?" he asked. "Mitch promised photos of merchants at the mall stringing up lights over the weekend. You got them?"

"Not yet," I said. "The Laskeys spent the weekend in Seattle."

Kip rubbed his neatly trimmed beard. "You mean Mitch didn't follow through? That's not like him."

"He probably took the pictures before leaving town," I said. "They spent Thanksgiving with their son in Monroe and then went on to Seattle. I'll ask him when he finishes his morning rounds."

"What's our lead?"

"I don't know," I admitted. "Milo found out this morning that Larry Petersen died over the weekend, but that's not a banner headline. Page one, below the fold, four or five inches, head shot—discreet, dignified."

Kip looked stunned. "Larry died in the slammer? Was he killed by another inmate?"

"It was a heart attack, according to the sheriff."

"Jesus!" Kip shook his head. "Larry was fairly young. All those Petersens seem to live forever." He grimaced. "I mean, unless they . . ."

"Kill each other?" I suggested.

Kip winced. "Yeah—I guess. But what I'm trying to say is . . . well, if you get stabbed or beaten to death, your heart stops, right? How can we be sure it was a real heart attack? Wouldn't the prison authorities just as soon cover up that kind of thing? You know—politics."

The thought had never crossed my mind. Or, apparently, anyone else's at the sheriff's office. "Milo talked to the warden. I suppose the guy could've lied, but if so, there's a much bigger story that goes far beyond Alpine. I wouldn't think one law enforcement official would do that to another. He'd be more likely to tell the truth, but ask for discretion."

Kip's expression was wry. "The Good-Old-Boy Cop Network? Dodge wouldn't cooperate."

"No, he wouldn't," I agreed. "Milo doesn't play games. The warden must be on the level. I can't see Larry in a prison fight. He had no history of violence until he strangled his sister." I realized I was thinking out loud. "He was driven to that by his father bypassing him for Linda to eventually become bank president. Larry always thought he was Marv's heir apparent, but his father and his sister betrayed him. That's a crime of passion."

"Family tradition," Kip murmured. "That's how it was with Marv taking over from his dad."

I nodded. "Larry had been in prison for ten years. I've no idea if JoAnne or his kids ever visited him. Or even his parents. I assume he was filled with remorse. That can drastically alter a person's physical and mental state."

Kip, who'd remained standing, leaned against my filing cabinet and looked unusually serious. "Maybe. Prison would be worse for a straight arrow like Larry than most perps." He moved closer to my desk, but still didn't sit down. "You covered the trial. How did Larry act?"

I thought back to those sessions in the Snohomish County Courthouse. I'd sat in on the trial a couple of times. The rest of the coverage was handled by my former reporter, Carla Steinmetz, who had quit after marrying Ryan Talliaferro, the current dean of students at Skykomish Community College. Carla had been prone to typos and a lack of attention to detail, but she'd flung herself into the drama of a murder trial and, as I recalled, had done one of her best reporting jobs.

"It's odd," I said after a long pause, "but what I remember

most was that Larry remained stoic, almost statue-like. He never did testify. I sat through most of voir dire because the case was being tried outside of SkyCo and I wanted to get a sense of who was on the jury. Even Vida couldn't help me. I don't remember anything unusual about Carla's account other than what she included in her articles." I paused again and smiled. "She did wonder why the courthouse had been built in Mission style instead of something more fitting for our woodsy world."

Kip grinned, a sign that he was rallying from the news of Larry's death. "Sounds like Carla. I wonder what Rick thinks about this. I suppose he's heard by now." He glanced at my wall calendar. "Gosh, Ginny's due back next Monday. It seems like she just left."

"It seems the same way to Ginny," I said. "She isn't ready to come back. I talked to her this morning."

Kip's brief cheer evaporated. "What's wrong? Is she okay?"

"Ginny claims she hasn't regained her strength yet." I pushed my chair back and stood up. "I told her she either had to come to work as planned or find someone to take her place."

"Oh, crap!" Kip slapped his hand against the filing cabinet. "Maybe she should just quit. Three kids must be a handful. Now that Rick's the bank manager, they should be able to get by on his salary."

"That crossed my mind," I admitted. "The Erlandsons aren't big spenders. The only vacations they've ever taken have been to visit relatives in Oregon and eastern Washington."

"Hey," Kip said, snapping his fingers. "Got a thought. Why not ask Carla to fill in? Won't she be on break from advising the college newspaper during most of December?"

It wasn't the best idea Kip had ever had, but it wasn't the worst, either. "Let me think about that. I gave Ginny a deadline to come up with somebody besides Denise Petersen. I mean, *Jensen*."

"Oh, no! Denise is a total airhead. She screwed up the last two deposits we made and put them into my brother's account."

"You're preaching to the choir," I said as I walked out of my office with Kip. "By the way, our lead story may be Alfred Cobb's resignation."

Kip looked vexed. "We won't know that until deadline. That's it?"

"At the moment," I said. "Would you like me to go out and assault the first passerby so Milo can arrest me?"

Kip's ruddy complexion grew even redder. "Sorry. I don't mean to pressure you. Spence hasn't had much today, either. I guess we're going through a news lull."

Kip's reference to Spencer Fleetwood's local radio station gave me an idea. "Milo mentioned how quiet it is around here after Thanksgiving. Maybe I should write a feature on what media moguls like the two of us do when there's nothing much to report. It might be interesting."

Kip looked dubious. I didn't blame him. He returned to the back shop while I pulled out the bound volume of *Advocate*s containing our coverage of the Petersen trial. It wouldn't hurt to refresh my memory. If nothing else, I might find a recyclable editorial. My mind was still blank.

A half-hour later, I remained unenlightened. There was nothing in the trial coverage that provided anything to suggest Larry's conviction wasn't justified. Nor did any of my largely outdated editorials inspire me with fresh ideas. By eleven-fifteen, I felt frustrated.

"Are you awake?" Mitch asked from the newsroom doorway.

I'd been sitting at his desk, which happened to be closest to our bound archives. "Barely," I confessed, picking up the volume I'd been perusing. "I still don't have an editorial. By the way, have you got those photos from the merchants' light-hanging shoot?"

Mitch clapped a hand to his forehead. "Oh, my God! I forgot all about that." His narrow shoulders sagged. "Brenda and I planned to come back to Alpine after we'd seen Troy in Monroe, but we decided we were more than halfway to Seattle and kept going. I'm sorry, Emma. What do you want me to do to fill the space?"

I'd moved away from his desk. "Fake it," I said, more harshly than I'd intended. "Get Clancy Barton and Cliff Stuart and whoever else you were thinking of to pretend they're putting up the lights at the mall. We have to run some kind of art on the front page."

Mitch looked so contrite that I felt sorry for him. In the few months that he'd worked for me, I'd found him totally reliable. Spending Thanksgiving with a jailbird son was enough to fog anybody's brain.

"Wait," I said, smiling ruefully. "I've got a better idea. Mountain View Gardens has an attractive display up and a ton of Christmas trees for sale. See if you can get a shot of a family buying a tree or a wreath or . . . just being . . . festive. The Hedstroms can help. They've taken out a quarter-page ad this week."

"Hedstrom," Mitch murmured, making a note. "First names?"

"Jerry and Mary Beth. Nice couple." I kept smiling.

Mitch still looked chagrined. "I feel like a dumbshit. If I have to dress up like Santa Claus, I'll get something good. Color, too."

"Forget it," I said. "I'm still in Monday-morning mode. Not quite with it, for some reason."

"A common condition," Mitch murmured. He grabbed his camera and saluted. "Back in a flash. Or as soon as I can find a happy family."

I figured that could take some time. But Mitch already knew that.

THREE

FIFTEEN MINUTES LATER, I'D FINISHED A BRIEF EDITORIAL saluting Alfred Cobb for his service to the county. If he didn't step down at the commissioners' meeting, I could save it for later. At least I felt as if I'd accomplished something. I was considering lunch options when Vida burst into my office.

"I found out from Al Driggers where the guest book from Linda's funeral is," she announced, looking pleased with herself. "It didn't go to Marvin and Cathleen Petersen after all. Linda's daughter, Alison, has it. Would you be interested in seeing it?"

I was puzzled. "Doesn't Alison live with her dad and stepmother in Everett?"

"She did," Vida replied with a smug expression, "but she's in Alpine now. She started teaching cosmetology at Skykomish Community College fall quarter."

"Oh!" I laughed wryly. "I haven't seen Alison since her mother was killed. I still think of her as a distraught twelve-year-old. She must be in her early twenties. How did Alison show up at SCC without us knowing about it?"

Vida's expression soured. "That's what I wanted to know. Or didn't Mitch tell you?"

"No." I made a face. "He didn't have time to tell me anything about his interview with the new science prof." I didn't want to tattle on my reporter's dereliction of duty regarding the mall lighting. "Mitch went to Mountain View Gardens for a photo op."

"Oh?" Vida seemed to sense my lack of candor, but apparently dismissed it. "Well now." She set her black leather purse on my desk and removed her kidskin gloves. "When the college listed the returning and incoming faculty for fall quarter in their news release, they neglected to mention instructors who didn't have an advanced degree. You might guess who wrote the story."

"Carla?"

Vida nodded, her hat's feathers swaying to and fro. "I ran into Mitch just before I went to the bank. I hadn't yet put in my paycheck over the weekend. He told me about the omission, but I'd already heard about it from Al Driggers. I'd suggest a feature on Alison and her new job, but the timing would be unfortunate, given that her uncle just passed away in prison."

"Definitely," I agreed. "Besides, she may be involved in the funeral. Does Al know if there'll be one?"

"No, but he's making discreet inquiries."

"Of course he is," I said, tongue in cheek.

Vida didn't respond in kind. "Why wouldn't he? The Petersens have always been buried here. I must dash," she said, putting her gloves back on. "I have a luncheon date. I may be a trifle late getting back." Vida whipped around, tromped out through the newsroom, and headed for the exit.

I was curious. It was only a quarter to twelve, and my House & Home editor seldom took extra time for lunch. In fact, she often stayed at her desk, working while she ate from a paper bag that held the same items—a hard-boiled egg, cottage cheese, celery, and sometimes carrot sticks. It was her diet menu, despite the fact that I could never tell if Vida had gained or lost weight. Her tall, broad frame disguised any added or lost pounds.

My own lunch involved a brisk trek to Pie-in-the-Sky Sandwich Shop at the mall. I had to wait at the stoplight on Alpine Way, where I felt a chill wind blowing down from Tonga Ridge. *More snow coming,* I thought, gazing up at the heavy gray clouds lurking overhead. Both Tonga and Mount Baldy were partially hidden from view. Next to the mall at Old Mill Park, I could swear that the statue of town founder Carl Clemans was shivering. The stoplight changed just as I felt a nudge at my back.

"Got some good shots," Mitch Laskey said. "You getting a sandwich, by any chance?"

"How'd you guess?"

"Same here," he said as we crossed the street. "It's the only decent food at the mall. Maybe we can find a table. Or do you want to go back to the office?"

"Your call," I replied, "though I still need to conjure up an editorial and a lead story."

"Why don't we take our sandwiches with us and brainstorm out of earshot," Mitch suggested as we entered the sandwich shop. "There's already a line and it's not quite noon."

"Sure," I agreed. The shop was small, with only a dozen tables, mostly for two. I recognized several of the customers, but merely smiled and nodded. My Monday-morning mood wasn't conducive to chitchat. Sticking to business was my antidote to self-pity.

Fifteen minutes later, Mitch and I were in my cubbyhole, he with his ham and cheese on rye, and me with chicken salad on white bread.

"You don't keep kosher?" I said, gesturing at Mitch's sandwich.

Mitch grinned. "That's 'kashrut,' you know. 'Kosher' is the Anglicized version."

"I didn't know," I admitted.

"That's okay," Mitch said. "I hadn't a clue about the Triduum until last Easter, when I had to write a feature about a family in Detroit that had triplets born on Good Friday."

"Uh . . . I assume they were Catholics."

Mitch nodded. "That was the hook. Mom said she was glad it didn't take all the way from Holy Thursday to Easter Sunday to deliver them. A feel-good piece. We needed all of those we could get in Detroit."

"I was thinking of doing one like that for this week's edition," I said after we'd both eaten some of our sandwiches. "But that's not a lead. I'm stumped."

"Tell me about this Petersen thing. Or should I look it up in the back issues?"

"Let's hope you don't have to," I said. "It was a huge story involving the Bank of Alpine. There was a rumor that a Seattle bank wanted to buy out the Petersen family, who had started up the bank with some other locals in the early thirties. As is typical of this town, nobody wanted big-city interlopers handling their money. The Seattle-based bunch dropped out, but not before the daughter of the local bank president, Marvin Petersen, was murdered. Marv had taken over from his father after the elder Petersen retired. Thus, the dynasty was established. But the next male heir apparent, Larry, found out his father was going to bypass him in favor of his sister, Linda. He reacted by killing her in a fit of sibling rage. Meanwhile, the Seattle folks discovered someone here was cooking the books and making off with chunks of money. The two cases weren't really connected, but that was enough to queer the buyout offer."

"Wow. That's a big story for a small town." Mitch paused to pop a couple of potato chips into his mouth. "Who did the cooking?"

I had to smile. "A bank employee who promptly fled to Michigan."

Mitch laughed. "Good thinking. Cops back home have enough locals to bust without fussing over a mere embezzler from some woodsy place two thousand miles away. So now the convicted sibling killer has gone to that bank vault in the sky. Why do we care? From the standpoint of a hard-news item, that is."

I hesitated. If the letters to Milo stopped after Larry died, there was no story. But if they didn't, then Mitch would get the assignment. I didn't feel right about leaving him out of the loop, so I told him why the sheriff had paid us an early-morning call.

"That's weird," Mitch said when I finished, "especially since Larry died over the weekend. Is there any reason you can think of that would set somebody off after all this time?"

I hadn't thought about that possibility. "The murder occurred in November ten years ago, shortly before Thanksgiving. Yes, I suppose there might be a connection. I'd like to think it's a crank, maybe somebody Milo picked up for speeding or a DUI. I can imagine the kind of weirdos you had in Detroit."

"The bigger the city, the bigger the nut pool."

For a few moments, we ate in silence. I took that as a good sign. I'd known Mitch for only a short time, but we were from the same generation, same blue-collar family background, both state university grads, had big-city newspaper experience—and both of us were now in semi-exile three thousand feet above sea level. We'd established an easy rapport and were comfortable with each other. Although I didn't know his wife very well, I sensed that they were devoted, if not necessarily happy. I changed the subject. "Do you know why Vida's taking a long lunch hour?"

Mitch chuckled. "I doubt it'll include three double martinis."

"I just wondered. It's not like her. I thought she might've said something."

"To me?" Mitch shook his head. "I don't think she's quite convinced that I wasn't involved in Jimmy Hoffa's disappearance."

"Were you at the *Free Press* when that happened?"

"No. I was cutting my journalistic teeth on the *Ypsilanti Courier*. A weekly, of all things." He chuckled again. "But I'd joined the *Free Press* staff by the time Jimmy was declared dead in 1982. I was neither shocked nor saddened. And nobody was surprised."

When we finished eating, Mitch showed me the photos he'd taken at Mountain View Gardens. Luckily, a young family named Curtis had been looking for a tree. Mom, Dad, a three-year-old, and a baby in a stroller made for an appealing shot.

"That works," I said. "In fact, I can't make up my mind between the second, fourth, and sixth photo. You and Kip can decide. How did the interview with . . . what's the new prof's name? It's odd."

Mitch grinned. "Beaufort Vard'i, of Anglo-Indian descent, born in San Francisco. He goes by Bo—that's B-O—and he told me there should be an apostrophe in Vard'i between the *d* and the *i*, don't know if the name was originally Arabic or Hindi, but his parents dropped it when they became American citizens."

I shook my head in confusion. "I think we can leave that part of the interview out. Names like O'Toole and Fong are about as exotic as we get around here. I hope the interview was more conventional."

"It was," Mitch assured me. "He's a sharp guy, and his real

interest is genetics, but he stuck to his theories of teaching biology and anthropology. Married, one kid in high school, moved here because he and his wife like the outdoors and it's a hell of a lot cheaper than living in San Francisco. I've got a couple of decent photos, too. He's good-looking, so one of these days he'll get hit with a sexual harassment suit that'll most likely be based not in fact but on hope, or the lack thereof."

"Got it," I said as the phone rang.

Mitch collected his gear and lunch leavings while I picked up the receiver. I was only mildly surprised to hear Ginny's sister-in-law, Donna Wickstrom, on the other end of the line.

"Emma," she began, "I feel so sorry about Ginny not being able to come back to work as soon as she planned. I talked to her a few minutes ago about part-time, but with Christmas and the art gallery and the day care at capacity anyway, I can't juggle her three without going crazy."

"It's not your fault, Donna," I assured her. "Ginny had a commitment, but if she's not feeling up to keeping it, we'll manage."

I could hear children's raised voices in the background. "Hold on, Emma," Donna said. "Derek! Jamie! Stop that!" The shrill cries faded into muted truculence. "It doesn't matter who started it," Donna said away from the receiver. "Stopping it is what counts. Santa's watching."

I smiled, remembering how often I'd used that line on Adam. I had to quit when he told me that if Santa was keeping an eye on him, who was watching the elves? That, he'd gone on to inform me, was probably why his toy tank had broken the day after the previous Christmas. The elves had gotten careless without proper "stuperfision." My son had made his point.

Donna sighed in my ear. "Actually, I'm hiring someone to help me, both here at the day care and at the art gallery. I have to keep the gallery open for longer hours in December."

"As I recall, you've had Evan Singer take up the slack from time to time," I said. "Is he unavailable or is this somebody new?"

"Both," Donna replied. "Evan's going to do some of it during the day because he works the 911 calls at night. Alison Lindahl is teaching at the college and she'll be on break in another week. Do you remember her? She's Linda Petersen Lindahl's daughter."

I paused. Judging from Donna's tone, she hadn't yet heard about Larry Petersen's death. "Yes, I just found out she's at the college, but—"

Donna had to interrupt me again as another melee erupted in the background. I waited at least a full minute while she sorted out Carlos, Destiny, and Esther. Or Hester. I couldn't quite make out the third miscreant's name. "I've got to go," Donna said breathlessly. "By the way, Craig Laurentis has a new painting at the gallery. He dropped it off at our house last night. You might want to take a look. Talk to you later."

I hung up. I owned a Craig Laurentis, the only piece of art I'd ever bought and my most prized possession, except for the Madonna and Child statue that Tom had given me when we'd visited Leavenworth on the other side of Stevens Pass. I made a note about the new Laurentis for "Scene" just as Vida entered the newsroom with Amanda Hanson. Vida took off her coat and hat; Amanda came into my office.

"Have you found my replacement yet?" she asked.

"No, unfortunately." Seeing that Amanda appeared apologetic, I hastened to forestall any guilt feelings. "It's not your fault. By the way, speaking of luck, any news about the foster kids?"

Amanda shook her head. "Walt and I didn't expect any, what with the long weekend. Vida just told me about an unwed teenager who's expecting a baby. Maybe that's the route we'll have to go. The only problem is that she doesn't know who the girl is."

"If anyone can find out, it's Vida," I said. "Are you still checking with adoption agencies?"

"We haven't followed up lately," she responded, her pretty face lacking its usual animation. "We've been focused on those three kids of Holly's." She lowered her voice. "It's a touchy subject with Vida. I know the baby is her great-grandson. What do you think will happen with that one? Roger seems totally irresponsible. Immature, too."

I couldn't help but roll my eyes. "An understatement. He's lucky to get out of that trailer park mess without being arrested. In fact, Milo went easy on him with only a fine for possession and driving without a license. The DUI charges were dropped."

Amanda leaned on the back of a visitor's chair. "That's another thing to consider," she said, now almost whispering. "The older kids may already be ruined. I mean, the way they've been raised is bound to have a negative effect on them. I hate to call little kids damaged goods, but Walt and I haven't had any experience with children. We've had enough problems just staying married."

This was the first time Amanda had really confided in me since I'd discovered the Hansons were considering adoption. Our work relationship had gotten off to a rocky start—mainly because her marriage was on the rocks at the time. The arrival of Ginny's new baby had somehow changed Amanda's way of thinking. Over time, the couple's childless state had turned into a blame game. His fault, her fault—until they realized it wasn't anybody's fault except Mother Nature's.

"I've wondered if you've considered breaking up the trio," I said, speaking as softly as Amanda despite being aware that Vida probably knew what we were talking about.

"That's a dilemma, too," Amanda said. "Holly got off with a fairly light sentence for second-degree manslaughter. She could be paroled in less than ten years. She may try to get the kids back. It's even possible she's learned her lesson. But I doubt it."

"Sadly, you may be right. Jail time doesn't ensure rehabilitation." I nodded in Vida's direction, noting her back was turned as she talked on the phone. "Have you asked about her grandson's baby?"

"No. I'm afraid to," Amanda admitted. "Has she told you where Holly's children are? I asked Marisa Foxx if she could find out since she's our lawyer, but so far we haven't heard anything."

The irony of our conversation didn't escape me. Amanda and I were discussing a topic that touched on a wide range of social problems we should address in the *Advocate*. It would have to be a series, of course, and I'd do it with Mitch.

"Oh!" Amanda said suddenly, handing me a phone message. "This came in while we were both at lunch. It's from one of the park rangers, Wes Amundson. Nothing urgent, but he thought you should know."

I wished the message *was* urgent. I might have a lead story. "Thanks, Amanda."

"Sure." She smiled faintly. "Thanks for listening."

"Any time." I paused. "I mean that."

Amanda's smile trembled ever so slightly. "I appreciate it."

She had just gone back to her post in the front office when Vida slammed down the phone, stood up, took a deep breath, and all but ran to the restroom. If it had been anyone but Vida, I would have assumed it was the flu, but she is never sick. No germ would dare attack her iron constitution.

I waited for her to emerge, but when she didn't after almost five minutes, I got up and went to knock on the restroom door. "Vida? Are you okay?" I inquired.

"Yes!" The single word sounded as if she'd bitten it off instead of spoken it. With a sigh, I returned to my cubbyhole and called Wes Amundson.

"Hi, Emma," he said. "Just wanted to tell you we've got another maple thief on the loose. Two trees this time, both a quarter of a mile down from the ranger station on the east side of the Icicle Creek Road. Dodge's guys are there now, so I thought you might want a photo."

"I do," I said, fortuitously seeing Mitch coming toward his desk from the back shop. "Any idea who's doing this?"

"Are you kidding?" Wes sounded annoyed. "If we knew, we'd collar the bastards ourselves. It's probably someone with logging experience, but there are plenty of suspects around here, especially with the ones who are out of work. These last two make twenty-five poached maples since August. You can't tell me the choppers are gathering firewood. If they were, I wish they'd take some of those cottonwoods and alders instead. I'm allergic to them. Unfortunately, none of those damned things grow in that section of the forest."

I agreed. "Are you sticking by the earlier forest service statement that the wood is probably sold to makers of musical instruments?"

"It's the best reason," Wes replied. "Violins, guitars—anything that requires high-grade maple like these trees. Good God, we finally get most of the meth labs cleaned out around here and we've hauled away literally tons of abandoned vehicles and boats and . . . oh, hell! There's my other line. Got to go."

Mitch was standing in the doorway. I told him about the call from Wes. "Can you go up there now while the deputies are searching the crime scene? Get a quote from one of them, and hope it's not Sam Heppner. He often says things that aren't fit to print."

"Sam would feel right at home in Detroit," Mitch remarked.

"No, he wouldn't," I declared. "Sam wouldn't last a week in any city that had a population over four digits."

"I'll be on my way as soon as I write the cutline for the Christmas tree photo and zap it to Kip."

Mitch went back to his desk. He left a few minutes later, but Vida was still in the restroom. I decided to check on her again. As I walked through the newsroom, I heard sirens. Maybe we had another story. Things were looking up. Bad news is good news in my world.

Vida came out just before I got to the restroom door. Her gray curls were in more disarray than usual, and her eyes were red. I'd rarely seen her so upset.

"What's wrong?" I asked, tentatively putting a hand on her arm.

"I can't talk about it," she said, shaking me off and proceeding to her desk. "Just leave me be. Please."

"No, I won't," I asserted, waiting for her to sit down before I plunked myself in her visitor's chair. "If you're distraught, I'm concerned. This isn't like you. Tell me what happened to cause you such distress."

Vida removed her glasses, took a crumpled handkerchief out of her purse, and dabbed at her eyes. It took a long time before she finally spoke. "It's Buck," she said, staring straight ahead. "He betrayed me."

I was startled. "I don't understand," I confessed. "How?"

Vida put her glasses back on, squared her shoulders, and finally looked at me. "He's talked Roger into joining the Marines."

"The Marines?" For some reason, that was all I could say.

Vida nodded. "He thinks Roger needs discipline and structure."

"Buck's probably right." I paused. "You think so, too." I paused again, this time waiting for a response. But Vida said nothing. "Well?" I went on. "You've spent over a month or more beating yourself up for spoiling Roger all these years. What other options would you suggest?"

She held her head. "I don't know. I really don't. I had no idea Buck was coercing Roger into joining the military until today. He took me to lunch in Sultan, where we couldn't be overheard by half of Alpine. He admitted he'd been talking to Roger for some time—behind my back. That's the part that's so hurtful. Buck should've told me what he was doing. It's as if he didn't trust me, as if he thought I'd interfere. Does that sound like me?"

I decided it was a rhetorical question. "Buck probably wants Roger to make the decision. Had he talked to Amy and Ted before telling you?"

Vida shook her head. "He felt the same way about them. Parents, he insisted, can be too protective. His four are scattered all over. Buck only sees his own grandchildren about twice a year. None of them have ever gone into the service."

"Maybe not," I said, "but plenty of moms and dads urge their kids to join the military to help them grow up. Boys in particular take a long time to choose a career. Adam's a good example of that. He changed his major about five times before he realized he had a religious vocation. The military provides various kinds of training to help young people figure out what they want to do with the rest of their lives."

"If they get to have them," Vida retorted. "What happens when Roger is sent off to somewhere like Iraq or Afghanistan? He could be killed or maimed or . . ." She turned away quickly, no doubt with visions of Roger in a body bag or confined to a wheelchair.

I, however, thought of enemies fleeing in droves at the very sight of Roger. After so many years of suffering through his self-ish, spoiled behavior, it was hard to think of him as a victim. To me, he was a one-man weapon of mass destruction.

"Nobody can force Roger to do anything," I finally said. "Maybe he'll find the Marines a challenge. He could not only find a career he'd enjoy, but see other parts of the world."

She stared at me with gray eyes hard as granite. "Such as Kabul?"

"Hey." I leaned closer to her. "It's possible he'll never see a war zone. How far has Roger traveled in his twenty-odd years?" *Very odd,* I thought to myself, while waiting for Vida's answer.

"He's been to Seattle and the ocean and eastern Washington," she responded. "Before you moved here, Amy and Ted took him to Disneyland and SeaWorld. Oh—he also drove up to British Columbia with his chums a couple of years ago to go camping."

And the Canadians let him in? The U.S. immigration officers let him come back to this country? "I forgot about that," I admitted. "I don't think you ever told me how the B.C. trip turned out."

Vida sniffed. "I didn't think you'd be interested."

"You didn't mention it in 'Scene,' so I assumed it was un-eventful."

Vida's color rose slightly. "It was young men enjoying them-selves. I didn't want to single out my grandson because of our staff policy to avoid promoting ourselves in the *Advocate.*"

I almost believed her, but before I could say more, I heard my phone ring. "Maybe I should get that," I said, rising from the chair. "I'm sorry about Buck causing you grief, but he's obviously trying to help. Men are sometimes . . . insensitive."

I managed to pick up my call just before it trunked back to Amanda. Milo's voice was at the other end.

"Looks like you've got a front-page story," he said. "Somebody shot that recluse guy, Laurentis. He's on his way to the hospital. If you need details, meet me there."

FOUR

CRAIG'S BEEN SHOT?" I EXCLAIMED IN HORROR. "WILL HE make it?"

"Don't know," Milo replied. "Gotta go." He hung up as the sirens sounded again.

Vida had heard my raised voice. She was on her feet when I came dashing out of my cubbyhole with my left arm in the right sleeve of my duffel coat.

"What is it?" she asked, all remnants of anguish and betrayal washed away by what she sensed must be a big story.

"Somebody shot Craig Laurentis," I said, discovering that I was putting my coat on backwards. "He's alive and is probably arriving at the hospital right now." I finally got my attire in proper order. "Did you hear the ambulance?"

"Yes. I wondered, of course. Shall I come with you?"

Vida rarely did hard news, but she needed someone else's suffering to get her mind off her own problems. "Yes. Bring a camera, just in case. Mitch is at the maple-poaching site."

"The what?" Vida asked over her shoulder as she reached for her coat and hat.

"I'll tell you about that later." The hospital was only two blocks from our office. Amanda was on the phone as we went past her. "Breaking news," I called out, following Vida through the front door.

"Who on earth would shoot a recluse like Old Nick?" Vida asked as we waited for the light to change at Fourth and Front.

"He does have a name," I said impatiently. "And he's not any older than I am. People only called him Old Nick because he had a gray beard. Prematurely, from what I figured out."

"Oh—yes. I keep forgetting," Vida said as we crossed the street. "You have one of his pictures." She sucked in her breath as we walked up the hill past the Bank of Alpine. "Dear me—I think they're all in shock by now at the bank. I feel sorry for Andy Cederberg and Rick Erlandson. All that old gossip's bound to resurface. Poor Andy has never felt like a real bank president since he took over from Marv. More like warming the chair for the next Petersen who goes into the business. As for Rick, I hope Ginny isn't carrying on like a sad sack at home."

"What next Petersen?" I asked, pausing for an SUV to go by at the corner of Fourth and Pine.

"Larry's sons," Vida replied, moving along briskly. "I assume at least one of them will return to Alpine eventually. Neither of the boys is as dim as their sister, Denise. I suppose Elmer and Thelma know what they're up to these days. If Milo doesn't inquire about them, I will."

We passed the medical and dental clinic, then crossed Third. It was still cold and windy, but so far there was no sign of rain or snow. "I don't remember the names of the Petersen boys," I said. "Were they at Linda's funeral?"

"Yes, but I never had a chance to speak to them," Vida replied. "Later they both came back to Alpine on winter break. Then they helped their mother move. That was in the spring, as I recall." We'd reached the hospital entrance. Vida pushed open the swinging doors. "Is Milo here?" she asked as we entered the lobby with its carved-wood panels of local flora and fauna.

"Probably at the ER entrance," I said, trying to smile at the pale-faced young woman behind the desk.

"Oh!" Vida exclaimed, revealing her toothy grin. "Jennifer, isn't it? Aren't you a Bjornson?"

The young woman smiled back. "Yes, I am, Mrs. Runkel."

Vida needed no introduction. "I understand your father still works part-time as a repairman for Sheriff Dodge. My, my, you've grown up since I last saw you. Jenny, I should've said. Have you been away?"

Jennifer—or Jenny, or both—nodded. "I spent two years at Edmonds Community College."

Vida's smile disappeared. "Oh. Isn't your mother still working at the college library here?"

"Yes," Jenny said, a trace of color rising in her cheeks, "but I thought it might be fun to go somewhere else to college."

"I see." Vida paused. "But you came back to Alpine. How nice." She didn't miss a beat. "We heard that Old Nick . . . I mean Mr. Laurentis, the artist, has been shot. Is that true?"

Jenny nodded again. "It must've been an accident. A hunter, probably. He hasn't been officially admitted, but I understand the ambulance pulled in about five minutes ago."

"You know Ms. Lord?" Vida said, waving a hand in my direction.

Jenny gave me a fleeting glance. "Yes, I remember from the time when Mr. Rasmussen was murdered at the college and my folks were both working there then."

As was often the case, I found it necessary to assert myself as something other than Vida's stooge. "Sheriff Dodge called and asked if I'd meet him at the hospital. Is he in the ER with Mr. Laurentis?"

Jenny's blue eyes widened. "I doubt it. Nonmedical person-

nel aren't usually allowed in that area. Maybe he's in the waiting room."

"The sheriff has a habit of doing what he needs to do," I
said. "Come on, Vida, let's find Milo."

We went down the corridor to the ER. "You certainly made
a point of being on intimate terms with Milo," Vida murmured.
"Is that wise?"

The comment irked me. "I've known Milo for fifteen years. I
also know you and Ginny and Kip intimately."

"It's not the same," Vida said.

"Why? Because I left out Ed?"

We turned the corner, following the arrows to the ER. "You
know perfectly well what I mean," Vida said.

I had no chance to argue. A white-coated orderly I didn't recognize opened one of the double doors for Vida and me to pass
into the waiting room. There were no patients in sight nor was
there any sign of the sheriff, but I knew the receptionist, Bree
Kendall. We had a rocky history, going back to her former job
with the local orthodontist, Carter Nystrom. For once, I was
more than willing to let Vida take the lead.

She marched up to Bree's post and placed both gloved hands
on the counter. "Sheriff Dodge told us to meet him here," Vida
said. "Where might he be?"

Bree shot me a baleful glance before responding. "Dodge
might be anywhere. He's not here."

Vida was unfazed. "Then tell us what's going on with Mr.
Laurentis. The sheriff informed us he'd been shot and was being
admitted. Has he already been taken into surgery?"

Bree folded her hands in her lap. She would've been pretty if
disdain hadn't puckered her face like a prune. "I'm sorry. That
information is confidential. You're not family, are you?"

I almost expected Vida to claim that she was. Half of Alpine seemed related to her by blood or by marriage. Bree wasn't a native, so she might have believed the lie. But my House & Home editor kept to the truth. "No," she said after a long pause, and began to peel off her gloves with the tantalizing finesse of a seasoned stripper. "I understand Mr. Laurentis has no family around here. But you probably know that." Vida paused to look at Bree—and drop one glove on the counter. "However, it appears that a crime may've been committed, which is why we were summoned here by the sheriff." She paused again and turned in my direction. "We, as you know perfectly well," Vida announced rather grandly as she dropped the other glove, "are The Press."

"Oh, crap!" I said under my breath as Spencer Fleetwood crossed the ER threshold from the street entrance.

Bree beamed at the sight of Mr. Radio. "Spence!" she cried. "I'm so glad you could come in person."

Spence flashed his big smile at all of us. "I'll break a leg for breaking news," he said. "Thanks, Bree, for giving me a heads-up."

Bree had the grace to look askance and blush—or maybe she was overcome by the attention from Spence. "Are you going to do a live broadcast from here?" she asked.

"That depends," he said, finally gazing at me before looking back at Bree. "What's happening with our recluse?"

"Well . . ." Bree cleared her throat. I sensed she would've loved to take Spence aside and share her knowledge only with him. "The ambulance brought him in just a few minutes ago. I can't leave my desk, so that's all I can tell you. Now." She gave him a meaningful look. "The hermit's condition is probably being evaluated before they decide to proceed with medical treatment."

I couldn't stand it. Shoving Spence aside, I stomped up to the counter, where Vida had moved off to one side. "What else would they be doing with someone who arrives in the ER by ambulance? And don't give me any of that 'triage' bunk. It's a battlefield or disaster term, and one patient doesn't require sorting through priorities. That's bullshit."

"Emma . . . ," Vida said softly.

I ignored her. "Furthermore, the victim has a name—Craig Laurentis. Give him some dignity as a human being. He's a brilliant artist, and how or where he lives is his business, you little twerp."

Bree's blue eyes widened in shock; Vida sucked in her breath; Spence let out a strangled sound between a laugh and a groan. I turned on my heel and practically ran to the door that led to the ER area.

Vida was right behind me. "Your language, Emma! Really. Quite shocking."

"Sorry," I mumbled. "You know what a pain Bree is."

"That's no excuse for—" Vida didn't finish her lecture. We were accosted by a tall, raw-boned nurse wearing the traditional white uniform both Old Doc and Young Doc Dewey insisted upon. "Excuse me," she said in a tight voice, "but you can't come in here."

Vida glanced at the nurse's nametag. "Astrid Overholt. I thought you lived in Everett."

Astrid peered at Vida through rimless bifocals. "Oh, for heaven's sake! I haven't seen you in years. I just moved back over the Thanksgiving weekend. My mother can't live alone anymore and there was a job opening at the hospital."

"How wonderful to see you," Vida enthused. "I'm glad I found out. I'll put it in this week's paper. We must have a chat. But business before pleasure, Astrid. I don't think you've met Emma Lord, the *Advocate*'s editor and publisher."

"I haven't," Astrid said, shaking my hand. "I'll bet you two are here about that poor soul who got shot. Is he homeless?"

"No," I said, making sure Astrid knew I could talk. "He lives out of town. Is he going to be okay?"

"I don't know," Astrid replied, a frown creasing her high forehead. "The wound didn't strike anything vital, but apparently he lost a great deal of blood. I understand he was found in the woods by—" She stopped as Milo and Spence came into the hallway.

". . . not a damned freak show," Milo was saying angrily to Spence. "There you are," he went on, approaching the three of us. "Any news?" The query was for Astrid.

"Not yet," she replied. "Dr. Sung is with him. I believe his main concern is blood loss before he removes the bullet."

"Right," Milo said, taking off his tall regulation hat. "I think Laurentis had been lying where the park rangers found him since last night. He was lucky anybody got to him before it was too late. Damned poachers. Hacking down trees is bad enough, but shooting people is worse. Make sure Sung gives me that bullet."

Astrid nodded. Spence, who had pinned a microphone on what looked like a top-of-the-line ski parka, moved closer to Milo. "Are you saying, Sheriff, that Mr. Laurentis was shot by someone who was poaching trees on forest service land?"

The sheriff scowled at Mr. Radio. "What did you think I said? They weren't kidnapping mountain goats on Mount Sawyer."

Spence retained his usual broadcasting aplomb, mellow voice and all. "This is for our KSKY listeners in the greater Highway 2 corridor."

"I don't care if it's for the Congress in Washington, D.C.,"

Milo retorted. "And it better not be live. I've got an attempted-murder case on my hands, Fleetwood. Hold your damned water and shut off that mike."

I'd managed to edge closer to the sheriff. "Will Craig make it?"

Milo turned his scowl on me. "How the hell do I know? Do I look like Dr. Kildare? Go back to the waiting room—all of you. I'll let you know when I find out."

At least the sheriff wasn't playing favorites. Vida, however, balked. "I need just a few minutes to talk to Astrid. She's a news item, too."

Milo regarded the two women warily. "Then do it at the nurses' station," he said, nodding toward the area by the ER entrance. "But don't get the nurse distracted if she's needed."

"I won't," Vida promised in a firm voice. "Come, Astrid, I must get caught up with you for my page."

Spence opened the door for me. "What do you know that I don't about the tree poachers?" he asked.

"Not much more than you do," I replied, noticing a teen-aged boy in a wheelchair with a woman I assumed was his mother. "You've reported the earlier thefts. Wes Amundson phoned to tell me about two more just before he was apparently called away by whoever found Craig."

We sat down by the waiting room's aquarium, out of Bree's line of sight. "I was coming from Monroe when I got word about the shooting," Spence said, keeping his voice down. "I've got some co-op Christmas ads from the local merchants there. That should cheer you up."

"It does," I said, pleased that Spence was keeping his word about sharing some of the ad revenue in east Snohomish County after KSKY's signal had been upgraded to reach beyond the county line. "And no," I went on, "we haven't had a chance to post anything about the shooting or the poachers on our web-site yet."

Spence flashed one of his almost-sincere smiles. "You can't complain much anymore about getting scooped by me. I think we've managed to put the rivalry to bed, don't you?"

The mischief in his brown eyes unsettled me. "Maybe." I craned my neck to make sure Bree couldn't see or hear us. "Speaking of bed, are you sleeping with the cranky Kendall?"

Spence chuckled. "Because she let me know about a possible news item? Has it occurred to you that she did it because she doesn't like you as well as she likes me?"

"That's what I meant," I said. "I thought she was dating the dashing *young* CPA, Freddy Bellman," I said, reminding Spence that he's in my peer group and old enough to be Bree's father.

"You're not making sense."

"About what?"

We both noticed that mother and son were staring at us. Apparently I'd raised my voice. "I meant," I said quietly and slowly, "that she has the hots for you and maybe the feeling is returned. A simple yes or no will do."

"Yes. No." He paused. "How's that?"

I turned away. "Forget it."

Astrid Overholt appeared in the ER doorway. "Logan Brooks?"

"Here, Nurse," the woman said, wheeling the boy across the waiting room. "I think Logan broke his ankle playing basket-ball."

Astrid smiled. "Let's have a look," she said. "Room Two is vacant."

The boy, who appeared to be about fourteen, didn't seem to be in pain. Maybe he was a stoic. Maybe his mother was overly

protective. An old pang of guilt resurfaced. When Adam was
eight, he'd fallen off some apparatus at the neighborhood play-
ground. Two of his buddies had helped him limp home. It was a
Sunday afternoon, and I had a deadline on the first of three articles for *The Oregonian* about the start of construction on
Portland's light rail system. It was a complicated assignment, re-
quiring most of my weekend to write the kick-off story for
Monday's edition. I looked at Adam's foot, told him it was only
a bruise, and went back to work. By Tuesday, he couldn't walk.
I finally took him to the ER that evening, where he was diag-
nosed with a broken bone. Needless to say, I felt like the worst
mother in Rip City.

"Where's your sidekick?" Spence asked.

The question yanked me out of my reverie. "What? Oh—
maybe she and Astrid haven't finished their chat."

Spence looked skeptical. "Nurse Astrid has a patient. I'd go
see what Vida's up to, but if I make her mad, she might threaten
to quit her weekly radio show."

"You're in a pickle," I remarked. "A lot of your bread and
butter is stored in *Vida's Cupboard*."

Spence nodded. "I'm glad we let her switch from Wednesdays to Thursdays. Too many midweek activities around this
town, including some of her church events. That program she
did with Roger and his parents after the trailer park debacle
practically blew our ratings right over Tonga Ridge. He didn't
say much, but he actually sounded contrite. I wonder how much
of it was real and how much was from the drama classes he
took during his off-and-on college career."

"Mostly off," I murmured. "I hope it was a wake-up call for
him, but my evil self tells me he may've only been sorry for getting caught."

Spence leaned back in the chair, long legs extended out onto the durable burgundy carpet. "It's quiet around here," he said after a pause.

"It's Monday," I pointed out. "A Monday after a holiday, at that. Besides, most people with sudden problems call Doc Dewey or Dr. Sung. Both are very good about seeing patients on an emergency basis—unless the patient arrives by ambulance. Then one of them rushes from the clinic across the street."

"We could use another doctor around here," Spence said. "You wrote an editorial on the subject a few weeks ago. Any response?"

I shot him an ironic glance. "Are you kidding? I'm lucky if anyone reads my editorials, let alone takes action, except for the perennial grouches. They jump me for wishing readers a happy Thanksgiving."

"How was yours?"

I shrugged. "Quiet. What about you?"

Spence looked away, apparently intrigued by the activity in the aquarium. "I took the holiday off and drove to Seattle. I'd done a couple of interviews that played while I was gone and had two college kids do the rest. There's plenty of canned programming I can use for Thanksgiving, even some of the old radio shows."

I looked at my watch. "It's almost two. I've got work to do. Maybe I'll let Vida stay here. If the surgery's complicated, it'll take a while."

Spence stood up before I did. "I've got a news show on the hour turn. Let me check."

Instead of heading back to the ER, Spence went to Bree's workstation. I followed—at a distance.

"Go ahead, Bree," Spence said. "If anybody comes in bleeding to death, I know how to make a tourniquet. Just try to get back to me in under four minutes, okay?"

"Well?" I said, after Bree had disappeared from my line of sight. "As Vida might say, have you sent a boy to the mill?"

"Probably not," Spence said. "Bree's worked here going on six months. She knows what she's doing. I think I'll interview her."

"Then I will, too," I said, feeling perverse. "Or maybe I should see if Vida's learned anything." I wasn't just being contrary. My concern for Craig Laurentis was real. I'd seen him only a handful of times, and we'd probably exchanged no more than a few words. Every time I looked at *Sky Autumn* on my living room wall, his presence was palpable. I felt some kind of visceral connection to the painting. The river rippling over the moss-covered rocks was so authentic that I could almost sniff the fragrant evergreens and the earth's sweet damp decay.

I abandoned Spence and went into the ER area. Vida was just coming from the nurses' station.

"Well?" I said. "What's going on with Craig?"

"I don't know," Vida said tersely. "Milo disappeared. He can't be in with Dr. Sung and the patient, or does he have some kind of medical training I don't know about?"

"He probably went out the back way to smoke," I said. "Did you get what you needed from Astrid about her move?"

"Enough," Vida said, stopping short of the exit doors. "She married Lyndon Overholt when they were both very young. He died a few years later in an unfortunate tractor accident on the family farm. They had no children, so she went to nursing school and has worked for years at Providence Hospital in Everett. She's temporarily living with her mother, Hertha Sundgren, but the old lady has dementia and Astrid will eventually have to put her in the nursing home here."

"That's a good three inches," I said.

"It's enough," Vida said, peering through the door's window. "Where's Spencer?"

"Covering for Bree," I replied. "She's trying to find out what's going on before his hourly newscast."

Vida looked at her watch. "It's two now. I didn't see Bree come through here. There's another way from her desk that comes out into the hall connecting the ER to the rest of the hospital."

"You're right," I said, and explained that I should get back to the office. "Do you mind staying here until Milo shows up with some news?"

"Of course not." She glanced at the nurses' station. "Very interesting information in there. I know who the teenaged girl is in the letter I received this morning. She miscarried shortly before seven A.M."

I shouldn't have been surprised by Vida's knowledge, though I felt it best not to ask how she'd obtained it. "Anybody we know?"

Vida grimaced. "Alas, no. The family name is Harlowe and they live between Baring and Skykomish with an RFD address. I suppose the mother mailed the letter while shopping in Alpine."

"How will you answer her?"

"Oh, with some Pollyanna cliché about how things work out for the best, but meanwhile you—meaning the idiot mother—should set a good example for your children and blah-blah. Not that it will do a bit of good. The advice is twenty years late. So many people have *no sense.*"

"You can't do much else," I said, "since you stated at the start you'd respond to all letters as long as they weren't salacious, libelous, or obvious fiction. You can't let on you already know how the pregnancy ended. And don't forget the pickled herring recipe." I gestured toward the other end of the hall. "I'll go out the back way. See you later."

My guess about where Milo had gone was right. He was stubbing out a cigarette in an empty planter box on the corner across from the clinic. He didn't seem surprised to see me.

"How long does it take you to shake off Vida and Fleetwood?" he asked. "I've smoked two cigarettes and damned near froze to death waiting for you to show up."

"You might've told me," I shot back. "I can't read your mind."

Milo snorted. "Yes, you can. Sometimes, anyway."

"What's wrong with Vida? Why couldn't she come out here, too?"

"Because I had to ditch all three of you to keep Fleetwood from tagging along."

"You really dislike him that much?"

"I don't dislike him," Milo said. "But . . . hell, I don't know. He's too damned slick, and I don't like being interviewed over the radio. It's an easy way to make a fool of yourself."

"So what's happening?"

Milo waved halfheartedly at one of the Blue Sky Dairy's truck drivers. "That's the other problem. I'm still piecing this together. Laurentis was barely conscious when the rangers found him. It was hard to get much out of the guy, but it sounds like he was shot last night or early this morning. He was about fifty yards away from where the maples had been harvested. I figure he caught the poachers in the act and they shot him. He ought to pull through, but it may be several hours before we can talk to him to find out if he can ID the perps. Poaching's bad enough, but now we've got attempted murder."

A few drops of icy rain blew into my face. I pulled the duffel coat's hood up further. "Where were these trees in relationship to the other ones that've been cut down?"

"Not that far from the last three, but closer to the road," Milo said, hunkering down into the turned-up collar of his jacket as the rain started coming down harder. "The other ones were between Burl Creek and the fish hatchery on the other side of town."

"But all of them have been well out of sight."

"Right," Milo responded. "They find maples off the beaten path, but all the cuttings seem to have been done at night. Only somebody like Laurentis who holes up God-only-knows-where would ever see them. The closest private property to those trees is my aunt and uncle's old farm. Even that's a good two, three hundred yards away with plenty of woods in between."

"Who owns that now? I forget."

"They sold the place to somebody from Kirkland named Holden or Hilton who wanted it for a vacation home. It sure as hell wasn't much of a farm the last few years that Aunt Thelma and Uncle Elmer owned it."

"Are the new owners staying there now?" I asked.

"Wes Amundson told me they haven't been around since late September, but they'll probably show up on weekends when the ski season starts." Milo looked up at the gloomy sky. "That could be sooner than usual, if the snow starts this early." He grabbed my arm. "Let's get the hell back inside. I should check on Laurentis's progress before I go back to the office."

I shook my head. "I'm on my way to the *Advocate*. Vida's standing by, though exactly where, I don't know. She may be assisting Dr. Sung in surgery by now."

"Okay," Milo said, but he didn't let go of my arm. "I haven't seen much of you lately. Want me to drop by after work and fill you in on what's happening?"

I wondered if "filling me in" was some kind of Freudian slip. Our off-and-on sexual relationship had been resumed recently after the harrowing trailer park tragedy. Still, I never wanted to get too close to Milo. Years ago there'd been a time when he'd talked about wanting to marry me, but Tom had still been alive—and still tied to his emotionally unstable wife. I'd told myself there was never going to be a second Mrs. Cavanaugh. I'd tried to excise him from my life. I couldn't. Sandra finally died and eventually Tom and I became engaged. It was like a fairy tale, until a bullet killed Tom and spoiled my "happily ever after."

As for the sheriff, his desire for a permanent arrangement between us was a stumbling block. Only once had he admitted he loved me. I'd never been able to tell him I returned his feelings. In recent years, neither of us had ever mentioned that scary four-letter word, "love." Maybe that was because we didn't know what it meant. "Call first," I said. "I may be running late."

He let go. "Right."

Milo turned away and went inside, leaving me out in the cold.

The first thing I did back at the office was to have Kip put the poaching and shooting story on our website. Spence would still beat me with his radio broadcast, but at least we'd have the news available online. Returning to my cubbyhole, I was hanging my wet coat on a peg above the baseboard heater when Mitch strolled in to see me.

"Turns out we've got more than just a poaching story," he said with that sparkle in his eyes only journalists and other kinds of ghouls get from death and near-death occasions. "Any word on the victim?"

"Dodge thinks he'll be okay," I said. "Any word on the poachers?"

"Nothing new." Mitch sat down. "I've got pictures of stumps and piles of leaves. Unfortunately, I didn't get to the scene until Laurentis was being loaded into the ambulance. I took a couple of shots, but you can't really see him or the medics. One of those guys is Del Amundson, Wes Amundson's brother, right?"

"No, they're cousins," I said. "Barney, who owns Alpine Meats, is Wes's brother. They're a fairly big family."

Mitch put a hand to his head. "I'm beginning to think I'll never get all these people straightened out. Are you sure everybody isn't related to everybody else?"

"Not really," I replied with a smile. "Just figure most of them are somehow connected to Vida and you'll be fine. I take it the deputies didn't find any usable evidence?"

"Dustin Fong told me they had some tire tracks, but they've gotten them before. In fact," Mitch went on, looking up at the ceiling, where we could hear the hard rain pelting the roof, "they're not even sure the tracks are from last night. The ground up there was frozen."

"If only they could find out who the buyer is," I said. "Maybe there's more than one, unless whoever they're selling to is fronting for several instrument makers."

"That's more likely. Somehow I can't picture the artisans who craft violins dirtying their talented hands by dealing directly with poachers."

"True," I allowed. "At least we have a solid lead story. It'd be a big help if Craig got a look at whoever shot him. Being a painter, he might be better than most at noticing things."

Mitch cocked his head at me. "You call him Craig? Do you actually know this guy?"

I gave a little shrug. "I've run into him a few times. In fact, he rescued me once when I had a bad fall in the woods. On another occasion he helped some people I knew who'd gotten . . . lost."

Mitch regarded me curiously. "Lost?"

I let out a sigh. "Lost in more ways than one. It's a long story." I wasn't going to blab about how Tom Cavanaugh's children had gotten mixed up in an attempted buyout of the *Advocate* or how they'd avoided being killed by the instigators.

Mitch took his cue and stood up. "I'll let you get to work. What's the deal? I write the poaching story and you write about the shooting?"

"No," I said, "you can do both. They're intertwined, and at this point, I don't know any more about . . . Laurentis's condition or any information he may have than you do. We can update that part just before we go to press with a sidebar."

"Got it." Mitch stood up and went back to the newsroom.

I decided to do some online research on tree poaching around the state. This latest theft was worthy of another editorial. I'd already published a short one after the first couple of trees were cut down, but we were reaching epidemic proportions. I'd ask readers for any information they could provide, knowing that although most responses would be worthless, there might be something helpful.

Unfortunately, my online talents are limited. I could find plenty of tree-poaching references, and most of them were related to gyppo loggers who cut trees on government or private property. There were a few references to maples as sources for guitars, but many others were for different types of maples that didn't grow in my part of the world. Certain varieties were desirable for their tonewood, which I learned was especially prized for making wonderful bongo drums.

I was about to wing it when Amanda came into my office.

"There's someone here to see you about the receptionist's job," she said, looking on her guard.

"Who is it?" I asked.

Amanda made a face. "Denise Petersen from the bank. Do you want to talk to her?"

FIVE

It took a moment to make up my mind. "Okay, where's the harm?"

Amanda shrugged. "Maybe she isn't as dumb as she acts. Denise says Rick Erlandson recommended her."

"He would, wouldn't he?"

Amanda blushed. "I should've thought of that. Yes, for all sorts of reasons. He's under the gun, isn't he?"

"You bet," I said. "Go ahead, I'll talk to her. Let's see if she can find the way to my office."

The pretty but dim young woman I remembered from the bank scandal didn't look much like the careworn creature who entered my cubbyhole a couple of minutes later. I'd glimpsed Denise since her return to the bank, but had avoided her teller's window. I could screw up my checking account without any help from someone as inept as she'd been on her first tour of duty behind the counter. To make matters worse, I'd forgotten that her father had just died in prison. I felt not only stupid but callous.

"Hi, Denise," I said, trying to sound friendly. "Have a seat. How are you doing?"

"Okay." Her face was thinner, with tiny wrinkles on her forehead and around her mouth. The blond and copper foil job on her hair was past its shelf date by at least a couple of months.

I felt sorry for her. "You must be upset about your father's death. I really don't know what to say, except I understand. My own parents both died at around the same age."

Denise barely looked at me. "Thanks."

I was at a loss for words, but finally cut to the chase. "Are you here about the temporary job opening?"

"Yes." Denise swallowed hard before continuing. "I never liked working at the bank, but it was the only job I could get after my divorce. It's not final yet, I mean, it will be," she went on speaking faster and faster, "but I never realized that a couple couldn't just split and move on. All these lawyer fees and filings and a bunch of other stuff take forever. Plus Greg has moved away, so he's in King County now. Or is it Snohomish? I can never remember which one Brier is in."

"Just inside Snohomish County," I said. "Have you discussed duties and hours and salary with Amanda?"

Denise nodded vaguely. "She told me what she did and how much she makes. It sounds fine."

I noticed her address was on Hope Court, a fairly new street on Second Hill near the Dithers sisters' horse farm. "Are you living in one of those townhouses the Bourgettes built a few years ago?"

She nodded. "Greg and I bought it when we got married. They were brand-new back then."

"Do you intend to stay now that you're divorced?"

Denise looked surprised. "Why wouldn't I? It's nice."

"Often when couples split, they sell the house or condo or whatever and split the proceeds, not just to avoid living amidst unhappy memories, but because Washington is a community property state."

Denise looked even more surprised. "It is? What if I don't want to move? It's such a hassle."

"You don't *have* to," I said, "but I assume Greg isn't paying his share of the mortgage." Realizing I was overstepping the boundaries of etiquette, not to mention violating Denise's privacy, I changed the subject. "Do you have other employment options when Ginny comes back to work?"

"Options?" Denise gazed around my office, as if she might find an option or two hanging on the walls. "I'm not sure. Maybe I'll take that new cosmetology course that my cousin's teaching at the college."

It had slipped my mind that Linda Petersen's daughter, Alison Lindahl, and Denise Petersen Jensen were related. "That might be a good idea," I said. "Stella Magruder seems to have a fairly high turnover rate at her salon. So many of the girls who work there don't stay long because they get married and have babies." *But not necessarily in that order,* I thought to myself. And then realized I wasn't one to criticize. I'd done the latter, but not the former—unfortunately.

"Really? I never noticed. Somehow those girls at the salon all look kind of alike." Denise ran a hand through her hair. "I should make an appointment to get my hair done before Christmas."

"Do you have a résumé?" I asked.

Denise looked blank. "No. I mean, I just heard about the job here from Rick Erlandson this morning. Do you need one?"

The question should've been, "Do *I* need one?" but I passed on saying so. "Do you have to give notice at the bank?"

"I don't think so. I mean, Rick wouldn't have told me about

the job if he thought we'd have to go through a bunch of stuff before I could quit. He's a nice guy. I think he understands."

And I understood that Rick probably couldn't wait to see the back of Denise. I wanted to stall, but I was facing more than one deadline. "Tomorrow is Amanda's last day. Could you spend at least part of it letting her show you the ropes?"

"Sure."

"Can you start Wednesday?"

"Sure."

I stood up. "Okay, let's go out and talk to Amanda."

My part of the conversation was brief. I left the two women after less than a minute and returned to my cubbyhole. I was halfway through the maple-poaching editorial when Vida arrived just before three o'clock.

"I can't believe it," she gasped. "Denise is out there in the front office with Amanda. Are you really going to hire that nitwit?"

"Would you prefer Ed Bronsky?" I asked.

Vida rocked on her heels. "Oh! Certainly not. But still . . ."

"I know. I considered Carla, but I doubt she'd do it. It'd be a comedown not only from her college job, but as a reporter here. She's got a family, too. We forget that Carla isn't a fresh-faced youth anymore. She probably needs the time off from her college duties to regroup, especially for the holidays."

Vida sighed. "I suppose." She shook her head before removing her hat, which now looked like a bunch of drowned birds. "Craig Laurentis is doing as well as can be expected. He's had one transfusion and will get another later on. Meanwhile, Dr. Sung removed the bullet. Milo can tell you about that."

"Has Craig said anything about who shot him?"

"No. He's been sedated and will stay that way at least until this evening." Vida studied her hat. "Dear me, I wonder if this will dry out." She sighed again. "Did Denise mention a funeral for her father?"

"No," I replied, "and from what I gathered, she's not terribly interested. She can come in tomorrow to learn the job and it sounds as if she'll be ready to go to work on Wednesday."

"I'll try to view that as good news," Vida said. "About her working here, I mean. The bank will be shorthanded, but there are plenty of college students who'd like to earn extra money while they're on break."

"True," I agreed. "I'd thought of hiring a student, but with finals still to come, fall quarter isn't officially over for another ten days. We'll manage somehow with Denise."

"I must get busy," Vida declared. "If you have anything for 'Scene,' let me know."

I promised I would. For a moment, I let myself slump in relief over the news that Craig's condition wasn't life-threatening. Then I remembered Donna Wickstrom had told me about his new painting. Maybe I'd stop by on my way home to see what it looked like. Ordinarily, it'd be an item for "Scene," but with Craig appearing so prominently on page one, I decided we should probably save that bit for another issue.

Just before five, I went out to see Vida. Mitch and Leo had already left, Amanda had reported that her get-acquainted session with Denise had gone relatively well, and Kip was still in the back shop. I'd finished my editorial shortly after three, and had spent the rest of the afternoon on the phone talking to people in Olympia about how the state land commissioner's office was dealing with tree poaching. After conversations with several well-meaning and seemingly intelligent staff personnel, I came away with only a few maybe-if-I-got-desperate quotes. Like our sheriff and the local rangers, they couldn't add much more than I already knew. There had been some arrests made, along with a conviction or two, but the problem still existed.

"You okay?" I asked Vida, leaning on her desk.

She peered at me from behind her big orange-framed glasses. "Of course. I shouldn't have gotten into such a state about Buck. You're quite right. Men are very insensitive. But the thought of Roger joining the Marines is still worrisome. Perhaps he'll change his mind."

"You don't think it'd help him get some structure in his life?"

"There are less dangerous ways," she said. "As much as I hate the idea, he might do better in college if he went to a school outside of Alpine. Not a big city, of course—too much temptation for any young man—but Everett, perhaps, or Bellingham. The latter would be my first choice, because my daughter Meg and her family live there. That would help make him feel at home. Roger's cousins are somewhat older, but he gets along with them when we're all together."

"I thought Meg's kids had moved away."

Vida nodded. "Temporarily," she finally said in a detached tone. "One's in graduate school at WSU in Pullman. The other is in Beijing, but only for a year. It's a temporary assignment with one of those computer companies."

Meg and the third daughter, Beth, who lived in Tacoma, both had children who were older than Roger. From what I'd gathered over the years, the other grandchildren survived their cousin's presence by exerting patience and tolerance.

"I assume Roger will make his own decision," I said, aware that Vida was probably in denial. "I'm off to Donna's art gallery. By coincidence, Craig Laurentis has a new painting there."

Vida's eyes sparked. "Indeed? Are you thinking of buying it?"

"I haven't even seen it," I said, "but I'm curious. The works that I've seen have always shown an amazing job of capturing the area around here. Don't you think *Sky Autumn* is special?"

"It's quite nice," she allowed, "but I've always preferred pictures of flowers—with or without fruit. I feel that art appreciation is a matter of individual taste. At least Laurentis's paintings are recognizable."

"Definitely," I said. "Take care. It's snowing, but not sticking."

Ten minutes later I was inside Donna's small gallery on Front Street between Seventh and Eighth. She had a hard-and-fast rule at her day care. Any parents who hadn't picked up their children before five o'clock were automatically assessed a twenty-five-dollar fine. Otherwise, she couldn't open the gallery on time to serve her weekday-evening art lovers.

So far, I was the only person on the premises besides Donna. She greeted me with a tired smile and an offer of hot chocolate. "I brought a thermos from home," she said. "I always make it for the children when it snows, but it started too late in the afternoon for them to drink it all."

"I'm fine," I said. "I'm anxious to see Craig's new painting."

Donna shook her head. "I could hardly believe it when I heard he'd been shot. Is there any further news?"

"No," I replied, "but what we do know is encouraging. I doubt there'll be an update on his condition until tomorrow."

"I can't imagine who'd do such a thing," Donna said, going behind the counter. "Are people who poach trees armed and dangerous?"

"It seems that this time they were," I said. "Maybe they carry guns in case they encounter bears or other animals that might attack them. That would make some kind of sense, I guess."

"Maybe." Donna bent down to wrestle with a three-by-five-foot package wrapped in wrinkled brown paper and tied with thick string. "To be honest, I haven't seen the painting in a decent light. Craig dropped it off last night while we were gone. We didn't get home from the late movie until after midnight, so I only took a quick look before rewrapping it to keep it safe from the children." She carefully cut the string with scissors and then made a long slice through the paper. "I put cardboard around the canvas because of the weather." She laughed, a light, tinkling sound like a little brass bell. "Craig's a bit careless when it comes to his deliveries. Steve and I would've missed this one if he hadn't hauled out the garbage after we got home."

"I take it your kids were with you?"

Donna shook her head. "Our oldest, Karen, is nineteen. Can you believe that?"

I could, though I hadn't thought about it. Karen wasn't Steve's daughter, but from Donna's first marriage, to Deputy Art Fremstad, who had been killed in the line of duty before I moved to Alpine. "I'm not sure I'd recognize Karen," I admitted. "I assume she doesn't want to help with the day care."

Donna had gotten down to the cardboard. "Not after all the babysitting she's done for us in the past few years. Anyway, she's a sophomore at the UW this year. She came home for the Thanksgiving holiday and stayed over last night because she had a late class today. We bought her a decent old car when she started college."

After removing two layers of cardboard, Donna revealed the painting. "Well? What do you think?"

I was stunned. "It's . . . different."

Donna stepped back for a longer look. "It is, but Craig's not the kind of artist who stays with the same old thing. That's good. It means he's still trying different ways to express himself." She turned to me. "You don't like it?"

I didn't know what to say. Admittedly, I'd seen only a few of

Craig's paintings, and while this was also a forest scene, it wasn't as realistic or as compelling. The colors were very dark, while the bare tree branches seemed distorted. If there was undergrowth, such as ferns, salal, or Oregon grape, I couldn't see their greenery. Even the jagged patches of sky were a murky shade of blue bordering on purple. The only bright spots were touches of gold on the ground, as if somehow the sun had broken through the clouds. Maybe it was a reflected sunset, maybe it was just a couple of blobs. Whatever the painting's statement was meant to convey eluded me.

I shrugged. "I'm not an art expert. It may be amazing to someone who understands painting, but it sort of throws me for a loop."

"You probably need to study it more closely," Donna said. "As I mentioned, I recognized that Craig was going in a different direction. But that can be a very good thing." She smiled at me. "I didn't tell you about this as a sales pitch. I just thought you'd like to see it."

"Oh, I do. He's very talented. Maybe it was rushed."

"No," Donna said, "I can tell it wasn't because of the paint layers. He worked on this for a long time. Not consistently, but whenever the mood struck him. He put a lot of himself in it, I think. It has a certain brooding quality. Maybe it shows something about why he chose his unusual lifestyle. That's just a guess, but do you see what I mean?"

"Maybe. I guess I'd have to reflect on that."

"I'll do the same," Donna said. "I like to understand an artist's motivation. It's not easy, and I'm probably wrong when I come up with a theory, but it makes me feel less like a dilettante."

"You do very well when it comes to your selections," I said. "I see you have some new vases. Who did those? I like the sort of shimmering shafts of . . . what?"

"Mother-of-pearl—real oyster shells," Donna explained. "They sort of swoop and swirl among the brighter colors. An eighty-year-old woman in Hoquiam does them. She only started working in this medium a couple of years ago."

"Nice," I said. "I wonder if my old pal Mavis down in Portland would like one for a Christmas present."

"Let me know," Donna said, scrunching up the used wrapping paper. "They run twenty to fifty dollars. I've got those four left. I sold two over the weekend."

I told her I'd mull a bit, and on that note I thanked Donna and took my leave. The wet snow was still coming down, but I'd parked just around the corner. I only needed to turn on my wipers to clear the windshield. It was almost six when I pulled into my carport. Every winter I promised myself I'd have a real garage built, but I never got around to it. Procrastination sometimes seems like my middle name. Maybe I'm that way because in my work life, I'm always up against deadlines.

I came inside through the kitchen door that leads from the carport, flipped on the lights, and went into the living room. Before taking my coat off, I gazed at *Sky Autumn* above the sofa. It was as mesmerizing as ever. I studied the details more closely than usual—the graceful bending branches of vine maples, with their silvery bark; broken twigs trapped in the water between rocks, looking anxious to move on; dark, dense forest in the background, with the slim gray trunks and a few brown leaves still clinging to the alders; the merest hint of patchy blue and white sky—it was autumn, a season of both sun and rain, of death on the ground and rebirth underneath.

This was definitely more appealing than Craig's most recent work. It suddenly dawned on me that I hadn't asked Donna what it was called. I took off my coat, went out to the kitchen to pour a Pepsi, grabbed a package of Gulf prawns from the freezer, and returned to the living room to call the gallery. Before I could dial the number, I discovered I had two phone messages. The first was from a charity with a name I didn't recognize, so I erased it and listened to the second call.

"It's almost five-thirty," Milo said. "If you want me to stop by, call before six. Otherwise, I'm going out to wrap my pipes."

It was now ten after six. I didn't know if I was more annoyed with Milo—or with myself. I'd forgotten his suggestion to "fill me in." On the other hand, how long would it take the sheriff to wrap his damned pipes? His house in the Icicle Creek development wasn't that much bigger than mine. Furthermore, he always took his cell with him—except when he was fishing. I knew Milo was miffed by my lack of enthusiasm for his offer, but he didn't usually play games. I pondered calling him anyway, but the phone rang before I could punch in his number.

"There you are," Vida said. "I thought you might be negotiating a price on that new picture."

"No," I replied, "but I did see it. It's not what I expected."

"You mean it's all squares and circles and cubes and clowns?"

I wasn't sure what Vida was talking about, unless it was some oblique reference to Picasso. "No," I repeated. "But it's quite different from Craig's usual work. It's still a landscape, though. I didn't particularly care for it."

"Just as well." She didn't pause for breath. "There won't be a funeral for Larry Petersen. Al Driggers called me right after I got home. He'd heard from JoAnne, and even though she divorced Larry after he went to prison, she's apparently still in charge of his estate. A guardianship, perhaps. She told Al that the family—I assume that means the three children, Denise, Cole, and Frankie—agree with her. She does want his cremated remains put in the mausoleum here. Apparently, and this is according to Al, she felt the Petersens should be together."

"But no service of any kind?"

"Only immediate family. However, it will be a few days before the remains are sent here. There's an autopsy, which I
gather is not unusual when someone dies in prison, especially if
the deceased is fairly young and not in obvious poor health. Al
says it has to do with some kind of government regulations, no
doubt to avoid lawsuits."

"That's understandable," I said. "So you'll write the obit?"

"Of course," Vida replied. "It will be tricky, though. Still,
everyone around here knows the background. Tact and taste are
required."

"You'll do it just fine," I said.

"I must cover Cupcake. He doesn't like snow, and I'm always afraid he'll catch a cold. I'd miss his singing."

I rang off so Vida could take care of her canary. After running the frozen prawns under hot water, I changed my mind
about calling Milo. The lonely holiday had given me an attack
of perversity, a not uncommon condition. I was still feeling
sorry for myself, and because I despise people who wallow in
self-pity, I'd inflict more misery as punishment for behaving so
childishly. It made no sense, but I'd do it anyway. That's why the
condition is perverse.

I called Donna instead. She answered on the third ring. I
asked her the name of Craig's new painting.

"His attached note says *Forest Watch,* though it doesn't
really fit the painting," Donna said. "I'm not sure what he means.
In fact, he crossed out something that I can barely read. I *think*
it says *Forest Leg* or *Forest Log.* Does that sound right to you?"

I thought for a moment. "Not really. As I recall, his titles are
usually self-explanatory."

"Well . . . it must mean something to him," Donna said. "I
wish I could actually speak with him about his work, but he's
too antisocial. Of course he's not the only one who doesn't like

to discuss his or her creativity. It's so personal. And then," she added with a little laugh, "there are the ones who won't shut up. I thought that since you're a writer, maybe you'd have an idea of what the title meant."

"Sorry. I really don't."

But I should have.

SIX

B Y MORNING, WE HAD TWO INCHES OF WET SNOW UNDER A clearing sky. I'd kept my eye on the weather off and on during the evening, in between going over my Christmas card list and catching some of the Monday Night Football game that had turned into a rout with Green Bay pounding St. Louis into the turf. Apparently, the wintry weather had moved east to the other side of the Cascades. By the time I left for work just before eight, my route had been traveled enough to make driving fairly easy.

Amanda had pulled in just ahead of me. I parked next to her red Miata. "Not a top-down day," I called out as she paused on the sidewalk.

"I haven't had the top down since Labor Day." Amanda opened the front door for me. "It's odd," she went on as we stepped inside and stomped slushy snow from our boots, "but I've gotten to like this job. What if Ginny decides not to come back?"

"You'd want to work for us full-time?"

Amanda sighed. "That's the problem. I've never worked

full-time, and it never was good for me, not just the lack of a regular income, but having too many empty hours to fill." She looked away. "It's gotten me into some bad situations. Now that I'm in my thirties, I realize I need either children or a regular job, whatever keeps me grounded. Walt and I both want a family, but who knows how long it'll take before that happens?" She finally stared me in the eye. "Yes, if Ginny doesn't come back and nothing happens on the adoption front, then I would like to work here. If you'd have me."

I smiled. "Of course I would. Once you settled in, you did a fine job. But let's not get ahead of ourselves. This is your last day, and you'll be busy at the post office until into the new year. A lot of dust will settle by that time."

To my amazement, Amanda hugged me. "Thanks. I really appreciate the vote of confidence." She stepped back, looking embarrassed. "That's another thing—I've never had a real girlfriend in Alpine. I can talk to you. That's nice."

I was touched. Making friends wasn't easy for anyone who moved to Alpine as an adult. I knew that from experience. "I'm glad to be a friend," I said, "but I'm almost old enough to be your mother."

"You don't seem that old," Amanda said. She looked at her watch. "It's after eight. Where's Denise? She told me she'd come by this morning for another round of instruction." Her brown eyes grew wide. "Oh, my God! I was late on my first day—remember?"

"Vaguely." I turned to look at the front entrance just as Denise came in. With a dog.

"Hi," she said, struggling to control a large black and tan animal tugging at its leash. "This is Doofus. I had to bring him along because he can chew his way out of the house when nobody's around and then I have to search all over the . . ." She grasped the dog's collar. "Come on, Doof. You'll like it here.

I've got your ball." With her free hand, she reached into her coat pocket and took out a beat-up tennis ball. "Fetch!" she cried, freeing the dog and tossing the ball toward the hall between the front office and the back shop. He raced past Amanda and me, brushing against both of us, but not quite knocking us down.

"Hey," I said sharply. "We don't allow pets here. You're going to have to—" Doofus just missed running into me as he brought the ball back to Denise. "You're going to have to take him home."

"I can't," Denise said, petting the panting dog. "He belongs to Greg. He dropped Doof off with me before Thanksgiving and he hasn't picked him up yet. I think Greg went to California."

"Why," I asked as Doofus sniffed my boots and then panted some more, "can't you take him back to your place?"

"Besides running off, he ate my down comforter yesterday. He's very gentle. In fact, he's scared of cats. I can't leave him alone."

Doofus was licking Amanda's Cole Haan leather boots that must've cost her several hundred dollars. She danced away from him and managed to get around to the other side of our reception counter. Doofus started to howl.

"You can't leave him here, and that's that," I said. "If you want to hang out with Amanda later today, that's fine, but you don't have to begin work until tomorrow." Before Denise could argue, I turned my back on her, stomped off through the newsroom to my cubbyhole, and slammed the door behind me.

Ten minutes later, someone knocked. "Emma?"

It was Leo. "Come in," I called to him. "No dogs allowed."

He opened the door. "The dog and its owner are gone," he said. "She literally had to lug that big mutt outside. What's with that action?"

"First of all," I responded, "Denise isn't the owner. The dog belongs to her ex, but she's mutt-sitting him. I wonder if Rick or Andy let her keep him at the bank."

"They could always lock him in the vault," Leo said. "Looks like he's part rottweiler. Denise called him a rescue dog. Does that mean he can rescue people or that people rescued him?"

"The latter, I think. What have I gotten us into?"

"We should never have complained about Ginny the Mope," Leo said. "I just ate breakfast at the diner with Fleetwood. He's got three more co-op ads for us this week."

"Excellent. Did he say anything about Craig Laurentis? I was just going to call the hospital."

Leo shook his head. "We were all business, though he did allude to hanging out with you in the ER yesterday. Has Fleetwood ever made a pass at you?"

The question might've seemed inappropriate, but I knew Leo was asking more out of concern than curiosity. "Never." I saw his skeptical expression. "We don't do anything for each other, except for occasional attacks of mutual aggravation. Are you trying to set me up?"

"God, no," Leo assured me. "I just wondered. He's the kind of guy I figured women might find attractive."

"I'm sure many of them do. I'm just not one of them."

Leo shrugged. "Forget I asked. I'm off to meet a deadline."

Vida and Mitch had also arrived. Now that my door was open, I could hear them talking about Denise and the dog. It sounded as if Vida had arrived before Doofus had been removed from the premises.

"... and an ugly animal to boot," my House & Home editor was saying. "Such big teeth! I'd be terrified around a creature like that."

"You mean the dog—or Denise?" Mitch responded.

"Oh, you know exactly what . . ."

My phone rang, forcing me to stop eavesdropping. "Get your butt down here pronto," Milo said without preamble.

"Why?"

"Just do it."

"Is it about Craig?"

"No." He hung up.

I put my coat on, grabbed my purse, and hurried through the newsroom. "Don't ask," I said over my shoulder. "The sheriff's in a tizzy."

Vida was agape. "Oh, for heaven's . . ." I was gone before she finished speaking.

Most of the snow had already melted off the sidewalks. It took me only a couple of minutes to reach the sheriff's office a block and a half away. Deputies Doe Jamison and Jack Mullins were talking to each other inside the curving counter; Lori Cobb, the receptionist and secretary, was on the phone.

"Where is he?" I asked.

Jack gestured at Milo's closed door. "Dodge got another letter. I think he's about to arrest Marlowe Whipp for delivering the mail."

"Damn. Dare I go in?"

"Damned if you do, damned if you don't," Jack said. "Maybe you can calm him down before he has a stroke."

I didn't bother to knock. "Well?" I said, immediately sitting down across the desk from the seething sheriff. "Is that fire and brimstone coming out of your nose or are you smoking?"

"Don't get cute," Milo snapped, picking up his cigarette from the ashtray. "Shit. I lighted two."

"Give the other one to me," I said resignedly. "This is going to be a bad day—again. Let's see the letter."

Milo handed me the longer of the two cigarettes and the single sheet of paper. It was typed in the same style as the others:

"TOO BAD SOMEBODY SHOT THE WRONG GUY—HOPE THEY
SAVED A BULLET FOR YOU, YOU BASTARD."

"Sent yesterday?" I asked.

The sheriff nodded. "Same kind of envelope, same postmark, same stamp, same frigging everything else except that this
son of a bitch is escalating the threats. Nut or not, I don't need
this shit."

"Of course you don't," I agreed after taking a puff on the
cigarette. It'd been so long since I'd smoked that I felt slightly
light-headed. "Do you have even the faintest idea of who might
be doing this?"

Milo glowered at me. "If I did, don't you think I'd do something about it?"

"Okay, okay. It was a dumb question." I hesitated, unwilling
to bring up what could elicit an even more explosive response
from the sheriff. "The reason I ask is that there was some confusion over the arrest of Clive Berentsen in the De Muth homicide last month." I saw Milo start to protest, but I kept on
talking. "I know he confessed, I know there were witnesses, I
know the whole sad story as well as you do, but the fact that
Clive didn't do it and had to be released later might have put an
idea into somebody's addled brain. The first letter mentioned
you'd made a mistake recently. The allusion could've been to
the Berentsen situation." I shrugged. "You know crazy people
get hold of even crazier notions and take off like rockets."

"Yeah, I know all that crap." Milo stubbed out his cigarette
and took a swig of coffee from his NRA mug. "What if it's not
a nut?"

"Why wouldn't it be?"

He rubbed at his graying sandy hair. "I mean somebody with
a serious grudge. It happens. It's part of the job description. But
I can't think of anyone connected to the Petersen case who'd do

something like this. The worst part about Linda's murder was that it involved one of the rock-solid Alpine families. Except for Larry feeling he wasn't worthy of running the bank and becoming head of the family when Marvin retired or died, nobody else was weird."

My mind's eye flashed back to Denise and the dog. But that wasn't weird, it was just poor judgment. As for being a bit dim, that was hardly a crime, or half of Alpine would be under suspicion. "I can't argue that point. By the way, Denise is taking Ginny's place for the month of December."

Milo leaned back in his chair and gazed at the ceiling. "Good luck. You must be desperate."

"I am." Since the sheriff seemed to have calmed down a bit, I broached the subject of Craig Laurentis.

"I stopped at the clinic and talked to Doc Dewey on my way to work," Milo replied. "He said Laurentis is listed in satisfactory condition, but to hold off until later this morning to question him. The guy's still kind of loopy from all the drugs."

"That's good news," I said.

"Yeah. We could use some." He lit another cigarette. "Where were you last night? Didn't you get my message?"

"I got it too late," I replied. "I stopped to see Craig's new painting at Donna's gallery. It's kind of strange."

"Oh?" Milo's interest seemed forced. "How so?"

"Just a different style. Sort of gloomy. Donna seemed to like it."

"She has to if she wants to sell it." He gestured at his mug. "You want coffee?"

"No thanks. I haven't even had a chance to get any at the office. You summoned me peremptorily."

"So I did." He glanced at the letter. "You think I'm overreacting."

"Not exactly," I hedged. "It's unsettling, but I doubt the writer is dangerous."

Milo regarded me with a wry expression. "Oh? Want to put that in writing?"

"Actually, that's my point. I get letters all the time telling me I'm the worst person in the world, I should be run out of town, I ought to be taken out and shot. Ninety-nine percent of them are unsigned or use phony names, so it's against my policy to print them in the paper. Almost half of them are repeat writers, the same goofballs who are always upset about something, which may or may not have to do with what's in the *Advocate*. They're letting off steam. It's a harmless safety valve. Your letters could be in the same category."

Milo thought for a minute. "Okay, I understand what you're saying. But what bothers me is that these letters started coming just a few days before Larry Petersen died." He held up a hand to keep me from responding. "I know what you're going to say—that it's a coincidence. But it's a damned strange one. You have to admit that."

"That's why the word 'coincidence' exists." It was the only explanation I could offer.

Milo puffed on his cigarette. "Let's hope you're right. But it still bothers the hell out of me."

I realized I'd let my own cigarette burn out and flipped the dead filter tip into the ashtray. "I don't know what else to tell you."

"What about the fact that these letters seem to be written by somebody who isn't a high school dropout?"

The correct spelling and decent grammar hadn't eluded me. "They were typed on a computer. The writer has spelling and grammar checks available. That tells me—along with the fact that the person's literate—he or she is also meticulous. It's someone who's concerned about not looking foolish or stupid."

Milo finished his coffee and set the mug aside. "And that doesn't disturb you?"

I made a face. "Well . . . I suppose it should. Maybe."

"It disturbs me." He waved a hand. "Okay, we're done here. I have to catch crooks who've committed actual crimes, like the poachers who shot Laurentis."

I stood up. "Will you let me know what Craig says?"

"I will if it's fit to print."

I thanked the sheriff and took my leave.

When I got back to the office, Leo and Mitch were both away from their desks, but Vida was ready to pounce. "Well?" she said the moment I set foot in the newsroom.

I brought her up to date on the letters Milo had received, then summed up the conjectures he and I had made. "If you have any other ideas," I said, "feel free to say so."

"I don't," she admitted, "but I may." Vida gestured at a handwritten letter on her desk. "Another pathetic creature, this one asking for advice about why her husband goes to sleep on his feet and sometimes while he's walking. It's signed 'Wide Awake Worrier.' I almost wish I required actual signatures, but of course most people don't want everyone in Alpine gossiping about their problems. I'd never get any letters at all even if I promised anonymity only in the paper. They'd know I'd know who they were. Not that I'd ever let on, but they can't be sure of that. Clearly, this husband needs to see a doctor. He's a narcoleptic."

"I hope he doesn't drive that way," I remarked. "I wish you'd get one from somebody complaining about a spouse or relative who writes crazy letters to the sheriff. It's beginning to get to me, even though I try to soothe Milo by telling him it's a nut."

Vida frowned. "I'll have to think about it. Right now I've got to find that pickled herring recipe for 'Stumpied.'"

I finally got my coffee along with a glazed French doughnut. An hour later I'd gone over most of Vida's page, all of Leo's ads that he'd submitted so far, and the local articles Mitch had finished. He wouldn't be done with the poaching/shooting lead until we had the latest information. The county commissioners' meeting also had to be put on hold except for the agenda.

Just before nine-thirty I got a call from my next-door neighbor, Viv Marsden. "Emma," she began, "didn't you notice that big package on your porch when you got home last night?"

"Package?" I echoed. "No. I came in through the kitchen and left the same way this morning. I didn't know it was there. Can you tell who it's from?"

"I didn't look." She laughed self-consciously. "I try not to be your nosy neighbor, and in fact I wouldn't have called you if I hadn't seen a FedEx truck parked on the verge between our houses yesterday afternoon. I thought maybe it was a Christmas present I'd ordered for Val, but the guy went to your house. Then this morning I decided to walk to Safeway to get some exercise and I noticed the package was still on your porch."

"Hunh," I said. "I haven't ordered anything lately. I'm not quite geared up for Christmas yet. If you don't mind, maybe you should get it and take it inside your house. I'll collect it tonight after work."

"No problem," Viv assured me. "I worry about things left outside for very long because of your other neighbors and their rotten kids. They've made off with some of Val's garden tools and his chainsaw. Fortunately, we got all the stuff back, but next time it happens, we're calling the sheriff."

"I don't blame you," I said. "So far, I don't think they've stolen anything of mine, but maybe I don't have items that appeal to them."

Viv harrumphed. "I'd hardly call Val's Weed Eater an entic-
ing object for teenagers except as a weapon. Those Nelson kids
are too lazy to do any work around their own house."

I agreed, and after a few more words of chitchat, I thanked
Viv and hung up. The rest of the morning flew by with the usual
busy work to meet our Tuesday deadline. It wasn't until after I
got back from getting my takeout lunch at the Burger Barn that
I heard from Milo.

"I've been at the hospital for over half an hour," he said,
sounding grumpy. "I'm waiting until Stella is finished and I'm
damned hungry and I won't eat any of this crap they call food
around here. I had enough of that when I was a so-called patient."

"Stella?" It was the one thing he'd said that grabbed my
attention. "You mean Stella Magruder, as in Stella's Styling
Salon?"

"Who else?" Milo snapped. "She's grooming Laurentis. Nobody else could untangle Laurentis's hair and beard. Jesus Christ,
you'd think I never interviewed somebody with lousy hygiene."

"I don't think that's exactly the point," I said. "Given Craig's
lifestyle, he could infect the hospital. I imagine the medics who
brought him in sanitized themselves after they left him in
the ER."

"Whatever. Anyway, I still haven't talked to the guy. In fact,
I'm going over to the Venison Inn and grab some lunch. I'll call
you whenever I've got something that isn't fleas or lice or whatever Laurentis might still be able to pass on to me."

"I'll be here," I said. "It's deadline day."

I changed my mind as soon as I hung up. Now that the rest
of this week's edition was almost wrapped up and we were playing a waiting game to finish the front page, I grew curious about
the mysterious package Viv Marsden had seen on my front
porch. It probably wasn't from Ben, who never Christmas-

shopped until the last minute. Besides, if my brother had sent something, he would've mentioned it when we spoke on the phone. As for Adam, his teachers at the seminary apparently had never taught him that Catholic dogma didn't prohibit the shipping of parcels both ways. Except for sending some knitwear that his native parishioners had made, my son believed that it was better to receive than to give, at least when it came from his mother.

I dialed Viv's number and asked if she'd had time to retrieve the package. She had, remarking that it was fairly heavy and bore a PERISHABLE sticker.

"Food?" I said. "Where was it sent from?"

"Ooh-la-la, Emma," she said, laughing. "It's from a shop in Paris."

Damn. I thought I'd heard the last of Rolf Fisher. My former so-called lover, for lack of a better term, had taken early retirement from the AP, exchanging his Seattle condo for a cottage in the Loire Valley. Or something like that. I was never sure what to believe with Rolf, which was probably why he intrigued me enough that I slept with him. Maybe I kept hoping I'd actually fall in love with the exasperating yet attractive and eligible jerk. He'd invited me to join him at his oh-so-charming *petite maison* in château country, but I'd repeatedly turned him down. I hadn't heard from him for at least six weeks, so I figured he'd finally decided I was a lost cause. But typical of Rolf, he didn't take no for an answer. Or so I assumed.

"No actual name on the package?" I asked Viv.

"Just the shop it came from," she replied. "I don't speak French, so bear with me. I can't pronounce the name, but the address is 27 Place de la Madeleine. Does that mean anything to you?"

It meant more to me than Viv could guess, since Tom and I'd

planned to spend our honeymoon in Paris. "All I know is it may be close to the opera house, which means it's in a fashionable part of the city."

"It's too big to put in the fridge," Viv said. "Maybe I should keep it on our back porch until you get home."

"No, keep it inside. I'll collect it when I get home from work. Thanks, Viv. Whatever is in it, I'll give you some for your trouble."

"No need," she insisted. "It isn't every day that I get to touch something that came from Paris. It's kind of exciting."

Speak for yourself, I thought. *How about "annoying" instead?*

"Do you know who it's from?" she asked before I could say anything I might regret.

"Not really," I replied, realizing that it was possible Rolf wasn't the sender. "These days anybody can order anything from anywhere. Maybe Ed Bronsky sent it as one last lavish gesture now that he has to live from paycheck to paycheck like the rest of us."

Viv laughed again. "You mean *Shirley's* paycheck. But I'm glad they finally got back into a real house. That big family of theirs must've been jammed like sardines in the mobile home. See you later, Emma."

Just after two o'clock, Mitch and I were going over the copy he'd already written for the lead story. "Maybe," I suggested, "you should go over to the hospital and see if Milo's ever going to talk to Laurentis. It's been almost two hours since I heard from the sheriff. Sometimes he forgets what the word 'deadline' means to us newspaper types."

"Will do." Mitch got up and headed out to the newsroom. Before he could put on his jacket, my phone rang.

"I could use some help over here," Milo declared in an irritable tone. "Laurentis won't talk to me. In fact, he won't talk to anybody, including Doc Dewey or Dr. Sung or the nurses."

"Won't or can't?" I said, wondering if Craig was suffering from some kind of trauma.

"Won't. He can sure as hell say 'no,'" the sheriff all but shouted.

"Hang on," I said, putting the phone down and calling to Mitch just as he was about to leave. "Change of plans." I relayed Milo's message. "Let me go over there, you hold down the fort, and then I'll call you if you're needed. Okay?"

"Sure." He started to take off his jacket. "I gather you can communicate with him."

"I *have* talked to him, but very briefly and not often," I admitted. "Still, it's worth a try."

After telling Milo I was on my way, I put on my coat, hoisted my handbag over my shoulder, and thanked God that Vida wasn't at her desk. She'd want to go with me and that might not be a good idea. In fact, trying to talk to Craig under any circumstances might not be a good idea, but I had to give it my best shot.

Once inside the hospital, I took the elevator to the second and top floor where the patient rooms were located. Debbie Murchison, a plump and pretty RN, was on duty.

"The sheriff sent for me," I informed her. "He didn't know the room number, but did say Mr. Laurentis had been moved from the ICU."

"Second door on the right," Debbie replied. "The patient has been fumigated." She wrinkled her nose and shook her head.

I tried to put on a sympathetic face, but for some reason, I felt protective about Craig. I thanked Debbie for pointing me in the right direction and went down the hall, where I found the door was closed. I knocked twice. Milo appeared a couple of seconds later, no doubt waiting impatiently for my arrival. He didn't say anything to me, but turned to the patient. "You've got a visitor. It's Ms. Lord from the newspaper."

I walked across the room, trying not to show the shock I felt. I didn't recognize the gaunt, pale, clean-shaven man in the bed. "Hello," I finally said in an unnatural voice. I had to clear my throat. Maybe it was the strong odor of disinfectant that was affecting my vocal cords. "How are you feeling?"

He gave a little shrug.

"Here," Milo said, shoving the visitor's chair at me. "Take a seat. I'm going out for a smoke."

I waited until the sheriff had left us alone. Craig seemed fixated on the blank screen of the TV set hanging from the wall. I took off my coat, stalling for time to figure out what I should say next.

"I saw your new painting last night," I finally announced, settling into a rail-back chair that looked as if it had been part of an old kitchen set. "You've altered your style."

He regarded me with those forest-green eyes I remembered so well from our first close encounter. "Well?"

The single word was raspy, another thing I remembered about Craig. Unless he talked to himself, I doubted that he used his voice very often. "I was surprised," I admitted. "It struck me as very different from *Sky Autumn* in terms of atmosphere." Maybe that wasn't the right word, but I was no art expert and lacked the proper vocabulary.

He shifted uncomfortably in the bed. There were three IVs running into his left hand, but I couldn't see any bandages, so I assumed he had been shot somewhere below his chest. "You hate it," he said at last.

I shook my head. "No. I just don't understand it. Your other paintings—and I have only seen two or three besides my own—

were all about primeval beauty. I can bond with that. I guess I was just put off by the difference in . . . *Forest Watch*."

Craig didn't comment. To break the awkward silence, I asked another question. "The original title was something else. Why did you change it?"

"It suited the final work better."

"I don't understand."

"You don't have to. You either respond or you don't. Titles aren't important except to the artist."

Feeling his dismissal for my lack of artistic understanding, I waited a few moments before I spoke again. "Where were you shot?"

He gestured with his free hand at the left side of his abdomen. "The doctor told me the bullet missed anything vital."

"That's good news. Are you in pain?"

"Yes."

"What are they giving you for it?"

He shrugged—and winced. "Morphine, I think."

I figured the medication was in one of the IVs. "Can you regulate the dosage?"

He stared at me. "Why would I do that?"

"To ease the pain."

"Pain is part of life." He looked away, toward the window with its view of the Clemans Building and the foothills that rose above the town.

This was no ordinary chat. I cut to the chase. "Who shot you?"

He waited for what seemed a long time before turning his gaze back on me. "I don't know. I never saw anyone at that time."

"How long did you lie there before you were found?"

"I kept going in and out, night and day, black and light."

"Did you know there were tree poachers in the woods?"

"Yes. They're plunderers. They're always around, in one form or another, despoiling Nature with their greed."

The more Craig talked, the less he rasped. I had a sudden vision of Dorothy pouring oil into the Tin Man's suit in *The Wizard of Oz*. "Have you ever seen any of these pillagers in the act?"

He shook his head. "I see what they leave behind. Stumps. Sawdust. Chunks of tree bark. Holes in the ground. Beer cans. Empty junk food bags. They left their consciences somewhere else a long time ago." He leaned toward me. "Are you putting this in the paper?"

I gave a start. "No. This isn't an interview."

"Then why are you here?"

The piercing green eyes seemed to bore a hole in my brain. "You wouldn't talk to the sheriff. He needs your help to find out who shot you and cut down the trees."

Craig lay back down on the pillows, the faintest of smiles at the corners of his mouth. I wondered how often he smiled. Except for his forehead, his face was curiously unlined. "You're the sheriff's stooge?"

"He knows we've met. He thought you might talk to me."

"He was right."

"He hoped you might be able to identify the shooter."

Craig shook his head. "Sorry. I can't."

"Maybe something will come to you later."

"I doubt it."

I didn't know what else to say. "You must be tired. I should go."

"I should go, too," he said. "I want out of here."

"You'll have to stay until the doctors are sure you can manage on your own."

"I always do."

"But you usually aren't recovering from a bullet wound."

"What difference does that make? I'll mend."

"You'll mend faster if you stay here for at least a couple of days."

He shook his head. "I don't think so."

Arguing with Craig was useless. I stood up. "I have to tell you how much I love *Sky Autumn*. I never tire of looking at it."

"That's good."

"Please take care of yourself," I said, hoisting my purse back over my shoulder.

He didn't respond. I was almost at the door when he spoke again. "Maybe I'll see you somewhere another time."

I swiveled around to look at him. "Yes. I hope so."

He nodded and shifted his gaze back to the window, probably looking not at Alpine's buildings, but the snow-dappled foothills that rose up the face of Mount Baldy.

SEVEN

"T WENTY MINUTES IN THERE AND YOU GOT NOTHING?" MILO practically shouted at me when I joined him at the nurses' station. "What were you doing, talking about the *Mona Lisa*?"

"Hey," I said irritably, "he didn't see the shooter. I don't think he's even sure when he was shot, let alone who pulled the trigger. What did you expect? A video of the crime?"

The sheriff let out a long, weary sigh. "I take it he talked to you."

"Yes." I avoided glancing at the eavesdropping Debbie Murchison, who was trying to look as if she were studying a patient's chart. "Why wouldn't he? He was my date at the Blanchet High School senior prom."

"I could almost believe that," Milo muttered. "If you gave *him* your frigid act, maybe that's why he became a hermit." The sheriff picked up his regulation hat. "I might as well go back to work."

It was all I could do not to say something waspish, but the conversation had already deteriorated enough. "Me too," I mumbled, refusing to look at Milo. Instead, I turned to Debbie. "How long will Mr. Laurentis be in the hospital?"

"That's up to the doctors," she replied primly.

"Of course," I said, ignoring Milo's departure. "How much of his stay is covered by welfare?"

Debbie blushed. "I wouldn't know. That's up to the billing department. Are you saying he has no health insurance?"

"I've no idea," I replied. "He's self-employed, of course."

Her blue eyes widened. "He is?"

I couldn't help but give her a withering look. "You didn't know he's an acclaimed painter?"

"No," she said. "Does he paint any of the places around here?"

I was still in perverse mode, enjoying Debbie's discomfiture. "You mean his subjects?"

"I mean, like buildings or houses or . . . you know."

"Oh!" I feigned surprise. "Not *that* kind of painter." I sounded even more condescending than I'd intended. "An artist—like Childe Hassam or Mark Tobey."

Luckily for Debbie, a patient's light went on. "Excuse me," she said, avoiding eye contact. "I must check on Mrs. Stuart."

On the way back to the *Advocate,* my less evil side surfaced and I felt guilty for my shabby treatment of Nurse Debbie. She probably did more to comfort and help other human beings in a day than I did in a month. I wondered if Ben would hear my confession over the phone. I suspect he'd tell me to get off my butt and go see Father Den at St. Mildred's. He knew I was long overdue for a confession session. Part of the reason for my reluctance was that I was always sure whoever was waiting in line outside could hear me, even if I whispered my sins into the screen that separated me from my pastor. Small towns have no anonymity. The other reason was that like so many Catholics, I dreaded the sacrament of penance, despite the fact that when I did go, I always felt much better after receiving absolution.

I was still dwelling on this conundrum when I reached the corner by the Bank of Alpine. Rick Erlandson was standing on the sidewalk talking to a husky young man who looked vaguely familiar. I nodded in their direction.

"Emma," Rick called, "got a minute?"

"Uh—sure." I walked over to join them, smiled a brief greeting at the man whose name proved elusive, and asked Rick if he wanted to talk about Ginny.

"I thought you were all squared away with that problem," Rick said. "You're not mad at Ginny, are you? Honest, she's really worn out. I try to help, but she insists on getting up at night to feed the baby."

"It's okay," I fibbed. "I'm just disappointed. We've got a replacement, thanks to you. How relieved are you to get rid of Denise?"

Rick looked stricken. "I don't . . ."

"Never mind," the other young man said grimly and offered me his hand. "I'm Frankie Petersen, Denise's older brother. Call me Strom. It's short for my middle name, after my mother's dad, Alf Bergstrom."

My hand was limp in Strom's firm grasp. "I don't know what to say. I made a terrible gaffe. I'm sorry."

He let go of my hand. "Denise is an airhead," he said, "but she can follow simple commands. Just don't try to make her do numbers."

"We can handle that part of the job," I assured him. "I didn't recognize you. It's been a long time. By the way, may I please offer my condolences on your father's death."

Strom made an indifferent gesture. "Thanks. Maybe he's in a better place now."

"True," I acknowledged.

"That's why Strom's in town," Rick said. "We still have

some family accounts at the bank. He's looking after them for his mom."

Strom nodded. "I haven't been to Alpine in almost ten years. It's changed a bit. Rick tells me it's grown since the college opened."

Rick put a hand on Strom's shoulder. "This guy's got an MBA from the University of Oregon. He works for an investment firm in Seattle. I could take lessons from him."

I noticed that despite wearing his suit jacket, Rick was shivering slightly. The wind had suddenly come up again and the blue sky was disappearing. "I'll let you two go back inside," I said. "It's getting chilly again and I've got a deadline to meet. Nice to see you, Strom." I gave him the friendliest smile I could offer and hurried across the street.

"I put my foot into that one," I told Vida, who was the only staffer in the newsroom.

She shot me a dark glance. "Interrogating Craig Laurentis?"

"No," I responded, taking off my coat. "Insulting Denise in front of her brother, Frankie. I mean Strom, as he likes to be called since he got his MBA and is working in high finance in the big city."

Vida eyed me even more keenly. "I heard he was in town," she said. "Where did you run into him?"

"Outside the bank, where he was chatting with Rick Erlandson. I didn't recognize him, and immediately opened my big mouth to criticize his sister for being a pinhead."

"An easy thing to do," Vida murmured. "I must talk to . . . Strom, you say? Well, why not? He should aspire to be like his grandfather. JoAnne Bergstrom's father was a fine man." She rested her chin on her hands. "Well now. I wonder if this is the point at which Strom takes over the bank."

"How old is he?"

"Early thirties? He was at WSU when the bank tragedy unfolded. He came back to help JoAnne move to Seattle." She frowned. "I wonder if Cole will come, too. He'd just started at Western Washington State back then. Denise will know what he's up to. I hope she knows *something*."

"If she doesn't, Strom will," I said as Mitch emerged from the back shop.

"Any late-breaking news?" he asked.

"Alas, no," I said, "except that Laurentis is improving. He insists he didn't see who shot him or when it happened. He lost track of time, which is understandable, given the bullet wound and blood loss. Besides, I don't think Craig owns a watch. Time isn't important to him."

"Dr. Sung figured it had to be after midnight, judging from the amount of blood he'd lost and given the type of wound," Mitch said.

"Yes," I agreed. "Craig wouldn't come into town until after dark, and he must've dropped the painting off while the Wickstroms were at the late movie. Their kids probably didn't hear him. He would've stopped by their house between nine-thirty or ten and midnight."

Vida wore a troubled expression. "Do we assume that Craig lives near the poaching site?"

"Nobody knows where he lives," I said. "I see what you're getting at. How did he happen upon the poachers unless he lived nearby?"

"It was beyond the old Petersen farm, correct?"

"That's what Milo told me," I replied.

Vida shuddered. "That's in the same vicinity where Roger found Linda Lindahl's body. I shall never get over that grisly experience. Poor Roger!" She suddenly stared at me. "Maybe that was so traumatic for him that he finally had to use drugs to cope with the memory."

"It took him a long time to get to that point," I said in a neu-

tral tone. "Unless he started much sooner than anyone thought."
Which is damned likely, I thought, *trauma or no trauma.* At the
time, Roger had taken a ghoulish delight in discovering Linda's
corpse.

Vida had ignored my last comment. "I must talk to Thelma
Petersen. She should be in touch with some of her husband's
family. Perhaps I'll stop at the retirement home after work." She
squared her shoulders. "Last call for 'Scene.' It's tasteless to use
the Strom Petersen sighting and the new Laurentis painting this
week. I need two more items to fill the four column inches."

Mitch and I exchanged glances. "Why," I asked, "can't we
mention Amanda returning to the post office? That's not self-
promotion for us."

Vida nodded. "That's fine. I might, however, mention that
she did a good job in her temporary post."

I agreed. Having done my duty, I looked back at Mitch.
"Your turn."

He frowned. "I wish I recognized more of the locals. I noticed somebody on the courthouse steps dropping a folder yesterday and chasing the papers all over the place in the wind."

"Man or woman?" Vida asked.

"Woman. Five-six, five-seven, thirties, good-looking, black
fur-trimmed jacket, red slacks."

"Ah!" Vida exclaimed. "Rosemary Bourgette, the prosecut-
ing attorney. The Bourgettes all have a sense of humor. Rosemary won't mind being in 'Scene.' Anything else? I can squeeze
in one more. Leo gave me three."

Mitch looked as if Vida had thrown down the gauntlet. "I was
out of town for a few days," he reminded her. "Let me think back
to last week after the Thanksgiving edition went to press . . ."

"You're a good photographer," Vida said. "Pretend your eye
is a camera. I often do that."

It occurred to me that Vida's mental photo album could probably reach around the world twice over. Mitch, however, was game. "Two preteen boys at Old Mill Park dressed like Pilgrims going down the big slide," he said, obediently shutting his eyes. "Irate curly-haired woman honking at car with flasher lights blocking her VW on Alpine Way and Fir. Older guy with telescope standing in the middle of the football field at the high school." He opened his eyes. "Any help?"

"That last one was undoubtedly Averill Fairbanks," Vida said. "I never put him in 'Scene.' He was probably looking for aliens who'd stolen his turkey drumstick. In a pinch, I could use the Pilgrim boys, but it does seem a bit dated now. By the way," she went on, turning to me, "I finished Larry's obit. See what you think."

I sat down by her desk, noticing that she had a file photo of Larry that had been taken at least fifteen years ago. "Do you think we should run that?" I asked.

"Why not? I'd do it if he hadn't died in prison," Vida replied. "Larry was a member of a very important Alpine family. I'm certainly not going to show any pictures of him from the trial or in his jail costume."

I tried not to wince at the word "costume," but agreed with Vida's rationale. "One column," I said, and began reading:

Lawrence (Larry) Franklin Petersen, 53, died Saturday in Walla Walla, Washington. A third-generation native of Alpine, Mr. Petersen had worked for many years at the Bank of Alpine, which had been co-founded by his grandfather, Franklin (Frank) Petersen. A graduate of Alpine High School and the University of Washington, where he received a bachelor's degree in Busi-

ness, Mr. Petersen's survivors include his parents, Marvin and Cathleen Petersen of Chandler,
Arizona; sons Franklin (Strom) of Seattle and
Cole Petersen of _____; and a daughter,
Denise Petersen Jensen of Alpine. He was pre-
deceased by his sister, Linda Petersen Lindahl. A
private service will be held at a later date.

"It sounds fine," I said. "Most people will know the story
behind it. How are you going to find out where Cole lives?"

"I'm going to call Rick right now," Vida replied. "If he
doesn't know, he can get hold of Strom—or Denise. I debated
about listing his memberships and affiliations, but decided not
to. Though Larry was very active in the community, it didn't
seem right to lavish too much praise on him."

"Probably not," I said. "I wonder if the family wants any
kind of memorial donations in Larry's name."

"That would be up to JoAnne," Vida said. "She seems to be
in charge, divorced or not. Maybe she hasn't made up her mind.
We could run something on that later." With an impatient sigh,
she picked up what looked like a handwritten letter. "One more
for the advice column. This idiot addressed it to 'Vida *Rankle*.'
Really, now!"

I laughed. "Is it from Carla?"

"It could be, given all her typos," Vida grumbled. "I will not
even repeat what she did with Darla Puckett's name years ago.
It's a good thing we caught it in time."

"Ah, yes." I stood up, glancing at the time. It was after four.
Leo entered the newsroom wearing a big grin. "Christmas
bonuses for everybody! I finally talked Gus Swanson into running a full-color double-truck co-op with two other Toyota
dealerships in the area for next week. Fleetwood's getting a
piece of the action, too."

Mitch chuckled. "There go a few hundred more jobs in Detroit."

I congratulated Leo.

"Just trying to make you stop regretting losing Ed all these years," he said with a twinkle in his eyes. "Oh—almost forgot." He reached into his briefcase. "I stopped by Le Gourmand to get the gift certificate for Amanda as a thank-you. Your fifty bucks and the other fifty the rest of us put in was gratefully appreciated, but I mentioned that since the Hansons' dinner there would probably be in 'Scene' and thus free advertising, they threw in another fifty, figuring it'd cost that much to get a really good bottle of wine."

I took the embossed envelope from him. "Nice," I said. "I'll give it to her just before she leaves."

An hour later, I was ready to go home, but not until I stopped by the front desk, where Amanda was packing up her belongings.

"Here's a little something for your good work." I slid the Le Gourmand envelope across the counter. "Take time out during the holidays to use this up."

Amanda looked genuinely surprised. "You didn't have to do anything. I was a real twit the first week. Or so."

"Then you became anything but a twit," I responded.

She opened the envelope and her eyes suddenly grew moist. "Oh, Emma!" She leaned across the counter and awkwardly hugged me. "Thank you! If you ever need me again . . ."

"Who knows?" I said as she let go of me. "It's not carved in stone that Ginny will come back. *Bon appétit*—and *merci beaucoup*."

She gathered up her belongings, and I opened the door for her. "Let me know if you hear any news kiddy-wise," I called after her.

"I will," she said over her shoulder. "But Vida will probably find out before we do. She always hears everything first in Alpine."

I returned to my cubbyhole and collected my coat and handbag. Everything except the county commissioners' meeting was set. I left Kip in charge, knowing if there were any last-minute problems, he'd let me know. After a brief stop at the Grocery Basket to pick up something ready-made for dinner, I pulled into the carport and went inside. I was unwrapping the fried chicken, mac and cheese, and small Caesar salad when I remembered to go over to the Marsdens' house to collect the package from Paris.

I got there just after Val had come home from work at the fish hatchery. "Hey, neighbor," he said, letting me in. "Viv tells me you got something from Gay Paree. How do you rate?"

"Maybe it's a bomb," I said, looking at Viv. "Does it tick?"

"If it does, I can't hear it. I'll bring it to the living room."

Val put a hand on his wife's shoulder. "Let me fetch and carry. I don't think I've ever handled a package from France."

Viv stepped aside. "Hop to it, then. I'm excited to see what it is. I'll bet you are, too, Emma."

"Well . . . that depends," I said.

Viv seemed surprised by my reaction. "On what?"

"It's a long and boring story."

"It can't be," Viv asserted. "Not if it involves Paris. Oh!" She put a hand to her mouth. "I'm so sorry! I forgot. That's . . . you and . . . oh, Emma . . . I'm an idiot."

The Marsdens had gotten to know Tom when he'd come to Alpine for a lengthy visit. We'd told them about our wedding and honeymoon plans. In a matter of hours after giving them our happy news, Tom was dead. And so was Paris, as far as I was concerned.

"Hey," I said, "don't feel bad. If I burst into tears every time

I hear somebody mention Paris, I'd have drowned a long time ago."

"I know, but still . . ." Viv couldn't stop looking chagrined.

Val entered the living room with the package. Before either of the Marsdens could say anything else that might embarrass them, I suggested we should open it together. Assuming the parcel had been sent by Rolf, the worst that could happen would be a gift of flimsy lingerie. The size and weight of the package, along with the sticker saying the contents were perishable, seemed to indicate something more substantial than sexy underwear.

I was right. It was a huge gift basket full of cheeses, chocolate truffles, cookies, crackers, crisp breads, jam, two kinds of pâté, and a single bottle of wine. There was also a small enclosure card, which I managed to palm before Viv and Val could see it.

"Wow!" Viv exclaimed. "Somebody must really like you! Who is it?"

I decided to tell the truth—or half of it. "A guy who worked for the AP and did a lot of digging for me when that college dean was murdered onstage a few years ago. He's retired now and living in France. Very nice of him." I gripped the sparkling Vouvray by the neck. "Here—I'm not a wine drinker. I'll give you some of the cheese, too. Take your pick."

"Oh, Emma," Viv protested, "you don't have to."

"I can't eat this all by myself," I said. "Even cheese doesn't keep forever. Take a box of crackers, too."

"What about your co-workers?" Val asked.

I shook my head. "I don't want to spoil them. They get plenty of pastries every morning from the Upper Crust." The truth was that I didn't want to have to explain to my staff where the gift basket had come from. The Marsdens finally made their modest choices. Val said he'd dispose of the wrappings. The basket was easy to carry; it was only the unread card tucked inside that felt heavy.

Once I got home, I put away the perishables, dished up the chicken and the mac and cheese on a plate to warm in the microwave, and poured some Canadian and 7-Up over ice. With drink in one hand and gift basket card in the other, I went into the living room. Before sitting down, I looked at *Sky Autumn*. Maybe, I'd reflected off and on since seeing *Forest Watch*, Craig's change of style wasn't as drastic as I'd first thought. But it was. Despite the tumbling water, the fallen leaves, the rotting tree trunks, *Sky Autumn* was vibrant, alive, comforting. The new work was gloom and doom—at least that had been my first reaction. Craig had undergone some sort of change between the two paintings. I wondered what, if anything, he'd produced in between. Donna might not know. He sold some of his work to other galleries in the region, though the owners who acquired them never met with Craig face-to-face. I always wondered how he conducted the nuts-and-bolts part of his artistic life. Donna had told me he had an account in a Monroe bank. She also said he'd contacted her from a pay phone a couple of times. According to her, he could sell his paintings for much more. Given his simple lifestyle, I understood that making money wasn't important to Craig. But his lack of social intercourse seemed to preclude any sort of tragedy that might alter his artistic style so drastically. The only thing I could think of was that even recluses can suffer midlife crises.

I sat down, took a sip from my drink, and looked at the envelope: "Emma," it read, purple ink in Rolf's spiky handwriting. I took another sip and removed the card.

"You don't know what you're missing in France," he'd written. "Me, I hope. I know you don't like wine, but Vouvray is sweet. You are not. But I still wish you were here." He signed it simply "Rolf."

Damn! The man didn't give up. Or did he delight in torturing me? I shoved the note back into the envelope, not caring if I
bent the elegant stationery that the galling words were written
on. Maybe Rolf thought it was a Christmas present. But Rolf
was Jewish. Hanukkah? No. There was nothing to indicate any
kind of holiday, celebration, or remembrance. Rolf was just
being Rolf. I took another sip from my drink.

Five minutes later, I'd put my salad in a bowl and was taking
my dinner out of the microwave when the phone rang. I'd left
the receiver on its cradle in the living room, so I had to hurry before the call trunked over to voice mail.

"I just got back from visiting Thelma Petersen," Vida announced. "She is surprisingly upset about Larry. Elmer, of
course, was uncommunicative. You'd think it might be the other
way around, since Elmer is Larry's blood relative."

"Elmer was never very communicative about anything," I
said.

"Except when it came to trouncing every Republican president since Abraham Lincoln," Vida noted with bitterness. "Old
fool. But to get back to Thelma. She's convinced that Larry was
killed by another inmate. She insists it happens all the time in
prison. I know that it does sometimes, of course, but I hate to
think there's a cover-up in Larry's situation. Do you think Milo
could find out?"

"I wondered about that," I admitted. "Maybe he should. If
Thelma's blabbing about it at the retirement home, everybody
in town will eventually hear the rumor. Why don't you ask your
nephew Bill to prod the sheriff?"

"I'll do that," Vida said, "though I believe Billy is on duty
tonight. I hope he's not out patrolling the highway if the weather
gets bad again."

"Was that all Thelma had to say?" I inquired.

"Oh, certainly not. Both of Elmer's sisters are dead. They

were older than the two boys. Thelma tried to get Elmer to call Marvin and Cathleen in Arizona, but he refused. He insists he's too deaf to hear his brother, and his brother's too addled to make sense. He never cared much for Cathleen, he thought she was snooty, but that's because she wouldn't let him bring his goat into their house. Marvin and Cathleen had lovely Persian carpets. I wonder if they took them to Arizona. I always picture people who live there wearing sandals for every occasion."

"I assure you, Vida, that Ben and most of his parishioners in Tuba City often wore real shoes."

"You told me yourself that Ben even wore sandals when he said Mass. I found that shocking."

"I think Jesus and his disciples wore sandals," I said, accustomed to Vida's occasional diversions from the topic at hand—or at foot, in this case. "People who live in the desert consider sandals appropriate footwear."

"Perhaps." Vida paused, no doubt shifting mental gears. "Thelma should call Marvin and Cathleen. Someone from the family certainly should. I ought to ring them and offer my condolences."

"Do it," I said. "You've known them forever. What about Cole?"

"Oh—yes. Now that was a surprise. Cole is in Alpine. He came to have Thanksgiving with Denise."

I was taken aback. "Why? I assumed he'd be with JoAnne and Strom in Seattle."

"Denise couldn't leave the dog, and she didn't have a carrier for him, so she was afraid to drive all that way with such a big animal loose in the car. She thought about putting him in the trunk, but that struck her as inhumane. It is over a hundred-and-fifty-mile round-trip, and not an easy drive with all that traffic."

"I'm surprised Denise had that much sense," I remarked. "So Cole's still here? Is he staying with Denise?"

"No," Vida replied. "He's allergic to dogs. He could manage, I suppose, for a few hours. He's staying with his cousin, Alison Lindahl. She rented an apartment at Parc Pines."

Something wasn't making sense. "It's been going on a week since Thanksgiving. How come Cole is staying on? Has it got something to do with his father's death over the weekend?"

"According to Thelma, it has more to do with Alison's roommate, Lori Cobb. She and Cole dated in high school."

"Lori is rooming with Alison? How did we miss that?"

"Lori didn't move in with Alison until the middle of November," Vida said. "I know, I should've found out about it, but apparently I slipped up with all the holiday goings-on. That's another thing I should mention to Billy. Working together as they do, he had to know Lori changed addresses. Surely she talked about moving. But you know men—they don't always listen."

My ear was beginning to hurt—from listening too much. "Okay, so where does Cole live when he isn't shacked up with Alison and Lori?"

"In Redmond," Vida said. "He works for Microsoft in marketing and travels quite a bit. Thelma told me he just got back from London."

"At least we can fill in that obit blank. Will you call Kip and let him know?"

"Of course." She paused again. "I've got quite a list of people to call. I think Billy should be off duty by ten. I'd better get going. I think I'll make one of those lovely casseroles from my recipe file for my supper and save the rest to take to the church potluck later this week."

Thanking God I wasn't a Presbyterian, I said good-bye

and hung up. While I ate my heated and reheated dinner, I pondered all the new information Vida had given me. Then I wondered why I was pondering.

Larry Petersen had died of a heart attack that might have struck him on the golf course, walking along Front Street, or behind the wheel of a car. It happened to people who weren't old, and occasionally to someone much younger than fifty-three.

Thelma Petersen's insistence that an inmate had killed her nephew was strictly speculation. But it'd be prudent for Milo to get the idea squelched before it ran the gamut of Alpine's grapevine.

Cole Petersen's presence in town wasn't suspicious just because of the coincidental timing of the letters accusing the sheriff of a wrongful arrest and conviction. Cole, like his brother and sister, had grown up in Alpine. They had friends here. For all I knew, Cole visited now and then, somehow sneaking in under Vida's radar. Even she couldn't keep track of every person who stopped by for old times' sake.

As for Milo's letters, I still believed they came from a nut. Maybe the sheriff should check with the judge who'd sentenced Larry or the jury members who had found him guilty. Milo might not be the only victim of someone with a bad case of malice.

On that note, I stopped thinking about the Petersens and tried to find something decent to watch on TV. SportsCenter was of mild interest. The movie offerings sounded like pap. Even PBS and HBO had little to offer. When I hadn't heard from Kip by ten-thirty, I called him to make sure everything in the back shop was ready to roll.

"Just about," he said. "Mitch is still here, finishing up the county commissioners' meeting piece. Alfred Cobb didn't resign. In fact, he stayed awake the whole two and a half hours. Mitch dozed off twice."

I laughed. "I don't blame him. Ed must've been disappointed. He didn't get a chance to make his big announcement."

"Ed's been disappointed before," Kip remarked. "Not to mention disappointing. Get a good night's sleep. Emma. Everything's under control."

I thanked Kip and rang off. I decided to make an early night of it and go to bed. But first I had to put away the nonperishable items from Rolf's gift basket. Jam, crackers, cookies . . . I sighed as I made room in one of the kitchen cupboards. Why couldn't Rolf leave me alone? Mr. and Mrs. Lord had made sure that their daughter received lessons in good manners. I'd have to thank Rolf for his largesse. Maybe I could get away with a brief notation on a Christmas card. Or a Hanukkah card. Or . . .

I stared at the labels in French. I thought about the Place de la Madeleine address. I visualized Paris. And then I shook myself and slammed the cupboard door shut. Tom and I had had a lot of things together, including a son. But we'd never had Paris.

EIGHT

WEDNESDAYS ARE A MIXED BAG. THE PAPER IS ON ITS WAY to porches, boxes, and newsstands. The pressure is off, but along with the sense of accomplishment, there's a letdown. One of my worst fears as editor and publisher of a weekly is that a huge story will break just as our carriers are delivering the most recent edition. Going online has helped to dispel that nightmare, but there's still the unease about the subtler occurrences that may hint at bigger stories, but are overlooked because our so-called nose for news is temporarily satisfied.

To my surprise, Denise arrived promptly at eight. I'd barely come in a couple of minutes earlier and was pouring coffee when she peeked into the newsroom.

"Hi," she said in a tentative voice. "Where is everybody?"

"Leo went to the Rotary Club's monthly breakfast. Kip's either in the back shop or he's coming in later because he probably didn't leave work last night until eleven or so." I paused to stir sugar into my coffee. "Mitch may also be late because he had to cover last night's county commissioners' meeting. It's Vida's turn to pick up the pastries this morning. You'll do it on

Friday, which was the day Amanda—and Ginny before her—did it. The money comes out of petty cash. Do you know where we keep that?"

"Um . . . I think so. What kind of pastry is Vida getting?"

"Whatever looks appealing to her," I replied. "That's how it works."

"So we can't ask for something special?"

"No, but you can pick out your favorites when it's your turn."

She nodded vaguely and went back to the front office. I took my coffee to my cubbyhole, wondering what we'd gotten ourselves into with Denise. I could only hope that she'd be as interested in some of her other job duties as she was in our pastry.

My first task was to check with the hospital to find out how Craig Laurentis was doing. According to the nurse on duty, he'd had a restless night, but was improving. I thanked her and hung up. I briefly considered visiting him on my lunch hour, but decided against it. Craig might feel I was intruding on his space. Even though he'd talked to me rather than to Milo, I was still a virtual stranger. I'd give the hospital another call after I got home.

When ten o'clock had come and gone, I realized there had been no further word from Milo about the sinister letters. I was still irked with him for his "frigid" comment in front of Nurse Debbie. He, of all people, knew how little it took to set the town gossips abuzz. I knew he'd been frustrated by Craig's refusal to talk to him; I figured that maybe the mysterious letters upset him more than I realized. He took his job seriously, if not always himself. He, like me, *was* his job. And I never could stay angry with him for very long. I picked up the phone and dialed his number.

"No letter today," he said, sounding relieved. "Maybe Marlowe Whipp delivered it to the wrong address or dropped it somewhere along his route. Let's hope that pain in the ass is over."

"Did Bill Blatt ask you about verifying how Larry Petersen died? Vida told me she mentioned it to him last night after he got off duty."

"Yeah. I put in a call to somebody who knows somebody who . . . et cetera. Meanwhile, I'm going to stop by the retirement home and tell Aunt Thelma to put a sock in it."

"Good idea," I said as Vida entered my office. "Talk to you later."

"I couldn't reach Marvin and Cathleen last night after I got home from the church potluck," she said, adjusting the band of her tweed skirt and tucking in her brown and white polka-dot blouse. "I left a message. Where on earth would they be at nine o'clock at night in Arizona?"

"I've no idea," I said. "The movies? Playing bingo? Visiting friends? It *is* a retirement community. They must have lots of activities."

"They wouldn't be playing bingo," Vida asserted. "They're not Catholic, they're Lutherans. Lutherans don't play bingo. I'm not sure if it's against their religion, but I've never known any Lutherans around here—and there are so many of them— who play bingo."

I tried not to smile. "Being a banker, Marv should be very good at keeping track of the called numbers."

"From what I hear, Marv is fortunate if he can keep track of his marbles," Vida retorted. "As for Cathleen, she was never very bright, at least not in school. I was four years ahead of her, and she could barely read in second grade."

I was almost afraid to ask the next question, but I plunged ahead. "Did you call JoAnne Petersen?"

Vida shook her head, the unruly gray curls going every

which way. "I thought I'd wait. If there's an autopsy, she probably doesn't yet know when the remains will be ready to put in the mausoleum."

"Milo will find that out," I said, seeing Denise talking to Mitch in the newsroom. "Did you get your mail?" I asked, lowering my voice.

"Most of it," Vida replied. "Leo ended up with three pieces and I got two of Mitch's. Oh—and one of yours, but it was some sort of ad for updating something-or-other with your cell phone. I tossed it."

"Okay," I said, and cleared my throat in what I hoped was a signal for Vida to shut up. Denise was coming our way.

"What do I do with the little advertisements?" she asked.

"The . . . you mean the classified ads?" I wasn't sure what she was talking about.

"Is that what you call them?" Denise frowned. "Doesn't 'classified' have something to do with secret information, like in the government?"

Oh, God, I thought, *what hath Emma wrought?* "Not in this case," I finally said as Vida left with what seemed to be an expression of despair. "Didn't Amanda explain the classified advertisements to you?"

Denise made a face. "Is that what she called those little ads?"

I nodded. "We put them in the paper and also online. That is, they go to Kip after they're checked for accuracy and authenticity." *Emma, you fool, don't use big words like that.* "I mean that sometimes people say things in their ads that aren't quite true, like with cars. The person who is selling the car might state that it's in excellent condition." I paused to see if Denise was grasping my words. I honestly couldn't tell, but at least she was looking at me. "Because this is a small town, we often know the person who is selling the car and we also know that the car is *not* in excellent condition—that it hasn't been well maintained, is rusted out in places, and has dents or a broken windshield, for example." I paused again. "If that's the case, we ask the seller if we can modify . . . that is, make a small change in the ad, leaving out the word 'excellent' or changing it to 'fair.' "

Denise looked puzzled. "Why not change it to 'bad'? Or," she went on, suddenly brightening, "'really, really bad,' because you charge by the word and that way you can make more money."

"That," I said wearily, "wouldn't be fair to the person buying the ad."

"But 'fair' isn't fair," she argued. "I mean, describing the car as 'fair,' not the person . . . wait. I think the phone's ringing." She rushed off.

I got up and went into the back shop to explain my predicament to Kip. "You are a very patient person," I told him. "You are very good at explaining things to people. Do you think you can help Denise with the classifieds? I can't even make her understand the basics."

Kip laughed. "Sure, I'll give it a shot. Every occupation has its own lingo. This is all new to her and she's probably nervous."

"That may be," I said. "Or she's the type of female who pays more attention to what men tell her than what women say. Besides, you're in her peer group. I sure don't want to spend the first few days trying to educate her about how newspapers work as opposed to banks. If I have to do that, I'll either fire her or kill her, and we'll end up with Averill Fairbanks or Crazy Eights Neffel in the front office."

"Don't worry, Emma," Kip said. "Maybe she's not as dim as you think. I know she got stuff screwed up sometimes at the bank, but it could be lack of focus on her part. You know, like ADD."

"Along with S-U-B-T-R-A-C-T?" I waved a dismissive hand. "Never mind. I know what you're saying and you could be right. At least she won't have to deal much with numbers around here."

The rest of the morning seemed to go smoothly. On my lunch hour, I started my Christmas shopping at the mall. Despite the merchants' ads in the paper promising "huge savings" and "shop early, shop smart," I didn't find any items worthy of my hard-earned money. Adam had sent his list the day after Thanksgiving, but most of it consisted of items I'd order online. Ben wouldn't tell me what he wanted until the last minute, so I didn't bother looking for possible presents. After flunking Thanksgiving, maybe my son or brother could join me for Christmas. It wasn't their fault that priestly duties had prevented them from visiting me, but I still took the defections personally.

During the afternoon, Vida fielded calls about Larry Petersen's obituary. Most of the people who phoned wanted to gossip, rehashing the whole horrible bank catastrophe. Vida became predictably irritated.

"I can take care of the silly questions they ask, but it's the self-centeredness that so annoys me. It's as if someone famous had died. Most people can only relate to such tragedies by what they were doing when they heard the terrible news. And such twaddle!" She gestured at the receiver. "Darla Puckett chattering away, saying, 'I discovered two overdraft charges I shouldn't have had at the very time Linda Lindahl must've been killed.' Or Brendan Shaw—'We were at Marv and Cathleen's that night, but had no idea what had gone on and neither did they. Imagine, just sitting there talking about golf with those two new attorneys the Petersens had invited—and I don't think either of them played golf.' And Edna Mae Dalrymple all a-twitter about Andy Cederberg staying late with her to figure out how the library's account had been mishandled by Denise, who'd gone home in tears, and then it turned out it wasn't Denise, it was Christie Johnston who was embezzling. Even Betsy O'Toole had to chime in about JoAnne Petersen shopping at the Grocery Basket late that afternoon and not realizing her husband was murdering his sister. At least Betsy asked me to give Leo a message about the special insert they're planning for next week with holiday recipes and the featured ingredients the store is selling on sale."

"Cut Betsy some slack," I said. "She and the rest of her family are still in shock over their own tragedy. It's going to be a rough Christmas for all the O'Tooles without Mike."

Vida nodded halfheartedly. "True. And so senseless—a young man dying while under the influence of those dreadful drugs." She stared up at the window that looked out onto Front Street. Only the lower legs of passersby could be seen, though Vida could identify most of Alpine from their footgear. I assumed she was thinking—again—of Roger and how easily he could've been the one who'd careened off of Highway 2 and ended up dead.

Having apparently run out of steam, Vida finally went back to work. So did I, catching up with my other staffers' duties.

Mitch had received at least three tips about the maple poachers, including one from Averill Fairbanks insisting that Venusians had stolen the trees for their excellent tonewood properties to improve intergalactic communication with earthlings. Mitch had told Averill that he thought maple trees grew on Venus. Averill responded that he didn't realize that and offered profuse thanks for the information.

Leo, going beyond the call of duty, had invited Denise to have lunch with him at the Venison Inn. She'd turned him down. It wasn't until later in the afternoon that I asked why.

"It's not because she thinks I'm a dirty old man," Leo said, noticing that we were out of coffee. "Well, maybe it is, but her reason was that she was going to work out at the gym for half an hour and then go home to check on her ex's dog. He still hasn't collected Doof or whatever his name is."

"Maybe he doesn't intend to," I suggested. "I'm not sure if Greg Jensen's from Alpine."

"Could be," Leo said. "I never met him." He went out to the front office to alert Denise about the need for more coffee.

Vida had just hung up the phone. "Do you know Denise's ex?" I asked quietly before our new hire could fetch the coffee makings and bring them into the news room.

"Of course," Vida replied. "He's Reba Cederberg's nephew. That's how . . ." Seeing Denise enter with a new bag of coffee, Vida stood up, but continued speaking. ". . . the old road into Index went. Come, I'll show you on the map in your office."

Vida hadn't missed a beat, even offering Denise a toothy smile on our way to my cubbyhole. I dutifully followed her to the county map on the wall, which was out of Denise's line of sight.

"As I was saying," she said in a normal voice, "the original road from the highway went off here." Vida didn't bother pointing to the map, but began to speak more softly. "That's how Denise met Greg Jensen. Reba was a Jensen before she married Andy Cederberg. Her older brother, Sig, was by their father's first wife, Dorothy. She died of an aneurysm when she was very young. Then her father married again and had two daughters, Reba and Rachel, by his second wife, Lucille. Sig, Greg's father and Reba's half-brother, and his wife, Diane, moved to Sultan at least ten years ago." She paused as Denise announced to whoever was within hearing range that fresh coffee was being made.

I leaned just far enough toward the door to see Denise go back to the front office. "The coast is clear," I said, and wished that the Cederberg-Jensen family tree was, too. I was utterly confused.

"Anyway," Vida continued, back up to normal volume, "Sig passed away three years ago. Greg may be living with his mother in Sultan, though Reba mentioned something to me about her sister-in-law spending winters in Palm Springs or Palm Desert or Palm something-or-other. I believe someone in the family has a time-share condo down there. It's not yet winter, so she still may be up here." Vida grimaced. "More sun worshippers. Whatever happened to savoring the seasons? Doesn't anybody over sixty appreciate the passages of time anymore?"

I didn't disagree, but my brain was still occupied with sorting out the Jensens and the Cederbergs. The only thing I could be sure of was that Denise and Andy had worked together at the bank, and at some point Andy or Reba had introduced her to Greg Jensen.

"I think," I said as Vida started out of my office, "I'll check with Kip to see how many people hate my tree-poaching editorial this week. I haven't gotten any calls, but some readers may have e-mailed their responses. Kip may not have had time to forward them on to me."

But Kip had nothing. The only allusions to the poaching incident were a couple of anti-gun diatribes, a topic that always raised hackles in a former logging town. He did, however, inform me that after a slow start, Denise had seemed to grasp how to handle the classifieds.

"Good," I said. "She's used to dealing with the public, so that shouldn't be a problem. You must've gone to school with the three Petersens. Did you know any of them well?"

Kip shook his head. "They were all younger than I was. I

remember Frankie, the older one, best, because he was only a year behind me and played football and basketball. He was a pretty good fullback and was able to muscle his way under the basket for rebounds, but he couldn't shoot, not even free throws."

"He now calls himself Strom. Apparently he outgrew 'Frankie.' "

"He was a jock," Kip said. "I always figured he'd end up as a high school coach someday."

"As a matter of fact, he has an MBA and works in finance."

Kip looked surprised. "Guess I misjudged him. Cole was more of a nerd, so I suppose he's a NASCAR driver."

"You're more on the mark with him," I said. "He works for Microsoft, but in marketing, not as a techie."

"That's kind of funny," Kip remarked, shaking his head. "People aren't always what they seem to be, are they?"

"You're right about that," I said, checking the entrance from the front office to the back shop to make sure the door was closed. "What about Greg Jensen?"

Kip looked momentarily puzzled. "Oh—Denise's ex? I don't remember much about him. Kind of quiet, maybe in the same class as Frankie. I mean *Strom*. Nice kid, not a troublemaker." Kip shrugged. "I think he was on the debate team."

I smiled. "Sounds too bright for Denise."

"He was no big brainiac. The high school was smaller when I went there. Anybody who liked to argue could get on the debate team then."

"I guess he argued once too often with Denise," I said.

Kip nodded. "Could be. Sorry I'm not much help about backgrounds. That's Vida's job."

"Ah, yes," I agreed, heading to the newsroom. "And she does it oh-so-well."

My House & Home editor was smirking when she came through the door. "You will never guess who my dinner date is."

"Probably not," I admitted. "Who?"

"Strom Petersen." She preened a bit. "I called Andy Cederberg at the bank and he gave me Strom's cell phone number, so I got hold of Strom and he's going with me to the Cederbergs' for dinner tonight."

I was only mildly taken aback. "What about Cole?"

"He already had plans," Vida said with a trace of regret.

I glanced over my shoulder to make sure Denise couldn't hear me in the front office. "With his sister?"

Vida shrugged. "Perhaps."

"I think I missed something," I said, eyeing Vida suspiciously. "Somewhere along the way, you left out Reba Cederberg's invitation."

"Oh." Vida feigned surprise. "Yes, well, certainly. I did call Reba—it'd be unfair to spring that sort of thing on her, but having known the Petersens so intimately, I knew she'd realize how I'd feel if I didn't get to see at least one of the boys while they were in town. My daughters all babysat for JoAnne and Larry years ago."

That was the first I'd heard about the connection between the Runkel sisters and the Petersens. Of course that didn't mean it wasn't true. Over the years, I'd discovered there were many things I didn't know about my closest friends and associates in Alpine. Newcomers are still outsiders even after decades in a small town. As such, they put natives on their guard and, in small, almost unnoticed ways, are kept at arm's length.

"Gee," I said, "I didn't realize you were so close."

Vida gave me a sour look. "My father and Frank Petersen were dear friends."

I kept a straight face, having heard an intriguing story about Mr. Blatt and Mr. Petersen from the usually uncommunicative Uncle Elmer. When the Bank of Alpine had been founded circa 1930, Elmer's father, Frank, and his investment partners had come up short of capital. A silent partner had been found, a reputable family man with a secret weakness for women and games of chance. Like most gamblers, he lost more than he won, until he hit the jackpot—big time. Unable to explain to his wife how he'd gotten the windfall, he'd wisely—and discreetly—handed over most of the money to help start the bank. For years I'd wondered why there were five medallions on the bank's lobby walls, but only four showed profiles and names of the founders: Frank Petersen, mill owner Carl Clemans, mill superintendent John Engstrom, and Vida's father-in-law, Rufus Runkel, who'd also built the ski lodge that saved the town from extinction after the original mill shut down. After the death of Linda Lindahl and the arrest of Larry Petersen, Uncle Elmer had confided in me. The blank medallion was for the rakish rascal who had been the silent partner—Vida's father, Earl Ennis Blatt. If Vida knew that I knew, she never let on.

I congratulated Vida on her coup. I was faintly envious, wishing I could find out more about the Petersen family now that I'd hired one of them. Maybe I could've gotten some insight about how to deal with Denise that didn't involve tearing out my hair.

When five o'clock rolled around, Denise was still behind the front desk, going over what looked like a checklist that Kip had made for her. "It's quitting time," I said with a smile. "You don't have to stick around until everybody else is gone."

She looked at me with a slightly startled air. "Oh, I'm leaving in a few minutes. I made a five-fifteen appointment at Stella's to have my hair done." She ran a hand through the straggly multicolored strands. "She's open until seven tonight. You could make an appointment, too."

I didn't take offense. I knew my unmanageable brown hair was overlong and overdue for cutting. "I'm going to do that either Friday or next week," I said before adding an obvious understatement. "I've never been very good about styling it on my own."

Denise eyed me critically. "It's the shape that's wrong. You need just a little height, and more tapering, because you have a round face. Stella should know that by now." She demonstrated by moving her hands over her own hair. "It wouldn't work for me. My face is too long."

Suddenly, she looked stricken. "I forgot about Doof! I've got to go home first." In a flurry of movement, she pushed the checklist to one side, grabbed her purse, and shrugged into her jacket. "Can you call Stella to let her know I'll be a few minutes late?"

"Okay." If I sounded unenthusiastic, Denise didn't seem to notice. She was out the door before I finished punching in Stella's number. Figuring that I might as well schedule an appointment for myself, I asked whichever stylist had answered the phone to set me up with the salon owner for next Wednesday at eleven. Feeling semi-virtuous, I collected my belongings and went home.

There were no calls, nothing but junk in the mail, and I made sure there were no parcels on the front porch. I'd hauled in some logs and kindling to build a fire. It hadn't started to snow again, but it felt as if the temperature might drop to below freezing. After finding nothing in the freezer more appetizing than a frozen chicken pot pie, I turned on the oven, poured a Pepsi, and went into the living room to call the hospital.

The nurse who answered sounded older and vaguely familiar. "Hi," I said, "this is Emma Lord. I'm calling about Craig Laurentis. How's he doing this evening?"

There was a long pause. "I don't know," the nurse finally replied. "Mr. Laurentis isn't here."

I was momentarily speechless. "You mean he was discharged?"

"No. I'm sorry, a patient is calling me."

The phone went dead.

NINE

IT WAS USELESS TO CALL BACK. NO ONE WOULD ANSWER, OR I'd get the reception desk in the main lobby. Whoever was working there wouldn't tell me anything. Or didn't know anything worth telling.

I dialed Milo's number. He answered on the third ring. "What do you mean, Laurentis isn't there?" the sheriff demanded. "Are you sure you got the right number?"

"Of course I did," I snapped. "I recognized the nurse's voice. She's a Peterson—not with an *e*, but an *o*. She's an LPN."

Milo didn't speak for a moment or two. "Shit. I just got home and was going to catch some NBA action. Okay, I'll send Dwight Gould over there to check it out and let you know what's going on." I could hear him cussing to himself as he hung up the phone.

I considered calling Vida, but remembered that she was going out to dinner at the Cederbergs' house. Even if she hadn't yet left, I didn't want to distract her from soaking up every ounce of information she could squeeze out of the Petersen brood.

I also thought about trying to reach Doc Dewey or Dr. Sung, but they both put in such long hours that I hated to bother them. Milo would find out what had happened to Craig.

After putting the frozen chicken pot pie in the oven, I checked my e-mail. The only one that wasn't junk had come from Adam less than an hour ago.

"Hi, Mom," he began. "In case you've lost my first two Christmas gift lists, I'm adding a couple of items I can really use. (*Needs*, not *wants*—trying to follow your mature advice, only taken me thirty-odd years to figure out what it means.) Go to Cabela's online and find the ColdGear outerwear Eras jacket and Coreman pants. I *need* these items because—in case you've forgotten—it's kind of chilly up here in western Alaska. You might also take a look at their Gore-Tex Trooper Parka. Dodge has one like it and he doesn't *need* it as much as I do. Remember—XL and Tall. Price is no object—for me. I work for God and He doesn't pay big bucks. Love and prayers, Adam."

I wrote back: "I work for me and I'm even stingier than God. I'll check out the items as soon as I rob the Bank of Alpine. Please give me absolution in advance. Love, Mom."

Adam didn't respond. His part of Alaska was two hours behind Pacific Standard Time, so it was just after four in his part of the world. He could be anywhere, which was always a cause for worry on my part. In blinding snow, the only way to get from one place to another was by following a rope. If the rope broke, the danger was worse than taking a mere tumble. Since Adam had been at St. Mary's Igloo, three people had suffered fatal falls, either going over cliffs or freezing to death. Every day I prayed that he'd be transferred to a less hazardous area, despite his dedication to his parishioners and the great beauty of his surroundings. When, of course, he could actually see them.

By seven o'clock, I was starved. I could've put the entrée in the microwave, but I preferred using the conventional oven, if only because it helped heat the house in cold weather. I went into the kitchen and checked the timer—fifteen minutes to go. And over an hour since I'd talked to Milo. I went back into the living room and was about to pick up the receiver when the phone rang.

"Laurentis apparently just walked out," the sheriff said, sounding irked. "The nursing shift changes at four and it takes a while to go over charts. Nobody saw him leave, but when the new nurse who was assigned to him looked in his room, he wasn't there. She thought maybe he'd gone to the can. Half an hour later, somebody named Enzo was delivering dinners and saw the bed wasn't just empty, but stripped, except for the bottom sheet. The IVs were unhooked, too. Sounds to me like your favorite recluse artist got tired of being around other people and took off. No telling where he went, since he didn't take his clothes. They'd been sent to the laundry."

"Jeez!" I shrieked. "Are you crazy? He's the one lead you've got in the poaching case, not to mention that the same perp tried to kill him. I don't get it. You're acting like your star witness played some kind of prank."

"Bullshit," Milo said, on the defensive. "The guy's a head case. He didn't see anybody, he doesn't know anything. How am I supposed to find him in the dark when we could never find him in broad daylight?"

"But he's not dressed for this kind of weather. He must've left the hospital in his gown with just a sheet and a couple of blankets over him. For God's sake, Milo, somebody must've seen him before he headed back to the woods. If he walked out before or during the shift change, it wasn't dark yet. The hospital's in the middle of town. Don't you dare tell me that Dwight or whoever else is on duty isn't trying to find him."

"You want to take over my job?" Milo shot back. "What's wrong with you? Tracking down Laurentis would be like finding a needle in a haystack. For all we know, he stole somebody's clothes before he left. Get real. I'm going to watch the Spurs finish hammering the Nuggets."

"You do that. I'm calling two Ts on you and tossing you out of the game. You're not scoring any points with me." I slammed the phone down.

By the time my chicken pot pie was done, I'd lost my appetite. I ate about half of it before tossing the rest into the garbage. Back in the living room, I stared at *Sky Autumn*. "Where are you, Craig?" I wondered. I couldn't bear the thought of him struggling to get wherever he was going with a bullet wound and hardly any clothes to ward off the chilly night. No shoes, only the flimsy bed socks provided by the hospital. No food since lunch. And no medicine to help him heal and ease his pain.

I finally turned away from the painting and told myself to worry about something else, like Adam falling over a cliff in St. Mary's Igloo or Ben being run down in a pedestrian crosswalk in Cleveland. After a few minutes of torturing myself with those mental images, I realized I was being irrational. If anybody could take care of himself in extreme circumstances, it was Craig Laurentis. He'd been living on the edge for most of his life.

I settled in with a novel Edna Mae Dalrymple had insisted I read. According to her, the author was the Second Coming of Jane Austen. After the first thirty pages, I wished that the author was going . . . somewhere, anywhere, but it seemed more like nowhere. Edna Mae was a fine librarian, but she and I didn't share the same taste in books. By the time I went to bed at eleven, I was already half-asleep.

Thursday morning there was no snow on the ground, just heavy frost on the grass and ice on a couple of puddles in my dormant garden. The gray clouds had lingered overnight, indicating that the wind had gone quiet, sleeping against the mountains like the rest of us.

Of course I thought about Craig as I drove to work. Hopefully, he'd made it safely home. Not for the first time, I wondered what "home" meant to him. A cabin, maybe, built with logs like my own little nest, but smaller and cruder. It could be an abandoned shack or a yurt or even a cave inside the granite cliffs. Wherever and whatever it was, I hoped he was there, nursing his wound.

Denise was on time, showing off her newly coiffed and foiled hair to Vida.

"Very nice," my House & Home editor said with a tight little smile.

I, too, complimented Denise on her new do.

"Thanks," she said. "You could do this. Not the cut, but the foil. You'd look good with blond in your dark hair."

"I've never colored my hair. I thought about it back in the days when it was called frosting, but I lacked the nerve." And the money. Raising Adam by myself, there was never much left over for luxuries like salon expenditures.

The day started on a busier note than the usual letdown of a Wednesday. As soon as my staff was assembled, I announced that we should all come up with some new and different holiday features. "Not just Christmas," I said, "but Hanukkah, Winter Solstice, Kwanzaa, St. Lucy's Day, St. Nicholas Day, Boxing Day—whatever."

"How about Debt Day?" Leo inquired. "Or is that in January?"

Mitch chuckled. "It's *every* day." He looked at me. "No offense, Emma. I wasn't getting rich on the Detroit paper, either."

Vida was looking at her wall calendar. "We'll have to combine St. Nicholas and St. Lucy. Their feast days are a week apart, the sixth and the thirteenth. I'll cover the Lutheran celebration for St. Lucy. Being on a Monday, they might have it Sunday." She looked quizzical. "I can't think of anyone in Alpine who does much for St. Nicholas. I believe that's mainly a Dutch and German custom."

"Clip art," Leo said. "There should be all kinds of stuff we can use from one of those holiday CDs. Kwanzaa isn't big around here, either. In fact," he went on, turning to Mitch, "where's the nearest temple or synagogue?"

"Everett," Mitch replied. "I think."

Leo's expression was wry. "Sounds like you're as lazy as I am when it comes to attending religious services. As Emma will vouch for me, I'm strictly a C & E-er."

"You should both be ashamed of yourselves," Vida said. "What's the point of believing in something if you only attend church at Christmas and Easter, Leo?"

Before my ad manager could defend himself, Denise staggered in with the morning mail. "Where do all these catalogs go? There must be two dozen of them."

"I'll take those," Leo said. "They'll probably end up in the recycling bin, but I'll check to make sure."

Denise's chin rested on top of the big stack that must've weighed close to twenty pounds. "What about the newspapers?"

"They're exchange copies," I replied. "You can put them on my desk. We get most of the state weeklies as part of the WNPA, but I rarely have time to look through them."

"The what?" Denise asked as she lifted her chin so Leo could remove the catalogs.

"The Washington Newspaper Publishers Association," I

said. "It's an organization and resource for smaller community papers like the *Advocate*. They also include some affiliate memberships for other kinds of publications."

Denise's eyes had seemed to glaze over after my first sentence. "Can you take them? Your regular mail is underneath."

"Sure." I waited for Leo to get out of the way. "Thanks, Denise," I said, unloading everything that seemed to be mine. "Try the apple fritters. They're Kip's favorite thing."

I carted off the foot-high stack of newspapers and dropped them in the sturdy plastic bin next to my filing cabinet. Every week, I vowed to flip through at least a few, but seldom got that far and always felt guilty when I dumped them to make room for the next pile. The only way I could soothe my conscience was knowing that the *Advocate* probably went unread in other editors' and publishers' offices. The rest was the usual promotions, solicitations, and other junk I rarely opened. There were two invitations to holiday media events that I wouldn't attend. The last piece of mail was a plain white envelope addressed to me. I figured it was a response to my editorial, though there was usually a two-day lag before I heard from readers who took the trouble to write a real letter.

I was wrong. As soon as I saw the typeface on the single sheet of paper, I froze in my chair.

"YOU ARE IN LEAGUE WITH THE SHERIFF. LARRY PETERSEN DIED AN INNOCENT MAN. YOUR STORY ABOUT HIM FAILED TO RECOGNIZE HIS WRONGFUL IMPRISONMENT. YOU WILL BE SORRY FOR THAT OMISSION."

Like Milo's letters, the words had been Scotch-taped onto the page. I looked again at the envelope. Another Cloudscape stamp had been affixed to the envelope. The postmark was Alpine, December 1.

I thought for a moment about showing Vida and whoever

else was still in the newsroom. Then I decided to call Milo, but changed my mind about that, too. Instead, I dialed the post office and asked for Amanda.

"Hi," I said when I heard her voice. "This is Emma. How's it going?"

"Fine," she replied, sounding surprised. "The big rush won't start until next week. In fact, they needed me last week. So many people mail their overseas parcels and cards around Thanksgiving."

"I've got a question for you," I said.

Amanda laughed. "Don't tell you've already fired my replacement and want me to come back."

"No," I responded. "She hasn't done anything ruinous yet. This is a post office query. Do you still have those Cloudscape stamps for sale?"

"Cloudscape," Amanda repeated, followed by a pause. "Yes, but only two sheets. They came out in October and won't be reordered. Most people are buying the Christmas stamps. Are you a collector?"

"No, though my son used to be. I've got his albums stored away someplace at home. I was just curious. Thanks, Amanda."

"Sure. Any time." We both hung up.

I sat motionless for a few moments, trying to make sense out of the letter writer's intentions. First me, then Milo. Finally I got up, put on my duffel coat, and headed out of the office. Both Vida and Denise were on the phone; Mitch and Leo had already gone on their rounds. When I reached the sheriff's headquarters, Mitch was going over the log with Lori Cobb and Sam Heppner. Milo was pouring himself a mug of coffee.

"Oh, God," he said when I approached the counter, "the nursemaid just arrived. You should've saved yourself a trip, Emma. Nothing new on Laurentis. I already told Mitch."

"That's not why I'm here," I said. "Can we talk?"

Milo sighed. "Why not?" He waited for me to come inside the area behind the counter before entering his office.

"Hey," Mitch called after me, "are you stealing my stuff?"

"Not even close," I said over my shoulder, and closed the door behind me.

Milo sank down in his chair. "This better be good."

"It's bad." I sat down, too, took the mailing out of my handbag, and pushed it toward him. "See for yourself."

Milo stared at the envelope. "Hell." He glanced at me in disgust before removing the letter and reading it in silence. "I thought this crap was over."

"I assume you didn't get one today."

He shook his head.

"Have you called the judge or the prosecutor or anyone from the jury to see if they're getting these?"

He shook his head again. "Maybe I should." He drummed his long, strong fingers on the desk. "A pain in the ass."

"I know."

"Not the letters." He stood up, went around the desk, locked the door, and took two steps toward me. "What you said last night. Did you mean that?"

I had to crane my neck to look up at him. "About what?"

"You know damned well what I mean."

I tried to recall exactly what I *had* said. "I was worried about Craig. Who wouldn't be? The guy had been shot, he didn't have warm clothes, and you haven't found any suspects or leads."

"How am I supposed to do that without any help from him and no evidence from the shooting site?" He'd raised his voice to a near shout. "Hell, Emma, with this lousy weather, we can't figure out *where* he was shot—and neither can he. All we know is where the rangers found him. It sure as hell doesn't help that now the sonuvabitch has taken off. Even when he's not wandering around in his hospital rig, we haven't a clue where he holes up in maybe twenty square miles of mountain forest."

I was getting a kink in my neck from looking up. "Okay, okay, but I still don't know what I did or said to make you mad at me."

His hazel eyes sparked with anger—at least that's what I thought I saw. "You *should* know unless your brain went south." He reached down and pulled me to my feet. "I'll spell it out for you. I'm talking about not scoring with you anymore."

I sucked in my breath and knew my eyes had widened in shock. "Oh, Milo . . . I . . ."

He had to lift me off the floor to kiss me. In all the years that we'd made love, he'd never kissed me like that. I felt as if I couldn't breathe. When he finally slackened his grip, I was gasping.

"Well?" His intense gaze seemed to singe my face. Or maybe I was blushing.

I sighed and laid my head against his chest. "It was just a figure of speech," I finally said. "I don't even remember saying it. Maybe it was because you were talking about basketball."

I felt rather than heard him laugh. "Maybe I should've been watching hockey. What would you've said if I'd mentioned 'puck'?"

"Goalie gee whiz?"

"That sounds like you." He let me go, but not before he kissed the top of my head. "I'll make some calls."

I didn't sit back down. "Do you still think it's a screwball?"

"You were the one who kept saying that," he reminded me. "After yesterday, I decided you were probably right. But not now." He nodded at the letter that was still lying on the desk. "This isn't good."

"I agree. Did you know that both Petersen boys are in town?"

"I found out from Bill Blatt," Milo replied. "He ran into Cole at the mall."

"Vida had dinner at the Cederbergs' last night. Strom— who used to be called Frankie—was there. I haven't had time to talk to her this morning." I picked up the envelope. "This distracted me."

"Bill told me she's having both Petersen kids on her radio show tonight," Milo said. "Did you know about that?"

I was flummoxed. "No. I thought *Vida's Cupboard* was going to focus on Mary Jane Bourgette and her antique Christmas decorations." I stood up, discovering my knees were a bit wobbly. "I'll talk to her as soon as I get back to the office."

"Hold it," Milo said. "You look like you were mauled by a bear. Put some lipstick on while I unlock the door."

"Some bear," I remarked, digging around for my lipstick.

The sheriff was at the door. "Want to listen to Vida together tonight?" he said as I heard the lock click. "I could pick up some steaks."

"I don't know. Maybe we shouldn't be in the same place at the same time if we're being stalked. Harder to hit moving targets."

For a split second, Milo looked wounded. Then he realized I was teasing him. "You look good, with or without lipstick."

"I need a haircut."

"I like your hair. I don't have to worry about messing it up." He opened the door. "See you around six?"

"Sure. Let me know what you hear from SnoCo."

"Will do."

Mitch was still jawing with Sam Heppner and Lori Cobb. All three of them stopped talking long enough to stare at me. "What?" I said, annoyed—and embarrassed. The sheriff's office wasn't soundproofed.

"Nothing," Mitch replied, trying to look innocent. "Don't worry, boss. I'm not malingering. In fact, I'm on my way." He left before I could reach the swinging half-door in the counter.

I, meanwhile, pretended to behave naturally and paused to ask Lori a question about her grandfather. "Is he or is he not retiring from the county commissioners?"

Lori's usually placid face registered impatience. "Who knows? One minute he says he is, and the next, he's talking about re-election. Somebody told him that Ed Bronsky wants to replace him. Grandpa doesn't like that. He thinks Ed's . . . unqualified."

I was in a bind, unable to defend Ed, yet frustrated by the trio of aged commissioners whose only current ability was to stall. SkyCo deserved to be represented by somebody, almost anybody, who could come up with fresh ideas and implement them.

"Why don't you take your grandfather's place?" I blurted. "Wouldn't he like to see the family tradition carried on?"

Lori seemed astonished. But Sam spoke up first. "Why not? You're smart, Lori. You could do that in your sleep." He grimaced, apparently realizing that was exactly how Alfred Cobb was doing it now. "I mean, you wouldn't have to quit your day job here."

"Think about it," I said to Lori, and on that note, I left, hoping that I had restored some of my dignity.

During the short block-and-a-half walk back to the office, I could still feel Milo's hungry kiss, the new coat of lipstick notwithstanding. I felt kind of silly. It wasn't as if we hadn't made love before. Sometimes it felt routine, and almost never impassioned. We were comfortable with each other, and that was good. But it wasn't enough.

When I came through the *Advocate*'s front door, Denise was

talking on the phone. I smiled at her and kept going, but she called out to me before I could reach the newsroom.

"I need help," she said, her hand over the receiver. "What do we do about personal classified ads? I mean really, *really* personal." She made a face and pointed to the receiver.

"You mean something sexual?"

"I think so," she whispered. "This guy may be drunk. He talks kind of slurred."

"Tell him to call later and ask for Leo," I said. "He'll handle it."

It wasn't the first time we'd been asked to run explicit ads in the personals, though it didn't happen often. I waited while Denise got rid of the caller, which took longer than I expected.

"Total head case," she said. "Why doesn't he put an ad in one of those weird Seattle papers or on Craigslist?"

"I guess he wants to buy local. How's your morning been going?"

"Okay." She gave me a vague smile. "Everybody here is nice. At least nobody's yelled at me yet."

"We try not to do that," I said. "You should take a copy of yesterday's paper as a souvenir. Or did you save it at home?"

Denise looked embarrassed. "I'm not a subscriber. I mean, I read the paper if I see it somewhere, but . . ." She shrugged. "I figure I know what's happening around town without having to read the news. Does that sound dumb?"

"Ah . . ." I had trouble answering her directly. "Not 'dumb,' but now that you're working here, it'd be a good idea to go through the paper when it comes out. You're the first person anyone sees when they walk through our front door. Sometimes readers stop in with some question about an item in the paper or why another item was left out. Ginny was always able to give them an answer so they didn't have to bother the rest of the staff. Sitting in the front office makes you the face of the *Advocate*. So to speak. Like a public relations person."

She giggled. "That's funny. I never thought I'd ever be in PR."

"It's not unlike your teller's job. You represented the bank to the customers."

"Huh. I guess that's right. I'll read the paper when I have time."

"Good idea." Trying not to feel discouraged, I continued on to my cubbyhole. At least Denise's muddleheaded attitude had made me stop thinking about the sheriff.

Vida was absent from the newsroom, but returned around a quarter to twelve. I suggested we eat at the Venison Inn. She demurred briefly, then agreed but warned me she would order only a light lunch. Reba Cederberg had served a lavish meal the previous evening, and my House & Home editor was afraid she'd gained at least two pounds.

We arrived five minutes before most of the crowd showed up, so Vida was pleased that we could sit at a window table near the front to provide her with excellent visibility of Alpiners' comings and goings during the lunch hour.

"Tell me about the Petersen boys," I said, even before we ordered. "I heard you've asked them to be on your radio show tonight."

"Yes," she replied, securing the faux ruby and rhinestone brooch on her navy beret. "I had qualms, but Strom was very open to my idea, so I thought it might be cathartic for him and for Cole to talk about their experiences with a father who was in prison while they were maturing from adolescence to manhood."

I tried not to look flabbergasted. "They agreed?"

"Cole wasn't there," Vida explained, "but Strom assured me his brother would be willing to join him. I'd already mentioned having Roger and his parents on my program after the problems at the trailer park. By the way, Spencer told me the ratings for that show were exceptional. He remarked at the time that it was very courageous of all of us to speak so freely about the situation and that what he termed 'edginess' of the content was the kind of programming that KSKY usually doesn't broadcast."

That was putting it mildly. *Vida's Cupboard* always had a huge listener base because it was the only live program that was all Alpine, all the time. Controversy was usually avoided, given that Vida stuck to local personalities, hobbies, recipes, gardening, and travel. Such topics were indeed tame, compared with Roger's involvement with drugs and the town hooker. Even so, Vida had trodden delicately with her daughter's family. It hadn't quite turned into an apologia, but the damage to the family's reputation had been minimized and no doubt the interview had squelched some of the more reprehensible rumors that had raced through the town in the wake of the trailer park tragedy.

"Not," Vida emphasized, "that I'll let the program become maudlin. I didn't do that with my own family, because I wanted to avoid being pitied. If my judgment about Strom and Cole is correct, they're quite bright and self-possessed. I intend to keep my questions to such things as acceptance, forgiveness, and family ties. Very appropriate for the Christmas season, don't you think? In a way, Larry's incarceration wasn't all that different from, say, a father who is serving abroad in the military or one who is no longer living under the same roof as the mother and rarely sees his offspring."

Vida sounded convincing. "I suppose," I allowed, but didn't elaborate. I'd intended to ask Lori Cobb about Cole's visit, but I'd been so rattled when I came out of Milo's office that I forgot they were an item. I was about to broach the subject of the young couple when Jessie Lott plodded down the aisle to take our orders.

"Jessie," Vida said, "I can tell your bunions are acting up. The cold weather, I suppose."

Jessie nodded. "Every winter, the same nuisance. The damp's even worse for my arthritis."

"Dear me, I can't imagine how difficult it is for you to keep working," Vida said. "Let Emma go first. I must mull."

I smiled at Jessie, who was only a few years younger than Vida. Like my House & Home editor, she'd been a single mother for many years and had stayed employed for the sake of her children and now for her grandchildren. "I'll have the pastrami and Havarti on light rye," I said. "Toasted, please, and a small salad with blue cheese dressing."

Jessie nodded and scribbled on her pad, plump fingers swollen at the knuckles.

Vida sighed. "Maybe the Cobb salad—with a bit of extra shredded cheddar. If you don't mind, I'd like the ranch dressing on the side, perhaps more than the usual amount as it seems skimpy with so much lettuce. Oh—does it come with one of those nice plump rolls?"

Jessie assured her that it did. She made her weary way back down the aisle just as Richie MacAvoy and another young man sat down across from us.

"Richie!" Vida exclaimed. "I don't believe my eyes. Is that you, Cole?"

Richie smiled. "Cole and I are getting caught up. We went through school together."

Cole Petersen came over to shake Vida's hand. "Mrs. Runkel, it's great to see you. Do we have to rehearse for your show?"

"I never rehearse," Vida responded. "Do you remember Emma Lord, the *Advocate*'s publisher?"

Cole looked dubious. He was taller but not as broad as his brother, Strom. "I think so," he said, and shook my hand, too. "It's been a while."

"Yes, it has," I agreed, accustomed to being in Vida's shadow. "You were still a teenager when I saw you last."

"Probably," he agreed. "I haven't been in Alpine much since my freshman year in college."

"We've been reminiscing," Richie said as Cole returned to his seat. "I worked at the bank not long after I got out of high school."

"So you did," Vida said, while nodding to an older couple who had just entered the restaurant. "My, but that seems like such a long time ago. How is your new baby? Chloe, isn't it?"

"Chunky little monkey," Richie replied, "keeping Cindy and me up half the night."

"How good of you to share duties with your wife," Vida said. "And Cole, I believe I heard you've been visiting your cousin, Alison, and her roommate, Lori Cobb. We must talk about that later. I haven't seen Alison since she moved from Everett." She paused as the Nordby brothers from the local GM dealership walked by, stopping long enough to pay their homage.

"How's that Buick running these days?" Skunk Nordby inquired.

"Quite well," Vida informed him.

"You're due for a tune-up the first of the year," Trout Nordby reminded her. "Put it on your calendar."

"I always do," Vida declared, "just as soon as Parker's Pharmacy sends me their new calendar." She leaned out into the aisle to wave at someone. "Speak of the devil," she said with her toothy smile, "here come Dot and Durwood Parker now. Yoo-hoo!"

I'd almost forgotten how wearing it was to lunch with Vida. Between her family disaster and it being the busy month of November, with the town's social activities in full swing, it had been at least six weeks since we'd shared a meal. Another dozen or more Alpiners had paused to meet and greet her by the time our food arrived. I'd begun to wonder if I could remember how to talk. When I finally had a chance to test my vocal cords, I refrained from telling her about the letter I'd received. Too many ears were too close to the ground in the Venison Inn, especially with Cole Petersen across the aisle. It was only after we got back to the office that I brought up the subject.

Vida, naturally, was appalled, but quick to zero in on practical matters. "If Milo finds out that other people involved in the murder trial are getting these peculiar mailings, that might help us understand the reason behind the letters, though the timing would still be odd. Why wait ten years?"

"How do we know this person did?" I said. "What if Milo finds out that the judge and the jury and everyone else involved in Snohomish County have been receiving similar letters since Larry went to jail?"

Vida dismissed the idea. "Surely *someone* would've said *something* over the years. Since the crime occurred here, we'd have heard."

What Vida meant, of course, was that *she* would've heard. But her argument was convincing. There had always been a strong link between not only the towns of Alpine and Snohomish but the city of Everett as well. Many former timber industry families had moved farther down the road when the original mill had closed, and later, when logging was sharply curtailed in the 1980s. Everett was as far west as you could go on Highway 2 without ending up in Puget Sound.

Later that afternoon, Vida received a phone call from Al Driggers informing her that the autopsy had been performed on Larry Petersen. The Walla Walla County medical examiner had confirmed that the deceased had died of heart failure.

"The interment will probably be Monday," Vida said after relaying the news to me. "Al talked to JoAnne. Cremation is in Walla Walla, perhaps even today, and the ashes will be shipped here."

"I assume Strom and Cole will stay on. Did Al mention if JoAnne was coming to Alpine?"

"He thought she would," Vida replied. "I'm going to try to reach Marv and Cathleen again. Maybe I should do that now. Certainly they can't be gadding around in the afternoon sun."

"Arizona can get rather cool in December," I said, then lowered my voice. "How come you aren't including Denise on your program tonight?"

Vida looked askance. "I simply couldn't deal with her on the air. Besides, it seemed like a conflict of interest now that she's working here."

That excuse sounded as good as any. "Does she know her brothers are going to be on your show?"

Vida sighed. "I've no idea. Strom told me he stopped to see her at the bank on Monday, but they didn't have much chance to visit. She was fairly busy. As for Cole, I couldn't say. It's rather sad. The rest of the family has all moved on, or at least away, except for Denise and Elmer. From what Thelma tells me, Denise doesn't visit very often."

"No surprise there," I murmured.

"Not that Thelma cares," Vida went on. "She's too upset about her great-niece Tanya being married in a windmill."

"I don't think Milo's daughter is actually being married *inside* the windmill," I said. "It's in a park."

"There's still a windmill involved," Vida said, obviously taking Thelma's side. "It's ridiculous. What if the day turns windy? That's dangerous with those big things blowing all over the place." She shuddered. "I mustn't think about that anymore. I have to finish a few things before I go to the radio station."

Just before I was about to leave, Leo showed me the mockup for the Grocery Basket special recipe insert. "Looks good so far," I said. "I like the nineteenth-century holiday art."

He pointed to a Thomas Nast Santa Claus. "It's easy to find Christmas and New Year's art from that era, but not for the other holidays. A dreidel, a menorah, yes. They don't change much."

"Just don't put a sprig of holly on it."

"No mistletoe, either. Isn't that a Druid thing?"

"I think we can skip Druid holidays," I said, "unless we include Winter Solstice. Now that I think about it, we probably should."

"Good idea. I'll find some Stonehenge art." Leo started out of my cubbyhole. "Did Denise put the pervert through to you this afternoon?"

I didn't know what Leo was talking about. "What pervert?"

"The guy who wanted to take out a too-personal personals ad," Leo replied. "She switched him over to me twice, but he hung up both times. I thought maybe she'd tried to let you handle him."

"No. He may be sleeping it off. Denise said he sounded drunk. And with the holidays approaching, we'll get more just like him," I said. "It's a bad time for lots of people."

"Oh—one other thing," Leo said, moving back closer to my desk. "Incredible as this may sound, my ex and our kids would like me to join them for Christmas this year. It's a Saturday, so I was wondering if I could take off Thursday and come back Sunday night. I'd have everything set for the next edition because so many of the merchants will be holding their post–holiday and pre-inventory sales."

"Sure, Leo," I said. "You haven't used up your vacation. We'll be fine." I smiled. "I'm glad. This will be your first family Christmas in a long time, right?"

"First one with all of us together in over ten years," he said. "I've burdened one or two of the kids with my presence—and presents—a few times. It's going to be sort of strange, but we made it through Thanksgiving." He shrugged. "We'll see. Maybe Liza won't make me sleep on the sofa this time. We're going to be grandparents in February."

"Congratulations," I said. "If you need an extra day, come back on Monday. You'll still have time for any last-minute work before deadline."

He blew me a kiss. "Thanks, babe. See you tomorrow."

I started getting ready to bail out, too. Kip poked his head in just as I was putting on my coat. "Did Denise say anything about not feeling good this afternoon?"

"No. Why?"

"It's sounds like she's in the restroom, throwing up."

"Oh. Well . . . it *is* flu season. Let's hope it's not contagious."

"That's for sure," Kip said. "Do you think it's okay to leave her all by herself if she's sick?"

"I can stay," I said.

"No, I will. I've got a couple of tech problems I want to resolve anyway. I'd rather get them taken care of now instead of waiting until morning. That sort of stuff always gets me off to a bad start."

"You're sure?"

Kip nodded and grinned. "I'll just keep my distance from Denise. I don't want to catch what she's got." He disappeared toward the back shop. It occurred to me that what was giving our new staffer the heaves might be something that Kip would never have to worry about catching.

TEN

MILO SHOWED UP AT SIX-FIFTEEN, BEARING TWO RIB steaks, a fifth of Scotch, and an apple pie. "Some woman in Monroe makes these," he said, showing me the label on the pie. "Jake O'Toole swears they're better than Betsy's."

"How could he remember that far back? Poor Betsy hasn't had time to make a pie since she began to help run the store ten years ago. And when Buzzy O'Toole took time off last month to recover after Mike died in the truck crash, Betsy managed the produce section, too. I know Jake told his brother not to worry about coming back until he and Laura had recovered from the initial shock of their son's death, but it's been over six weeks and this is a busy time at the store."

"Buzzy started work again just before Thanksgiving," Milo said, opening the cupboard where I kept my liquor. "Canadian or bourbon?"

"Whichever is easier to reach." I opened the oven to check the potatoes. "The younger generation around here has been through the mill lately. If it isn't drugs or road fatalities, it's emotional trauma. I'm surprised the Petersen boys agreed to be on Vida's show tonight. What do you make of it?"

"Not much," Milo said, pouring our drinks. "Is this going to turn into one of those 'let's search our souls' evenings or what?"

I'd just opened the package of steaks. "You want to jump into the sack right now and skip Vida's program? I thought you must be hungry." I gestured at the counter. "You're the one who brought a special pie."

"It looked good." Milo had the grace to seem contrite. "You look good, too."

I held up one of the steaks. "Well? This meat or . . . ?"

"Oh, hell," the sheriff said, taking a big gulp of Scotch. "Let's eat first. We can't miss Vida and her damned show."

It didn't surprise me that Vida could win out even over sex. "Fine," I said. "I'll put your steak on now so it'll get done to your usual old-catcher's-mitt preference. Grab my drink and go sit down in the living room. Better yet, start the fireplace. I set it up last night, but never got around to lighting it."

Milo obeyed wordlessly. When I joined him a couple of minutes later, the regional section of the *Seattle Times* was burning under the kindling and the sheriff was studying *Sky Autumn*. "It's realistic, all right," he said. "Where is it?"

"The creek? I'm not sure," I admitted. "Carroll Creek, maybe, above the town? Or it might not be a specific creek. Craig could've taken different elements from anywhere around here."

Milo shook his head. "I don't think so. It looks familiar." He took another sip of Scotch. "It's late spring. The leaves are out on the vine maples, the water's a runoff from higher up. We've had two, almost three years of drought. I figure he painted this awhile back. Otherwise, the creek would be trickling, not rushing, over those rocks."

I realized what Milo meant. I'd always reacted to the painting on a visual and emotional level. But typical of the sheriff's approach to just about everything, especially his job, he responded to the basics. Who, what, when, and why—that was how his mind worked, and everything had to fit before he could come up with an answer.

"It's odd that you should mention that," I said. "When I saw his latest painting at Donna's gallery, I almost wondered if this one had been painted a long time ago. The style was radically different. Artists seldom go off on tangents. Their work changes more slowly. I don't know how long it takes Craig to paint a picture or if he starts one and stops, does something else, then goes back to the other one, or what. I've no idea how he makes decisions about selling his art. Given the way he lives, I can't imagine he has a weatherproof storage facility."

Milo chuckled. "For all you know, he lives in a downtown Seattle penthouse and pretends he's a hermit just to sound interesting. He can probably make more money as a weirdo."

It wasn't the craziest idea I'd ever heard, but I didn't believe it. "He's been sighted around here for years," I pointed out. "Furthermore, Donna says he could charge more if he wanted to because he's so talented. The really peculiar part is why nobody has come across where he lives and works."

Milo finally sat down in the easy chair by the hearth. The logs had started to catch. I could feel the fire's warmth as I took my usual spot on the sofa across the room. I could smell the wood smoke, too. My little log house felt cozy. The irony wasn't lost on me as I recalled that only a week ago I'd been miserable, spending Thanksgiving alone and full of self-pity.

"Maybe," Milo said after lighting a cigarette, "somebody has found his place, but didn't live to tell the tale."

"Oh, no." I was vehement. "Sure, there are hermits who kill anyone venturing onto their turf. You've told me horror stories about the forest freaks who decorate their hideaways with intruders' skulls, but Craig's not that type." I craned my neck in the direction of the painting above me on the wall. "The man who did that could never kill anyone."

"Don't kid yourself. Anybody can do anything, if they're desperate. Good God, haven't you seen enough of that as a newshound?"

I grudgingly admitted that was true. "Never mind. I hope Craig got back to wherever he lives. Did anyone see him after he left the hospital?"

"If they did, nobody told me," Milo said with irritating indifference. "I got busy following up some leads on those tree poachers."

"What?" I practically shrieked. "Why didn't you tell me?"

"They're *leads*, damnit. If we arrest somebody, it'll be in the log."

I was used to the sheriff's closemouthed attitude about investigations, but the poachers and Craig were linked in my mind. And his, of course. "Okay, okay. I have to turn your steak and put mine on. We'll eat out here and listen to Vida's show."

Five minutes later, I started back to the living room, but the sheriff was coming into the kitchen, seeking a refill of his drink. "Just half a shot," he said. "Did you know you were almost out of Scotch?"

"That's because you haven't been here for a while," I said. "You know I don't drink that stuff. I can't stand it."

Milo glanced at the kettle on the stove. "Fresh green beans?"

"Canned. I don't buy fresh beans this time of year unless I have company. They're too expensive."

"I'm not company?"

"I didn't have time to stop at the store."

"I did." He reached for the almost empty bottle of Scotch and poured what was left into his glass before opening the fridge to get more ice. "What's with all this fancy French cheese?"

I was hoping Milo wouldn't notice. "A gift."

The sheriff dropped two ice cubes in his drink, closed the refrigerator door, and looked at me with obvious disappointment. "I thought you were done with that AP guy."

"I am," I said. "I didn't solicit the cheese or any of the other expensive delicacies he sent from Paris. If I had, I'd have asked him to overnight *haricots verts* for your dinner."

"What the hell is an 'arocover'? It sounds like it should be in a zoo along with the asshole from the AP. And why is there smoke coming out of your stove?"

"Oh!" I yanked the oven door open, filling the kitchen with more smoke. "It's grease. I meant to clean it over the weekend, but . . ."

I started to cough and my eyes began to water. Milo elbowed me out of the way. "Go sit down. You're a mess."

By the time the sheriff had opened the back door, turned the oven off, and rescued the potatoes, it was five to seven. "All clear," he called. "Come and get whatever's left of it."

I'd already set the plates and the cutlery on the counter. "Thanks," I said in a sheepish voice. "The last week or so has been a real downer."

"That's okay." He used a big cooking fork to put my steak on a plate. "At least you didn't have to spend Thanksgiving finding out that you're going to be bankrupted by your daughter's wedding. I keep hoping she'll dump him like she did with her last couple of future bridegrooms. Tanya's not a good picker when it comes to men."

"How many are on the invitation list?"

"Would you believe three hundred? Mulehide and I didn't have more than thirty when we got married, and that included the two of us."

"As the mother of a priest, that's one problem I'll never have," I said as I finished filling my plate. "I'll turn on the radio."

One of Spence's college students was updating the weather

and traffic. Possible chance of snow at the three-thousand-foot level, temperatures tonight in the high twenties, winds up to twenty miles an hour, ice and snow possible on Highway 2 and surrounding areas as well as in Alpine itself. Traction tires required for going over the pass. In other words, normal for December in SkyCo.

A trio of commercials followed, first for Harvey's Hardware, second for Barton's Bootery, and third for the Grocery Basket. Next was Spence's recorded voice saying, "Here's what we've all been waiting for on Thursday nights from KSKY-AM—it's *Vida's Cupboard*. Let's open the door for an intimate chat with Alpine's favorite neighbor, Vida Runkel."

The sound of a creaking door could be heard, followed by a slight pause before Vida greeted her listeners. "Good evening, dear friends and neighbors. Tonight I have the great pleasure of chatting with two members of one of Alpine's first families, Franklin and Cole Petersen. How lovely to have you . . ."

Vida continued briefly, explaining that the elder brother preferred going by Strom these days in honor of his Bergstrom grandfather. "Like any family," she continued, "you've had your triumphs and your tragedies, just like the Windsors and the Kennedys and the Roosevelts."

I marveled that Vida could get out the latter two famous names—unless she was referring to the Roosevelt named Teddy rather than FDR.

Vida continued. "We were saddened by your father's death this past weekend, and also by the circumstances in which he found himself at the time of his demise. Do you think that his situation had an adverse effect on his health?"

"Christ," Milo muttered in disgust.

"Prison," Strom—at least it sounded like Strom—said, "is a harsh environment. Still, it wouldn't be right for either Cole or me or anyone else to determine if that contributed to his death."

"Good answer," I murmured.

Vida asked her next question: "Did either of you visit your father while he was in prison?"

"Yes." It was Strom again. "I saw him . . . oh, maybe a dozen times over the past ten years. He seemed resigned to his fate. We never talked about what had led up to . . . how things turned out for him."

"Understandable," Vida said. "Not a pleasant subject for father or son. And you, Cole?"

"I only visited him three times," Cole said, his voice low. "It was really rough to see him in a place like that. It turned out that the last time I saw him was the weekend before he died. It was a real bummer."

"But how timely," Vida declared. "I imagine that despite your sadness, you were thankful to have made what turned out to be the final visit." She paused, apparently expecting Cole to respond. "Or," Vida went on, apparently realizing he wasn't going to pick up on her cue, "did you regret you hadn't seen him more often?"

"I haven't figured that out," Cole replied. "I'm working on it. It's not easy."

"Ah," Vida said, sounding pleased, "that is the crux of our chat. Surely you'd agree that family ties may bend but rarely break in the face of heartache and tragedy. I've found it to be so. Don't you feel the same way?"

There was another pause. I envisioned Cole and Strom exchanging looks to see which brother would answer the question. Seniority won out. "You have to define 'family,' " Strom said. "Obviously, people related to you by blood are family, but that doesn't exclude others you meet along the way and bond with. I think family is often a duty, rather than a sense of love.

That's not to say I don't love the members of my family, but over the years, I've made friends who are as close to me or even closer than blood relations."

Milo snorted. "That's the truth."

"You're saying that," Cole put in, "because you guilt-tripped yourself into going to Walla Walla at least once a year. It made you feel good. Did you ever think how Dad felt?"

"Hey, bro—you spent two years just up the pike at Wazzu in Pullman. You could've practically walked to the slammer, but you didn't bother. You were too busy making out with coeds or cows or whatever Cougars do at Moo U."

"You ought to know," Cole snapped. "You were there for a couple of years yourself. You never got over Jim Lambright cutting you from the football team even before the season started, but I heard the real reason you left the U Dub was to follow a she-goat to Wazzu because she missed her mother."

"Such brotherly fun!" Vida exclaimed. "Isn't it wonderful to be able to say how we feel to our loved ones?"

"Oh," Cole said, "we could say plenty. Like Mom never going to see Dad except to get him to sign the divorce papers. One trip, over and out. What made it worse was every time I'd go to see her in that condo on Queen Anne Hill in Seattle, she had their wedding picture on the mantel. She'd go on and on about how happy they'd been, all the sacrifices they made for the family, the so-called difficult years that made them bond. It was a freaking farce. If they were ever happy, I never noticed it."

"That's because you were always a sniveling, self-centered little brat," Strom said with fervor. "Dad and Mom loved each other, but they weren't the demonstrative kind, especially in front of us kids. I don't think they wanted us to know they ever had sex. How the heck did they think we got here? The freaking stork?"

"Aha!" Vida exclaimed loudly. "That's a perfect example of

parents who consider the feelings of their children. Not cod-
dling, of course, but gently bringing them into the adult world.
So much to learn, but not all at once. Now we must take a brief
break for a word from our fine local sponsors." She hadn't
paused for breath.

Milo was laughing. "Holy crap! Vida didn't know what she
was getting into. Doesn't Fleetwood have a three-second delay
on his programs? I thought he told me that when I backed out
of the show last month. He wanted to assure me that if I said
something dumb, it wouldn't get on the air."

I was laughing, too. "That's probably up to whoever is
working as the engineer. If it's an inexperienced college kid, he
may not have acted fast enough. Or else he got too enthralled in
the bickering brothers."

"Talk about reality shows." Milo shook his head. "I wish we
could hear what Vida's telling the Petersen boys now. I'll bet, as
she'd put it, she's fit to be tied."

"Maybe," I said, "but it certainly gets the listeners' attention. What do you want to bet that Fleetwood gets requests to
replay the show for people who missed it?"

Milo shook his head. "I'd never bet against Vida on anything."

We waited in silence for the second commercial to end.

"It's your friend and neighbor, Vida Runkel, here with Strom
and Cole Petersen in a lively discussion of family ties. Indeed,
they don't always seem to bind in the way we'd want them to,
but they still remain *strong*." The last word was spoken em-
phatically, as if in warning to her squabbling guests. "Now I'd
like to move on to what you two have in the way of future
plans. Until your grandfather, Marvin Petersen, retired, there
had always been a Petersen at the Bank of Alpine. Is it possible that either of you is interested in moving back here and tak-

ing up on what I can only call the Petersen dynasty's banking responsibility?"

"Not a chance," Cole responded. "I like what I do at Microsoft. I'm no genius when it comes to technology, but I like marketing the company's products because I believe in them. The travel I get to do is great, seeing all those cool places around the world and how other people live. I just got back from Bangkok, and before that, Beijing and Hong Kong. I couldn't do that here."

"No, I suppose you couldn't," Vida said in a voice that indicated she wondered why Cole would want to go to anywhere else in the world besides Alpine. "What about you, Strom?"

"I haven't given it much thought," he replied disinterestedly.

"I understand." Vida sounded sympathetic. "You're going through the grieving process. It's never wise to make big decisions at such a time. I assume you'll both be staying on for the private memorial service at the mausoleum."

"Maybe," Strom hedged.

"Probably," Cole said.

"When is your mother, JoAnne, due to arrive in town?" Vida asked.

There was yet another pause. "I don't know," Strom finally admitted. "Maybe over the weekend. I'll call her tomorrow and find out."

"I already talked to her," Cole said. "She's not coming until Monday morning."

"You didn't tell me that," Strom shot back.

"I didn't have a chance," Cole retorted. "She phoned me just before I headed here."

"So now you both know. That's so comforting," Vida said. "At this point, I'd like to hear your Christmas plans as a family. Do you . . ." Pause. ". . . mind if we move on, as I see our time is running out." Milo and I exchanged looks as Vida switched gears, no doubt due to angry glares from one or both Petersens. "Is there anything else either of you would like to say about being part of a family that has done so much for Alpine over the past eighty years?"

"We had some good times growing up here," Cole said, almost as if he meant it. "It's always cool to hook up with old buddies."

"The town's changed," Strom said. "I think the college has helped move Alpine into the twentieth century."

"You mean the twenty-first," Vida corrected.

"Actually, I didn't," Strom said.

If Vida had gasped, it was inaudible, but she recovered quickly. "Any last words for our loyal listeners?"

"You mean," Cole inquired, "from my dad?"

"Well . . . yes, of course. That'd be lovely."

"He told me the weekend before he died he didn't kill Aunt Linda."

Instead of the usual farewell from Vida, there was only a sharp intake of breath, followed by the door closing on her cupboard.

ELEVEN

"FOR CHRISSAKES!" MILO EXPLODED. "WHERE DID *THAT* come from?"

I was stunned, too. "I've no idea."

The sheriff had bolted out of the easy chair, swearing a blue streak. "Now I've got to talk to those two sonsuvbitches before they leave town. Call the station. Tell them . . . tell *Vida* to keep them on hold until I get there."

"But even she can't—"

"She sure as hell can," Milo said, grabbing his jacket. "Do it!" He was out the door before I could say another word.

I knew KSKY's number by heart. I punched it in, thankful that I didn't misdial. A young man answered. "Is Mrs. Runkel still there?" I asked, and added quickly, "along with the Petersens?"

"The guys are headed for the door," the young man replied. "Mrs. Runkel's still here."

"Tell them to stay put," I said. "This is Emma Lord, from the newspaper. The sheriff is on his way to talk to all of them." That was a stretch, but I didn't want to single out Strom and

Cole. Maybe they'd think that some FCC rule had been violated. "If you let them leave, your ass is grass," I added, and hung up.

Making sure everything was turned off in the kitchen, I gathered up my coat and purse. The sheriff wasn't leaving me out of this confrontation. I, too, was a victim of the letter writing. It also occurred to me as I backed out of the driveway that Vida had come close to breaching our agreement that she would never break any kind of news on her radio program before the *Advocate* had the story. I'd already been a bit miffed when she'd teetered on the brink by asking the Petersens if either of them intended to work for the Bank of Alpine. But it was the last part of the interview that made me angry. She couldn't have known what Cole would say, but the entire segment had been newsworthy. Both of us should've guessed that from the start, or so I told myself as I drove through the cold, hard rain that pelted my windshield.

I figured I was less than five minutes behind the sheriff. Turning off the Burl Creek Road, I saw his Grand Cherokee parked at an angle blocking the exit of Vida's Buick and three other cars on the narrow gravel track that led to the radio station. I had to stop my Honda on the verge, almost halfway into the encroaching underbrush, and get out on the passenger side.

Trudging through the small parking lot with my vision impaired by the freezing rain, I realized that Milo was in the doorway, his back turned to me, and his long arms spread out to prevent the brothers from leaving the studio. The Petersens' combined ages might total the sheriff's, and Strom's husky frame hadn't yet turned to fat, but when duty called, Milo exuded authority and strength.

"I'm not going to tell you again," he said sharply. "Get back inside. Or should I cuff you right now?"

"Hey, man," Cole said, "we haven't done anything."

"It's not 'man,' sonny," Milo informed the younger Petersen, "it's 'sir.' Move it."

The brothers moved. Backwards. Milo was about to shut the door when I called to him. "Not so fast. Do you want me to drown out here in the rain?"

"Oh, shit!" he said under his breath. But he waited. "I should've guessed you couldn't stay put and clean your damned oven."

Vida was standing by the desk that served as most of the station's receiving area. I could see into the studio through a big window. A young Asian man was at the controls, flipping switches or whatever radio engineers did when there was no live broadcasting.

"This," Vida declared, arms folded across her impressive bosom, "is a pretty kettle of fish. May I ask why you're here?" She suddenly saw me behind Milo. "Emma! What is this?"

"Can it, Vida," Milo said, keeping his eyes on Strom and Cole. "We can talk here or we can go to headquarters. Your choice."

"Hey," Cole said, "I don't get it. Really. What's wrong? All we did was a radio show. Whatever happened to free speech?"

"That's what we're going to talk about," the sheriff replied, pausing to take in the confined quarters. "I need some answers to some simple questions. Dare I trust you two to come to my office or do I need to call for backup?"

"What kind of questions?" Strom asked, his face turning red.

"I'll explain that when we get to headquarters." Milo was keeping his temper under control, but I could tell it wasn't easy. "I want to show you something, but what I've got is at my office. Well?"

The brothers reluctantly looked at each other. "This is stupid," Strom declared. "But we'll play along. There better be a big payoff. I planned to drive back to Seattle tonight."

"You still can," Milo said. "Here's what we'll do. Emma, you go first to clear the way to the road. I'll go next. Then . . ." He stopped, gazing at the Petersens. "Did you come together or did you each bring your own car?"

"I got my Jeep," Cole said.

"Mine's the Lexus." Strom seemed embarrassed by the status symbol. Or maybe he was still angry.

I left before the rest of the cavalcade got organized. As it turned out, Milo followed me, the brothers followed the sheriff, and Vida took up the rear. I wondered what the poor kid in the booth was thinking. If he had any sense, he'd contact Spence as soon as we left. Selfishly, I hoped he was slow on the uptake. I had my own rear end to cover. As soon as I pulled up in front of the sheriff's headquarters, I called Kip.

"Emma!" he said when he heard my voice. "What do we do about Vida's show?"

"That's why I'm calling," I said, and briefly explained what was going on. "Anybody who's still semiconscious in town probably knows what happened, even if they somehow missed the program. Just get a brief summary online for now. I may have more later. Don't mention that the brothers are being questioned. And for God's sake, make sure you get Cole's version of what Larry told him exactly right. But no direct quotes from either of them."

"Will do." Kip hung up just as Milo pulled in next to me, got out of the Cherokee, and went inside.

I managed to follow him in time to grab the swinging door before it shut in my face. Brushing wet hair off my forehead, I staggered to the counter, where Jack Mullins was regarding the sheriff and me with a wry expression. "Splish-splash, you were taking a bath, along about a—"

"Shut the hell up, Mullins," Milo growled. "I've got camp followers. Anybody else around here besides you?"

Jack shook his head. "Just Evan Singer doing the 911 thing in his hidey-hole. Quiet so far until you two showed up." He glanced at the entrance, espying the Petersens and Vida. "Oh, jeez!" Jack cried. "I forgot about her show tonight! I keep thinking it's still on Wednesdays."

"With any luck, the rest of Alpine did, too," Milo muttered as the rest of our not-so-festive party tromped into the sheriff's domain.

"Really, Milo," Vida began, "you must tell these boys—"

"Not now," he interrupted, before softening his tone. "For once, just be quiet. Please." The sheriff beckoned to Strom and Cole. "We're going into my office." Before opening up the swinging half-door, he shot hard looks at Vida and me. "You'll get your turn later. No arguments."

"Well!" Vida exclaimed as the Petersens were ushered into Milo's inner sanctum. "Doesn't that beat all! Was I or was I not on the program with those boys?"

I grudgingly had to defend the sheriff. "This is police business, Vida. You know exactly what Milo is doing. All he wants to know is if Strom and Cole have any knowledge about the letters."

"The letters?" Jack said. "You mean the ones Dodge got from the nutcase? What happened?"

Vida took umbrage. "You didn't listen to my program?"

"Hey," Jack said, backing away even though the counter separated him from my House & Home editor. "I'm on the job. I have to man the phones and keep track of the patrol deputies."

The explanation was reasonable, but Vida knew better. "You forgot."

Jack's impish face grew sheepish. "I did. My brain hadn't gotten the message. Sorry, Vida. You know I wouldn't miss it."

The phone rang. "But I *am* on the job," he added, picking up the receiver.

"It's been an entire month," Vida muttered. "People simply don't pay attention. Tsk, tsk."

I put a finger to my lips and gestured discreetly at Jack, who was obviously speaking not to someone reporting a prowler or a runaway teenager, but to his wife, Nina. "No kidding! But, Sweet Lips, I'm *working*. I can't be . . . hey, that was the World Series . . . How could I watch Monday Night Football here this week? I wasn't on duty . . . Who said that about JoAnne? . . . No kidding. Hey, Love Muffin, got to go. The sheriff's on the prowl. I'll tell you when I get home, Kitty Cat." He put the phone down. "That was my Lawful Dreaded Wife telling me about your shocker of a show, Mrs. R. So that's what this Petersen thing is all about?"

"Yes." Vida looked severe. "I must say first that you shouldn't malign Nina in front of others. You know perfectly well she's the best thing that ever happened to you."

Jack didn't back down. "Aside from the chicken pox and getting shot in the groin by an irate husband back in 1988?"

"You're impossible," Vida declared. "What did Nina say about JoAnne? I assume she meant JoAnne Petersen."

"Debra Barton heard from JoAnne, who said she's coming to town tomorrow. The Bartons and the Petersens used to be kind of tight."

"So they were," Vida conceded. "Odd that JoAnne should change her plans from what she told her son earlier. Why such urgency?"

Jack held up his hands as if to defend himself. "Don't ask me. I'm just an innocent bystander."

Vida grew thoughtful. "JoAnne has visited the Bartons a few times since she moved. She still has some of her family here, not to mention friends. She golfed, you know."

"Oh." Jack glanced at the closed door to his boss's office. "I don't hear any screaming. Dodge must not have gotten out the thumbscrews yet. I still say those letters he got were from a head case."

"I got one, too," I said. "I brought it to him this morning."

Jack grinned. "I heard you brought the boss more than a letter."

I ignored Vida's stare and gave Jack a disgusted look. "You people should spend more time catching bad guys than speculating about what goes on behind closed doors. Which, I must admit, is what I'm wondering about right now."

I'd hardly gotten the words out of my mouth when the door opened. Strom and Cole emerged first, looking no worse for wear. In fact, they both seemed in much better humor.

"Okay," Milo said, pausing in the doorway to light a cigarette. "You're on, Lois Lane and Brenda Starr." He waved the hand that wasn't holding the cigarette at the entrance. "Looks like you've got competition. Here comes Fleetwood."

"Why not?" I mumbled, watching Spence stride through the door managing to look as if he'd just stepped out of Brooks Brothers. Even his perfectly styled graying black hair wasn't damp. Maybe he was encased in some invisible weatherproofing.

"Good evening, all," he said in his Mr. Radio voice. "Vida, my dear, the phones are ringing everywhere. You've done it again." He beamed and she preened. Then he turned to the Petersen brothers and put out his hand. "My pleasure and gratitude, gentlemen. I'm delighted to meet two young men who can light up the airwaves with such candor and lack of self-consciousness. Very rare."

As they shook Spence's hand, Strom looked wary; Cole appeared stunned. Both mumbled their thanks, though for what, I didn't know.

"Are you done here?" Spence asked Milo.

I held my breath, waiting for the sheriff to answer. But he merely shrugged. "I have what I need. Why don't you media giants work it out between yourselves? I've got an apple pie waiting for me." He ambled through the half-door and held his hand out to me. "I need your key. I don't want to have to break down the door."

I heard Vida suck in her breath. I didn't dare glance at her, knowing her eyes must look like gooseberries behind those big glasses. I ignored Jack, too, certain that he was leering in his puckish manner. Trying to stay calm, I scrambled through my purse and handed Milo my key chain. "You take it off. I don't want to break a fingernail."

"Got it," the sheriff said, deftly running the key along the metal loop and palming it. "See you later." He loped out the front door.

Spence acted blasé, but I sensed he was peeved. "I hoped," he said after an awkward silence, "I could do a live interview here." He looked at Jack. "Is that possible?"

The deputy shrugged. "How would I know? I just work here, catching crooks and saving lives. Do you need some kind of equipment?"

Before Spence could reply, Strom spoke up. "I'm leaving. The weather sucks and I want to get back to Seattle before this rain turns to snow. I'm out of here." As good as his word, he bolted for the door.

"Chicken shit!" Cole called after him.

Vida wagged a finger. "Now, now. Let's all settle down. I'm sure you can tell us what went on with the sheriff." She turned to Jack. "Do you think we could go into Milo's office to stay out of your way?"

"Not a chance," Jack said. "I'm looking forward to full retirement."

"Well then," Vida asked patiently, "where can we go?"

Jack grinned. "You don't want me to tell you." He held up both hands before there were any repercussions. "How about one of the cells? They're all empty. Would you like the deluxe or economy size?"

Vida was dismayed. "You have a break room. What's wrong with that? Or should I get my nephew Billy over here to help us?"

Jack folded faster than a Texas Hold'em player with a deuce and a six in the hole and nothing but face cards in the flop. "Go ahead," he said, "but Lori only cleans the place up in the morning."

Cole suddenly balked. "Did I say I wanted to do this?"

"You can't *not* do it," Vida said, "and may I add that my daughters always told me you were much better behaved than Strom when they babysat the two of you and your sister, Denise."

Denise. I wondered if she'd listened to her brothers on the radio, and if so, how she'd reacted. Her name had never come up, due either to an oversight or a kindness. I didn't know which. It was as if she was out of the family loop.

"I suppose," Spence said as we followed Vida down the hall to the break room, "we could do this as a four-way sort of roundtable. But it'd be simpler if it was just Q & A, don't you think?"

"I assume it's not live," I replied as Vida switched on the lights in the small break room that wasn't much better appointed than the prison cells and considerably less tidy. "When would you air it?"

"Good question," Spence said, pulling out a chair for Vida. The furniture looked like someone's discarded dinette set. Or sets, maybe, since only two of the four chairs matched. "It's eight o'clock now," he said, checking his Movado watch. "A Thursday." He cogitated while Cole and I seated ourselves.

"Too soon for nine, not enough promo, too late for ten on a work night. Probably tomorrow, maybe at six following the news. That way, people who are going out for the evening can catch it." He turned to Vida. "I might replay your program, too. Would you object?"

Vida didn't answer immediately. "I suppose not. I assume you won't tamper with it."

Spence put a hand on Vida's arm. "Rest assured I would never do anything to upset you. We'll talk again tomorrow." He looked at me. "When I decide how to handle this, could you post it on your website?"

"Sure," I said. There was no point in being ornery. Vida's ratings had probably gone over the top again, and both KSKY and the *Advocate* might garner some more advertising, especially with Christmas coming up. "Just let me know as soon as you make up your mind."

"Okay," Spence said, handing Cole a clip-on microphone. "Let's do it. I'll record the intro later to save time." He cleared his throat. "First off, let me say to you, Cole, that I'm sorry your brother, Strom, had to head back to Seattle this evening, but with snow in the forecast around SkyCo, I don't blame him. You and your brother's appearance on *Vida's Cupboard* have created quite a stir around here. What do you make of it from a personal angle?"

"I don't know," Cole replied, looking genuinely stumped. "I suppose it's because Strom and I don't see much of each other. He's four years older, and after he went off to college, I was still in high school. I'd only see him three or four times a year. The age gap got wider as we got older while growing up. It shouldn't make a difference now, but we lead separate lives, even though we're both based in the Seattle area."

"So," Spence said, "you hadn't seized an opportunity to air

your sibling grievances since becoming adults until now. I dislike terming your exchange a meltdown, but your father's death makes you both vulnerable. Do I sense suppressed emotions with you and Strom in the ten years since the original tragedy occurred?"

"Yeah, that's right," Cole agreed. "When we started answering Mrs. Runkel's questions, it was like somebody turned on a faucet. Everything came pouring out. We just let loose. It probably wasn't a good idea."

"How do you mean?" Spence probed, sounding like a caring shrink.

"Oh . . ." Cole gazed up at the ceiling and drummed his fingers on the soiled plastic tablecloth. "It's hard to explain. Just sibling stuff, kind of dumb when I think about it. Embarrassing, too. It's like we forgot we were on the radio."

Spence chuckled softly. "Mrs. Runkel has that effect on people, doesn't she? That's why we call her programs a chat." He offered Vida a warm glance. "I think, though," he went on, "that what's most intriguing here is the aftermath. For our listeners at home, we're at the sheriff's headquarters, where Milo Dodge asked Strom and Cole Petersen to join him after the door closed on *Vida's Cupboard*. Can you tell us why the sheriff did that, Cole? Was it something you mentioned on the air?"

Cole squirmed a bit. "I saw my dad the weekend before he passed away. I didn't know that'd be the last time I . . . you know what I mean. Anyway, we usually just talked about . . . stuff. Like my job and if I was seeing anybody and sports and whatever. But looking back now, maybe he had some kind of . . . intuition about what was going to happen to him. Just before I was about to leave, he said there was something I should know. I asked him what. He said he didn't kill Aunt Linda. I was stunned. I must've looked stupid, because he asked if I believed him. I didn't know what to think—he never denied it after he was arrested or during the trial. None of us kids went to the trial. Mom and Dad thought we shouldn't, and anyway Strom and I were in college and couldn't take time off. I told him if he didn't kill Aunt Linda, he should've said so at the time. But he just shook his head and gave me this weird look." Cole spread his hands. "Our visiting time was up. I had to leave. I didn't mention it to anybody until tonight. It creeped me out."

"Understandable," Spence said. "Is that why Sheriff Dodge wanted to talk to you? Did he have doubts of his own about your father's guilt?"

"Uh . . ." Cole grimaced. "I don't think so. But he wanted to know if we knew anything about some anonymous letters that had been sent to people around here insisting that my dad didn't do it. I guess the letters started showing up a few days before Dad died. Anyway, neither of us had a clue. That sounded pretty weird to both of us. We couldn't think of anybody who'd have a reason to do something like that, unless Dad had done it before he died. But Dodge told us the most recent letter had shown up today and that all of the envelopes were postmarked from Alpine. It doesn't make any sense."

I was annoyed that the letters had been mentioned, but at least Milo apparently hadn't given out the recipients' names. Vida and I exchanged peeved expressions.

Spence was nodding sagely. "It's often difficult to understand what motivates certain deranged—if sometimes well-meaning—people to act so irrationally. I gather the sheriff didn't name any of the persons who received these letters?"

"He showed us one, but we couldn't tell who got it. There wasn't much to it, just that Dad wasn't guilty. It was written on a computer and taped to the page, but Dodge covered up part of the message. He wanted to see if we knew anything about it—or maybe how we'd react."

"Interesting," Spence remarked, his eyes shifting in my direction. "I'd also be interested to know in the days to come how you—and your brother, Strom—will feel about those last words from your father. I imagine you both, as well as other family members, would be comforted greatly if you believed he was innocent."

Cole seemed to have tuned out Mr. Radio. He was staring at the red-and-white-checkered tablecloth. *Zoned out,* I thought. *Emotionally drained.* I didn't blame him.

Spence sensed as much. "Thank you, Cole. I know our listeners appreciate your candor. All our good wishes at KSKY go out to you at this sad time." He shut off the recorder and unclipped his mike. "Well. That was quite a tour de force, Cole. Seriously, I thank you for being so open. Does doing that feel cathartic?"

Cole seemed to haul himself back into reality. "Cathartic? I don't know. It's just . . . strange. Can I go now?"

"Sure." Spence stood up. "In fact, you want to have a beer?"

Cole shook his head. "No. I'm staying with friends. They were going to order a pizza after I got back from the station. They're probably wondering what happened to me." He allowed Spence to shake his hand, murmured his thanks to Vida, and gave me a bleak glance. Then he left the break room, moving like a much older man.

Spence gathered up his gear. "I guess I won't ask either of you out for a beer," he said, flashing his bright, white smile. "Unless, Vida, you'd join me for a glass of wine? I owe you."

"I think I'll go home," Vida said. "I dislike leaving Cupcake alone at night if it snows."

I was already out in the hall when Vida caught up with me. "Apple pie indeed! I will never understand what goes on with you and Milo. You're like children!" She shook herself like a big bird after a bath and stalked on out through the open area.

I didn't try to keep up. Jack was on the phone. It sounded as if he was trying to calm someone who was panicking about a porcupine in his or her woodshed. He looked up and leered at me. I ignored him and made my exit. I was already in my Honda when Spence came out into the rain that was beginning to turn to wet snow. He approached the driver's side of my car. I reluctantly rolled down the window.

"No point in asking you, is there, Emma?" he said, with a wicked grin. "I assume you've got something else on your plate besides pie."

"Don't be a jackass," I snapped. "Milo and I've been friends for—"

Spence laughed. "Stop. All I want to say is that Dodge is one lucky bastard. I don't understand why. G'night." He hurried off to wherever he'd parked his Beemer. I turned on the ignition and reversed out of the diagonal parking space so fast that I narrowly avoided getting hit by Vida's Buick. She honked at me and swerved out of the way. *Great,* I thought, *she probably thinks I can't wait to jump into Milo's arms instead of running over Spence.*

The truth was that I wasn't sure if I wanted to do either— or both.

I was locked out of my own house. I'd forgotten that Milo had my key. To leave my driveway open, he'd parked the Grand Cherokee in front of my house, just off the street, half on the dirt, half on the grass. There are no sidewalks south of Cedar and west of Fifth. Local Improvement District bond issues are always voted down by Alpine's stingy electorate.

I pulled into the carport to enter through the kitchen. Both front and back doors have the same lock, the result of my first few years in Alpine, when Adam was in and out on visits from college and kept losing either one or the other of the two original, but different, keys. It seemed simpler to have only one key for both locks, though in retrospect it was a bad idea. If my careless son lost *the* key, he was really in a jam and only GORM could help him. He'd devised the acronym for his frazzled mother, which stood for Good Old Rescue Mom.

Looking through the back door window, I could see the light was on in the kitchen, the apple pie sat on the table with a large chunk missing, and the sound of the TV emanated from the living room. Hopefully, Milo would hear me knock.

Apparently he couldn't. Maybe he was in the bathroom. I waited a moment or two, wishing the wind wasn't blowing the wet snow through the carport. I knocked again and called the sheriff's name.

No response. I traipsed around to the front and rang the doorbell. If he was in the easy chair, the door was only four feet away. I pushed the doorbell twice. Nothing. I was starting to worry. And shiver. I'd closed the living room drapes after coming home from work, so there was no way to peer inside. Frustrated, I fumbled for my cell and dialed Milo's number. After four rings, I heard a muffled voice say, "Dodge here."

"Emma here. On the front porch. Let me in! I'm freezing."

"Huh? Oh. Right. Sure. Hold on."

Just as I was wiping wet snow out of my eyes, the sheriff opened the door. "You were asleep!" I yelled, pushing past him to get inside. "I've been outside for ten minutes!"

He peered at whatever NBA game he'd been watching. "You couldn't have. There's still eight and a half minutes to go in the quarter. There was under eleven the last time I checked."

"They must've taken about six time-outs," I said angrily, struggling with stiff fingers to get out of my coat. "Maybe they had a bench-clearing brawl. Give me back my key before you forget it belongs to me."

"Oh. It's over there on your end table." Milo yawned, picked up the remote, and muted the sound. "What happened with Fleetwood and the rest of the gang?"

"They're all dead," I said, still annoyed. And cold. "How was your damned pie?"

"Good. I tried some of that French cheese with it." He made a face. "Not as good as local cheddar. You want a piece?"

"No." I took a deep breath and sank onto the sofa. "I have to call Kip. Or do I? I'm not sure we can add anything to our online edition."

Milo was on his haunches, banking up the fire. "Are you talking to me or the sofa cushions?" he asked over his shoulder.

I sighed. "Who knows? Strom took off right after you left."

Milo nodded. "I saw him get into his Lexus as I pulled out." He stood up and stretched. "What'd Fleetwood do? Make Cole sing solo?"

"Exactly," I replied. "All things considered, Cole did a decent job. Spence is going to play the interview tomorrow, probably after the six o'clock news. I assume you'll want to hear it before then."

Milo leaned on the back of the easy chair. "I'd better. It might be evidence." He saw my curious expression and shook his head. "Don't get excited. I'm guessing, but I'll bet Cole repeated what Larry told him about being innocent."

"He did," I said, "and elaborated on his reaction at the time. He still doesn't know what to make of it."

The sheriff looked rueful. "I don't either. I'm beginning to wonder if there's more to all this than some oddball trying to make trouble. I'm not sure Fleetwood should air the damned thing—unless it'd make the creep crawl out of the woodwork."

He picked up the remote and turned off the TV. "I wonder if I should go listen to that tape now. I wouldn't put it past Fleetwood to pull a fast one and broadcast it sooner."

With some effort, I hauled myself off the sofa. "Did you ever check with anyone at SnoCo to find out if they'd gotten any strange letters?"

He made a dismissive gesture. "I got stonewalled by some halfwit assistant to the judge who tried the case. I have the name of the jury foreman, but it turns out that the guy is out of town until just before Christmas. I'll call the judge again tomorrow. Not that I expect to hear anything helpful. Sometimes those big shots in SnoCo treat us like stepchildren. Screw 'em. If anybody did get a letter over there, they should've let us know. Since they didn't, I figure no news is bad news—for us."

"Are you that worried about the chance you actually did arrest the wrong suspect?"

Milo scowled at me. "It happens. Did you lose your memory between here and the radio station? I arrested the wrong guy less than two months ago in the De Muth homicide, for God's sake. You don't think that still bugs the hell out of me? I hear all kinds of morons making cracks about that, even on my own staff. It may be a joke to them, but it sure as shit isn't to me."

"Clive confessed after the two of them got into the tavern fight and De Muth dropped dead," I reminded him. "You had no choice."

"Bull. You think anybody else remembers that part? All they know is that Clive ended up spending jail time before the whole mess got squared away." Milo was pacing in front of the fireplace, rubbing his head as if he could erase the memory. "People around here probably think I'm losing it, been too long on the job, gotten soft—and old."

"Oh, good grief!" I cried. "That's crazy! Maybe whoever is

writing the letters picked up on the Berentsen arrest and it gave them some nutty idea. Or else it's just bad timing."

The sheriff stopped moving a couple of feet from me. "Don't try to whitewash it. It is what it is."

"And what the hell does that mean? I hate that phrase," I said in disgust. "If you don't want Spence to play the tape, confiscate it."

Milo's expression was mocking. "You want me to get into a free-speech war with Fleetwood? That's all I need. Get your head screwed on straight and come up with something that's not a bunch of crap."

"Hey," I yelled, "I'm only trying to help. Don't be such a jackass! What do you want me to do, write an editorial about how terrific you are and anybody in SkyCo who criticizes you is mad as a hatter?"

"Go ahead. It sounds like some of your other shit-brained ideas." He glared at me with a fierceness that should have been frightening, but only made me angrier. I turned my back on him and stomped off toward the kitchen. Just as I got to the open doorway between the two rooms, Milo grabbed me by both shoulders and turned me around so fast that my neck squeaked.

"You're such a pain in the ass," he said, his voice suddenly low as he leaned down so that his face almost touched mine. And then it did, and the next thing I knew we were on the floor by the fireplace and I couldn't remember anything except that this wasn't the Milo Dodge I thought I knew so well and it wasn't Emma Lord, either. It was two wild, ravenous, fierce human animals suddenly risking pride for passion and not giving a damn. The past wasn't present; the future didn't matter. There was only us, no babes in the woods, no orphans of the storm, just two scarred veterans of love's bittersweet wars. I couldn't think, and I didn't want to. It was enough to lose myself in this stranger named Milo and let whoever he was lose himself in the me I didn't recognize.

"Oh!" I gasped after we were both spent and my head rested on Milo's chest. "Guess you can forget the 'old' part."

"I can't hear you. You're all fuzzy. Or else my ears are ringing."

"Mmm."

Neither of us said anything for a long time. I didn't move, content to feel the rhythm of his breathing, and vaguely wondering if he'd gone to sleep. But after a while, I realized I was cold. I lifted my head to look at the fireplace. There were no flames, just a scattering of orange embers in the grate. I checked my watch, the only thing I was still wearing.

"My God," I said in shock, "it's going on eleven!"

Milo opened his eyes. "What?" He raised his head. "Jesus. It can't be." His left arm was still around me. "I can't see my watch."

"I can move."

"Don't. You feel good like this."

"We can't stay here forever."

"Can't we?" He ruffled my hair with his free hand. "Why not? The rest of the world's a bunch of crap."

"It's also winter out in that crappy world. Aren't you chilly?"

"No. Want me to warm you up again?"

I smiled at him. "I'm sure you could, but one of us has to act like a responsible adult or else we'll never get off the floor."

His hazel eyes studied my face for a long moment. Then he pulled me closer and kissed my nose. "You're right. Roll over so I can get up."

I scooted off of him and put a hand on the side table next to the easy chair to steady myself. I felt shaky, a discovery that made me giggle. The sheriff was sitting up, his back to me.

"If you want something funny," he said in faint dismay, "my watch says it's nine-fifteen. The damned thing's stopped."

"I'm not surprised. If I can walk, I'm going to get my bathrobe."

When I returned, Milo had put all of his clothes back on except for his socks and boots. "I'd better head on out," he said wistfully.

I peeked between the drapes to see what the weather was doing. "It's sticking. An inch, maybe."

"No problem." He sat down to put on his boots. "You're right. It is cold in here now."

"My furnace turns off at ten every night, then comes back on at seven in the morning."

He gestured at the end table by the sofa. "Don't forget your key."

"I won't. In fact, I'll do that now." I picked up the key, clasping it in my hand.

Boots on, the sheriff stood up. "I'll talk to Fleetwood first thing tomorrow. I want to hear that tape."

"You should," I said as he put on his all-weather jacket. "Take the rest of the pie with you."

"Don't you want some?"

"I'll cut out a slice. Come on, you can leave through the kitchen."

Milo stood by the window over the sink, looking out to the carport. "It's still blowing, coming in from the north."

"It could get bad by morning," I said, taking a fairly generous piece of pie and putting it on a plate. I covered the rest with the plastic lid and handed it over. "I do have regular cheddar, extra sharp. It's in one of the crisper drawers."

The sheriff nodded absently. I knew what he was thinking— the same thing that was going through my mind. Whatever we'd

had there on the living room floor had evaporated once we covered ourselves. I felt close to tears and had to turn away. "I'd
better put the key on my loop right now. Be careful."

"You too. Thanks for everything."

A burst of icy air filled the kitchen as he went out the door.
I'd never felt so cold—or so alone.

TWELVE

K IP CONFRONTED ME FIRST THING THE NEXT MORNING AS soon as I walked through the *Advocate*'s front door. "I waited up until after eleven, but I never heard back. Did I miss a call from you?"

I tried to act as if I hadn't forgotten Kip existed during the hour or more that he'd waited for the phone to ring. "There wasn't anything to add. Spence is supposed to let us know when he's going to air the interview, but Milo wants to hear it first."

Kip looked puzzled. "Dodge wasn't there at headquarters?"

"He'd already finished talking to the Petersens," I explained. "Strom didn't stick around, either. He took off for Seattle. It was a one-on-one between Spence and Cole." I forced an apologetic smile. "I'm really sorry. I should've called to let you know there was nothing new."

Kip shrugged. "No big deal. Did the original posting look okay?"

I didn't want to admit that I'd never bothered to check. "Fine," I said, and hoped it was true. "I always trust your judgment." That *was* true. "Where's Denise?"

"Not here yet," Kip replied. "Maybe she's still sick. She left the reception area in kind of a mess. I had to shut down her computer, wash her coffee mug, empty the wastebasket, and rescue a copy of this week's paper from under her chair."

"Thanks," I said. "Maybe I can give you a five-dollar bonus. Oh! I forgot that she has the bakery run."

"I'll bet she didn't plug the coffee in before she left," Kip said. "Or did you tell her about that?"

"No, I figured Amanda did."

We both went into the newsroom. Leo was coming out of the back shop. "If you're in search of coffee, you'll have to wait. It wasn't set up and I plugged it in about three minutes ago."

"No sign of Denise?" I asked.

Leo shook his head. "Maybe she's skiing to work. There must be four inches out there, but at least it's stopped now."

"It's ten after eight," I pointed out. "Did she call?"

"I got here about ten to," Kip replied. "No messages from her. A bunch for Vida about her show last night." He grinned. "You'd expect that, though. She gets plenty of calls even when somebody has a new chocolate cake recipe on *Cupboard*."

At least he hadn't said "apple pie," I thought to myself. "Then I'll call her. Denise, I mean."

Even as I spoke, my eye was caught by a pretty, breathless blonde coming through the front door. I went out to greet the newcomer, leaving Leo and Kip to stare at the coffeemaker.

"Ms. Lord?" the newcomer said with a tentative smile. "You don't remember me, but I'm Alison Lindahl."

"Oh, Alison!" I exclaimed, taking her hand. "You're beautiful! How are you?"

She laughed. "How am I beautiful? It's all smoke and mirrors, which is why I'm teaching cosmetology now." Alison quickly sobered. "In fact, I'm not teaching today. My students are working on their finals projects. But my cousin Denise called to say that Aunt JoAnne is coming to town this morning and could I fill in here for her. I didn't know what to say, so I thought I'd better come by to see if you'd want me to take her place for the day."

If Alison's physical transformation wasn't as natural as it looked, I remembered that her brain was inborn. "That'd be great," I assured her, "but do you want to do it?"

"It's better than staying home and watching Denise's brother play kissy-face with my roommate, Lori. She's taking the day off, too. If Cole stays through the weekend, I'll spend more time at Donna's art gallery to keep my distance."

I'd also forgotten about the Alison-Lori-Cole connection. "Has Cole recovered from being on Vida's program last night?"

Alison shook her head. "I wouldn't know. I haven't seen him or Lori this morning. Anyway, I worked as a temp, usually a receptionist, while I was going to college. Oh! I just remembered—I brought the legacy book or whatever it's called from my mom's funeral. Mrs. Runkel wanted to see it for some reason. Is she here yet?"

"No, but she will be." I stepped aside so Alison could go behind the counter. "In fact, she's running a bit late."

"Maybe she's worn out from listening to my cousins." Alison suddenly looked wistful. "Frankly, I could barely stand it. I don't remember Uncle Larry all that well, but he seemed like a nice man. It's weird he'd say he hadn't killed my mother. If he *did* say that, and Cole isn't making it up." She looked at me as if I had some kind of answer for her. I considered telling her about the letters Milo and I had received, but decided against it—for now.

"Cole sounded sincere," I said.

"He seems like a good guy, but you never know, do you?"

Alison sighed. "Maybe Uncle Larry realized he wasn't well or maybe he wasn't in his right mind when Cole saw him. Who knows? After all those years in prison, Uncle Larry might've been out of his head and wanted to believe he hadn't murdered his own sister." She paused again, her face frozen. "Wouldn't you think that after all this time since my mother died, I could finally put the past behind me? It wasn't as if we were really close." Her artfully mauve-colored lips barely moved.

"I marvel that you've done so well despite undergoing such traumatic circumstances at a very impressionable age," I said. "But you always were a brave as well as a smart girl."

"Brave?" Alison shrugged. "No, just worried about my dad getting railroaded as the ex-husband turned prime suspect. As for smart, at least I was able to understand early on that my stepmother was the real deal when it came to mothering."

"How are your folks?" I inquired, trying to remember the last time I'd seen Howard Lindahl and his second wife, Susan. It had probably been at the trial, almost ten years ago.

"They're good," Alison replied. "Oh—here comes Mrs. Runkel. It looks as if she's been to the bakery. Omigod, what's that on her head?"

"A fried egg," I said under my breath as my House & Home editor entered the front office.

"Alison!" Vida exclaimed, echoing my own greeting, but without surprise. "I knew you'd be a good trouper." She set the bakery box on the counter and undid her headgear, a white knit wool cap tied under her chin with a yellow starburst on top. "Denise called me to say she couldn't do the bakery run. She forgot to mention it to you. I'm glad your aunt JoAnne is coming to town. I must have a chat to catch up with her. She's usually so busy, with her old friends and family."

"I'm sure my aunt would enjoy that," Alison said. "This isn't a happy visit, according to Denise. In fact, she tried to talk her mother out of coming. I guess Uncle Larry's death really upset Aunt Jo."

If Alison's statement surprised Vida, she hid it. "Of course. Losing a spouse, even an ex-spouse, can be devastating. Now," she went on, picking up the bakery box, "I must set out these delicious goodies. I managed to get quite an assortment. The snow must've gotten some of the early customers off to a late start."

As Vida tromped into the newsroom, I asked Alison if there was anything she needed to know about Denise's duties.

"I can play it by ear," she insisted. "I know about the classifieds, but if anything stumps me, I'll ask. That's a big part of temping."

"Wonderful," I said. "I'll let you get to it."

The coffeemaker had finished its job as I went back to the newsroom. Leo and Kip were ogling the Italian slippers, three kinds of bear claws, a dozen various doughnuts, and a half-dozen napoleons.

"Duchess," Leo said, "you must've drained all the petty cash on this stuff. Should we all bring in some store-bought cookies Monday?"

"My treat," Vida responded. "I used my own money, since this wasn't my usual bakery day. Besides," she went on, standing back to inspect her handiwork on the tray, "I always think people get hungrier when the first snowfall in Alpine is deeper than an inch or two."

"Not to mention," Leo remarked, "that you must've sent KSKY's ratings right over Mount Baldy. Fleetwood owes you a big Christmas bonus."

Kip nodded enthusiastically. "That was killer, Vida," he declared. "You really rocked last night. I expected the cupboard door to fall off its hinges. Ah—your phone's ringing—again."

"So it is," Vida said a bit smugly. "I'll answer it."

I poured a mug of coffee and took a sugared doughnut. Leo nudged me. "I wonder what Denise thought about her brothers going at each other over the airways. Maybe that's the real reason why she isn't here this morning."

"Being Denise," I said, dropping my voice while trying to block out Vida's animated chatter on the phone, "she may be the only person in Alpine who doesn't regularly tune in to Vida's show."

"Are you adding anything to last night's online posting?"

"I don't know yet," I replied. "The sheriff wants to hear the interview with Cole, and Spence may air the original again if he gets a lot of listener requests."

Leo shook his head. "I wouldn't do that if I were him. He'd better talk to whoever his lawyer is first. One or all of the Petersens might sue him for exploitation or inciting harassment or God only knows what else. I remember one occasion when I was working in Orange County and the paper there ran photos of local firefighters who'd posed for a fund-raising calendar. It was such a hot item with all those good-looking studs that they were asked to run it again—in color. Within two months of publication, two of the guys had dumped their wives for women who'd contacted them after seeing their pictures. Both ex-wives filed a lawsuit against the paper for . . . I forget the exact reason, but basically it was for provoking alienation of affection, charging the publisher had violated their privacy and ruined their marriages."

"Did they win the lawsuit?" I asked.

"No. Tom had smarter attorneys than the exes." Leo suddenly looked embarrassed. "Sorry, babe. Didn't mean to . . . you know."

"It's okay," I said. "I can hear his name and not burst into tears. You worked for him a long time. It's occurred to me that you knew him better than I did."

"Maybe, maybe not." He shrugged. "You look tired. Do you feel all right?"

"Yes," I answered, wishing it were true. "It's been a long week. I haven't had time to get out my Nativity set and start putting the pieces up one by one."

"Kip told me Denise was sick last night before she left," Leo said. "I thought that was another reason she didn't show up." He gestured with what was left of his bear claw. "Here comes our star reporter now. Hi, Mitch. How do you like the new blonde?"

"Nice," Mitch said, nodding to Vida, who was now on a second phone call. "I'd have introduced myself, but she seems to have her hands—and her ears—full with fielding calls for our radio star." He removed his jacket before glancing at the pastry tray. "Wow. This is sumptuous. Italian slippers are my special vice."

"Have you already checked the sheriff's log?" I asked.

Mitch nodded. "Six vehicle accidents, none serious, mostly caused by the snow, including two in town. One porcupine on the loose at the Overholt farm, unapprehended so far. Grace Grundle thought one of her cats had been kidnapped, but she found Toodles later, trapped in the kitchen cupboard where she keeps some of her many kitty treats. Speaking of cupboards, how 'bout those Petersen boys?"

"Indeed," I said vaguely. "Do you know if the sheriff has listened to the tape?"

Mitch had already taken a bite from his Italian slipper. "Mmm—pear filling. What tape?"

"Spence made a second tape with Cole," I said. "Dodge wanted to hear it before it went on the air."

"No," Mitch said, sitting down at his desk. "I didn't talk

much to the sheriff. He seemed to be grumpy, probably because Lori took a vacation day while her light-o'-love is still in town. He's got Doe Jamison answering the phones, and it's obvious she doesn't like playing that particular role. Doe's not one for female stereotyping."

"She wouldn't be," I murmured. "Okay, I'll check with him later. I'd better get to work." I trudged into my cubbyhole, feeling a bit stiff in joints and muscles I hadn't used for a long time.

It was after ten by the time Alison delivered the mail. "Sorry," she said, "but Marlowe Whipp was late and I've been answering the phones, especially for Vida. Her ears must be about to fall off by now."

"She loves it," I said, looking apprehensively at the stack of mail Alison couldn't fit into my inbox. "Just set it down in any reasonably spare space. I'll be pitching most of it anyway."

I waited to start going through the pile until after Alison left. She'd put all the catalogs on the bottom, the exchange papers in the middle, and the smaller pieces on top. Gritting my teeth, I picked up the smaller envelopes and sifted through them quickly. To my surprise and relief, there was no plain white envelope addressed to me.

If it had been an ordinary morning, I'd have called Milo by now to find out if he'd listened to Spence's tape. I would've also asked if he, too, had been spared another ugly, anonymous letter about Larry Petersen's innocence. But it wasn't an ordinary morning. Or maybe it was, as morning must follow night, but what had come before was not ordinary. I felt foolish for my lack of better recovery powers.

Vida finally had a moment to spare, and headed straight for me. "Well now!" she exclaimed, plunking herself in one of the visitor's chairs. "How am I going to get any work done today? I think I'll ask Alison to hold my calls for a while."

"Anything of interest in what your fans had to say?"

Vida shuddered. "You wouldn't believe—yes, of course you would—what nonsense people come up with. Darla Puckett insisted she knew Larry was innocent all along because he had such an honest face. Darla has always had the brains of a chicken. Ella—my sister-in-law—said she had doubts from the start because she saw someone or something very peculiar that night, though she couldn't remember what it was. Of course she wouldn't—she had that stroke a while ago and she hasn't regained what little she ever had of her mind. Then there was Garth Wesley, who should have *some* sense, being a pharmacist. He'd heard a rumor that Linda Lindahl was poisoned before she was allegedly strangled and that he'd prescribed sleeping pills for Reba Cederberg just two days before the murder, and all these years he's wondered and felt guilty. Doesn't that beat all?"

My head was swimming. "I don't recall anything odd about the autopsy," I finally said after trying to piece together the spate of rumors and conjectures. "It was quite straightforward. Cause of death was strangulation. The only thing that was unclear at first was whether Linda's scarf or a rope had been used to do it."

"True," Vida said. She gave my desk a once-over. "No strange letter today?"

"No, thank goodness. I wonder why. It couldn't have anything to do with your show, because the last pickup even at the post office is six P.M. I suppose it's possible that Marlowe lost it along his route. It wouldn't be the first time."

"No," Vida said thoughtfully. "I wonder if Milo got one." She cocked her head to one side. "Emma, you look dreadful. What's wrong?"

"Nothing," I snapped. "Why should it be?"

Vida's gray eyebrows raised above the rims of her glasses.

"I'm sure I don't know," she said, but her words lacked conviction. "I must make a call of my own," she went on, getting out of the chair. "Poor Pastor Purebeck ended up in the ER after our potluck Wednesday night. Doc Dewey said it was food poisoning. Can you imagine? Presbyterians *always* wash their hands." Shaking her head, she exited my cubbyhole.

I found myself smiling as I wondered how much of Vida's casserole the good reverend had eaten. Maybe Garth Wesley wasn't the right person to feel guilty about poison.

Over the course of the next hour and a half, I started to call the sheriff three times, but stopped before I punched in the last two digits. I couldn't understand why he hadn't called me. He knew I'd want to know how he'd reacted to Spence's tape. Then it occurred to me that Mr. Radio hadn't phoned, either. He was supposed to let me know when the segment would be aired so I could post it on our website.

I was pondering the matter when Mitch poked his head in. "What do you think about a feature on animals encroaching on civilization because their own habitat is disappearing? I'd use the porcupine bit as the hook."

"We've done stories like that in the past," I said. "It's not uncommon around here, as you'll discover when you find a bear in your bathtub. But," I added, "you have a knack for humor. Make it funny, start off with maybe something about kids watching for Santa's reindeer and instead, they blah-blah."

"Good idea," Mitch agreed, still leaning against the door frame. "Is it okay if I put a bit of myself into it as a big-city boy dealing with a new environment? Not that we didn't have plenty of wild animals in Detroit, but they usually had only two feet."

"Sure," I agreed. "By the way, would you mind calling the sheriff and asking about that tape Spence did with Cole Petersen last night? If you can't get Dodge, try Fleetwood. One of them must know by now."

"I'll do it ASAP," he said, with a snappy salute before turning on his heel and going back to his desk.

It was going on noon. I wasn't hungry. Maybe I'd eat another doughnut and call it lunch. Staying in might help me focus on other matters such as a meaningful editorial for the upcoming issue. Nothing came to mind. Maybe I was brain-dead. Finally I thought about Craig Laurentis, wondering if he was on the mend. His fate was out of my hands, even if I couldn't put him entirely out of my mind.

Mitch was back in the doorway. "I can't get hold of either Dodge or Fleetwood. Doe told me the sheriff had been out for most of the morning, and whoever is covering for Spence said he'd been in and out but probably wouldn't be back until after lunch. The kid on backup duty didn't know anything about the tape, except that there was one somewhere, but he hadn't heard it."

"Swell," I said glumly. "Well, I guess that's Spence's problem, not ours. Maybe we'll hear something later, or I'll let Vida take on that task. It is partly her responsibility."

Mitch nodded and started to turn away, but I called to him. "When you were at the sheriff's this morning, was there anything mentioned about the tree poachers? Milo made some comment about a lead yesterday, but of course he wouldn't give any details."

"Interesting," Mitch said, having stepped inside my office. "You know, we actually have trees in Michigan. Ever hear of the white pine?"

I thought for a moment. "Maybe, but not around here."

"That's because it only grows in the central and northeast parts of this country and Canada. In the days of sailing ships, the trees were lusted after for mast making. About ten years ago, some yacht builder helped himself to a stand of white pine to add more class for his status-crazed customers. He zeroed in on the Upper Peninsula's Porcupine Mountains State Park on Lake Superior. But he didn't want to get his hands dirty, so he hired a couple of unemployed gyppo loggers. Problem was they decided to keep the trees for themselves and cut out the middle-man. Unfortunately, the yacht builder caught on to them and there was a confrontation. Bad idea. His hirelings shot him, right in the middle of a campground with about twenty startled witnesses."

"And your point is . . . ?"

"The same if we were talking drugs," Mitch replied. "The masterminds don't do the dog work. How hard is it to cut down a maple? I've done it myself twice. They grow too damned fast, at least the ones we had did. If I were Dodge—and he probably knows more about it than I do—I wouldn't look for loggers as the culprits. I'd look for kids, especially dropouts."

"Teenage dropouts with guns?"

Mitch raked his long, thin fingers through the swatch of graying hair that always seemed to be in danger of impairing his vision. "That's the part that bothers me. If we were talking drugs in Detroit or any other city, the shooting would be a no-brainer. But not around here."

"A lot of kids grow up with guns in this area," I pointed out. "Dads—and moms—who hunt, want self-defense, collectors. It's part of the local culture here in the mountains. Don't broad-cast it, but Father Kelly's dad was a career army man who had a bunch of souvenirs from Korea, including guns. They're locked up in a safe at the rectory."

"I get all that," Mitch said. "It's not the fact that the poach-ers would *have* guns, but the fact that they *used* them. It's not like they were committing a capital crime. The maple wood is probably being used to make guitars, for God's sake!" He mulled for a moment. "Do you think I should say something to Dodge about my qualms?"

"Ah . . ." I was flummoxed. The last thing Milo needed about now was a rookie Alpiner giving him law enforcement advice. "Maybe you should hold that thought." I noticed a hint of disappointment on Mitch's face. "As a matter of fact," I went on, "my first reaction was that I couldn't believe Laurentis had been shot by tree poachers. Not because of the poachers, but because of Craig. If there's anybody more attuned to the forest, it's him. He could smell danger from a mile away."

"You actually know this guy?" Mitch asked.

"Sort of," I said. "Remember when you and Brenda came to dinner at my house after you moved here? You both admired the painting above my sofa. That's a Laurentis."

"I'll be damned." Mitch grinned. "I didn't make the connection. I mean, I'd heard something about the hermit being a so-called artist, but . . ." He shrugged. "The guy's good. Brenda thought he was more than good, and she's got an artist's eye of her own, just a different medium with her weaving." He made another pass at his hair. "So what you're saying is the question doesn't involve the shooter as much as it does the victim."

I hadn't thought it through that far, but Mitch was right. "Yes," I said, "I guess it does."

And the awful conclusion I drew was that if we were right, Craig Laurentis was still in grave danger.

After Mitch left my cubbyhole, I wondered if Milo had considered the same possibility. I doubted it, because that wasn't the way his mind worked. I knew him too well.

Except I didn't. In fact, I was beginning to wonder if I knew him at all. Or even if I knew myself.

THIRTEEN

B Y TWO O'CLOCK, THERE WAS STILL NO WORD FROM EITHER the sheriff or Mr. Radio. Vida had just come back from interviewing Charlene Vickers about her trip to Dallas over the Thanksgiving weekend.

"Dallas!" she exclaimed disdainfully. "Why would Marguerite and her husband ever move to such a place? All that oil and cowboy boots and hats and barbecue."

"As I recall, Marguerite's husband got an offer he couldn't refuse from a big residential landscaping company in Dallas many years ago."

"Big!" Vida almost spat out the word. "Yes, everything there is *big*. 'Big D,' isn't that what they call it? As if bigger is better."

"How did Cal like the trip?" I asked.

"Charlene insisted he had a pleasant time," Vida said in obvious disbelief. "I know better. I don't think Cal has any time for those big oil companies since he was forced to turn his Texaco station into a Chevron. Most Alpiners will take forever to get used to the change. Everyone I know still refers to it as Cal's Texaco. And so does he, in private."

I didn't argue. I'd been known to do it myself since the switch. "Have you had a chance to look at the guest book from Linda's funeral?"

"No," Vida replied in disgust. "I haven't had a spare minute. In fact, we should go through it together. Would you like to have supper at my house tonight?"

Visions of Pastor Purebeck clutching his stomach lurched in my mind's eye. "Why don't you come to my place? I've got some imported food items that won't keep forever in the fridge."

Vida looked wary. "Imported? From where?"

"Paris," I said, and went on before she could comment. "Rolf Fisher sent them. I thought he was dead. He is to me, anyway."

"Well now." Vida regarded me speculatively. "I didn't much care for the man—too slick by far—but I thought the two of you had some enjoyable times together. You shared so many mutual interests."

"We can hardly share them from more than ten thousand miles away," I said. "Besides, I never knew whether to believe anything he told me. Not an actual liar, but . . ." I shrugged. "That relationship was never going anywhere. Especially since half of it went to France."

Vida didn't say anything right away, but then she posed an unexpected question. "Do you think it's safe?"

"Safe? What? France?"

"The food," she replied. "Foreign countries don't have the same standards, you know. I've heard they allow flies in German restaurants. Imagine! It's no wonder they lost two wars."

"I'll ask Doc Dewey to run the stuff through the lab, okay?"

"Emma." She regarded me with a mixture of reproof and amusement. "I suppose the French do know how to prepare food. Yes, I'll come to your house. Don't go to a lot of trouble.

I can still feel the extra pounds I gained at the Cederbergs' the other night." She stood up. "I must write up the Vickers' trip before I forget the details."

Amazingly enough, Vida never took notes. She had a memory like an HD camcorder. "By the way, I meant to ask if Reba mentioned anything about her nephew Greg. Apparently Denise still has his dog."

Vida made a face. "I think Greg and Denise are a sore subject with Reba. His name came up after Strom left, but in an odd context. We were talking about Roger." She paused, looking faintly embarrassed. "I mentioned something about Roger's emotional trauma, and Andy told me I shouldn't feel bad about that because he thought most young people had emotional problems these days. Then he looked at Reba and said, 'Take Greg for a prime example.' Reba turned very red and replied that we shouldn't discuss such things at the dinner table. Andy drew in his horns, mumbling an apology. Naturally, I was curious, but I couldn't press them for an explanation."

I was surprised that she hadn't given it a try. "Maybe that's what broke up the marriage."

"Very likely," Vida agreed. "*I'd* have emotional problems if I were married to someone like Denise. In fact, I may have a nervous breakdown before she finishes working here."

"Not you, Vida," I said. "You're too tough."

She looked askance. "Perhaps."

"By the way, after Cole arrived with Richie MacAvoy at lunch, I never got a chance to ask if Strom was upset about his father's death."

"Not outwardly," Vida replied. "In fact, he literally ate and ran. These young people—always so busy, wound up like tops. But of course he has a great deal of catching up to do in Alpine."

"Maybe it's just as well Adam never lived here full-time after we moved from Portland," I said. "He didn't have any long-standing ties. At least on the rare occasions he shows up, I get him all to myself."

"Yes," Vida agreed. "Meg and Beth always have to see old friends when they visit. I understand, but still . . ." She turned to make her exit. "Six o'clock?"

"That sounds fine." It also sounded like an echo of what Milo had said the night before—which reminded me that we hadn't heard anything about Spence's plans for the second interview. "Wait," I called after Vida. "Can you call Spence and ask if he's going to air the tape with Cole?"

"Oh!" Vida clapped her hands to her cheeks. "He called while I was out. I'll take care of that right now."

I followed her out of the newsroom. Mitch was working on something, maybe the wild animal feature, and Leo was talking on the phone. I glimpsed Alison in the front office, where she was chatting with Belinda Poole, the Baptist minister's wife.

"You are?" I heard Vida say, making eye contact with me. "I see. Then you'll let us know?" She rolled her eyes. "Excuse me, I didn't quite catch that . . . Oh, certainly. You take care and do feel better . . . Try steam . . . I will. Thank you." Vida rang off. "Spencer has a dreadful cold. I could hardly understand him. He has to wait on the Cole interview as well as a possible re-broadcast of my program. He can't do a live introduction with impaired vocal cords."

"Of course not."

I left Vida to her Vickers Texas tale. Half an hour later, Donna Wickstrom called. "Emma," she said in almost a whisper, "can you come to the gallery?"

I looked at my watch. It was ten to three. "You're open early."

"Just come. Please."

Her desperation alarmed me. "Be right there," I said, and hung up.

Making my exit, I announced that I had to leave for a few minutes. I didn't say where I was going, an omission I knew Vida found galling. Fortunately, the merchants along Front—including Kip—had cleared their sidewalks. It hadn't snowed again, but it hadn't melted, either. We were probably due for some black ice by nightfall.

To my surprise, the Closed sign was on the gallery door and the shade was drawn. I knocked three times. Donna let me in at once.

"Thank goodness!" she cried softly. "I didn't know who else to call. It's Craig. He's in the back, and he's a mess."

"Why didn't you call 911?" I asked as we hurried through the gallery's showroom.

"He wouldn't let me. I didn't know what to do."

I managed not to gasp in shock when I saw Craig Laurentis. He was huddled on the floor, wrapped in a dirty hospital blanket. One foot was bare; the other still wore what was left of the treaded sock he'd worn during his brief stay. His face was even gaunter than when I'd last seen him. There was dried blood on one hand and I didn't think I could bear to examine the bullet wound that was hidden by the blanket.

I cleared my throat. "Craig," I said softly but firmly, "I'm calling the doctor. You can't stop me."

He couldn't seem to speak, though his mouth was open and he tried vainly to raise the bloodied hand in protest. I turned my back on him and went into the showroom, where I dialed Doc's office number. Marje Blatt, one of Vida's many nieces, answered. I cut to the chase, telling her I had to talk to Doc immediately.

"He's with a patient, Emma," Marje replied in her usual efficient manner. "If it's an emergency, you should call 911."

I snapped. "Do you want me to send your aunt over to wring your neck? Let me talk to Doc. Now!"

Marje didn't say anything, but I heard some noise in the background. Maybe she'd fallen out of her chair. I didn't care, as long as she put her boss on the line. While I waited impatiently, I tried to see into the back room, but Donna was in the way, hovering over Craig.

"Emma?" Doc said. "What's wrong?"

"It's Craig Laurentis. He's in a very bad way at Donna Wickstrom's art gallery. Can you please come?"

"Why don't you . . . never mind," Doc said briskly. "Is there a parking place in front of the gallery? It'll be quicker if I drive."

I glanced outside. "One door down, toward the corner of Eighth. I'll stand in it until you get here."

"Fine." He rang off.

I decided I had two, maybe three minutes to wait outside, but first I asked Donna to come with me. She started to argue, but I was already at the door.

"Quick," I said as we went outside. "How and where did you find Craig?"

"He called me from the gallery about half an hour ago," she said. "He'd broken a back window to get in. I don't know how he had the strength. He could barely speak, but I don't think he got very far after he left the hospital. For all I know, he's been sleeping by the dumpster in the alley. I *thought* he told me he'd tried to call you, but maybe he meant he wanted me to call you now. So I did."

I suddenly remembered the incoherent and allegedly drunken calls Denise had taken the previous day. God only knew how she'd interpreted what he'd actually said if he could barely speak. If Craig had wanted to talk only to me, then that explained why he'd hung up on Leo.

I realized Donna was shivering in her lambswool sweater and light wool slacks. "Go back inside," I said. "I don't want Doc to have to hospitalize you with pneumonia."

"Okay. I should call home anyway to see how Ginny's managing with the little ones," she said, backpedaling to the gallery. "I had to ask her to stand in for me, but I didn't say why."

"Good thinking," I remarked, though Donna didn't hear me. She'd already ducked in out of the cold.

I felt slightly embarrassed standing in the gutter on Front Street. At least two cars and one truck honked at me, probably figuring I was about to jaywalk. Or maybe it was somebody I knew. I was so focused on watching for Doc that I didn't notice.

After what seemed like a long time, but probably was less than five minutes, I saw his metallic blue Land Rover. I retreated to the curb and waited for him to get out.

"I alerted the medics," he said, skipping any greeting. "This doesn't sound good."

Like his father before him, Doc was never one to gloss over medical problems. "It isn't," I said as we hurried inside. "Donna thinks he's been outside until today."

"Damn," Doc said under his breath. "What fools these mortals be." He took one look at Craig and made a shooing motion at Donna. "Out, out, young lady. You too, Emma."

We both retreated to the showroom, seeing Doc on his knees, mumbling to himself—or to Craig. I whispered a question to Donna, asking if Craig was conscious.

"Barely," she replied. "He must be starved and maybe dehydrated. This is so awful—I can't imagine what he's been through."

"He should never have left the hospital," I said. "But I wasn't really surprised." I gazed around the gallery. "Where's that new painting?"

"I'm not finished framing it," she replied, nodding in the direction of the back room. "It's kind of a . . . challenge."

I nodded. "I can imagine. I hear sirens."

"Thank heavens," Donna murmured. "Maybe this time those nurses will keep a better eye on him."

"It's the best place for him," I said as Donna went to the door.

"Oh, of course," she agreed, leaning out to look for the medics.

I didn't say anything. It occurred to me that if Craig pulled through, he needed more than nurses to look out for him. If my fears for his safety were justified, he needed a deputy on duty, too.

Wes Amundson and a recent hire, Tony Lynch, entered the gallery with the gurney, IVs and oxygen at the ready. They barely looked at Donna and me on their way to the back room.

"I'm closing the door until they're ready to leave," Donna said. "We're already collecting gawkers. I can't deal with that right now."

I couldn't, either. "I think I'll go to the hospital," I said, "if Doc will let me ride with him."

"Should I go with you?" Donna asked.

I shook my head. "Go home. Ginny may have passed out from exhaustion by now. But keep this disaster to yourself. You can tell Ginny if you can get her alone, but if any of your little charges overhears anything, God only knows what they'll say to their parents. We don't want rumors running amok about you, Craig, the gallery—whatever."

"Yes," Donna murmured. "Kids really do say the darnedest things."

"So do adults," I said, trying to see what was going on in the rear of the gallery. I couldn't tell. There were too many people, too much movement, and too much pain, judging from Craig's weak moans.

"I'll wait until they're gone," Donna said after a long pause. "I have to get that window fixed, too. Maybe Steve can do it. He should be home from the high school a little after four. I'll call him now." She shot me a quick look before picking up the phone. "Don't worry—Steve's very discreet. You have to be when you're a teacher."

I went to the other side of the gallery, where I dialed the *Advocate*'s number. Alison answered. I asked her to put me through to Mitch. The Laurentis story was his, but I knew Vida would be irked anyway at not being the first to know.

"Do you want me to meet you at the hospital?" Mitch asked after I explained what had happened.

My initial reaction was to say yes, but I had second thoughts. None of us would learn any details until Craig was able to talk—assuming he ever could, given his perilous state. If Mitch came, nothing short of tying Vida up would stop her from joining him. "Hold off. For all I know, he has to have more surgery."

"Got it," Mitch said. "I'll stick to my rollicking wildlife feature. Do you want me to tell Kip in case we need to put something about Laurentis on the website?"

I glanced at my watch. "It's not quite three-fifteen. I should be back no later than four. Got to go. They're taking Craig out to the ambulance."

Donna and I hung up our phones almost simultaneously. Neither of us spoke as Wes and Tony rolled Craig through the gallery. Doc followed them, looking grim. With a wave to Donna, I followed Doc.

"Could I ride to the hospital with you?" I asked as we waited for the medics to maneuver the gurney through the front door.

Doc frowned at me. "Are you sure you want to do that?"

"Yes."

"Okay. But once we get there, I'm not available for comment."

"I understand. Thanks."

The ambulance was blocking traffic on Front. Doc was parked just east of the gallery, so his Land Rover wasn't impeded. He didn't wait for the medics to load their burden.

"I have to be there when they arrive," he said after we'd gotten into the SUV. "If you've got any questions, ask them now."

"Is Craig going to make it?"

"Depends," he said, turning onto Eighth and driving up the hill past Cascade Dry Cleaners. "I can't tell how much more blood he's lost, but it looks as if an infection's set in. Damn fool. Anyway," he continued, turning onto Pine, "the other problems, like lack of nourishment and dehydration, can be fixed. Elvis Sung and I both figure he's basically healthy. Darned if I know what the guy eats, but he was probably in decent shape before he was shot."

"How old is he?"

Doc chuckled. "He told Elvis he was a hundred and one. I figure mid-fifties. From what I recall about sightings around town over the years, he went gray prematurely. Maybe that's how he got to be a recluse."

I didn't understand. "You don't mean vanity, I assume?"

"No, no," Doc replied as we passed McDonald's and Posies Unlimited. "It's not a myth that trauma can turn a human being's hair white virtually overnight. Maybe he served in Nam. That might do it."

"He'd be the right age. Milo was in Nam."

"So he was. Ever see his medals?"

"Medals? No. He never talks about it."

"Typical." We passed the Baptist church on the right and then St. Mildred's on the left before reaching the hospital's underground parking entrance. "A lot of Vietnam vets don't talk about it, at least not the real stuff. Most vets of any war don't." He pulled into the garage, parking the Rover in his private space. "Come on, Emma. You can take the staff elevator up to the first floor with me, but you're on your own after that."

"I understand," I said.

We didn't speak on the brief ride from the garage. Doc had already put on his game face and merely gave me a pat on the shoulder after we arrived in a hallway off the lobby. He went down the hall; I assumed I should go through the door directly in front of me.

Jenny Bjornson was behind the front desk, reading an issue of *People* magazine. "Hi, Ms. Lord," she said in a chipper voice. "It sounds like we've got some excitement going on around here. I heard sirens."

"Your escaped patient has been caught," I said, figuring she'd find out what had happened soon enough. "It turned out that freedom wasn't good for him."

"Oh—you mean the hermit guy." She giggled. "What would you expect from somebody like that? He must be crazy."

I kept my temper in check. "I would've thought the nurses or someone else on the floor would notice his departure. Mr. Laurentis left in broad daylight."

Jenny's pale face showed a spot of color. "The nurses get so busy with charts and doctors' orders and other patients. I'd hate to have their jobs. You wouldn't believe how tired they are at the end of a shift."

"No, I guess I wouldn't."

The irony was lost on Jenny. "So how come he's being brought back?" she inquired.

Again, I tried to hide my irritation. "He's not healing properly."

"Oh. That's probably because he took off so soon."

I nodded slightly. "Can you do me a favor?"

She suddenly looked wary. "Like what?"

"Call the sheriff's office and let them know that Mr. Laurentis is back in the hospital."

"You can use our phone," she said.

It wasn't what I *could* do, it was what I *couldn't* do. I didn't want to talk to Milo. No, that wasn't true. I didn't want to be the one to call him before he called me. After what had passed between us the previous night—the naked emotion, the unbridled passion, the loss not just of self-control but of self—I was embarrassed. No, that wasn't true, either. I was afraid it hadn't meant as much to him as it had to me. All these thoughts and contradictions flew through my brain at warp speed. I cursed myself for acting like a chicken-livered adolescent. At the moment, Jenny Bjornson was the least shallow and most mature person in the hospital lobby.

"Oh—thanks," I said after a long pause, and then told an outright lie. "I would've used my cell, but the battery's low." I took the receiver from her and turned away to dial the sheriff's main headquarters number. I could hear clucking sounds inside my head.

Doe Jamison answered. I relayed my message to her as concisely as I could manage.

"That was a dumb stunt on Laurentis's part," she declared in disgust. "Do you want to talk to Dodge? He's in his office, and I'll warn you he's as pissed off as I am. The next thing I know he'll have me scrubbing floors. This hasn't been a good day around here. Thank God it's almost over."

"No argument here." I bit the bullet. "Okay, put me through."

"Sure. Good luck."

The chicken clucking in my head got louder. As soon as I heard the phone start to ring, I hung up.

FOURTEEN

"Hunh," I said, handing the receiver back to Jenny, "we got cut off. Lori Cobb's taking a vacation day and I guess her sub isn't used to transferring calls."

Jenny shrugged. "It happens. I still do it wrong sometimes."

I stood by the reception desk, considering my options. It dawned on me that I didn't know why I'd come to the hospital in the first place. I'd told Mitch we wouldn't learn anything for a while, but apparently I hadn't taken my own advice. It was useless to waste time hanging around and listening to Jenny's inane chatter. I asked her to have Doc Dewey call me as soon as he knew anything.

"I've got to get back to the office," I added. "It's going on four."

"Sure," Jenny said. "But I get off at five, so if I don't see Doc, I'll leave word with the nurses."

"Try the OR, too," I said, halfway to the door. "Mr. Laurentis may need surgery."

Jenny looked puzzled. "Mr. La . . . ?"

I wanted to strangle the little twit. "Craig Laurentis. The

patient who was just readmitted. Can you remember that for more than two minutes?" As I shoved the door open, I left Jenny looking stricken, and I didn't give a damn.

It was starting to get dark as I walked down Fourth, the gray clouds overhead hanging in like dirty laundry. Once again, I passed the Bank of Alpine—and once again, I saw a familiar figure coming through the door.

"Emma?" JoAnne Petersen called.

I moved toward her, trying to smile. "I don't think I've seen you in years." Ten to be exact, but I didn't want to pinpoint the time of the family tragedy. She hadn't aged well. I remembered her as a rather pretty woman with good skin and rich brown hair. The skin was not only sallow but wrinkled, and the hair was turning gray. JoAnne had to be fifty or thereabouts, but she looked ten years older.

"I never seem to have time to visit anyone other than family or a few close friends," she said, a faint smile on her thin lips. "I got a call from Vida, inviting me for tea tomorrow afternoon. I might be able to do that. I understand she's had her own share of problems recently."

"Vida will ride them out," I assured JoAnne. "She's a very strong person. Are you staying with Denise?"

"I planned to," she replied, "but I didn't realize she had Greg's dog. I'm allergic to dogs, so I'm going to stay with my cousin Olga. She's still working at the hospital on night duty, but has the weekend off."

I vaguely recalled Olga Bergstrom, an old-school, no-nonsense kind of woman. "Is she the one you sold your house to?"

JoAnne shook her head. "That was one of the younger Bergstroms, Carol Ann. She and her husband, Doug Larson, were expecting their first baby back then. I thought it'd be good to keep some sort of family connection, even though I lost money on the sale." She smiled wanly. "There was a time when it was a happy house. I hope it is again."

My glance strayed to the iron tower clock that had stood on the sidewalk in front of the bank since it opened. It was five minutes to four. "I think I know the Larsons," I said, feeling antsy. "He owns the gym and she works there part-time."

JoAnne nodded. "Do you go there often?"

I laughed. "No. I'm not the workout type. I get enough exercise chasing stories."

JoAnne's smile was slightly wider. "I walk for exercise. Denise is a fanatic for going to the gym. When we lived here, I worked a lot in our garden. I always feel that exercise should accomplish more than getting muscles. But now, in the condo, I . . . well, all my gardening is in pots and planters." Her expression was wistful as she looked away from me. "Life's strange, isn't it?"

"Very," I agreed. "Nobody told me it was easy."

"No." JoAnne held out her hand. "It's cold. I should be on my way. Nice to see you, Emma."

We shook hands. "You too, JoAnne. Take care."

As she crossed Third, I waited for a few vehicles to pass on Front. I hadn't offered JoAnne condolences on Larry's death. I suppose I didn't need to. It's always the same—"I don't know what to say, but . . ." I remembered the well-meaning people who tried to console me after Tom was killed. So inadequate, so impossible to convey compassion for the inevitable. I'd wanted to say, *Don't bother. I know you're trying to be kind, but Tom's dead. That's the bottom line. Nothing you or I can say or do will change that.* I wondered if JoAnne felt the same way.

Vida, who had been talking to Alison, glared at me when I came through the *Advocate*'s front door. "Well? Is it Florence Nightingale flapping her wings back into the coop?"

The chicken allusion wasn't lost on me, given my recent attack of cowardice. But even Vida wouldn't realize that. I saw Alison stifle a laugh from where she was sitting behind the counter. "I don't know anything more than I did when I called Mitch," I said. "I went with Doc to the hospital, but he dumped me off and warned me it might be hours before he had any word about Craig."

Vida expelled an impatient breath. "You don't know how to talk to Young Doc. I've known him since he was knee-high to a sheep. As much as he'd like to think he's the reincarnation of his father, Gerald is not as crusty or as clever as Cecil. Nobody could be. You simply have to stand up to Young Doc. Then he tells you what you want to know."

"He can't tell me what he doesn't know. Even Old Doc didn't have a crystal ball." To forestall further argument from my House & Home editor, I headed for the newsroom.

Vida was at my heels. "The least you can do is fill me in on what happened," she said, waving a hand to indicate that neither Mitch nor Leo was at his desk. "You can also tell me why Spencer ended up in the ER this afternoon."

I turned around so fast that I almost bumped into Vida. "What do you mean?"

"What did I say?" Vida demanded. "Marje Blatt called me after you called Doc. He'd been tending to Spencer and had to leave him before he could complete his treatment, so Doc told him to go to the ER and Dr. Sung would take care of him there. He had a nosebleed that wouldn't stop, but that sounds very strange for just a bad cold."

"Don't ask me," I said. "I don't have a medical degree."

Vida finally went over to her desk and sat down. "Really, I don't know what's going on around here. Everybody seems to be in such a mess. Maybe it's the weather."

I plunked myself in her visitor's chair. "Snow in December

isn't exactly unexpected," I murmured. "Honestly, Vida, I don't know much about anything. I just ran into JoAnne Petersen by the bank. It sounds as if you're having tea with her tomorrow."

"It does? She hasn't informed me of that."

"She will. At least that's what she told me."

"Well." Vida simmered down. "That will be very nice. Perhaps I'll call her this evening before I come to your house. I suppose she and Denise will be having dinner. Maybe Cole will join them."

"I wouldn't know about that, either," I said. "She's changed plans and is staying with her cousin Olga Bergstrom. JoAnne's allergic to Greg's dog. And before you ask, she looks kind of haggard. Somehow, I expected her to be a new and improved, if somewhat older, version of the JoAnne Petersen I remembered."

Vida gave me her gimlet eye. "She did just lose her husband."

"Ex-husband," I said. "An ex she reportedly never visited after he signed off on their divorce papers."

Vida nodded twice. "Yes. That *is* odd, in a way." She shrugged. "Now tell me about what happened with Laurentis at the art gallery."

I recounted the story, step by step. Brief summations never work with Vida. Any uncertainty or omission would be pounced on by my House & Home editor.

"Poor man," she said when I was finished. "But so foolish."

I heard Alison talking to a man in the front office. So did Vida. "It's Rick Erlandson," she whispered before I could lean forward to see the visitor. "Oh, my. I hope it's not about Ginny quitting permanently."

Rick entered the newsroom before I could say anything. He looked worried. Maybe Vida was right.

"Hi," he said. "Have you two got a minute?"

"Yes," I said, getting up. "Take a seat. I'll grab Leo's chair."

Rick sat down. "I just talked to Ginny. She's home now, but

that was quite a shocker about the hermit guy at Donna's gallery."

I agreed. "Ginny's not calling everyone in town, I hope."

"No, no," Rick assured me. "Donna told her to keep it quiet. But Ginny had to talk to somebody, so she called me."

Vida leaned closer to Rick. "Is there something about Craig Laurentis that we should know?"

Rick shook his head. "That's not why I'm here. I mean, it's awful and all that, but it's Andy Cederberg that's upset me." His lean face seemed to get longer. "JoAnne Petersen came by the bank an hour or so ago and had a long talk behind closed doors with Andy. After she left, he stayed in his office and kept his door closed. That's not like him. I had a question for him about the Doukas account that needed an answer right away, but he wouldn't let me in. That's way beyond weird for Andy. The next thing I knew, he went home without saying a word to anybody. That was just five minutes ago." He stopped to blow his nose. "Sorry—I've got a cold. Anyway," he went on, looking at Vida, "I knew you'd been at Andy and Reba's house for dinner the other night. I wondered if you knew what might be bothering him, although he seemed fine until JoAnne showed up today. If there's some huge problem, I've got to be the one running the bank, and frankly, that scares me."

"My, my," Vida murmured. "This is all very strange. The only thing that comes to mind—and it wasn't mentioned when I was at the Cederbergs' house—is that despite what Strom and Cole said on my program last night, perhaps one of them is indeed going to work for the bank. JoAnne would know, I should imagine. That would certainly upset Andy if either of the Petersen boys wanted to step in right away as president. Andy would be demoted or out of a job."

Rick nodded. "I wondered about that. I might be out the door, too, if both of them wanted to work for the bank. But why would they say on the radio that they weren't interested in following the Petersen tradition?"

"Because," I suggested, "they don't want to make a formal announcement so soon after their father died?"

Vida bristled. "How dare they lie on my program! If they did, I'll seek more than just an apology."

I held up my hands. "Let's not jump to conclusions. There may be some other explanation for Andy's distress." I looked at Rick. "I've always assumed that JoAnne still had an account at the bank. I realize you can't divulge private information, but you did say some of the Petersens still have financial dealings with the bank."

Rick nodded. "For one thing, they own the property and the building. That's a matter of public record."

"Oh, certainly." Vida smiled sympathetically. "Of course Denise would have her accounts at the bank, having worked there off and on." She inclined her head to one side, allowing time for Rick to contradict her. He didn't, so she continued applying her own brand of genteel pressure. "I can't imagine that Marvin and Cathleen wouldn't keep most of their money here since he still owns the bank." Her gray eyes seemed to grow larger behind the big glasses. I wondered if she was hypnotizing Rick. "It's all so worrisome, isn't it? I'm not surprised Andy is distressed. And you, too. Emma's right about JoAnne—I can't help but think that she's kept money in the bank if only because she sold her house to her relatives here. My, my—if only one could be sure . . ." She let her voice trail off, but those mesmerizing eyes stayed fixed on Rick as if she was literally reading his mind.

He cleared his throat. "You really know these people," he murmured—and blew his nose again.

"My, yes!" Vida agreed. "My family goes back to the first generation of Petersens. Very close links. Naturally, I have a certain understanding of how they think. I also assume that Strom and Cole probably don't keep accounts in town. They've been gone for such a long time."

Rick nodded. "But sometimes you can't tell who actually owns certain investments if they're in a trust or under a business name."

"So I'm told." Vida frowned slightly. "I never heard if Alison inherited Linda's estate, but I would imagine Howard and Susan Lindahl would have been appointed guardians because she was a minor at the time of her mother's death. The Lindahls are Everett people, so it's likely they transferred whatever Alison inherited to a more convenient bank."

"That's what usually happens when somebody moves away," Rick conceded. "After Howard Lindahl remarried, he never lived in Alpine."

"Understandable," Vida allowed, "but now Alison has moved here." Her voice held a note of triumph, as if Alpine had just scored the winning run over Everett in the bottom of the ninth inning. She certainly seemed to have been victorious in eliciting information from Rick. Like most people, he was helpless in the hands of a masterful inquisitor. Torquemada should've been so lucky.

"By the way," I put in, turning to Vida, "did you ever get hold of Marvin and Cathleen?"

She shook her head. "They must be gadabouts down there in Arizona. Or else they've both gone deaf and can't hear the phone ring."

"They're on a cruise," Rick said. "Denise showed us a post-card she got from them the day before she left the bank. They were in Samoa."

Vida heaved an exasperated sigh. "Why didn't she tell me? I could've put that in 'Scene.'"

I gave her a dubious glance. "Right next to Larry's obit?"

"Well . . ." Vida paused. "This coming week, perhaps."

I couldn't resist. "Right next to the brief story about his interment?"

Vida glared at me again. "Ooooh . . ." I expected her to whip off her glasses and rub her eyes until they squeaked, a habit that made me wince. Thankfully, she thought better of it with Larry sitting next to her. "I'll mention it after they get back," she said. "I assume Denise will know."

Rick pushed his chair back and stood up. "I'd better go. The bank's semi-rudderless with Andy and me both gone. I thought you might know why he's a mess. He still has back problems from whoever tried to run him down ten years ago. Did they ever find out who did it?"

"It was Christie and Troy Johnston," I replied, "but the charge was dropped after she was arrested for embezzlement. As you recall, the Feds took over after the Johnstons fled to Michigan. It was pointless to bring them back here to prosecute the incident. Christie's still in prison, but Troy may be out by now. He got less time as a co-conspirator."

Rick looked puzzled. "I don't think Andy ever told me about that."

Vida had also gotten to her feet. "Andy probably thought everyone at the bank had enough to worry about at the time. As for his back, those aftereffects don't always surface immediately. I suspect part of it is heredity. His father, Stilts, has had a bad back for years. That's one of the problems with being so tall—and thin." Vida put a hand to the waistband of her skirt, as if to feel any loss of the two pounds she'd gained at the Cederbergs' dinner. "Now that I think back to the other night, there was something that was mentioned. A family problem, nothing serious, but Reba didn't want to discuss it."

Rick stared at Vida. "With the Cederbergs?"

"Not precisely," Vida responded. "Come, I'll walk you to

the door." She took Rick's arm. "I want to buy a Christmas present for your new baby. And something for the other two as well. What do you think . . ."

I put Leo's chair back in place and went into my cubbyhole. Two minutes later, Vida charged through the doorway.

"It's something to do with Greg Jensen," she declared. "If I were a betting woman, I'd put money on it."

"Did you say that to Rick?" I asked.

"No. It's speculation on my part, so there's no point starting rumors." Vida sighed. "What's puzzling is why JoAnne would be so concerned. Denise and Greg are divorced. The only link they seem to have is the dog. I wonder why Greg doesn't collect him. It *was* a him, wasn't it?"

"Yes. Greg's probably waiting for the weekend to come here. Denise said he lives in Brier. That's over an hour away."

"I almost wish Denise was here," Vida murmured, "if only to ask about Greg. Of course she's so impossibly vague that I doubt she'd know—or care. Perhaps I can get JoAnne to confide in me. I can't see why she'd mention it to Andy Cederberg, and even if she did, why would he be so upset? Greg is Reba's nephew, not Andy's. My, my, this is very perplexing."

I felt as if Vida was talking to herself rather than to me. It was almost four-thirty. I'd wasted the entire day, and yet I was tired—very tired. "I'm going home," I said, turning off my computer. "It may take me a while to figure out what to do with that French food."

Vida studied me closely. "Are you sure you want company?"

"Yes. Why wouldn't I?"

She bit her lip before speaking. "I think you've had too much company."

I couldn't look her in the eye. "If that's what you think, maybe that's why I don't want to be alone tonight."

"Oh, my goodness!" she exclaimed under her breath. "Yes,

of course I'll come. Oh, dear!" Shaking her head, she walked out of my cubbyhole in her splay-footed manner.

Instead of heading first for the fridge when I got home, I went into Adam's closet and dug out the box that held my Nativity set. The Holy Family, two shepherds, three sheep, one angel, and three Wise Men had belonged to my parents. The original stable was already a shambles when I inherited it, so I'd bought a new one, and over the years I'd added more sheep, more angels, and three camels. I'd quit at twenty-four pieces so that I'd come out even on Christmas Eve when I put Baby Jesus in his crib. I was already two days behind. Carrying the battered carton into the living room, I removed the stable first, dusted it off, rearranged the straw inside, and put it on the mantel. Then I placed two sheep near the stable. And prayed.

Forgiveness. Mercy. Wisdom. Guidance. Healing. My litany of requests to God was longer than Adam's Christmas gift list. And harder to get. Or maybe harder to accept. God's more generous than willful humans like me.

After putting the box and the rest of the figures in the hall closet, I went into the kitchen. Sorting through Rolf's delicacies, I realized that there was nothing basic for an actual dinner. Most of the food was intended for appetizers. I considered thawing something out of the freezer, but decided I'd let Vida forage. She might actually enjoy it, once she got over the notion that she was being poisoned by rabid French anti-Americans.

At precisely six, the doorbell rang. "It's snowing again," Vida informed me as she swept into the living room. "We may be in for it tonight." Before taking off her coat, she put the funeral guest book on my end table. "I still haven't gone through it," she said. "I recall Reverend Nielsen was tedious and long-winded, but that's typical of Lutherans." She espied my Nativity set. "Oh. I see you're doing your Advent set. I'm rather puzzled. Pastor Purebeck is beginning to talk more about Advent. Sometimes I feel as if there's a shift in the wind when it comes to religion these days. I wonder if it's some sort of backlash because of the Born Again people. They tend to get carried away. I suppose there's no real harm in Protestants—the more established sects, I mean—resurrecting some Roman traditions. At least there's history to that."

I sensed that Vida was trying to divert me from whatever suffering she thought I was enduring. "I've always felt that eventually all Christians would band together again," I said. "Not in our lifetime, but someday. We've got too much in common to be separated brethren. How do you feel about cheeses?"

"Very strongly, of course," Vida said, with a perplexed expression. "Do you think we Presbyterians don't consider Him as our Lord and Savior?"

"Huh?" I burst out laughing. "I said *cheeses*, not *Jesus*."

"Oh." She looked sincere, but I had a feeling she'd heard me correctly the first time. It was yet another attempt at rousing me from my state of gloom. "I'll have to study the different varieties first."

We went into the kitchen, where I began to haul various packages from the fridge. After ten minutes of debate and conjecture, we ended up with a chèvre, a Boursin, and a Brie de Meaux. I unwrapped the pâté de foie gras and a box of crispbreads. Insisting that we needed a vegetable, Vida asked me to open a jar of black olives. I complied, refraining from telling her that I didn't much like olives in any color, form, or size. I could always eat carrot sticks later on.

While I set out everything on the kitchen table, she fetched the funeral book from the living room. "We might as well

go through this while we eat," she said, sitting down and opening the book. "We must be careful not to get any food on it."

"Right," I agreed, placing two cheese knives on the table before I sat down, too.

"Hmm," Vida murmured. "It seems as if no one has opened
this until now. Some of the pages are still stuck together."

"Maybe Alison couldn't bear it," I said.

"Very likely." She closed the book. "Let's start by thinking
back to the funeral. What do you recall about it?"

"The Wailers," I answered promptly. "It was my first time
hearing them shriek their way through a funeral."

"So it was," Vida said grimly. "At least one of my sisters-in-
law, Nell Blatt, dropped out years ago. Unfortunately, they
found a replacement for her. I do wish our local clergymen
would unite to ban them from such outlandish displays of grief.
Half the time they hardly know the deceased."

"They've still never managed to invade St. Mildred's."

"Nor Trinity Episcopal. Regis Bartleby is as firm about their
exclusion as Father Fitzgerald and Father Kelly." She thought
for a moment. "I can visualize the pallbearers—Rick and Andy
from the bank, JoAnne's brother, Duane Bergstrom, a Gus-
tavson . . ." She closed her eyes and tipped her head back.
"Which one? There was an Everson . . . or an Iverson? Oh,
goodness! My memory is failing." She shook her head and nib-
bled on a plump olive. "Roy Everson," she said suddenly.
"From the post office. He'd been a golfing chum of Marv's, and
maybe Larry's, too. Oh, Karl Erdahl. He retired from the forest
service and moved to some lake outside of Spokane. I can't
think why."

"You're amazing," I said after swallowing some of the
Boursin cheese. "The only pallbearers I remember are Rick and
Andy."

"Understandable," Vida said in a charitable voice. "You'd lived in Alpine a mere five years. There was one odd thing, though. All the Petersens were in the family room except Alison. I realize that Howard and Susan Lindahl wanted to keep her with them, but she was Linda's daughter, after all. Still, I remember thinking it odd. It was if the Lindahls wanted to disassociate Alison from all of the Petersens, including her birth mother."

"I can't blame them," I said. "Linda hadn't been much of a mother to Alison for a long time."

Vida wagged a finger. "True—except that not long before Linda was killed, she'd made overtures to Alison. Taking her shopping, spending more time with her. In retrospect, that's odd, too." Vida ate some pâté before speaking again. "Let's move on to the reception in the church basement. There really was quite a crowd."

I cut off another piece of chèvre. "Why are we doing this?"

Vida's face was somber. "Because we missed something."

"'We'? What do you mean?"

"You, me, Milo, everybody involved." She took off her glasses and rubbed her eyes. Gently. "Ever since that first letter came to Milo, I've had this peculiar feeling that the person who sent it is right. Then, after what Cole said on my program about his father telling him he didn't kill Linda, my feeling became stronger. I believe Larry was innocent. If no one else will help me, I intend to prove he was telling the truth."

FIFTEEN

Y OU SOUND AS IF LARRY'S WORDS WERE A DEATHBED CON-
fession," I said. "Or I should say 'retraction'?"

Vida had put her glasses back on. "I think that's what it was.
He had—as Cole sensed—a premonition that he was dying. Perhaps he'd had other symptoms of heart trouble. In any event, he
didn't want to leave this world without making sure the rest of
his family—and everyone else—knew he was not a murderer."

I considered Vida's words carefully. "That's not impossible,"
I finally allowed. "Do you think he knew who killed Linda?"

"I can't be sure," she admitted. "But I suspect he did, which
means he was shielding someone very dear to him."

"His three children," I said, thinking out loud. "JoAnne.
Even his father, Marv. Who else meant so much to Larry?"

"There may be a dark horse." Vida sighed. "I can't think
who. I never heard any rumors of Larry and another woman,
but you never can be sure about people, can you? Deep down,
we don't always know others as well as we think."

"No," I said, my eyes fixed on the tablecloth's butterfly pat-
tern. "We don't."

"So," she went on more briskly, "let's go through the list of people who signed the guest book. That will help us envision the reception." Vida scanned the first page. "Marv's handwriting was very shaky. If he and Cathleen are on a cruise, I wonder if he knows about Larry's death. In fact, I wonder if Marv knows he's on a cruise."

"Surely someone would've notified him," I said. "Are you sure Marv has Alzheimer's?"

"That's what Thelma Petersen told me," Vida replied. "Of course she's never been fond of her in-laws. She certainly had no time for Cathleen, and always took Elmer's side when he and Marv got into some sort of sibling set-to. So silly. The brothers couldn't be more different."

"I think the only time I saw Cathleen up close was at the funeral reception," I said. "I don't recall speaking with her."

"You wouldn't even if you did," Vida said. "Cathleen never had anything to say that was worth listening to. Nice woman, decent taste in home decorating, but quite empty in the brains department. She was rather pretty before she went to fat."

"Big Mike Brockelman," I said suddenly. "He wasn't at the funeral or the reception."

Vida regarded me with a curious look. "Why would he be?"

"It was rumored he and Linda were having an affair," I said, and then remembered mentioning his absence at the time to Milo. "I suppose Big Mike's wife wouldn't give him permission to leave Monroe for his girlfriend's funeral."

"Oh!" Vida obviously had thought of something important. "Yes, there was talk about Linda and Mike. In fact, on the night she was killed, hadn't he gone to visit her at Parc Pines? She wasn't home, so he ended up with Amanda Hanson instead. Remember?"

I'd forgotten that tidbit. "Oh, yes, back in Amanda's wanton-wife era. I hope she really is beyond that now."

Vida leaned back in her chair. "I'm trying to recall alibis, of which there seemed to be aplenty. Howard Lindahl was a prime suspect at one point, being Linda's ex, but it turned out he was set up, apparently by the killer. So hard on his wife, Susan, and Alison, of course."

"Even at twelve, Alison was a trouper," I said.

Vida nodded. "Credit for that goes to Susan for being such a fine stepmother. Let me think about the seemingly solid alibis . . . Mike and Amanda, Marv and Cathleen giving a dinner party, Larry and JoAnne hosting guests, too." She stopped, biting her lip. "What was it Betsy O'Toole told me about her recollections of the night Linda was killed? I used it in 'Scene'—innocently, of course." Her gray eyes sparked. "It was about JoAnne rushing around the Grocery Basket, having forgotten she and Larry were having a card party that evening. How could you forget that?"

"It's not impossible," I said, recalling a few incidents, mostly, but not all, in Edna Mae Dalrymple's case, when members of my bridge group had become confused about whose turn it was to be hostess. "There's another factor to consider. Larry was supposed to be home, but he had no alibi for that time period because JoAnne was shopping. If you flip that around, it could work the other way."

"Ah." Vida nodded. "JoAnne may have been seen rushing because she was doing something besides going to the Grocery Basket, such as murdering her sister-in-law. Betsy was her unwitting alibi. My, my. That *is* interesting."

"Motive?"

"The same as Larry's," Vida replied. "JoAnne couldn't bear the thought of her husband being passed over in favor of his sister to run the bank. JoAnne always struck me as a social climber. Some of the other Bergstroms have been like that."

The interweaving of longtime Alpine families still confused

me. Despite having lived here for over fifteen years, I'd never been able to sort through all the more notable dynasties, including Vida's. In fact, I'd given up trying, content to rely on her flawless and copious knowledge of the town's residents. Complicating matters for me was that a whole new generation had come of age in that time span—marrying, divorcing, birthing, and in some cases, dying.

I had another question. "Could JoAnne have carried Linda's body from Parc Pines to the forest where you and Roger found her body in the rotted-out log?"

"Linda was larger than JoAnne." Vida paused, apparently to think through the scenario. "If Larry was protecting someone, he still might be the one who moved Linda. That would make sense."

"I talked to Denise at the funeral reception," I said, "but I never realized that Strom and Cole were there, too. I wouldn't have seen them during the service if they were in the family room."

"You wouldn't know who they were," Vida pointed out. "Ten years ago they were still boys. Now they're men. I spoke to them briefly, but they didn't linger. You know how young people are when it comes to functions such as funerals. And of course they both had to get back to their respective colleges."

"Right." I was silent for a moment. "Is JoAnne's the only breakable alibi among the suspects?"

Vida grew thoughtful again. "Christie Johnston had a strong motive for killing Linda, in a more immediate way than Larry or JoAnne. That is, Marv could've changed his mind about whether Linda or Larry should be his heir apparent as president. Linda had discovered that Christie was stealing money from the bank. At the time, I thought Christie and her husband, Troy, were the murderers. They said they were home together watching TV. That's no alibi at all. But why would Larry want to give up his freedom for an embezzler?"

"He might if Christie was his lover," I suggested. "Maybe he thought it was better to be known as a killer than an adulterer."

Vida shook her head. "I understand what you're saying, but JoAnne ended up divorcing him anyway. That's another thing— I thought she'd remarry eventually. But she hasn't."

"According to Strom, his parents loved each other deeply," I said. "When I talked to JoAnne today, she behaved like a grieving widow. Maybe the divorce was a legal thing, with Larry in prison."

"Possibly," Vida murmured.

"Who represented JoAnne when she got the divorce?"

"Simon Doukas. His mother was a Bergstrom."

"I'd forgotten that," I admitted, getting up. "Here, have some chocolate truffles. Maybe they'll recharge our brains."

"My brain is fine," Vida assured me, "but I shouldn't eat candy. I'm dieting, you know." She peered into the elegant little box holding the chocolates. "Hmm. I suppose one wouldn't do any harm. I see they have a flavor key. My high school French is quite rusty, but 'orange' is the same in both languages. I'll try that one. The fruit will cut down on the calories." She plucked the dark chocolate Grande Seville from the box, took a bite, and sighed with pleasure. "Is there a raspberry one?"

"Here." I handed over a second truffle.

"Olives and oranges and raspberries," Vida said after she'd polished off both chocolates. "That's a wholesome combination. Aren't you going to eat one?"

"Not right now," I said. "I'll stick to the pâté and some of the crackers I haven't opened yet."

"Did I see apple pie in the refrigerator? You could eat that and get some fruit."

"I'm fine. Let's get back to business. Who can we eliminate?"

"Marv and Cathleen," Vida answered promptly, though her expression was wistful as I put the lid back on the truffles box. "Marv would never harm his own child, and Cathleen wouldn't know how to go about killing someone. Their alibi is solid, too. I know how their dinner parties were conducted. Guests arrive at six-fifteen, a cocktail or two, sit down at the table at seven or a few minutes after, two or three courses, then a slight lull to digest before dessert and coffee. After that, they'd move back to the living room and visit for an hour or so. Occasionally a liqueur might be served. Guests usually departed by ten, giving Cathleen time to clean up before bed. She's never been one to face a mess in the morning."

"You amaze me," I said.

"Nonsense. I've been to many of their dinner parties. Cathleen always kept to the same routine. There's never been anything spontaneous about her. Nor Marv. Neither of them has an ounce of imagination. Adhering to a strict schedule is suited to a banker. It's part of the mind-set, dealing with all those numbers. Like his father before him, Marv was very disciplined in his habits. I believe Larry and Linda inherited those same traits. But Linda was smarter than Larry."

"Marv and Cathleen out," I said, writing their names on a clean paper napkin. "Who else?"

Vida was silent for so long that I wondered if I'd have to give her another truffle to make her talk. "I don't think I ever heard where Cole and Strom were that night," she said at last. "They were both college students—Strom at the UW before he transferred to WSU, just before Cole decided to leave Western Washington State University and finish at Pullman. Like ships passing in the night, if you think about it. There was talk that Strom followed a girl there, but apparently nothing came of that romance. He went on to get a graduate degree at . . . dear me, I forget. The University of Oregon, perhaps. So much switching around between schools by young people these days."

"Don't I know it," I murmured, recalling Adam's college hopping until he finally settled at Arizona State.

Vida continued her recital. "Both Petersen boys might've come home that weekend, especially Cole, who was still going to school in Bellingham, being closer to Alpine than Pullman. Do you recall Milo asking about their whereabouts the night of the murder?"

"If you don't remember, I sure don't," I said. "I assume they weren't in Alpine. What about Andy and Reba?"

"They were home," Vida said. "Their children were with them, but they were quite young and might not have been questioned." She frowned. "That alibi is rather shaky, though I can't see a motive."

"Andy's running the bank," I reminded Vida.

She shook her head. "No, that doesn't fit. How could he guess Marv would retire so soon? I doubt he'd know that Linda was the heir apparent. If the murder was premeditated, it'd take a very different kind of mind than Andy's. He's reasonably bright, very thorough, but not the least bit cunning or ambitious."

"True," I agreed. "Who else?"

"Rick and Denise were at a movie," Vida recalled. "We couldn't forget that if we wanted to. Ginny was so jealous of that relationship. She and Carla were both having man trouble. It was dreadful, listening to them moan and groan about their love lives, or lack thereof. That was the period where Carla was dating Dr. Flake, a romance I was glad to see end. He was much better off marrying Marilynn Lewis. I wonder how he's getting along with his practice in North Bend. We need a third doctor in Alpine."

"I thought Doc Dewey and Dr. Sung were trying to find someone."

"They are, but it's not easy," Vida said. "They'd prefer another GP who's just finished his or her residency, but so many MDs want to specialize. It's a serious problem everywhere."

"I know." I glanced at the napkin with Marv's and Cathleen's names checked. "Cross off Rick and Denise, too?"

"Yes," Vida said. "Denise is too dim to carry out a murder, and Rick . . . well, he's simply too nice. Besides, his motive is even weaker than Andy's. It seems we're looking for that dark horse."

My mind reverted to the original prime suspect, Howard Lindahl. "Who set Howard up? It was a man, supposedly a business client who never showed up. After Larry was arrested, we figured he'd made the phone call so Howard wouldn't have an alibi for the time of the murder. I don't recall if Larry admitted he'd done that, but we assumed he did."

Vida agreed. "Milo should be here. He could answer some of these questions and put an end to this guesswork. Why don't you call him?"

I shook my head. "Doe told me he was in a bad mood. I don't think he'd like being pestered when he's off duty."

"Oh." Vida backed down—too quickly, I thought. She seemed to realize she'd made a gaffe. "Yes. He'd probably have to check his case file. Let's see . . . we might ask Alison what she remembers, though I hate to bother her outside of the office. It's a Friday night and she may have plans to—"

The phone rang. I jumped. Vida stared at me, but I was on my feet and headed for the living room before she could say anything. I grabbed the receiver on the third ring.

"Emma?" Doc Dewey said. "I've just finished with Craig Laurentis. His wound is infected, and we're giving him enough antibiotics to cure an elephant. The prognosis is fairly good, but once we get him stabilized, I'll take some tests, just in case."

"I'm relieved," I said, sinking onto the sofa. It was true. But I was also disappointed. I had hoped the call was from someone other than Doc. "I assume he's out of it, as far as being able to tell what happened after he left the hospital."

"He won't be up to that until sometime tomorrow," Doc said. "He's spending the night in the ICU. I'm going home. Elvis is on call tonight. Take care of yourself."

"Doc," I said before he could hang up. "One quick question—is Spencer Fleetwood okay?"

"As far as I know. Good night, Emma." Doc disconnected the call.

Vida had come into the living room. "Doc?" She saw me nod and sat down in the armchair on the other side of the fireplace from the easy chair. "I gather Craig is recovering?"

I gave her the few details I'd learned. "I asked about Spence, but Doc only told me he thought he was okay. Did Marje say anything other than that he had a bad nosebleed?"

"No. As I mentioned earlier, this seems to be a bad time for health problems around here." She leaned back in the chair and stared at the ceiling. "I feel stupid. I thought we were going to get somewhere this evening, but we seem to have hit a brick wall. What if I'm wrong?"

"That seems unlikely."

Her head swerved around to look at me. "Is that sarcasm?"

"No. I trust your instincts." I shrugged. "I suppose you *could* be wrong, but even Milo has begun to wonder if Larry wasn't guilty."

"He has?" She looked surprised. "Men rarely admit they're wrong, especially men like Milo."

I had no intention of responding or elaborating. I redirected the conversation. "There was that rope and the map that was planted at the Lindahl house the night before the murder. Ten years ago only very expensive private labs had the kind of DNA testing that would've been able to tell who had handled the rope and strangled Linda. The charge was premeditated homicide. That's another thing—why did Larry go to trial? Why didn't he plea-bargain? I recall thinking that at the time."

"Larry was never put on the stand," Vida said. "I understood he didn't want to be. He also hired an outsider for his defense, someone from Everett. Horsfeld or Hirschfield or something like that. I only attended one session, and that was during the summation. Frankly, his lawyer was unconvincing about the temporary insanity defense."

I nodded. "Hard to call it 'temporary' when he'd apparently plotted the crime at least a day ahead."

The phone rang again. I gritted my teeth and answered after the first ring. This time it was Kip MacDuff on the other end. "Did you hear the seven o'clock news on KSKY?" he asked.

"You know I avoid KSKY like the plague," I said, "except for Vida, of course. What's happened?"

"Whoever is filling in for Fleetwood said an arrest has been made in the poaching incident," Kip said, and I could hear the excitement in his voice. "The suspect is Greg Jensen."

"What?" I shouted, causing Vida to rocket out of her chair like a sharp line drive to left-center field.

"You heard me right," Kip said. "The sheriff's office got a tip. They arrested Greg at the house he and Denise own. He'd come from Brier to collect his dog."

Vida hovered over me, trying to listen in. "Is he being booked?"

"It's Friday," Kip said, "so I suppose he's stuck in jail until he can be formally charged Monday. Shall I put it on the website?"

"Only after you call the sheriff and verify it," I cautioned him. "Who made the arrest?"

"Dwight Gould and Doe Jamison. I'll call right now. I guess this all happened between five-thirty and six."

"Okay. Keep me posted," I said, and hung up.

"Who? Who?" Vida repeated like an impatient owl.

"Greg Jensen."

She was goggle-eyed. "That's incredible."

"Maybe. I recall Ginny saying something about Greg being in a band. He may know a guitar maker who wants the wood. Or maybe he wants it for himself."

Vida had wandered over to the hearth. "Yes. I believe Greg and his chums occasionally played at Mugs Ahoy. I've no idea if they were any good. Roger might know. He's always up on all the bands, local and otherwise." She gazed at the crèche. "Have you ever wondered if John the Baptist was a hippie?"

"I'm sure he was regarded as such in whatever the vernacular of the day was."

Vida nodded. "All that strange clothing and eating bugs and such. It's understandable how he could be misjudged."

I hoped Vida wasn't thinking that Alpiners were misjudging Roger. If he became a saint, I might morph into Queen Esther. Or Jezebel.

I suddenly swore out loud. "Goddamnit!"

"Emma!" Vida shouted even more loudly. "What's wrong with you? You never swear like that."

"Why didn't Milo call me? He said he had a lead. I'd like to strangle that son of a—"

"Stop!" Vida took a couple of threatening steps toward me. "I don't blame you," she said, lowering her voice. "It's unconscionable of him. But that's no excuse for your outrageous as well as blasphemous language, and in front your crèche, too."

"Sorry." I held my head while trying to regain my equanimity. "Greg Jensen. Armed and dangerous?"

Vida returned to her chair. "Did Kip say Greg was a person of interest in the shooting?"

"No. I'm sure he'd have mentioned it if it was on the news. Unless Spence's stand-in omitted that part. As you know, the hour-turn news at seven is a brief update."

"Sometimes those youngsters have poor judgment." Vida adjusted her glasses before assuming a resolute manner. "What's wrong with us? We should be covering this story."

"It's not ours to cover," I said, inwardly cursing myself for not thinking immediately of relaying the news to Mitch. "I hope he's home." Ignoring Vida's annoyed expression, I checked the Laskeys' number and dialed it. Brenda answered in a wary voice.

"Is Mitch busy?" I inquired after identifying myself.

"He's not here," Brenda replied, sounding more at ease. "He left about fifteen minutes ago to follow up on something about that poacher being arrested. We heard it on the news."

"Good," I said. "That's what I was calling about. Do you know where he went?"

"The sheriff's headquarters," Brenda informed me. "Did you want to talk to him? I assume you have his cell number."

I assured her I did. "Mitch is at the sheriff's," I said to Vida as I dialed his cell. "The Laskeys listen to KSKY and . . . Mitch? It's Emma. Can you give me the details of Jensen's arrest?"

"Hang on," he said. "I'll move where I can hear you. Doe and Dwight are talking up a storm."

Vida had gotten to her feet again, but at least she wasn't hanging over my shoulder.

"Okay," Mitch said at the other end. "Somebody called in here just after five to say Greg Jensen was the poacher. Dwight had just come on duty, but he had to wait for backup."

"Who called?"

"They don't know. The caller ID showed only 'security screen.' Doe said it was someone who sounded as if he or maybe she was disguising his or her voice. Very low, very hushed. Whoever it was only said, and this is a quote, 'Greg Jensen poached the maples.' Doe called Denise to find out if she might know where he was. Denise said he was at their house on Second Hill. That's where they found him and made the arrest."

"Okay, but I'm confused," I said. "You told me Dwight had to wait for backup, but Doe was there, filling in for Lori. If she was still on the job, why didn't they leave right away?"

"Doe was about to leave," Mitch replied. "Her shift was over. Jack Mullins was due for the night shift, but he's on suspension."

I tried to hide my surprise lest Vida wrest the phone out of my hand and take over. "That's odd," I said as calmly as possible. "Why?"

"I don't know," Mitch said. "Doe saw his pickup pull in a little before five, but he never officially reported for duty."

"Where was the sheriff?"

"He'd just left." Mitch paused. "You're not going to believe this, Emma. Dodge not only suspended Mullins, but he suspended himself, too. Is that crazy or what?"

SIXTEEN

I WAS TOO STUNNED TO SPEAK. VIDA MUST'VE THOUGHT I'D had a stroke or something. She snatched the phone out of my hand.

"This is Vida," she said. "Emma seems to be having a spell. The weather, no doubt. Now tell me everything we need to know."

I was too upset to be angry. Sitting on the sofa, I could only stare into space and vaguely hear what Vida was saying to Mitch. It seemed as if she was on the phone forever. I actually did feel sick. Maybe it was the flu, passed on from Denise. But JoAnne hadn't mentioned that her daughter was ill. I'd assumed Denise was pregnant. Maybe she was. I didn't know what was wrong with her. I wasn't sure what was wrong with me, except that the world seemed to have slipped off its axis. Nothing made sense. I hoped I was dreaming. It certainly felt as if I was in some kind of nightmare.

Finally Vida hung up. "Well, that beats all." She looked at me with a worried expression. "You're very pale, Emma. I think you should lie down. I'll make tea."

As she bustled out to the kitchen, I curled up into a ball on the sofa and started to shiver. Before Vida returned, I realized I was sick. I got up and staggered into the bathroom, where I threw up several times. *Damn,* I thought miserably, *it is the flu. Terrible timing.* I heard Vida on the other side of the door.

"Do you need help?" she called to me.

I managed to eke out something that sounded like "No." Vida apparently went out of the hall, probably to the kitchen to check on the teakettle. I sat on the bathroom floor for a long time, leaning against the cupboard under the sink.

A half-hour must have passed before I could get up, clean the bathroom, and wobble out to the living room. Vida was flipping through the new issue of *Vanity Fair* I'd bought to read Christopher Hitchens's article on the recent election shenanigans in Ohio. Maybe I thought I'd get some ideas to perk up the locals the next time they went to the ballot box.

"Oh, my word!" she exclaimed when I flopped onto the sofa. "You look absolutely dreadful. It's the flu, isn't it?"

"I guess."

"I'll stay with you," she declared, "but I'll have to dash home and check on Cupcake and fetch some night things."

"No," I said, "I don't want you catching it. We both can't be incapacitated. Besides, I feel a little better."

"If I haven't caught it from you by now, I won't," she insisted. "Do you feel like drinking some tea?"

"Not just yet. Tell me what you found out about what's going on with the sheriff's gang."

"Greg Jensen claims he's innocent," Vida said, after taking a sip of tea. "They did ask him about the shooting and he swears he's never shot at anyone or anything in his life. He claims he was in Brier Monday night watching football with a friend at a local pub."

"Friends can lie for friends."

"They can also perjure themselves if it comes to a court case," Vida noted. "Dwight, however, asked him about the football game—Dwight had watched it, too—and said Greg sounded as if he'd seen the game, but pointed out that he— Greg, I mean—could have read about it later."

"True." I was less interested in Greg and maple trees and Monday Night Football than I was in Milo and Jack. "So what about the suspensions?"

"Neither Dwight nor Doe would discuss that," Vida said in disgust. "Closing ranks, of course. But it's certainly news. I haven't heard of such a thing since Eeeny Moroni was sheriff."

"Oh, God," I moaned, putting a hand to my head, "I hope Spence doesn't hear about this. Maybe he won't if he's out of commission, too."

Vida took another sip of tea and stood up. "Will you be all right if I go home now? I should be back in twenty minutes."

"Go ahead. But you really needn't—"

"Hush," Vida said firmly, picking up her mug and heading for the kitchen. "You can't stay alone," she added, raising her voice after leaving the room. "I'll clear away our supper things after I get back."

As ever, there was no point arguing with Vida, even if I'd had the strength to try. Two minutes later, she was out the door. I lay on the sofa like a lump, but I was starting to feel better. Maybe I had a twenty-four-hour variety and the worst was over. After another five minutes had passed, I sat up, wondering if I could clean the kitchen. The phone rang before I made the effort.

"Emma," Vida said in a weak voice I hardly recognized, "I'm sick, too. I'm sorry. I've already . . . oh, dear . . ." She hung up.

I sank back on the sofa. At least it was the weekend. Hope-fully, Mitch, Leo, and Kip would stay germ-free. Vida and I had two full days to recover. I felt sleepy, but I wanted to change my clothes. I finally got up, surprised at how shaky I still was. Moving slowly, I went into the bedroom and took off my sweater and slacks. I was slipping into my robe when I heard the front door open. I froze with my hands on the bathrobe's ties. Had Vida left the door unlocked? Of course she had, I thought stupidly. She had no key. I started to call out, but my vocal cords were paralyzed.

"Emma?"

It was Milo. I still couldn't utter a sound.

A moment later, he was in the hallway. "You can stand up, but you can't talk?"

I stumbled toward him, tripped over my own feet, and started to fall. He caught me before I hit the floor. "Where should I put you?" he asked.

"Sofa?" I finally managed to say.

"You sure?"

I nodded, my head against his chest.

"Okay. Vida called. She's sick, too."

I nodded again. He carried me into the living room. It was only then that I noticed his lower lip was cut. "Oh," I said, barely audible even to myself. "You're hurt."

"You ought to see the other guys," he muttered, setting me down on the sofa.

I stared at him. *"Guys?"*

He stood up, thumbs hooked in his wide leather belt. "Yeah, *guys.* You need a pillow?"

It felt like I was smiling. "We did this before."

"Right. You managed to fall over your own feet, sprain your ankle, get drunk and then high on Demerol. Pillow or no pillow?"

"No. Tell me what happened with those *guys.*"

Milo sat down on the floor next to me. "I can only take so much crap about certain things." He didn't look at me but off toward the far end of the living room. "Fleetwood opened his big mouth once too often. Then Mullins did the same thing. I decked both of them. End of story."

"Oh, no!"

"Oh, yes. Did you eat the rest of that pie?"

"No."

"Maybe I will." He turned back to look at me. "How do you feel?"

"Better. Really." My voice was almost normal. "What about the suspensions?"

Milo rubbed the back of his head. "I suspended Jack after I hit him. Then I decided it was only fair to suspend myself, too. I was officially off duty, but Jack was just coming on."

I wanted to laugh, but I didn't have the strength. "Oh, Milo! For how long?"

"Forty-eight hours."

"Dare I ask why you . . . ?"

He reached out and put a big hand over my mouth. "No. And don't even think about licking my hand. You're sick."

My eyes widened. His hand stayed put.

"Damn, but you've got pretty eyes," he said. "Soft, like fur on a brown bear." He stared at me for another moment or two before taking his hand away.

"Brown bears don't have soft fur," I said after taking a couple of breaths. "Couldn't you say 'kitten'?"

"I could've said 'pit bull.'"

"Speaking of dogs, what do you make of Greg Jensen's arrest?"

"Not much. I'm on suspension, remember?" He stretched out on the floor, leaning on his elbow.

"Why didn't you call me today?"

"Why didn't you call me?"

"Are we really fifteen?"

"You're fourteen, I'm seventeen."

I shifted around on the sofa, trying to get into a more comfortable position. I still felt stiff and sore from our impassioned adventures the previous night.

"What's wrong?"

I narrowed my eyes at him. "You're a load, Dodge."

He stopped just short of smirking. "I haven't gained more than twenty-five pounds since I was twenty. If you're hurting, it's the flu."

"You outweigh me by a hundred pounds, big guy. I can tell one ache from another. Which," I went on, "reminds me. Have you considered that the poaching and the shooting could be two different incidents?"

"I don't like coincidences," he said, "but given that Laurentis hasn't been much help telling us what he saw or where he was when he was shot, I'm sticking with the obvious—for now, anyway. We can't get a blood trail in this weather."

"Maybe something will come back to him later," I said.

"Maybe." Milo got up. "I'm going to get that pie. You want anything?"

"Yes. There's some 7-Up in the fridge. Ice, please."

He ambled off to the kitchen. A moment later I heard him swear. "For chrissakes, did you and Vida eat this French crap?"

"Yes," I called back as loudly as I could manage.

"No wonder you're both puking. That Fisher bastard probably tried to poison you in revenge for not traipsing after him to France. I'm tossing the stuff you opened."

"Milo . . ." I gave up. He could be partly right. The food might've spoiled in transit. I heard him sweep off the table, open the garbage can, and dump the offending delicacies. "*Adieu,* Rolf," I murmured. My only regret was for the truffles. I would've liked to try one. Feeling sleepy, I closed my eyes. I could hear the sheriff rummaging around in the kitchen. Then I heard the faint ring of a phone. Not mine—it was on the end table next to the sofa. *My cell?* I wondered vaguely. But it wasn't the same ring. Maybe my ears were buzzing.

I heard Milo's voice. "I'm on suspension, damnit. I don't give a rat's ass if Jensen calls the attorney general. Tell me on Monday."

Silence. A few moments later, he was back in the living room, pie in one hand, a Henry Weinhard's dark ale in the other. He sat down in the easy chair. "You asleep?" he asked.

"With my eyes open?" I turned onto my side to get a better look at him. "Greg asked for a lawyer?"

"Marisa Foxx," he said. "She'll probably get him bailed out."

"That doesn't bother you?"

"Hell, no. Don't tell me *you* forgot I'm suspended?"

"No. But I know you pretty well, big guy. You don't take off the uniform and stop being a lawman."

His expression was droll. "You sure about that? If I didn't, I'd have arrested both of us last night for indecent behavior."

I flung a hand to my forehead. "Oh, Milo! Stop!"

He didn't say anything. Suddenly he seemed preoccupied with his pie. I dozed off and on for what seemed like a long time. Then I realized I was thirsty. I stretched my neck and sat up. "Where's my 7-Up?"

Milo was thumbing through the *Vanity Fair* Vida had been reading. "Oh—I forgot." He tossed the magazine aside and stood up. "Ice, right?"

"Yes. What time is it?"

He glanced at his watch. "How would I know? I never got

around to getting a new battery. Maybe I'll just buy another watch. I kind of like the time this one stopped."

The sheriff went out to the kitchen.

I was speechless. Milo was not sentimental. Not ever. I tried to look at my watch, but I hadn't turned on the end-table light.

"Ten-forty-seven, according to the clock on your stove," he called to me.

I'd managed to sit up and turn the lamp on. "That's right. What's the weather doing?"

"Six inches and still snowing," he answered after a brief pause. "We could have a foot by morning."

"You'd better get home," I said as he came into the living room and handed me a glass with 7-Up and ice.

"I'm not going home," he said, nodding toward the front door. "I brought my stuff with me in that kit."

"Do I dare ask where you plan to sleep?"

He shrugged. "Wouldn't you be better off alone? I can bunk in Adam's room."

My bed was a double; Adam's was a single. My son was six-three, the same height his father had been. But Milo was six-five and more big-boned than either Adam or Tom. "You can sleep with me," I said.

The sheriff shook his head. "Can't do that."

"Why not?" I realized it was a stupid question as soon as it came out of my mouth. "Never mind. I'll sleep in Adam's bed and you can sleep in mine."

"No. You need to be in your own kip. I'll manage. I did it before when you damn near totaled yourself in the kitchen."

"I'd been in a collision and a fight before that happened. Cut me some slack."

"Face it, you're a klutz, a human train wreck about to happen."

"I've got the flu," I said stubbornly. "Or something like it."

"Did I say I give a damn if you're not a ballet dancer? You've got some good moves of your own, but walking isn't one of them." He reached out and mussed my already disheveled hair. "Drink your pop. I'm going to the can."

He'd barely disappeared when the phone rang. Startled, I fumbled for the receiver and was surprised when I heard Vida— or a pale imitation thereof—at the other end.

"Billy came to check on me," she said. "I *am* better. How are you?"

"Improving," I replied.

"Good. Billy told me about Greg. Marisa Foxx posted bail for him. She took him back to the house he and Denise bought, but Greg wouldn't go in. He refused to spend any more time with his ex. I can hardly blame him." She stopped for a moment, probably to catch her breath.

"Did Greg say anything about Denise being sick?" I asked.

"Pardon? Oh—I've no idea. But he asked Marisa to get the dog for him. She wasn't keen on the idea, but he pleaded with her and she finally gave in. Denise came to the door and then went to fetch the dog. She was up and about, so maybe she'll come to work Monday. Anyway, while Marisa waited on the porch, Greg got into his own car and roared off."

I was surprised. "What did Marisa do then?"

"Billy wasn't explicit, as he has a tendency to omit details and I wasn't feeling well enough to prod him. He described Marisa as upset. She's afraid he may be fleeing the county or even the state."

It took a moment to absorb the news. "Marisa related all this directly to Bill or . . . who?"

"Billy," Vida replied wearily. "He took over for Doe at ten. She'd put in a fourteen-hour day and has to get up early tomorrow to help her mother give a baby shower for a cousin in Marysville. Naturally, she wanted to get ahead of the snow before the pass is closed."

"I wouldn't think Greg would leave the dog," I said.

"That's what Marisa thought, too. But now she thinks that all he really wanted was a ride back to where his car was parked and that he'd already planned to make his getaway. The dog was a ruse."

"That sounds right," I agreed.

"Of course," Vida continued, "I assume he'd intended to take—Doukas? No, no, I'm confusing the name with the Doukas family. How silly of me."

"It's Doofus," I said. "Very apt for Denise. Go on, what then?"

"What? Oh." Vida wasn't tracking as well as usual. "I assume Greg did come up here to get Doofus."

"Probably," I agreed.

Milo had come out of the bathroom. "Who the hell are you talking to at eleven o'clock?" he asked gruffly.

"Vida," I said, making a face at him.

Shaking his head, he collected his kit. "If you're going to jaw on the phone all night, I'm heading for bed. Can you make it on your own?"

I'd put my hand over the mouthpiece, but knew that Milo's deep voice carried to Vida's house on Tyee Street. "Yes. Good night."

He paused to kiss the top of my head. "Yell if you need me."

I nodded. He headed for Adam's room. Vida hadn't spoken since Milo had come into the living room. "Are you going to be all right tonight?" I asked her, trying to sound natural.

"Oh, yes," she replied. "Amy offered to stay with me, but I told her that wasn't necessary. Besides, Diddy has croup."

Now I was wondering if Vida was feverish and delusional. "Diddy? Or Daddy?"

"Ah—I'll explain when I feel better. Good night, Em—" She hung up so abruptly that I didn't hear the last syllable of my name.

Unless I'd missed something in the last fifteen years, I'd never heard Vida refer to her son-in-law, Ted, as "Daddy" and certainly not as "Diddy." There could be an explanation that was suggested by the old-fashioned word "croup" to describe a baby's cough or cold. Had the Hibberts taken in Roger's baby by Holly Gross? It was possible, even likely. That struck me as a bad idea. Roger was about to join the Marines, usually a four-year hitch. Amy and Ted were almost fifty. The idea of people in my peer group raising a baby dismayed me. Couples were now waiting much longer to have children, but even in their younger years, the Hibberts hadn't been shining examples of parenthood. Maybe they'd learned from the Rotten Roger experience, but I doubted it.

It wasn't my problem, I told myself as I finally got off the sofa. I walked gingerly into the kitchen. Milo had cleaned up except for a couple of plates, the cheese knives, and Vida's tea mug. I put everything in the dishwasher, made sure the stove was off, looked outside at the snow still coming down, and turned off the light.

Ten minutes later, I emerged from the bathroom. Milo had left the door to Adam's room open. In case, I guessed, I needed help.

I left my door open, too. In case I needed Milo.

It was after nine when I woke up, feeling slightly disoriented. Rolling over, I lifted the shade so I could look outside. The world was white, with drifts almost up to the windowsill. And quiet. Only a few fitful flakes were still coming down. I sank back down, collecting my thoughts and my strength. A few minutes later, I got up, heading for the bathroom. The door to Adam's room was still open. The bed was made. There was no sign of Milo. Maybe he'd risen early and gone home.

I went into the bathroom, taking longer than usual with my morning ritual. It seemed useless to get fully dressed, so I put the bathrobe back on over my bra, pants, a long-sleeved Jamie Moyer Mariners' T-shirt, and thick wool socks. I'd already washed my hair in the shower, so I wrapped a big towel around my head. When I finally got to the living room, I already felt worn out. The drapes were still closed. I was about to open them when Milo's voice startled me from behind.

"Don't," he said. "It'll stay warmer if you keep them shut. The temperature's dropping."

"I thought you left," I said, turning around.

"Why would I? I can't go steelheading and I don't feel like shoveling half a foot of snow to get out of your driveway." He put his hands on my shoulders. "How do you feel, Swami?"

Involuntarily, I touched the towel on my head. "Depleted, weak, but not really sick."

"You look washed out. Are up to eating something?"

"Not really. When did you get up?"

"A little before eight." He dropped his hands. "I made some scrambled eggs, bacon, and toast. You want coffee?"

I shook my head. "I'll drink some ice water." I looked up at him. "You didn't shave."

Milo rubbed his long chin. "I forgot my razor. I'm thinking of growing a beard. Maybe I'll suspend myself for a couple more days and see how it looks before I go back to work." He frowned at me. "You think it's a bad idea?"

"I won't know until I see it," I said. "It might be . . . fine."

"Too scratchy for you?"

I shrugged. "I have limited experience with bearded men. Or bearded ladies, for that matter."

"Come again? Fisher had a beard."

"It was more like a goatee."

Milo virtually sneered. "Whatever. It must've scratched."

"Is that why you're growing a beard?"

He shot me an exasperated look. "No. I only met the guy once. I forgot what he looked like until you said '*limited* experience.' Those goatees look silly. If I grow an honest-to-God beard, you can experiment with me." Milo cocked his head to one side. "You're still kind of shaky. Sit. I'll get your ice water."

I didn't protest, but I followed him to the kitchen and sat down at the table. The sheriff was putting ice in a glass when his cell rang.

"Shit," he barked, "why didn't I turn this sucker off? Screw it." He ignored the ringing. It stopped after seven rings. Milo had finished pouring water into the glass. "You sure you're not hungry?"

"I'm empty, but not hungry," I said, "if you know what I mean. Maybe toast later on."

"Sure." He poured himself more coffee and was about to sit down when his phone rang again. "Who is this asshole?" He picked up the cell and looked at the screen. "Oh, damn! It's Mulehide." He kept staring at the screen through the next four rings, finally muttered, "She won't give up," and clicked the phone on. "What now, Tricia?"

I could hear a woman's high-pitched voice rattling away at the other end while the sheriff leaned back in the chair and began to look increasingly annoyed. Finally, his ex-wife stopped for breath.

"What the hell am I supposed to do about it? We've got a foot of snow up here. I'm stuck."

Mulehide had gotten her second wind. Milo winced and held the phone out from his ear. I could make out only a few words—"meltdown," "terrified," and "you coldhearted bastard." Tricia was bordering on hysteria. In fact, the next sound I heard was of sobbing. Milo finally moved the cell back within hearing and speaking range.

"If it's that bad, call the cops," he said. "Or are you exaggerating?"

I could hear Tricia's blubbering protests, though I couldn't make out what she was actually saying. I tried to read the sheriff's reaction, which had changed from aggravation to unease and, finally, resignation.

"Okay, okay, cool down," he said. "I'll see if I can get out of here. I don't know what this section of Highway 2 is like between here and Monroe, but I—"

I could hear her interrupt him. "Yeah," he responded impatiently, "you already told me it's forty degrees and raining in Bellevue. Get real. I'm in Alpine. I'll call you back after I've checked my options. In the meantime, pull yourself together, keep the doors locked, and make Tanya unlock her bedroom door." He hung up. "That really tears it," he said, clutching the cell phone so tightly I thought he'd break it.

"What's going on?"

Milo slowly shook his head. "If I can sort through what Mulehide told me, Tanya and her freaking idiot of a fiancé, Buster Van Stoop or whatever the hell his name is, had a huge fight and she's threatening to kill herself and Buster's threatening to kill her. Tanya's locked herself in her bedroom and won't come out. Buster's howling at the moon or some damned thing. Mulehide thinks the situation is a tinder box and only good old What's-His-Name-Besides-Sap Dodge can rescue everybody. If

Mulehide hadn't dumped her most recent ex, she could ask him to handle it. Hell, he's spent more time with my kids than I have in the last sixteen years. Suddenly I'm not the bad guy anymore, but the Great White Hope. 'Dope' is more like it, at least from Mulehide's point of view."

"Do you think she's really exaggerating?"

"Oh . . ." He sighed. "I don't know. Tanya and this guy aren't kids. I mean, they may act like it, and I still think of all three of my kids as . . . kids, but they're allegedly grown-ups. Tanya must be . . . thirty? I suppose Buster's about the same age."

"Is his name really Buster?"

"No. I never can remember it. I've only met him twice."

"Tanya must've gone through school with the Petersens," I said.

"All our kids did. Brandon was the same year as Frankie," Milo said. "I mean Strom. See what I mean? What difference does it make if I call Buster Buster? These kids change their names anyway. Michelle is Mike now. No wonder her marriage didn't last more than ten minutes. She says she's a lesbian. Why not? Her mother's a witch. Some role model for a girl. I'm lucky if any of our three didn't turn out to be axe murderers. The closest they've come so far is Bran getting arrested for a hit-and-run a few years ago. How did he expect not to get caught right in front of Bellevue Square? I still don't understand where he found the brains to become a vet." Milo drank his coffee and picked up his cell. "Let's see if Dwight can do me a favor, even if I'm not his official boss right now."

"Who is?" I asked, still taking in Milo's revelations about his offspring. He hadn't talked about them that much at one time in all the years we'd known each other.

"Sam?" He shook his head as he dialed. "No, Dwight's got seniority. He's his own boss."

"What kind of favor?" I asked.

Milo didn't answer. He already had Dwight on the line. "This is your non-boss. Does your snowplow still work?" He paused. "Yeah, I need you to get me out of here. Family emergency in Bellevue." He paused again. "No. I'm at Emma's. If you say just one word, you'll end up like Mullins. Get your ass up here ASAP. And thanks."

"You're going to Bellevue? What about the highway?"

"It'll be fine. That Grand Cherokee's so damned heavy, it couldn't slide if it wanted to. I'm chained up, too." He got out of the chair and put his coffee mug in the sink. "Will you be okay while I'm gone?"

"Yes."

He looked uncertain. "You sure?"

"Yes."

He still seemed indecisive. "I could stay. Maybe Mulehide can pull herself together and get everybody straightened out."

"But you know she can't."

He sighed even more heavily. "You're right. I'm going to go out and make sure the Cherokee'll start. I don't usually leave it outside in this weather." Milo went into the living room to get his jacket. After I heard the front door close, I got up and went into the bedroom. I might as well get fully dressed. A heavy sweater on top of the T-shirt and wool slacks would be warmer than my bathrobe. My hair was still damp, so I made a haphazard attempt at finishing the job with the blow-dryer and a brush. By the time I was finished, Milo was back inside.

"Dwight's here," he said. "Offer him a cup of coffee after I pull out. He'll do just about anything for decent coffee. He used to bitch all the time about the coffee at work before we hired Lori."

"He had a right to," I said, recalling the dismal dark dishwater that had been dispensed at the sheriff's headquarters for years. "Did the Cherokee start?"

Milo nodded. "I thought it would." He took a step forward and enveloped me in his arms. He was holding me so tight and for so long that I could hardly breathe. It scared me. I felt as if he didn't want to let go because if he did, he'd never hold me again. Worse yet, I was thinking the same thing. At last he eased up on his grip. "I'm not going to kiss you good-bye."

I nodded. "Save it to kiss me hello."

Without another word, he released me and went out into the cold, white mountain morning.

SEVENTEEN

THE SHERIFF WAS RIGHT ABOUT DWIGHT GOULD. AS SOON as the deputy finished plowing all the way up to my Honda, I came out into the carport and asked if he'd like some coffee.

"You didn't have to do the whole driveway," I told him as he entered the kitchen.

"The plow's fun, better than a horse," he said. "Horses are too much like people—unpredictable and a damned nuisance."

Dwight wasn't the most affable of Milo's deputies, running a close second to Sam Heppner when it came to a cynical view of human nature. He'd been married once many years ago, but it hadn't lasted long. His wife, Kay, had left him for mill owner Jack Blackwell, who later dumped her. Jack, whose oily charm eluded me, had a serious history of discarding wives and girl-friends. I'd lost count over the years.

Dwight lived alone in a small house off the Burl Creek Road and seemed to enjoy his own company. He was at least five years older than Milo, and I always wondered if he resented having a boss who was younger. But Dwight was a hard and thorough worker, traits much appreciated by his boss. They weren't actual friends, though they'd occasionally gone hunting and fishing together. I assumed the sheriff preferred Dwight's taciturn company to more talkative types. Milo liked to fish alone, but if he had to have someone with him, only certain words were permissible, such as "Got anything yet?" "Nice fish," or "That a snag or a bite?"

I poured coffee into a mug for Dwight. "You're off duty, I gather."

He nodded. "Fong and Heppner are on. Poor bastards."

"Sugar? Cream?"

Dwight shook his head.

"Take a seat," I offered.

"Well . . ." He eyed the chair suspiciously. "Okay."

"I hear your poaching suspect took off last night," I said, sitting down across from Dwight.

"Damned fool. Now he's really in for it."

"Do you think he cut the trees?"

Dwight shrugged. "I'm not on a jury. I just follow orders."

"His alibi sounded credible."

Dwight scowled at me. He was short and stocky, with a pugnacious bulldog face. "Who's telling tales?"

"Vida."

He snorted. "That figures. Bill Blatt should stand up to that bigmouthed aunt of his."

Making conversation with Dwight wasn't easy, especially when my strength was depleted. "Was Greg a troublemaker growing up?"

He shook his head. "No more than most teenagers. They're all a pain in the butt."

"Maybe he just wanted to go home to his place in Brier."

Dwight didn't comment.

"Do you think he had help cutting down the maples?"

"Maybe, but he could do it with a decent gas chainsaw."

"Does he own one?"

Dwight scowled again. "How do I know? That's up to Dodge to get SnoCo to check out his place in Brier."

"The sheriff says you're in charge while he's on suspension."

"He does?" Dwight looked shocked. "That's crazy. How can he expect me to run his operation?"

"You might start by getting a warrant for the house Greg and Denise own here."

"Hey," he said, clenching his hands into fists on the table, "are you trying to make trouble?"

I was annoyed. "No. Don't be a jerk, Dwight. Just because Milo's not around doesn't mean the rest of you are on vacation."

His small jet-black eyes narrowed for just an instant. "What'd he do, deputize you after he . . . skip it." Dwight took a big gulp of coffee. "We can check his alibi. If he was at a pub watching football Monday night, he'd have more witnesses than just his so-called buddy."

"True." I tried to be pleasant. "I assume the pub was in Brier."

"That means SnoCo, too. But Jensen knew the game. He thinks the Patriots will end up in the Super Bowl. I'm not sure about that."

At last we'd reached neutral ground—or turf. "Who's your pick?"

"The Chiefs, maybe. They beat New England in that game. Only two points, but KC still looks good. You like football?"

"Not as well as baseball or basketball, but . . ." I stopped. "The Monday night game wasn't New England and Kansas City. That was the week before."

Dwight's small eyes grew wide. "It was?"

"You watched it, didn't you?"

"Yeah, yeah, sure, but . . ." He looked genuinely puzzled. "Maybe I nodded off. I'd worked over the weekend. I could've sworn . . . hell, maybe I'm thinking of one of the ESPN highlight shows."

"The Packers-Rams game would've put anybody to sleep this last Monday," I said kindly. "No contest."

Dwight took a final swig of coffee and stood up. "I'd better go. Maybe I should do some homework before Dodge gets back on the job."

"Thanks for the plow job," I said, getting up to open the door.

"Thanks for the coffee," Dwight said. "It's the real deal." He paused. "I hope you are, too."

As he walked through the carport, I pondered his last remark. If nothing else, it indicated he liked his boss.

Half an hour later, I finally felt like eating something. I made a soft-boiled egg and two pieces of finger toast. I poured myself some coffee, but the first sip didn't taste right. I dumped it out along with what was left in the pot. Then I realized that Milo had made it. Maybe Dwight had been kinder than I thought about both his coffee and his boss.

Shortly before noon, the city plows had arrived on my street. Life was returning to normal. I stepped outside to check the temperature. It was hovering under thirty and the wind was blowing. It felt like a Chinook, which meant the weather was warming up. Returning inside, I called Vida to ask how she was getting along.

"Much better," she replied, sounding more like herself. "Buck says the forecast calls for rain by later today. You must be recovering, too."

"I am," I said. "I might even try to get out of the house."

"My street was plowed earlier. I finally reached JoAnne, but she has to meet with Al Driggers this afternoon to finalize the interment and decide on the inscription. She may come tomorrow after I get home from church. It's possible that if I feel up to it, Buck and I will have dinner at the ski lodge. That was our original plan for this evening."

"Don't push it," I cautioned. "If I decide to run errands, I'll drop by to see you. I've got some things to talk about regarding the poaching."

"Oh, don't bother," she said hastily. "I'm fine. You mustn't overdo, either. We can talk tomorrow. I should hang up now. I'm going to have some soup. Take care, Emma." Vida rang off.

My brain shifted into overdrive. It had crossed my mind that Vida hadn't inquired about Milo, or made any comment last night when she could hear him in the background. I laughed to myself. Buck had spent the night with Vida. He must've shown up after Amy had checked on her mother. And Vida, of course, had forgiven him for his alleged betrayal. Age is no barrier when it comes to matters of the heart. It was a comforting thought.

But I felt at loose ends. Talking through puzzling occurrences such as Greg Jensen's behavior always helped me find clarity, or at least direction. After ten minutes of mulling, I dialed Marisa Foxx's number.

For the first couple of minutes we exchanged clichéd conversation. Marisa and I had formed a friendship in the past couple of years, but we both always seemed so focused on our careers that we didn't see each other very often.

"Okay, Emma," she said in her droll manner, "you're not calling to talk about the weather. Go ahead, put me on the witness stand."

"First of all, how'd you get to be Greg's attorney?"

"Let me think how much client confidentially I can contravene here," Marisa said dryly. "It's a matter of record that I've represented other Petersens in the past few years. When Simon Doukas retired, Jonathan Sibley and I took over all but a few of his clients. As you probably know, Simon's mother was a Bergstrom, as is JoAnne Petersen. Marvin and Cathleen Petersen were very gracious to both Jonathan and me when we joined the Doukas firm ten years ago. I represented Denise in the divorce, though. It was uncontested by Greg."

"I don't know about you," I said, "but all these family connections still sometimes mystify me. Now, don't take this wrong, but how come you were the one who posted bail for Greg?"

"I didn't," Marisa replied. "That is, I handled the bail through the bondsman I use in Monroe. Again, as a matter of public record, it was Reba Cederberg who put up the money. She's his aunt."

"That I know," I said. "And I won't bother you about the intricacies of bail amounts or that Greg hasn't been arraigned or any of that until we see how this plays out. I'll also refrain from asking if you think he's guilty or even if you think he's the kind of guy who'd do such a thing. But because you know you can trust me and vice versa, I admit I'm curious about your reaction to his decision to take off without his dog."

Marisa laughed. "I'd hate to have to question you as a witness. Your interrogatory style's enough to make me request a sidebar."

"Just answer the question, Ms. Foxx," I said in a mock-stern voice.

"It really surprised me," Marisa admitted. "I understood why he didn't want to face his ex. I've had plenty of divorced clients like that. But I had no inkling that Greg intended to bolt. I almost wonder if he did. I mean," she went on hastily, "Greg waited in my car until Denise came to the door. Then, when she went to fetch Doofus, he got out and took off in his VW, which he'd parked a few feet away when he originally came to get the dog, but got arrested instead. I didn't see Greg until I heard him gun the engine. It was too late to stop him."

"How was Denise?"

"You mean her attitude?"

"That, too, but did she seem sick? Denise is filling in for Ginny," I explained. "Denise was sick before she went home Thursday, then Vida and I both got the flu yesterday, or something like it. I wondered if she'd be able to come in Monday."

"Denise did look pale," Marisa said. "But otherwise, she seemed okay. I only saw her for a couple of minutes. How do you feel now?"

"Better. So's Vida. I couldn't believe she got sick, having the constitution of an ox. I guess it just proves she's human." I didn't want to get sidetracked. "How did Denise react when Greg drove off?"

Marisa laughed again. "She just sighed and remarked something like 'There goes your poacher. Greg's so lame. Now I'm still stuck with the dog and his stupid guitar.' Then she excused herself because Doofus was barking his head off. If Denise hadn't had a leash on him, I suppose he'd have run after Greg. I'd think she'd like the company up there on Second Hill. Except for the other two townhouses, it's still not very populated that high up."

"Apparently Doofus isn't much of a guard dog," I said. "That's it?"

"Yes. I had to leave to notify the sheriff's office."

"I assume you haven't heard from Greg since?"

"No. I don't expect to."

"How did Reba take it? She must be responsible for the full bail money if he's actually fleeing justice."

"Reba's very upset. I don't blame her. She can't believe . . . oops. Time to remember I'm an attorney."

"I get the picture," I said. "Thanks, Marisa."

"I'm not much help, really. We have to get together soon. In fact, poker night is Wednesday at my place, potluck dinner at seven. Can you come? Somebody always begs off this time of year."

I'd played poker with Marisa's group of far-flung professionals on a half-dozen occasions. I'd enjoyed myself, but didn't want to become a regular, because two players lived in Monroe and another was in Mukilteo. The drives were too long after a workday.

"I might do that," I said. "I'll let you know by Monday, okay?"

"Fine. And I'll call you in case we've got a full house—so to speak."

On that note, we hung up.

My idea of running errands faded when the rain started thirty minutes later. Driving would be relatively easy, but I wasn't up to slogging through slush and mud. Instead, I retrieved my holiday mailing list and the four boxes of cards I'd bought at Parker's Pharmacy for half price after last Christmas. I'd written five notes and addressed twice that many envelopes when I suddenly remembered to call the hospital to find out if Craig Laurentis's condition had been upgraded.

To my surprise, the nurse on duty was Julie Canby, wife of Spike Canby, who owned the Icicle Creek Tavern. "Julie," I exclaimed when I immediately recognized her voice, "when did you go back to work?"

"Emma?" There was a smile in her voice. "Last weekend, for Thanksgiving relief. After our little October adventure going to the trailer park, I realized how much I missed nursing. Spike can get kitchen help easily enough with the food service program at the college, and I wanted to go back to the work I really love, instead of frying burgers and making onion rings. What can I do for you?"

I told her how I knew Craig Laurentis. "What's his status?"

"Improving, but still out of it," she said. "They transferred him out of the ICU to a room a couple of hours ago. Dr. Sung was here this morning and thought Mr. Laurentis would pull through, but that's one nasty infection he's got. Did he really sleep in a dumpster?"

"Donna Wickstrom thought he did," I said. "How soon will he be able to talk and make sense?"

"He can talk now," she responded, "but he's not making sense. Sort of in and out. That's perfectly normal after what he's been through."

It suddenly dawned on me that I'd forgotten about asking Milo to have a deputy keep an eye on Craig. So much had happened, and somewhere in the back of my mind, I must've figured that as long as Craig remained in the ICU, he was safe. Now Milo was gone and the sheriff's department was short-handed. Maybe I was worrying unnecessarily. None of the patient rooms were far from the nurses' station. "If Craig starts to make sense, would you let me know?"

"I will if I don't get stuck going over charts before I leave at four," Julie responded. "Frankly, I figure it'll be tomorrow before he's rational. I'll be on duty again, so feel free to give me a buzz."

I thanked Julie and hung up. By the time I'd finished another dozen cards—without notes—I was hungry again. Vida had chosen soup. That sounded good to me, so I opened a can of Campbell's chicken noodle and was pouring it into a kettle when the phone rang.

I hardly recognized Spencer Fleetwood's voice. "Emma," he said, sounding like a ghost of Mr. Radio, "have you got the radio or TV on?"

"No." *Oh, damn,* I thought, *I'm about to get scooped again.* "Why?"

"KOMO-TV broke into a football game a few minutes ago with a story about a hostage situation in Bellevue. The family's last name is Sellers. Does that ring any bells?"

Offhand, it didn't. "No. Should it?"

"Well . . ." A long pause followed. "The reporter identified the home owner as Tricia Sellers. A few years ago I was seeing a woman who worked for one of the classical music FM stations and taught at Interlake High School. There was a Jake Sellers on the faculty, and she mentioned that he'd taught in Alpine before moving to Bellevue. Anyway, the reporter said that Ms. Sellers, her daughter, her daughter's fiancé, and the woman's ex-husband were in the house. I wondered if it could be Dodge's family. Have you talked to him today?"

The name had come back to me. Milo always called Tricia's second husband Jake the Snake. He'd been a teacher at Alpine High when he swept Mulehide off her feet and carried her all the way to Bellevue. But that had happened before I moved to town.

Those thoughts were muddled fragments in my brain as I struggled to take in what Spence was saying. I couldn't speak for so long that he had to call my name three times to get my attention.

"Yes," I finally said, breathless. "But not since he went to Bellevue."

"Dodge went to Bellevue?" It was Spence's turn to sound startled.

I cringed, wishing I hadn't confided in the man that Milo had put in the ER. But I couldn't take the words back. "Tricia wanted his help with a family problem. I assume he went to Bellevue."

"You're hedging," Spence shot back. "Look," he went on, "I *assume* you know what went down between Dodge and me yesterday. I was out of line and misjudged his feelings. I'm sorry."

"Okay," I said quietly. "That doesn't matter now. Can you find out what's happening with the hostage situation? I've lost my AP contact in Seattle." I wouldn't confess that I'd also lost the strength to act like a professional journalist.

"I know a couple of people at KOMO," Spence replied. "They may not work Saturdays, but I'll give it a try. Do you want me to come over?"

The offer stupefied me. "No, I'm fine." *Liar, liar, liar . . .*

"It'd be easier than calling back and forth."

Spence was right about that. "Oh . . ." I didn't know what to say.

"Emma," he said solemnly, "do you remember how you had to prop me up when I was on the edge a few years ago? It's pay-back time."

Hazily, I recalled the horrific incident that had practically destroyed the Spencer Fleetwood I thought I knew. In fact, that was when I found out he wasn't Spencer Fleetwood. It was his radio name. Somewhere at the back of my brain, I heard Ben's voice lecturing me about charity. It was a sin not to be charitable; it was also a sin—a lack of humility—to reject charity when offered.

"Okay."

"I'll be there in ten minutes." He hung up.

I turned on the TV to KOMO on Channel 4, the local ABC affiliate. A college football game was on, but I didn't bother to see who was playing. It could have been a Ping-Pong match for all I cared. I kept waiting for an update on the Bellevue situation, but the teams kept running, passing, fumbling, punting. I switched to KING, KIRO, and a couple of other local stations. Nothing. Just more football, situation comedy reruns, and a cooking show.

I suddenly remembered the soup. Had I turned on the stove? I hurried into the kitchen. The burner was off, but I'd lost my appetite. I put the soup kettle in the fridge before going back to the living room to wait for Spence.

He was as good as his word. Ten minutes later, at three-twenty, he pulled his BMW into the driveway. I let him in through the front door and tried to conceal my shock. There was a big bandage on his nose and his eyes were bloodshot. The usually debonair Spencer Fleetwood looked like a wino who'd gotten into an alley brawl over the dregs in a bottle of Two Buck Chuck.

"Go ahead," he said, still not sounding like himself. "Say it. I'm a mess."

I shook my head. Spence could look like a werewolf for all I cared at the moment. "Did you find anybody at KOMO?"

He took off his expensive ski parka, which appeared undamaged. "I got lucky. One of their marketing guys who worked with me twenty-five years ago in Milwaukee happened to be in. He'd left his homework at the office yesterday and was collecting it. He gave me the name of one of their people who is working on the story at the station. Her name's Mia Fong, and guess what?"

"She's Dustin's sister?"

"Cousin. Small world, huh?"

"Dustin's on duty today," I said. "Have you talked to Mia?"

He'd gotten out his state-of-the-art cell phone. "I waited until I got here. Mind if I sit before I call her?"

Somehow, I couldn't offer Spence the easy chair that was

Milo's favorite seat. I waved at the sofa. "Please." I sat down in the easy chair.

I'd already muted the TV, but I used the remote to switch channels and see if there was any coverage from Bellevue. There wasn't. While Spence waited to have his call put through, I wondered if Buck watched football when he was at Vida's house. Even if he did, though, the hostage situation in Bellevue wouldn't mean anything to him. And despite Vida's fondness for Buck, I couldn't quite see her sitting down with him to watch college football. The only team she'd ever followed was the Alpine High School Buckers. It also occurred to me that at least one of the sheriff's deputies might have seen the breaking news story. But would any of them except Dwight realize their boss was involved?

My fretful musings stopped when I heard Spence speak to Mia, inquiring about the latest from Bellevue. He listened for some time before speaking again. "So basically," he said, glancing at me, "nobody knows what's going on inside the house except that the fiancé of the younger woman who lives there is threatening to shoot her and the other family members?"

I wondered if Milo was armed. I wondered if Buster was crazy. I wondered if I could endure the suspense without going to pieces.

"When was that?" Spence asked Mia. A moment later, he spoke again. "But nobody's heard gunshots, right? What's the SWAT team doing? . . . That's good. Staying out of sight is smart. It's lucky they've got that kind of landscaping for cover. When will you update the story?" He leaned forward to look at the TV screen. "A little over three minutes to go. Not close, so the game should end about three-forty. Mind if I check in with you again? . . . Good. Thanks. By the way, your cousin's on duty today . . . Right, he's a good guy. You've got my number . . . Yes, that's it. Bye." He put the cell on the end table. "As soon as the game's over, they're cutting straight to the Bellevue situation. The house is in a cul-de-sac of an older development. In Bellevue terms, that means it's probably at least ten years old."

"It's grown so," I remarked. "I haven't been there lately. I always get lost." I put a hand to my head. "I need some Excedrin."

Spence followed me out to the kitchen. "Can you fill me in? You were very discreet on the phone."

"That's because I thought you were hoping Milo would get killed in Bellevue," I said, pouring some water into the glass I'd already used. I didn't say anything more until I'd gotten the Excedrin bottle out of the cupboard and swallowed two tablets. "Get yourself something to drink. You sound awful."

"I can't blow my nose," Spence said wryly. "I really do have a cold, the first one in three years."

"Are you going to put this on the news?"

"Not if I can help it," he replied, opening the fridge. "Where did all this French cheese come from?"

"Oh, God!" I reeled against the sink. "Never mind. It's probably poisoned. Take anything you want."

"Henry's dark ale's fine with me."

"Of course it is," I said. "I'm going to sit down again."

When Spence came out from the kitchen, he regarded me with a bemused expression. "I think we ought to talk about something other than what's uppermost in our minds. What did you make of the Petersen brothers the other night?"

"I'm not sure," I admitted. "I can't figure out if they were going through some kind of catharsis, or it's just that they don't really like each other much. Naturally, I'm allowing for typical sibling rivalry."

"Very different personalities," Spence said. "Cole called me yesterday to apologize. He also wanted to make sure I got a favorable impression of his mother. I don't know why—I've never met JoAnne, but he insisted that the reason she never visited Larry after presenting him with the divorce papers was because of the children. They were her priority now as a single parent. Larry himself told Cole that. What struck me as odd was that those kids were already raised by the time Larry went to prison. I also got the impression that none of them ever lived with JoAnne after she moved to Seattle."

"That's probably true," I said. "Denise stayed here, Cole had started college in Bellingham, but transferred to Pullman, and Vida thought Strom got his MBA from the University of Oregon."

"That's what was on the form he filled out for the program." Spence drank from the highball glass that held his dark ale. That figured. Milo always drank beer out of the bottle or can. I don't know why, but I found the difference endearing on the sheriff's part.

Spence nodded at the TV. "Hit the sound. They're letting the clock run out. If there's a wrap-up, it'll be quick."

Mr. Radio knew his broadcasting. The final score was barely flashed, the play-by-play announcer signed off, and suddenly a fair-haired young man stood in front of some upper-middle-class suburban homes that were partly hidden by King County and City of Bellevue police vehicles. He held a mike in one hand and an umbrella in the other as heavy rain poured down.

"This is a special report on the tense situation at a . . ."

"Rookie," Spence murmured. "They always get stuck with weekend assignments."

The young man continued: ". . . after a 911 call to Bellevue police this morning around noon today that family members were being threatened by an as yet unidentified young man thought by neighbors to be the daughter of the family's fiancé."

Spence winced. "Please. Sentence structure, kid."

I bumped up the sound two notches for fear of missing something despite the fact that Spence was keeping his voice low.

"King County and Bellevue police have been in contact with the allegedly armed man, but there's been no response from inside the house during the past forty-five minutes." The reporter turned away from the house, the camera following him to the cul-de-sac's entrance, where a dozen or more citizens stood outside a barricade. "One of the neighbors who lives two doors away is a longtime friend of the family." He'd reached the barricade and held the microphone in front of a pretty middle-aged woman in a bright red rain slicker. A caption appeared on the screen identifying her as "Elaine Fulke, neighbor." "Can you tell us what you heard or saw earlier, Ms. Fulke?" the reporter asked.

"I was walking my dog just before noon," the woman replied, looking at the mike as if it might bite her. "A car came into the cul-de-sac and parked half on the grass and half on the driveway to the Sellerses' house." The camera swung around to show a light blue Acura. Milo's Grand Cherokee was parked in front of the house. I let out a little gasp.

"You okay?" Spence asked.

I nodded, though he knew damned well I wasn't okay. But there was nothing he or I could do about it.

The reporter, whose name now showed on the screen as John something-or-other I didn't quite catch, asked if Ms. Fulke had seen the driver get out.

"Yes," she replied. "I've seen him several times. In fact, I've met him and talked to him. He seems very nice, rather quiet, but pleasant."

"Did you talk to him this morning?" John inquired.

"No," she answered, looking worried. "He was in a hurry,

and I didn't want to bother him. Besides, it had started raining quite hard and I wanted to get indoors with Pluto."

"So you recognized the young man," John said, stating the obvious. He paused, fumbling with the umbrella as he touched his earphone. "What's his connection with the family?"

"Instructions from the station," Spence said softly. "Warning not to name names."

"He's engaged to Ms. Sellers's elder daughter. They're getting married in August." Ms. Fulke looked sad. "At least that was the plan."

"When did you realize there was a problem at the Sellerses' house?"

"When a police car showed up about fifteen minutes later. I couldn't imagine what was going on. This is a very quiet neighborhood."

"Thank you, Ms. Fulke," John said, turning away. "According to the 911 call, Ms. Sellers was afraid that a volatile situation was getting out of hand and feared for her life and that of her daughter. She reportedly told the dispatcher that the young man had a gun and was behaving erratically. After police arrived at the scene, they weren't given access to the house. The alleged gunman appeared at an upstairs window and told them to go away, it was a private matter. Phone contact was finally made twice, ordering the suspect to come out with his hands up, but he refused and said he was staying until, and I quote, 'this problem is resolved, one way or another.' For now, we're playing a waiting game here in a usually peaceful Bellevue neighborhood where the threat of violence looms overhead just like the heavy dark rain clouds."

"Oh, God." Spence shook his head as John disappeared from the screen and was replaced by a bald, broad-shouldered black man who looked suitably somber.

"Thank you, John. KOMO-TV will remain at the scene while this tense drama unfolds. Stay tuned for further developments and a full report on our regular five o'clock newscast."

A dog food commercial followed. I turned off the sound again. "They didn't mention Milo," I said, sounding overwrought. "I saw his car. Where is he? Didn't you tell me Tricia's ex-husband was inside?"

"That's what I heard earlier," Spence asserted. "Stop tying yourself into knots. This kind of on-the-spot news isn't always a hundred percent accurate, especially when the reporter is still on training wheels. We can try one of the other stations later."

"I'm calling Milo," I said, starting for the phone on the end table.

Spence grabbed my wrist. "Don't. If he's in there with the rest of them, you could stir something up. I've covered these situations. They're a powder keg. You never know what even the smallest thing can do to somebody who's unstable and is holding a gun."

I wasn't convinced. "Shouldn't the Bellevue and King County police know there's a law enforcement officer inside the house?"

"Listen to me." Spence's gaze was so compelling that I didn't dare lose eye contact with him. "Think this through. Would you stake your life—or Milo's—on the fact that he *is* inside that house? You're making a lot of assumptions, and as a journalist, you know that's not smart."

"I saw his Cherokee," I declared, still mulelike.

"Could you see the license plate? How do you know it's his? There must be a hundred just like it in Bellevue alone. Furthermore," Spence went on, no doubt aware that I'd begun to waver, "do you want the guy with the gun to know Milo's a lawman?"

"He probably already does," I said. "They've met."

"That doesn't mean the . . . what's his name?"

"Ah . . ." I made a face. "I don't know. Milo calls him Buster. I don't think he knows what the fiancé's real name is."

"You see? Not much communication between them. Let it alone," Spence said sternly. "The cops at the scene don't need interference. Not only would they resent it, they know what they're doing. We don't."

Spence was right. Reluctantly, I went back to the easy chair and collapsed. "I feel so damned helpless," I wailed.

"I know. Do you want a drink?"

I shook my head. "My stomach's still not quite right."

"Do you have any brandy? A couple of sips won't hurt."

I couldn't remember. I only kept brandy on hand for the holidays, but without Adam or Ben coming for Thanksgiving, I hadn't been to the liquor store in weeks. "Check the top cupboard across from the sink."

Spence started for the kitchen. I got up and followed him. "I thought you were going to call Mia."

"I am," he said, opening the cupboard. "But not yet. If they know anything more at KOMO, they'd have said so."

"They know the names of who's inside, don't they?"

Spence took out Milo's bottle of Scotch, a half-empty fifth of Jack Daniel's, a pint of Crown Royal, and a bottle of Napoleon brandy with less than two inches in it. "Probably," he finally replied. "Where's a snifter?"

"For God's sake," I said impatiently, "I'll drink it out of the bottle." Before Spence could say anything, I grabbed the brandy and opened it. "Call Mia and ask her." I took a swig of brandy, grimacing as it sent fire down my throat. "Well?"

Spence shrugged. "Okay. Sit down before you drink any more." He was returning the other bottles to the shelf. I stayed put. I wasn't taking any more orders from Mr. Radio, no matter how well intentioned.

"Milo's deputies have to know what's going on," I said.

"Why?" Spence asked, closing the cupboard. "You want them to organize a posse and rescue their boss?"

"Milo doesn't need anybody to rescue him," I snapped. "It's a matter of professional courtesy. If it was you, I'd notify your employees at the station."

Spence grinned, though not nearly as widely as usual with the bandage's edges almost touching the corners of his mouth. "Thanks. But are you sure you want everybody in town to know what's going on with the sheriff's private life?"

"They'll probably find out eventually," I said. "Dwight Gould knew Milo was going to Bellevue because there was a family crisis. Lots of people will remember Tricia and Jake. As you might imagine, it was quite a scandal at the time. The current situation is probably already spreading from Mount Baldy to Tonga Ridge." My phone rang. "See?" I said, hurrying back to the living room. "I'll bet that's Vida."

It wasn't. "Emma?" Julie Canby said. "I'm about to leave, but you asked me to call if there was anything new about Craig Laurentis. He's not really lucid, but he keeps saying your name, and it sounds as if he wants to see you. He's very agitated, which isn't good for him. Could you come by before we have to knock him out?"

EIGHTEEN

I WAS SPEECHLESS FOR A MOMENT OR TWO. "I . . ." SPENCE HAD reentered the living room and was staring at me. "Yes, I'll try. Thanks, Julie. I appreciate the call."

I took another sip of brandy and shook myself.

"What was that all about?" Spence asked.

I had to tell him, news rival or not. "Laurentis is still gaga, but he keeps asking for me. I'd better go to the hospital and see if there's anything I can do."

His bloodshot eyes twinkled—at least it looked like they did. It was hard to tell. "I didn't realize you had a nursing degree."

"Oh, shut up." I set the brandy bottle down on the end table. "Call Mia now before I go. Please."

He made a little bow. "As you wish, Your Grace."

I moved out of the way so Spence could pick up his cell from the end table. "Mia?" he said as I stood a few feet away by the coat closet. "I assume there's nothing new to tell me." He paused. "Right. That's what I figured. Do you have names for the alleged hostages?" He paused again, then frowned. "I see. Okay, thanks for now. How late are you working? . . . I assumed you would. I owe you lunch. Say, does your cousin know about this? . . . I was just curious. Thanks again." He disconnected and looked at me. "First, the ex-husband hasn't been IDed. The only reason they know he's an ex is because one of the neighbors has seen him at the house before. Not Ms. Fulke, but—"

I interrupted him. "Did the neighbor give a description?"

"No. Just hold on. Mia's staying with the story as long as it takes to unfold. She hasn't talked to Dustin because she couldn't think of any reason why she should. Ergo, no apparent Alpine connection unless they've done a deep background on Tricia and Jake Sellers, which I doubt they have. Now I wish I hadn't asked. If Mia's as sharp as she sounds, she's probably trying to figure out why I'm interested in the first place and why I'd ask about her cousin."

"I'm beyond caring about that part," I said, taking my car coat out of the closet. "I'll be back as soon as I can." Grabbing my purse, I started to go out the front door.

"Hold it." Spence was putting on his parka. "I'm coming, too."

"No. You have to stay here and watch for breaking news."

His expression was typically sardonic. "How will you get your car out with my Beemer in the way? My BlackBerry can't pick up TV, but it has other remarkable functions. Your cell's a dinosaur. Let's go."

"BlackBerry," I muttered. "I never heard of that. Is it edible?"

"Ah. The brandy did you some good," he said as we crossed the slushy grass to the driveway. "I can find a TV at the hospital, probably in Laurentis's room."

"Okay, okay, but," I warned him before we got in the car, "Craig may not talk if you're there. He wouldn't when I was with Dodge."

"Oh, God, Emma," Spence said in mock dismay, "how many men are madly in love with you in this town?"

I didn't answer him. In fact, we didn't speak during the five-

minute drive to the hospital. He kept the radio turned to
KOMO-AM, but there was no news, only talk, talk, talk. To my
amazement, Spence pulled into the area reserved for the doctors
and other staff.

"Hey," I said, "how can you do this?"

"I have friends in high places," he replied. "Elvis Sung gave
me a special permit to park here when I interviewed him on the
radio after he first started to work up here."

"Scott Chamoud didn't get one when he interviewed him for
the *Advocate*."

"That's probably because Elvis put some moves on the future
Mrs. Chamoud before she married Scott and they moved away."

"I never knew that," I said before getting out of the car. "My
former reporter kept that to himself."

We got into the same elevator Doc Dewey had used. Spence
clearly knew his way around. Reaching the second floor, he
stopped short of the nurses' station. "You check in to see Craig
and I'll have my way with . . ." He glanced at the prune-faced
woman who was studying patient charts at the desk. "Well, we
all have to make sacrifices," he said resignedly.

I approached Prune Face, whose nametag identified her as
Ruth Sharp, RN. I recalled her from an encounter in the ER a
few years back. "I'm here to see Mr. Laurentis," I said. "He's
been asking—"

She cut me off. "I know. You're Ms. Lord. Go ahead. He's the
last door down on the left. If you can shut him up, I'd be grateful.
That man's a nuisance." She went back to reading her charts.

The location of Craig's room struck me as symbolic of his
recluse's reputation. Or maybe whoever was in charge of bed assignments believed that such a strange human being should be
kept out of sight. Eccentricity trumped talent in the minds of
most Alpiners.

Craig was moaning when I entered the room by the stairwell door. He looked better than when I'd last seen him at the gallery. That wasn't much comfort. Despite Doc Dewey's and Dr. Sung's prognoses, I wondered if he'd ever regain the strength and vigor of the man I'd come to know. If he'd been agitated when Julie called, he was merely restless now. I assumed he must be exhausted. I hauled a chair over to the bed, sat down, and put my hand on the one of his that wasn't pierced with IVs. "Craig," I said softly "it's Emma."

His eyelids flickered. The moaning stopped. But he didn't look in my direction. In fact, his eyes had closed. I waited, patting his hand. The TV in his room was off. I fought an urge to get up and turn it on. I wondered what Spence was doing. I wondered if Craig had gone to sleep. Most of all, I wondered what was happening with Milo.

Finally, after several minutes had passed, I tightened my hold on his hand. "Craig," I said softly but urgently. "It's Emma."

His eyes fluttered open. He seemed to focus, but I couldn't be sure. I could also feel him relax.

"Long . . . saw . . . not sure . . . but knew . . . wasn't . . ."

Craig winced. It almost looked as if there were tears in his eyes.

"Wasn't what?" I asked. "Wasn't a saw?" Maybe he was talking about the poachers.

But he shook his head. If not tears, there was perspiration on his gaunt face. Whatever he was trying to tell me was at a great cost to him mentally and maybe emotionally as well. I felt so sorry for him that I was about to insist that he didn't expend any further effort.

Before I could say anything, Craig spoke again. "Go," he said in a voice that was more like a sigh. "Go."

"Go? You want me to go?"

He shook his head almost imperceptibly. "Go," he repeated.

I rubbed my aching head with my free hand. The Excedrin hadn't yet started to work. "Go where?"

Craig grimaced and shook his head again. "For . . ." He closed his eyes, obviously exhausted as well as frustrated.

"Go for what?" I asked as patiently as I could manage.

"Donna." His gaze fixed on me, waiting for my response.

"Donna Wickstrom? The art gallery?"

A single nod.

"Your new painting?"

The nod that followed sapped his strength. His eyes closed again. I tried to decode what he meant, other than something to do with *Forest Watch*. "Go," he'd said. Craig must've meant I should go to the gallery.

"You want me to go to Donna's?" I asked.

There was no response. His whole body had gone slack. Slowly, I withdrew my hand. I was frightened. Then I looked at the monitor that showed his vitals. I understood the green lines enough to know that Craig was still alive and relatively stable. I got up and went out to the nurses' station. Ruth Sharp had just hung up the phone.

"Did you give Mr. Laurentis a sedative?" I asked.

"Yes," she replied, looking self-righteous. Her rigid demeanor wasn't softened by the round pleated cap she wore on her short gray hair. "Just before you came. Someone on the previous shift should've done that sooner. It serves no purpose for a patient in his condition to become so distraught. It upsets hospital routine as well."

There was no point in further discussion. Nurse Sharp was probably right. "It's working," I informed her. "Where's Mr. Fleetwood?"

"In the visitors' lounge," she replied. "I assume he has no intention of broadcasting from here? That would also upset hospital routine."

"Of course," I murmured, turning to head for the lounge.

Spence appeared immediately. "I heard your voice. Nothing worth watching on TV," he said lightly, with a quick glance at Nurse Sharp.

I looked at my watch. "It's almost four-thirty."

"So?" Spence hit the elevator button. "We've got plenty of time to get back to your place for the news at five."

"We aren't going to my place," I said, loudly for the sake of Nurse Sharp. I didn't need any more tittle-tattle about my private life. "We're going to the art gallery."

The doors slid open and we got in. "Why?" Spence asked.

"I don't know." I leaned against the back of the elevator. "I'm so torn. Craig's trying to tell me something important about his new painting. I can't think what, but I feel that at least I have to see if Donna knows what he might be talking about. Can you do me a huge favor?"

"What is it?"

We'd reached the parking garage level, so I withheld my answer until we were in the Beemer. "Drop me off at the gallery. Ginny and Rick Erlandson live one block up on Pine, between Seventh and Eighth. It's the second house from the corner on the southeast side of the street. You can watch the TV there. I'll call them now, if you'll do it."

"I can handle it," Spence said. "I hope I don't scare the children with my hideous appearance. How will you explain why I'm there?"

I was already dialing the Erlandsons' number. "I'm winging it."

Ginny answered on the first ring. "Oh, Emma," she said before I could get out more than a quick hello. "I'm really still worn out. You wouldn't believe the week I've had. First, Brett fell off his—"

"Stop," I said sharply. "This has nothing to do with the *Advocate*. Spencer Fleetwood wants to watch your TV."

There was dead silence at the other end, broken by a child's shriek. "I have to go, Emma. Brad just—"

I hung up on her. "Brazen it out, Spence. Tell Ginny you're from CPS. Or use the charm you didn't waste on Prune Face at the hospital."

"That was one hopeless case," he murmured, taking a left off Pine. "Don't worry. I'll tell Rick that his sister needs your artistic opinion on a new painting. Are you going to be okay?"

I glared at him. "I've been through a lot of crap in my life, too. Whatever doesn't kill you makes you stronger. I hope."

He pulled up to double-park outside the gallery. "Go, girl. Call me when you're done."

I all but flew out of the car and stumbled on the curb. If it hadn't been for being able to steady myself on an *Advocate* box on the sidewalk, I'd have fallen flat on my face. I patted the box in gratitude and went into the gallery. Donna was chatting with Warren Wells, who was studying a Kenneth Callahan numbered print from the Pacific Northwest artist's later period.

Both Donna and Warren greeted me warmly. Warren even offered his hand. "You've been working too hard, Emma. Francine hasn't seen you in the store for months. She's afraid you're going around town in a barrel. Or are you waiting for her pre-Christmas clearance?"

I didn't have time for chitchat, even for the sake of fellow parishioners and Francine's Fine Apparel weekly ad revenue. "Tell your wife to mark down all her Max Mara pieces to fifty bucks each, and I'll be there when she opens the door." I turned to Donna. "Is the Laurentis still in back?"

"Yes. Is something wrong?"

"I don't know." I moved on through the gallery. "Ignore me. Sell Warren something expensive."

Forest Watch was on a table surrounded by various matting and frame samples. Obviously, Donna hadn't made up her mind about how to show the work off to its best advantage. There was a light on a chain overhead, but it was turned off. I clicked the switch, realized that it had more than one setting, and turned it up as high as it would go.

The painting was still disturbing, even more so than it had seemed the first time I saw it. What was I supposed to see? Time of day? It looked like evening, but only because the background was so dark. Time of year? Not spring or summer—too bleak. Craig's style was so unrealistic compared to *Sky Autumn* that if there were any deciduous trees, such as the vine maples in my painting, I couldn't tell. He'd used some green, but the shades were murky, even sinister.

I heard Donna say good-bye to Warren. A moment later she joined me in the back room. "Warren's buying that Callahan print for Francine," she said. "It's a Christmas . . ." She stopped, probably realizing that I wasn't paying much attention. "What it is, Emma? Has something happened to Craig? Or to you?"

"Both," I said, finally looking at her. "Craig's actually improving, but he wanted to see me. By the time I got to the hospital, they'd given him a sedative. He could barely speak. I figured out that he was trying to tell me something about *Forest Watch*. I haven't a clue what he meant. Do you know?"

Donna shook her head. "Let's try magnifying it."

She moved a Daylight Naturalight tabletop magnifier over to the table. I should've noticed it sooner. Kip used a less expensive version in the back shop when we needed to get a better look at blurry photos submitted by our readers who were involved in group activities.

Donna and I both studied every inch of the painting in silence. Nothing we saw inspired any revelations. I posed a question. "Can you tell when Craig painted this?"

"You mean from the paint itself?" Donna shook her head. "I can guess. It's probably not very recent. Craig used different paints—acrylic, oil, some watercolor. If you touch certain parts of the canvas, you can tell that by the thickness of one kind on top of the other. It's as if he was having trouble getting the effect he wanted. My point, I guess, is that I have a feeling it took him a long time to finish this."

"In other words," I suggested, "he wanted to get it right. But why? It's . . ." I shook my head. "I don't like it. There. I've said it out loud. In fact, when I saw Craig the first time in the hospital, he knew I didn't. Have you ever seen any of his other work that looks like this?"

"Not the actual paintings," Donna replied. "I've seen photographs in catalogs from a couple of other galleries that show his works. There was one in this style three or four years ago at a Bellingham gallery, and another last spring in Boise. I'll admit they weren't as different as this one, yet I could tell Craig was experimenting. That's what artists do. Callahan's a good example."

"I know," I said. "I interviewed him years ago for *The Oregonian*. I wasn't quite as fond of his later works, either, though they certainly weren't depressing." I gestured at *Forest Watch*. "That one is. Or maybe 'disturbing' is more appropriate."

Donna shrugged. "A painting definitely can evoke the artist's mood at the time while he's working on it."

"I understand that, but . . ." I stared at Donna. "What did you say?"

Donna frowned. "That an artist's work reflects his state of mind. Why do you ask?"

"No. It was *how* you said it. I was reminded of something,

but I don't know what it is." I sighed. "Let me take another look with the magnifier." Peering through the three-and-a-half-inch glass, I went over every detail. "Those two small gold blobs are the only bright spots. What are they? I can't tell even with the enlargement." I stepped aside so Donna could take a look.

"It could be moonlight reflecting off of something," she said. "Or symbolic of the gold mining around here a hundred years ago."

"Gold," I murmured, thinking back to what Craig had been trying to say in his hospital bed. "I thought he was telling me to 'go,' as in go here to the gallery. But I might be wrong."

Donna glanced at the painting. "Has any gold been found near Alpine in recent years?"

"Not that I ever heard," I admitted. "Do you have any idea where Craig lives?"

"Only that it's somewhere nobody else seems to go," Donna said, turning as she heard the gallery door open.

I checked my watch. It was five straight up. "I've got to dash. You take care of your customer. Is it okay if I go out the back way?"

If the request puzzled Donna, she didn't show it. "The key's in the lock." She lowered her voice. "It's Mary Lou Blatt, Vida's sister-in-law. She'll talk my ear off and not buy anything." With a little wave, Donna headed back into the gallery. "Mary Lou! How nice to see you! Is there something I can show . . ."

I was out in the alley before Mary Lou could start driving Donna crazy. The dumpster that Craig had apparently slept in was on my left. I shook my head, sorry for him, sorry for me, but even sorrier for Milo.

By going out the back way, it was only half a block to Ginny and Rick's house. I should be able to catch most of the newscast. I walked uphill as fast as I could through the downpour. Melted snow water was rushing into the drains next to the curb. Red, green, and yellow streetlights lit up the dark December evening like Christmas decorations. My mood, however, was far from festive. As I reached the Erlandsons' front door, I realized my heart was beating far too fast. My hands were shaking as I pressed the doorbell. It seemed like it took a long time for Rick to open the door.

"Hi, Emma," he said. "Kind of nasty out, huh?"

"Better than being snowed in," I said. "Where's Spence?"

"Watching the news," Rick said, leading me into the small entryway. "Gosh, he's got a worse cold than I do, poor guy. At least I don't have to wear a bandage on my nose. I guess he's following some news story for the station. Is it one you're doing for the *Advocate,* too?"

"That's what we're both trying to determine," I said, hoping to sound casual.

Ginny, carrying the new baby, came out of the kitchen into the hall. "Oh, hi, Emma. Can you take Bando? That's what the other boys call him. Rick, you need to run to the store," she went on, after handing off the infant to me as if he were a football. "I forgot I didn't have any sauce for the lasagna."

A loud crash sounded from the kitchen. "Brett?" Ginny cried. "Brad?" She raced back down the hall.

"I'd better go," Rick said. "See you later, Emma." He grabbed his heavy jacket from a peg near the front door. "What kind of sauce?" he yelled to his wife, who was out of sight if not out of hearing range.

I carried baby Bando into the living room. Spence was sitting on one half of a two-piece sectional. The TV showed what looked like another Iraqi neighborhood destroyed by one side or the other—or both.

"Well?" I said, sitting on the other sectional while the baby stared up at me with what seemed like a quizzical expression.

"Nothing." Spence looked disgusted. "I missed the very beginning because one of the kids grabbed the remote and turned it to a cartoon. God, I'm glad I never had kids."

Bando objected to the remark, letting out a piercing yowl. Or maybe he'd realized I wasn't his mother. "What shall we do?" I asked, trying to jiggle the baby to shut him up.

"This is all international stuff," Spence said, standing up. "Next will come the national after the commercials, and then we'll get to local news. Since they haven't broken in, I assume nothing's happening. Or the situation is over."

A chill ran up my spine. "But . . ." Bando was crying in earnest. Ginny appeared in the living room before I could say anything else.

"Oh, Emma, let me take him. You wouldn't believe the mess in the kitchen." She reached out to remove the screaming baby. "Did you want to stay for dinner? Whenever I make lasagna, there's plenty left over. Once Rick gets back, it'll only take half an hour or so to bake."

"No thanks, Ginny," I shouted. "But we're grateful that Spence got to keep up with the news."

Bando was calming down as his mother held him against her shoulder and patted his back. "Gas," she remarked. "Oops!" The baby blurped all over the place. "Oh, darn! Mind if I don't see you out?"

"Not at all," Spence said, managing to sound unperturbed. "Enjoy your dinner. Cute kids," he added over his shoulder as he opened the front door for me. "Thanks."

We both ran to the Beemer that was parked just one space down from the Erlandsons' house. After I collapsed in the passenger seat, Spence reached over and patted my knee. "Take it easy, Emma. And hang on. We're going to break the speed limit to get back to your place."

He wasn't kidding, especially since there wasn't much traffic at five-fifteen on a Saturday night. We pulled into my driveway at five-eighteen and were in the house a minute later. While Spence turned on the TV, I fell into the easy chair, still wearing my wet coat.

The anchors had moved on to national news. Spence hung up his parka, then stood next to me. "Coat, madam. Why don't you finish that brandy? You look like you could use it. I'll get another Henry's. Then you can tell me about the painting."

I merely nodded, before struggling to take the coat off. "Thanks."

Spence went about his self-imposed duties. He was in the kitchen when the male anchor announced that there was breaking news from "the Bellevue hostage standoff." I yelled to him before I practically fell out of the easy chair.

A grim-faced John was waiting for his cue. I held my breath. Spence had picked up the remote and turned the sound up a notch, as if he could force the reporter to speak.

"The Bellevue crisis has come to a tragic conclusion just minutes ago," he said, as blue and red lights flashed in the background. "Despite the efforts of Bellevue and King County police to get the alleged gunman to free his hostages and surrender . . ."

"Say it, say it!" I screamed.

Spence rushed over to the chair and put his arm around me. "Shhh," he said, tightening his grip.

". . . when the gunman wounded the young woman thought by neighbors to be his fiancée before turning the gun on himself. Official identification is being withheld until the dead man's next of kin have been notified. The injured young woman has been airlifted to Harborview Hospital in Seattle. Meanwhile, the other two hostages, Tricia Sellers, owner of the house, and her former husband, Jacob Sellers of Lake Sammamish, are being treated for shock at Overlake Hospital here in Bellevue.

So ends this sad drama in what until now had been a serene syl-van suburban neighborhood."

"Hissing sibilant serpent sound-bite shit," Spence said in dis-gust.

The picture switched back to the studio. "Thank you, John," the pert blond anchorwoman intoned solemnly. "So ends an-other domestic tragedy involving . . ."

I barely heard her. I didn't even realize I was crying until I felt the salt on my tongue. "Where's Milo?" I whispered hoarsely.

Spence let me go and stood up. "How do I know? At least he's not dead."

"You don't know that!" I shouted, staggering to my feet. "Maybe Buster shot him in some other part of the house and they haven't found his body!"

"Oh, for . . ." He caught me as I succumbed to a weak-kneed fit of hysteria. "Good God. Emma." I was out of control, beat-ing my fists against his chest. He shook me. "Emma! Stop it!"

I stopped. And passed out.

NINETEEN

The next thing I knew, I opened my eyes and tried to focus. I was on the sofa under the comforter from my bed. At first I had no idea why I was there or why Spencer Fleetwood was in my living room, seated in the side chair and talking on his damned BlackBerry. *I must be dreaming. Why is Mr. Radio at my house and why does he have a bandage on his nose? This is crazy. I've got the flu, and Milo should be in the easy chair leafing through* Vanity Fair.

Then reality set in, like a knife to the heart. I struggled to sit up. "Spence?" I called shakily. "What's happening?"

He motioned for me to be quiet. "What did he look like?" Spence said into his cell, and waited for an answer from whoever was talking at the other end. "Okay, let me know when you see him . . . What? Oh. Can you give me his home number?"

The ringing of my phone on the end table startled me. Still trembling, I twisted around to pick up the receiver on the third ring.

"Emma," Vida said, "have you heard the news?"

"Yes," I said, trying to sound normal. "It's very upsetting."

"Should we tell Kip?"

"I think we should wait," I replied.

"What if Spencer gets it first?"

I glanced at Spence, who was jotting something down in a small leather-encased notebook. "He already knows."

"How could he?" she demanded. "I only heard about it fifteen minutes ago. Did Doc call you?"

"Doc?" I said, wondering if I wasn't dreaming after all. "Why would Doc call me?"

"Then who told you about JoAnne Petersen?"

"JoAnne?" I echoed. "What about her?"

"Really, Emma, you sound addled," Vida declared. "What do you think I'm talking about? Buck and I had just arrived at the ski lodge for dinner. The early-bird special, you know. Doc and Nancy came in just ahead of us. Before they could look at a menu, he was called away. JoAnne apparently tried to kill herself with an overdose of sleeping pills."

I fell back on the cushion, incredulous. "Why?"

"I've no idea," Vida replied. "It's a good thing she was staying with Olga. Being a nurse, she figured out what had happened. JoAnne took her cousin's pills. Olga seldom uses them, but being on the night shift, she occasionally has trouble going to sleep when it's light outside. I must go. Buck is ordering for both of us."

She rang off. It occurred to me that many of my recent phone calls had ended abruptly, a symptom of the last few days of stress and strain that had infected not only me but much of Alpine.

Spence had also concluded his call. "What was that all about?"

I told him as succinctly as I could.

"That's a strange turn of events," he said. "Depression, maybe? Guilt for not visiting Larry? Feeling like a flop for having raised two boys who may hate each other and a daughter who's a dimwit?"

"I don't know," I admitted. "How long was I out?"

"Two, three minutes." He shrugged. "You just sort of caved. You probably need to eat something."

"Who were you talking to?"

"Mia at KOMO," Spence said, standing up and fiddling with the bandage on his nose. "This is beginning to itch. I asked her if anybody who looked like Milo had been spotted at the scene in Bellevue."

I pulled myself into a sitting position. "What did she say?"

"She had to look at film they hadn't shown on TV. There were some plainclothes guys mingling around with the cops, but she didn't know if they were Bellevue or KingCo detectives or some other official presence, like doctors. John the Rookie was going home to recover from his first big-time reporting assignment, but she gave me his number. I'll call him in a few minutes after he dries himself out."

"Have the cops gone through the house?"

Spence scowled at me. "Searching for Milo's bullet-ridden body? Come on, Emma, get real. Don't you think somebody would've heard the shots?" He started into the hallway. "I'm going to try to do something about this damned bandage. It's driving me nuts. I can't even blow my nose. How am I supposed to get over this damned head cold? I've probably got a sinus infection by now."

"Tough," I muttered as he went out of sight. Realizing that the receiver was still in my lap, I picked it up to set it in the cradle. That's when I noticed my message light was on. It hadn't occurred to me to check for missed calls after returning home. I dialed the number and code to retrieve my messages. There were three. The first had come in at four-forty, just after Spence and I had left for the hospital.

"Hello, Emma dear," Edna Mae Dalrymple chirped in her birdlike voice. "I'm calling to remind you that bridge club is moved to Thursday this week. Or did I tell you earlier? Maybe not, since I wasn't sure until today. We have to change dates because Charlene Vickers and Janet Driggers have other engagements on Wednesday, and this time of year it's so difficult to get substitutes. See you soon. Bye-bye."

The second call, fifteen minutes later, was also from Edna Mae. "Oh, Emma, we forgot Thursday is Vida's program. The change in dates, you know. And after her last show—well, we're all agog. We've decided on Tuesday unless we wait to start after *Cupboard*. I'll get back to you as soon as I can. Do you have Vida's recipe for glögg? I called her, but she's not home. Thank you, dear."

I sighed. Edna Mae and the rest of the bridge players hadn't considered that Tuesdays were deadline night for me. If our current lead stories were still evolving by then, they'd have to find a sub for *me*.

My ear was getting tired and my headache had only just begun to ebb. I took a deep breath before listening to the third and last message, logged at five-fourteen.

"Where the hell are you?" Milo asked angrily. "Pick up the damned phone." A pause. "I'm on my way to Harborview with Tanya. That sonuvabitch Buster shot her and then blew his own brains out. Don't call back. I won't be able to use my cell at the hospital." I could hear raised voices in the background and a loud whirring noise. "I'm coming, dickhead, just hold—" The line went dead.

I went limp with relief, dropping the receiver out of my hand onto the floor. Spence came into the living room. "Emma!" he shouted. "Good God, what now?"

I couldn't answer right away. Spence just stood there, looking aggravated. Fleetingly, I noticed that the bandage had been replaced by two large Band-Aids.

"Milo's alive," I finally said. "He's gone to Harborview with Tanya."

"Well." Spence grinned, looking, if not yet sounding, more normal. He retrieved my phone from the floor and set it back in the cradle. "Didn't I say he was alive and well and being his usual belligerent self?"

"Milo's not belligerent," I said hotly, though realizing that whoever he'd called a "dickhead" was probably another law officer or a medic. If he hadn't been extremely upset, he'd never have spoken that harshly.

Spence touched his nose. "Huh. You could've fooled me." He went to the coat closet and took out his parka. "In that case, you don't need me anymore. My work here is done."

I was surprised. "You're leaving?"

"Hey—I've got a radio station to run. You know where to find me." With that parting sally, he was out the door.

For about five seconds, I was sorry to see him go. Then I realized that the bastard had used me. It was typical Spencer Fleetwood MO. He'd milked what he could get out of a story—*my* story, at that. I was so angry that I got up, locked the front door, went into the kitchen, and drank the rest of the brandy while I tried to think of how to handle the situation.

It was six-fifteen. The usual quarter-hour newscast was over. Would Spence break into his regular canned programming with the story about Sheriff Dodge's family disaster? In his place, I would. The only thing I could do about that was to have Kip put the news on our website. But I hesitated. This wasn't just any news coverage, this was Milo's private life. I'd once violated my ethics as a journalist by suppressing certain facts in a homicide story involving Vida. More recently, I'd handled Roger's participation in the trailer park incident with kid gloves. But what came first? My responsibility to the newspaper or my concern for people I cared about deeply? Journalist or human being? The answer seemed easy, but it wasn't, especially if Spence was going to broadcast the whole sordid mess over KSKY.

Going back to the living room, I turned on the radio. Due to my perverse nature and the semi-rivalry between the spoken and the printed word, I'm not a regular listener. The music was soft rock. After two songs, a presumably live female voice came on.

"You've just heard Lionel Richie's 'My Love,' the Mamas and the Papas' classic 'California Dreamin',' and the Little River Band performing 'Cool Change.' This is Bree Kendall, filling in for Spencer Fleetwood, with KSKY's usual Saturday night soft rock, two hours of oldies, but always goodies, and easy on the ear. Now let's hear from one of our local sponsors."

A commercial voiced by Spence for Nordby Brothers GM dealership followed. Now I knew why Spence and Bree were so chummy. If nothing else, Spence or even Bree should've informed us that she was working part-time at the station. It was worth a mention in Vida's "Scene."

Bree was back. "Don't forget, KSKY is always local, all the time. Our next trio of oh-so-soft rock starts with Paul McCartney and Wings, doing 'With a Little' . . ."

I turned Bree, Paul, and Wings down low. Nothing about breaking news. Maybe Spence hadn't finished putting together his hot news item for Bree to read. I couldn't imagine his vanity would permit him to do it live in his current stuffed-up vocal state. Or maybe he was checking on the JoAnne Petersen attempted suicide. I tried to put my wrath aside and think through the occurrences of the last hour or more. It was frustrating. I didn't have Vida to lean on; she was too busy eating dinner with Buck at the ski lodge. My best bet was Mitch

Laskey. Somehow, the obvious had eluded me. I wondered what had caused my brain to misfire. Then I wondered why I was wondering—I knew why, and cursed myself for behaving like an adolescent idiot. It had been a long time since I'd let my heart rule my head.

"Mitch," I said when he answered the phone, "are you in the middle of dinner?"

"Not yet," he replied, "but Brenda's in the middle of the kitchen, thinking about it. Is Alpine being attacked by some of Averill Fairbanks's aliens?"

"Not that simple," I said. "Could you meet me at the office? I need your brain for half an hour."

"It'll take Brenda that long to find her recipe," Mitch said. "She's been weaving all day, trying to fill Christmas orders. As soon as I find my brain, I'm on my way."

"Okay, I'll see you there."

I rang Kip next, but he didn't pick up. I left a message for him to call me on my cell. Before putting on my coat, I upped the radio's volume. KSKY was still playing music. I could listen to it in the car on my way to the *Advocate*.

Seven minutes, two commercials, and half of Men at Work's "Down Under" later, I parked the Honda and unlocked the *Advocate*'s front door. I'd just turned on the lights in the newsroom when Mitch arrived. "What's up?" he asked, shrugging out of his all-weather jacket.

"Have you watched the news on TV today?" I asked.

"I flipped to CNN a few times between football games," he replied. "Did I miss something?"

"I meant the local news—Bellevue, that is."

"No. In fact, Brenda and I've only been to Bellevue twice since we moved out here. What's going on there and why should we care?"

I'd sat down at Leo's desk. Mitch joined me in my ad manager's visitor's chair. "I don't know where to start."

"The beginning usually works for me. You know—who, what, when, why, and how."

Mitch's laid-back style soothed me. "I'll have to give you some background first," I said, and launched into the wreckage of Milo's marriage and divorce. "Until the past month or two, he hasn't had a lot of contact with his ex or even his kids, but today he got a call from Tricia about a serious domestic crisis involving his daughter, Tanya, and her fiancé. Milo had to go to Bellevue to help her sort it out. It turned out to be even worse than—" My cell rang. "I'd better take this. Sorry." I answered with my name, and was surprised to hear the agitated voice of Reba Cederberg on the other end of the line.

"Emma, I'm sorry to bother you," she said, "but I can't get hold of Vida, and I have to talk to her. Do you know where she is?"

"Yes, Reba," I said, hoping Mitch recognized the name. "She's having dinner at the ski lodge. It's the one occasion when she ignores a call. Vida feels strongly about observing phone etiquette in public. You should be able to reach her at home in about an hour. Is there anything I can do? You sound upset."

"Oh, I am," Reba said. "An hour? Oh, dear. Well . . . maybe I'll have to wait. Or . . . I don't know *what* to do. Maybe I should call the police."

I'd scribbled a note for Mitch to turn on KSKY. "Where's Andy?" I asked as my reporter got up and went over to his desk.

"He's here, but he doesn't know what to do, either. Just a minute."

Reba apparently muffled the receiver with her hand. I could hear voices but not what was being said at the other end of the line. Mitch had turned on KSKY, shrugging and giving me a questioning look as a band I didn't recognize played a song I didn't know. Somehow it seemed like a metaphor for what was going on with the call from Reba.

"It's my sister-in-law, Diane, Greg's mother," Reba said. "She just phoned from Palm Desert. Greg's in terrible trouble. We don't know how to help him out of this mess."

I motioned for Mitch to pick up his phone. "You mean about Greg skipping town after you posted bail?" I asked, raising my voice to keep Reba from hearing the sound of the second phone connecting to the line.

"Not just that," Reba replied. "It's such a mess. Diane's beside herself. She's afraid that Greg's on his way to Palm Desert, and that means he's jumping bail. That's bad enough, but what's more disturbing is he . . . well, he's done something very foolish. His intentions were well meant, I think. Still, it was unfair of him to involve innocent people."

I exchanged beleaguered looks with Mitch, who'd turned the radio down so he could hear the phone conversation. I tried to prod Reba. "Can you tell me what he did?"

She began to cry. My headache was coming back. Mitch was holding the phone away from his ear and leaning back in his chair so far that I thought he'd tip over. I could hear a phone ringing somewhere, but it wasn't in the newsroom. The front office? My cubbyhole? The back shop? The ringing stopped. Reba's sobs had grown fainter. I heard Andy's voice in the background. The ringing must have been another phone at the Cederberg house.

"What's happening?" I said softly to Mitch.

He'd straightened up in the chair. "Maybe they forgot to disconnect the call to you."

We both sat in silence for at least a minute. I could still hear Andy's voice, though his words weren't audible. Suddenly a high-pitched howl assaulted my ear. I cringed; Mitch grimaced. It had to be Reba. But it was Andy who spoke into the phone. "Emma?" He'd raised his voice to be heard over Reba's fresh outburst of sobs. "Can we call you later? We have to go to the hospital."

Why not? I thought. *Everybody else is going there these days.* "You mean Reba's collapsed?"

"No," Andy said, his voice suddenly breaking. "JoAnne Petersen just died."

TWENTY

I THINK," MITCH SAID DRYLY, "YOU'D BETTER FILL ME IN ON the rest of the story while we go to the hospital."

"We won't have time," I said, trying to collect myself from the latest shock. "In fact, let's not go to the hospital. We've got some work to do here instead."

"In that case," Mitch said, "shall I make coffee?"

"I will. I don't know if Alison cleaned out the coffeemaker Friday."

Mitch had gotten to his feet. "I'll do it. You look tired, Emma. Bad night before what I assume was a bad day?"

"Both Vida and I've had a touch of flu," I said.

"It's that time of year," Mitch remarked, inspecting the coffeemaker. "Clean as a whistle. Too bad Alison can't stick around instead of Denise. Or is Ginny coming back Monday?"

"I don't even want to think about that mess right now," I said, letting Mitch perform the coffee duty. "I don't even remember where I left off. Can you turn that radio up a bit?"

"You got a thing for nostalgia?" he asked. "What about going back even further for some Motown Sound?"

"I'm waiting to see what Spence is up to," I said. "I'll tell you why."

Ten minutes later, I'd finished recounting not only Milo's saga, but Craig's fruitless attempt to convey something he felt was important about his new painting. Almost out of breath, I ended with JoAnne's apparently successful suicide. As ever, Mitch was a good listener, asking questions and making comments only when necessary, skills he'd honed during his career with the *Detroit Free Press*.

"Hmm," he murmured when I'd finished. "Let's see—two dead, two wounded—I'm counting Laurentis being back in the hospital—and a bail-jumping poacher with an unspeakable secret. Not bad for a weekend, Emma. Even in Detroit, I didn't usually get that much on my plate in less than twenty-four hours. That doesn't mean it didn't all happen—we just had a bigger staff. No wonder you look tired."

I admitted I'd probably left something out. "My head not only aches, it's spinning. And I keep waiting for the other shoe to drop with Spence breaking all this on the radio."

"I wonder why he hasn't." He glanced at the radio. "We missed the news recap at seven while we were listening to Reba go ballistic."

I'd lost track of time. "Damn. You're right. But if Spence broke the story about Milo and the Bellevue catastrophe, it would've taken more than the usual five-minute news segment that always includes sports, weather, and traffic conditions."

"What's holding Spence back, I wonder?"

I had omitted something, but that was intentional. I was not going to mention that the sheriff had sent Mr. Radio to the ER. For the first time, it occurred to me that maybe Spence had decided discretion was the better part of valor. He only had one nose. He probably didn't want the sheriff to go for his golden throat the next time.

"Checking sources, maybe," I said. "So what do we do besides wait for official confirmation from Doc Dewey about JoAnne's death?"

"Call the hospital in Seattle to see how Dodge's daughter is doing?" Mitch suggested. "Did you hear how badly she was wounded?"

"No," I replied. "But it had to be more than a graze or they wouldn't have airlifted her to Harborview."

"Do you know her very well?"

I shook my head. "I never met her or any of his children. Or Tricia, for that matter, although you may recall that she was up here in October to discuss Tanya's wedding plans with Milo."

"Sounds like Dodge just saved himself big bucks on a wedding." Mitch cocked his head to one side. "You sure the sheriff didn't shoot Buster just to save ten, twenty grand?"

Ordinarily, I would've laughed, but all I could manage was a weak smile. "I don't think Milo was ever inside his ex-wife's house today. You're right. We should call Harborview. It's your story. You do it."

Mitch looked uncertain. "It is? No problem, but I didn't realize I'd gotten the assignment. Isn't it better if you handle this one? You know Dodge better than I do. I sense he's kind of touchy about personal stuff."

It occurred to me that Mitch might be one of the few people in town who didn't know that Milo and I had a long and often tumultuous history. "Well . . . let me think about it. But would you mind calling Harborview? I've already had my share of dealing with the medical profession the last few days."

"Sure." He pulled a Seattle phone book out from somewhere under his desk. "You want me to call the local hospital, too? That *is* my story."

"What?" My mind was eighty-five miles away, high on a hill overlooking Elliott Bay, wondering what Milo was doing and how he felt. "Oh—yes. I'm going to see if Vida's home yet."

I left Mitch to his calls and went into my cubbyhole to make my own. Vida didn't answer at her home, which meant she was probably still at the ski lodge. I tried to call Kip again, but he didn't pick up. Then, gritting my teeth, I dialed KSKY's number.

Bree answered. Her warm, chummy radio voice turned frosty when she heard my voice. "Spencer is busy. Can he call you back later if he has time?"

"No," I said, and hung up. I, too, could play the cut-off game.

Mitch was still on the phone when I went back into the newsroom. He held up his index finger to indicate the call was almost finished. "Thanks, Olga. I'm sorry about your loss. Take care."

"Death confirmed?" I said.

"Afraid so," Mitch replied. "That was JoAnne's sister, the nurse. She'd ridden to the hospital in the ambulance."

"Cousin," I said, crossing myself in a haphazard manner for JoAnne and the rest of her family.

"Oh." Mitch wasn't fazed, either by my correction or my prayerful gesture. "Lucky I knew they were related. All the Petersen offspring were at the hospital when their mother died. Maybe they'll try to get along better with two dead parents on their hands."

"A truce anyway," I remarked. "My God, that family's had more than its share of misery." But my priority wasn't what was left of the once-exalted Petersen dynasty. "Did you get through to anybody at Harborview? I got nowhere trying to talk to Fleetwood. That blond bitch he's got working for him is probably sleeping with him, too."

"Moonlighting?"

"In more ways than one," I said. "Well? What about Tanya?"

Mitch shook his head. "Zip. Unless I was family, they weren't giving out any information regarding Tanya Dodge's condition. I tried the local press angle, but it didn't cut any ice. I don't suppose you have any contacts with hospital personnel there."

"Not that I can think of." It had been thirty years since I'd lived in my hometown of Seattle. "They'd talk to Doc, I'll bet."

"There you go," Mitch said, leaning back in his chair again. "Meanwhile, since you can't get Kip, do you want me to post JoAnne's demise on the website? I've got the time of death, and I can tactfully phrase the overdose as accidental for now."

"Hold off," I said. "I'm going to the hospital."

"You think Doc's still there?"

"I don't know."

Mitch regarded me curiously. "You want me to tag along?"

"No. I want you to talk to the Cederbergs. In person." I picked up a blank piece of paper off Leo's desk and wrote down two sentences and a question. "Here's what I want you to ask them, and don't let either of them stonewall you. I don't care if you have to use bodily force. They may be the only ones in town who have the answer."

Mitch took his time absorbing what I'd written. "Well." He chuckled softly. "I'm not sure how you came to this conclusion or even exactly what it all means, but I can do this."

"You'd better. It's your story." I grabbed my purse, shrugged into my coat, and hurried out of the newsroom.

The rain had let up, just a drizzle that required the lowest setting on my windshield wipers. There was a parking place right across the street from the hospital's main entrance. Whoever was behind the front desk wasn't Jenny Bjornson. I didn't pause to find out who the dark-haired older woman was, but went straight to the elevator and up to the second floor.

Ruth Sharp was still on duty, but she'd lost her aura of taut composure. When I approached the desk, she gave a start. "Visiting hours are almost over," she said in an uncertain voice.

"Where are all the Petersens?" I asked.

Ruth licked her thin lips. "They're in the visitors' lounge with Mr. Driggers. You mustn't bother them."

"I won't," I said. "I'm here to see Mr. Laurentis. How is he?"

"I haven't made rounds yet," she responded. "We've had a hectic evening in the ER. I was called away for some time. So was the other nurse on duty."

"Right." I headed down the hall to Craig's room. He was asleep. At least I hoped he was asleep. A glance at the monitor showed me that he hadn't flatlined, but his pulse, heartbeat, and blood pressure were all dropping at what looked like an alarming rate. I pressed the call button, wishing I'd dragged Ruth Sharp along with me.

"Craig!" I called, shaking the mattress. "Craig! Can you hear me?"

There was no response except for the faint sound of shallow breathing. I ran out into the hall. "Nurse! Ruth!" I couldn't see the station from the end of the hall where Craig's room was located. Glancing into the room opposite his, I could make out only an inert form under a couple of blankets. No help there. I spotted a service cart a few feet away. Grabbing with all my might, I tilted it until it crashed on its side. Basins, towels, cleaning bottles, and God-only-knew-what-else clattered onto the floor.

Ruth Sharp appeared in the hallway at once, as if someone had shot a rocket up her prim rear end. "What on earth are you doing?" she demanded, stomping toward me. "Are you insane?"

"Craig's dying," I said. "Can't you read a monitor, you dumbshit?"

Ruth was shocked. "I'm calling the police." She started to

turn away, but I dove after her, yanking at the back of her uniform. "Do your job! *I'll* call the police!"

I don't know if it was my reminder of her vocation or the wild look in my eyes, but suddenly she seemed to realize I wasn't kidding. I followed her to Craig's room, but didn't go beyond the threshold. I saw her checking the patient and the monitor before picking up the phone, pressing a single button, and saying loudly, "Crash cart, Room 210!"

I knew that was my signal to get out of the way. Feeling guilty, I hastily began picking up the debris I'd dumped on the floor in my attempt to get Ruth's attention. The last thing I wanted was to be blamed for turning the hall into an obstacle course for the crash cart. I managed to remove almost everything when I heard voices from the other end of the hall. Stepping into a recessed supply nook to make way, I held my breath until two orderlies and a man I recognized as a physician's assistant came racing past with the cart. By the time they entered Craig's room, Elvis Sung entered the hallway from the stairwell. If he saw me, he gave no sign. Dr. Sung had a life to save.

And I had prayers to say. It dawned on me how little I'd prayed in the past chaotic twenty-four hours. I'd even fallen behind with my Nativity set—again. St. Mildred's was catty-corner from the hospital. Father Kelly would have said a five o'clock vigil Mass, but the church was probably closed and locked now. When the hospital had been built fifty years ago, Old Doc Dewey had wanted to put in a chapel. But Old Doc, like Young Doc, was an Episcopalian, and the Lutheran majority had been convinced that whatever he had in mind would be "too Romish." The Baptists and the Methodists felt that an Episcopal overseer would create something "too Anglican." And the Presbyterians didn't want to spend the money. Or so Vida had explained to me years ago. "It's a *medical* facility," she'd added, defending her own religion. "It wasn't prudent to spend money on frills. We already had plenty of churches."

Thus, I was resigned to standing in the stairwell to say my prayers. I was still there when I heard footsteps from lower down, apparently coming up from the first floor. The owner's tread was light and unrushed. I had a feeling I knew who was approaching the second floor in what I guessed was a stealthy manner. I moved closer to the door, out of sight until the new arrival reached the top step.

"Hi, Denise," I said. "Are you making rounds tonight?"

"Oh. Hi. I left something up here." She waited for me to move away from the door.

I stayed put. "What was it?" I asked, trying to sound casual.

There was a slight pause. "My bracelet. The clasp broke."

"What does it look like?"

"It's . . . gold." She licked her lips, which seemed to have gone dry. "Small links. It's really thin and hard to see."

"I know where it is," I said. "Come on, I'll show you."

She frowned. "Are you sure it's mine?"

I shrugged. "Who else would it belong to?"

"I can get it myself." She made a lunge for the door, trying to shove me out of the way.

I wouldn't budge. But I'd underestimated Denise's strength. She elbowed me so hard that I doubled over, gasping for breath. Then, with a frenzied look in her eyes, she came at me again, her arms wrapping my upper body in a painful grip. The battleground was small, only a few square feet between the door and the top of the steps. I tried to shake her off, but it was useless. Denise was younger, stronger, and desperate.

My only chance was to use my feet. Just as I felt she was about to send me plummeting down the stairwell, I managed to hook my right foot around her left ankle. I used the heel of my boot to gain enough leverage on the handrail to get her off-balance. Her grip slackened just enough for me to twist around and gain a momentary advantage. I caught my breath. Denise let out a growl like a cornered animal, clawing at my face and hair. I raised my left knee and caught her in the stomach. She gaped at me in shocked horror. Her hands dropped to her sides, her footing gave way, and she fell backwards, tumbling down the cement stairs to the first landing. Gasping for breath, I stared at her. She was lying on her back, eyes still open. But Denise wasn't seeing anything. At least nothing that was of this world.

I sank to the floor, leaned against the door, and threw up just before I passed out.

The first person I saw after I came to was Ruth Sharp. She wasn't the last person I wanted to see, but she was pretty low on the list. "I'm taking your vitals," she said. "Please do not ask me any questions other than about your condition."

"What is my condition?"

"Shh." Nurse Sharp was taking my pulse. She didn't look much better than I felt. Her uniform was no longer crisp or unblemished, and the little pleated cap was askew.

I realized I was on a cot by the nurses' station. I could see Dwight Gould and Doe Jamison in the hallway, talking to Dr. Sung. Ruth Sharp finished with my vitals. "Well?" I said.

"Your blood pressure is elevated, one-fifty over eighty-five, but your pulse and heart rates are satisfactory. I suggest that you lie here for a few minutes and try not to become agitated." She moved away from me, taking the portable monitor with her.

Doe hurried over to the cot. "What's happened around here? Denise Petersen is dead."

"Am I being charged?" I asked in all seriousness.

"I don't know. I mean . . ." Doe, who is usually the stoic type, looked rattled. "Maybe you should wait to say anything more."

"Fine. How's Craig Laurentis?"

"They don't know yet, but they sound hopeful." Doe lowered her voice. "Dr. Sung thinks somebody put the wrong medication into Laurentis's IV. That's malpractice, if I ever heard of it."

"It wasn't malpractice," I said. "It was attempted homicide."

Doe's eyes widened and her mouth fell open. "Are you serious?"

"Yes. It was Denise. She came back to make sure her second attempt to kill Craig was successful."

Doe still looked incredulous. "Denise is a semi-moron. Is she crazy, too? I mean, *was*. Damn, I don't know what I mean."

"That's okay, Doe," I assured her. "We all thought she didn't have a brain in her head. But she certainly was a cunning piece of work." I made an effort to sit up. "What's going on?"

"They've taken Denise down to the morgue," Doe replied. "Doc Dewey is going to do a postmortem. My God, Emma, Denise is down there with her mother! I can't get my head around this."

Out of the corner of my eye, I spotted Mitch Laskey, who was now talking to Dwight. Maybe Mitch had been there all along, but I hadn't seen him until I raised my head. "Hang on, Doe. Can you tell Mitch to come over here when he's finished with Dwight?"

"Sure." She started to turn around, but I stopped her.

"Any word on Tanya Dodge?"

Doe threw up her hands. "That's the other thing! We didn't

know anything about the Bellevue catastrophe until one of Dustin's relatives called from Seattle a couple of hours ago."

"But is Tanya going to be okay?"

"Dodge checked in with Dwight about fifteen minutes ago. Tanya's still in surgery. The bullet just missed her heart."

"Oh, God. Poor Milo."

"I know." Doe shook her head. "He doesn't need this."

"Nobody needs what's happened around here lately," I murmured.

"Right," Doe conceded, "but as much of a jerk as he can be sometimes as a boss, I like Dodge. I respect him, too. He's had kind of a crappy life, hasn't he?"

I sensed it wasn't a rhetorical question. Those dark Muckleshoot eyes of Doe's had a mystical quality, perhaps tribal wisdom passed from generation to generation. Her people had lived in the region for thousands of years, back to when the Cascades' last glaciers had receded. But I didn't know how to answer the question. Maybe Doe thought I was responsible for a share of Milo's misfortune. Or maybe she believed I was the answer. Fortunately, Mitch rescued me from saying anything at all.

"Damn!" he said cheerfully. "I missed my chance to be a superhero. I guess I'll never see the headline 'Reporter Saves Publisher from Crazed Killer.'"

Doe literally backed off, presumably to give Mitch and me some privacy.

"What did the Cederbergs tell you?" I asked him.

"Just what you thought they would," Mitch replied, half kneeling next to the cot. "Greg sent those letters. He'd figured out that Denise was a head case fairly early on in their marriage. But he got scared once he began to realize that maybe it was her, not her father, who'd murdered Linda. She'd say or do things that made him realize Larry had taken the rap for her. Sometimes she'd lash out at Greg for some minor criticism, and then rant about her aunt and how mean and critical and nasty she could be. Or else she'd talk about her father, how he'd always been so protective of her and never let anything bad happen to his little princess. Then she'd ask Greg questions like 'Would you take a bullet for me?' It tore the poor guy to pieces."

I was surprised by the depth of Mitch's knowledge. "Andy and Reba told you all this?"

Mitch shook his head. "No. Andy finally got hold of Greg on the phone to tell him about JoAnne. Greg was in Sultan, at his mother's house, trying to figure out what to do. He showed up at the Cederbergs' just as I was leaving. Andy and Reba had already told me about Greg sending the letters. He'd called them last night after he took off from the townhouse. I got to spend at least ten minutes with Greg at the Cederbergs' before I came over here. He'd originally planned to spend Thanksgiving in Palm Desert, where his mother's spending the winter, but when he dropped Doofus off with Denise last week, he suddenly felt that he had to act on his suspicions. That's why he screwed up about being at the pub watching football. Wrong Monday night. You can imagine the state his mind was in the past week or so, and probably even before that."

"What set him off when he saw Denise again?"

"He wasn't sure," Mitch replied. "The best he could come up with was that Denise acted too nice. He almost changed his mind about leaving the dog with her, then decided not to do anything that might set her off. He canceled the California trip and tried to figure out how to get Dodge to reopen the murder investigation. The letters were his answer."

"Why did he word them in such a threatening manner?" I asked.

"His reasoning was fairly sound," Mitch said. "Greg was

afraid to come right out with his suspicions, but he wanted to get the attention of someone in authority that he could trust. He had no way of knowing Larry was going to die. That really threw him, which is why there was a lapse between the last letter to Milo and the one to you. He wondered if somehow he'd hexed Larry."

I nodded. "That's understandable, if off-base."

Mitch nodded. "He shook off that idea pretty fast, though he didn't feel he'd made any impression on Dodge. After he heard Laurentis had been shot, Greg realized that he and Denise often walked the dog in that part of the woods. She seemed to have an affinity—not his word for it, but I knew what he meant—for the area. He wondered if Denise had taken Doofus there, but couldn't imagine why she'd shoot the recluse."

Doe had brought Mitch a visitor's chair from one of the patient rooms. "You look uncomfortable," she said. "As long as you're entertaining your boss, you might as well sit."

Mitch smiled in gratitude. "Thanks, Doe. Did I ever tell you you're my favorite deputy?"

Doe looked startled. "I thought everybody liked Dustin Fong best."

"Fong's great," Mitch said, "but you've got more soul. I know all about soul, being from Detroit. Run along before I start singing to you."

Doe giggled. I'd never heard her do that before. "You're funny," she said before moving away.

"You do have a way with you," I remarked.

"It's a sham," Mitch said diffidently. "Where did I leave off?"

"Did Greg know Denise had a gun?"

"It was his gun," Mitch said. "He brought it along on those walks because something creeped him out. It took him a while to understand that it wasn't the woods, it was his wife. When he finally split with Denise, he forgot to take the gun with him. All he wanted was out—and the dog."

"So what about the letters?"

"Greg felt he had to keep writing but switch to another recipient. You were it." Mitch shrugged. "In a weird way, his campaign worked. In fact, when he was arrested he thought it was for sending the letters. He thought the stamps had given him away."

"The stamps?"

Mitch grinned. "He used Cloudscape stamps. By coincidence, that was the name of his band. He bought a bunch of them when they first came out."

"Oh, good Lord!" I shook my aching head. "I never knew that."

"Who did, among us aging adults?"

"But guitar notwithstanding, Greg's not the poacher," I said, recalling what Marisa had told me when she went to get Doofus. "Denise remarked that Greg was so lame and how dumb it was to poach the maple trees. But Marisa never mentioned why Greg was with her. I'll bet Denise made that anonymous call accusing her ex of being the poacher."

Mitch considered my words. "Sounds right. Maybe she thought he knew too much about her. Putting him in jail would get him out of the way. At least she didn't shoot him."

"Incredible," I murmured, shaking my head. "A real sociopath. Does Greg know Denise is dead?"

"He didn't when I talked to him." Mitch turned somber. "I suppose he does now. Maybe that's the best ending for everybody."

"It stinks," I said. "JoAnne must've been aware of the truth. If she knew all along, she and Larry probably realized Denise wouldn't last long in prison, and institutionalizing her was an ugly scenario, too. The Laurentis shooting must've scared the hell out of JoAnne. I'm guessing that's why she came to Alpine sooner than she'd planned. It may be the real reason she didn't want to stay with Denise. No wonder JoAnne looked so haggard when I ran into her the other day. She's lived her own lie for ten years."

"If she knew all along, her life must've been as much of a prison as Larry's."

I paused. "It'd explain why she was so anxious to move away from here. It could also be the reason she didn't visit Larry. JoAnne probably couldn't bear to see her husband as a martyr. Or maybe he didn't want to put her through that torture."

Mitch looked off into space. "Guilt." He paused for a moment. "I know all about Jewish guilt," he finally said wryly, looking at me again, "but I suppose Lutherans can feel as guilty as anybody else. The Petersens must have wondered how they'd created a monster in Denise."

"The family's had a history of sibling rivalry," I said, thinking of Marv and Elmer as well as their two older sisters, who had cut their ties to Alpine long ago. "JoAnne went along with Larry's lie. Even if she didn't see him, she knew he was still there. Maybe she didn't want to live in a world without him."

"My God," Mitch said softly. "The things people do for and to each other." He shook his head. "So we've still got a poacher on the loose. And no office manager *pro tem*."

"We can worry about all that on Monday," I said. "I'm tapped."

A familiar voice reached my ears: "Well now, Ruthie," Vida said from somewhere behind Mitch, "what kind of ward are you running around here? Didn't I always say you spent too much time reading charts and not enough time reading people? You ought to be ashamed of yourself! Look at my poor Emma! You're lucky she's not dead, too. If she were, I'd have had your head on a silver platter, and it wouldn't be wearing that funny little cupcake of a cap you have on now!"

TWENTY-ONE

THE ENORMITY OF WHAT I'D DONE TO DENISE DIDN'T STRIKE me until I was home an hour later. Vida had made tea. Buck had built a fire. I was back on the sofa. All of a sudden I burst into tears.

"Whatever is wrong?" Vida asked, exchanging concerned glances with Buck.

"I killed somebody!" I wailed. "I can't believe I did such a horrible thing."

"Oh, for heaven's sake!" Vida exclaimed. "It was self-defense. Would you rather be lying in the morgue with JoAnne Petersen? Besides, Doc told Dwight it was an accidental death. Denise could have fallen down those stairs ten times and not suffered more than a bruise."

Buck nodded. "Seen it happen many times in the military. Some poor devil takes three, four bullets, recovers, and then gets run over by a messenger on a motorbike. When your name gets called, you go. In any case, your hand-to-hand fighting was combat. I can't tell you how much of that I've seen, even in the air force. Sometimes the fight was between men on the same side."

"Now, Buck," Vida said, patting his broad shoulder, "don't start in on your war stories. Poor Emma's had enough of that."

"Okay, Munkie-Runkie. I'll retire to that easy chair."

I didn't object. Somehow it didn't seem like sacrilege for Buck to take temporary residence there. He was almost as tall as Milo and even broader, at least through the midsection. Buck and Vida made a very imposing couple. "Munkie-Runkie" had not only stopped my tears, but it also made me wonder what rhyming pet name she had for Buck.

Vida had pulled one of my dining table chairs over to the sofa. "You must fill me in on how you concluded that Denise killed Linda. I feel very left out."

That, of course, was unthinkable for Vida. "I only put it all together tonight," I said. "The keys to figuring it out were both subtle and not so subtle. From the get-go, I never believed the poacher was the shooter. Milo had to consider they might be connected, if only because of the timing, but that's how he works a case. Everything has to be considered to see if it fits— and it didn't."

"Sound," Buck murmured. "Dodge served in Nam, right?"

Vida nodded, giving the colonel a fond smile. "Let Emma finish."

I picked up where I left off. "Looking back at my first visit with Craig in the hospital, I realized he didn't link the two incidents, either. So what was the motive for the attempt on Craig's life? He'd also said something I should've caught when I heard it, but didn't until Donna was talking about how artists work. It was the same phrase—'at that time.' Donna's remark wasn't important, but the phrasing was. Craig had been referring to the shooting when he said he hadn't seen anyone 'at that time.' It dawned on me that there must've been another time when he *had* seen someone. I finally realized that the answer was in the painting. There were also bare branches in the scene. They had to be maples because Wes Amundson had mentioned there were no other deciduous trees at the poaching site. Craig might not have seen anyone or recalled exactly how far he'd dragged himself after he was shot, but it wasn't far from those maples."

Vida shook herself. "My, my! That was quite clever of you."

"Devil's in the details," Buck said.

"True," I agreed. "But neither Donna nor I could figure out what it meant. Then—and I reminded Mitch of this when he walked me to my car after we left the hospital—that he'd given me part of the answer while we were talking about Bree Kendall working for Spencer Fleetwood."

"What?" Vida shrieked. "Bree is on the radio?"

"Never mind—we can talk about that later," I said. "I referred to Bree as—excuse my language—a 'blond bitch.' Then Mitch made a crack about her moonlighting. Craig's new painting has two muted golden spots on the ground that might be highlighted by an unseen moon. I should've paid more attention to the title, *Forest Watch*. In fact, he'd originally called it something else, and one of the words was 'leg' or 'log.'"

"The log!" Vida exclaimed before turning to Buck. "That's where poor Roger found her body. Both Linda and Denise were blondes."

"Exactly," I said. "Craig repeated the word 'saw,' but I thought he was referring to the poachers sawing down the maples—even though he insisted that wasn't what he meant. It was what he actually *saw* when Denise hid her aunt's body in the forest. She must've seen him as well, but as a local, Denise assumed—as everybody else did back then—that the man known as Old Nick was much older and probably crazy. It was barely a couple of years ago that we found out his name, his age, and that he might be a recluse, but he was also a talented artist. Even if Denise had wanted to silence Craig, she didn't know where to find him—until the night he came the same way to deliver the new painting to Donna Wickstrom. I suppose she'd seen him while she was walking Doofus. If she didn't have the gun with her then, it wouldn't take her long to go back to the townhouse and get it. All she had to do was lie in wait for Craig to go back the way he'd come—and shoot him."

Vida nodded. "So cold-blooded. I wonder if she enjoyed visiting the site where she'd put Linda's body. A ghastly thought, but perhaps she savored her ultimate triumph over her more accomplished aunt."

I agreed. "Denise saw herself as a cipher in the family. I remember her alluding to that at the time of the murder. Denise felt like an outsider, despite Larry's apparent affection for her. I can't begin to figure how a twisted mind like Denise's would respond to what she considered being an isolated member of the revered Petersen dynasty. I finally remembered her allusion to that after Linda was killed. She'd told me when she was about to quit working at the bank."

Buck shifted his weight in the easy chair. "If this Craig hermit saw what was going on, why didn't he call the police?"

I smiled at Buck. "Recluses don't always make credible witnesses. Nor do they want any involvement with society, let alone authority figures. Craig's opinion of human nature is not only low but detached."

Vida nodded. "Possibly paranoid, too. He may have been afraid of becoming the prime suspect. When the Rafferty house was set on fire, there was talk that Old Nick—as he was known then—had done it."

"Hmm," Buck murmured. "I wonder if he was in Nam. Way too many of those vets never did get their heads screwed back on straight when they finished their tours. Lots of dropouts." He shook his head. "Darned shame. Why did Denise take a gun with her? She had a dog."

"It wasn't her dog," I replied. "It belonged to her ex, and according to Denise, Doofus—the dog—was very timid. She may've always carried a gun when she went alone into the woods."

Buck snorted. "I hope she had a concealed-weapon permit. Irresponsible gun owners make the rest of us look bad."

"Really, Buckums," Vida said, "that's the least of the trouble Denise has caused."

I tried not to smile. Vida's pet name could have been a lot worse. She looked at me again. "I can't get over Denise's ability to carry out such a plan in the first place. You recall that Larry supposedly set up Linda's ex-husband, Howard Lindahl, as the prime suspect. Are you telling us that Denise was that ingenious?"

"Yes, strange as it may seem. The break-in to plant phony evidence implicating Howard was staged by her. That's another reason why I figure Larry refused to testify on his own behalf at the trial. He couldn't answer many of the questions he'd be asked about the murder, the stashing of the body, and the break-in. The jury might have begun to wonder if he really was innocent."

"But," Vida objected, "a man claiming to be a potential customer called Howard to get him out of the house the night of the murder."

I cocked my head at Vida. "You think Denise couldn't sweet-talk some guy into doing that for her as a harmless practical joke?"

"Well . . ." She frowned. "Goodness. That happened while Rick was dating Denise. Ginny was in the dumps. In fact," she went on, "Denise's alibi for the night of the murder was that she and Rick went to a movie."

"I think we could ask Rick about that," I said. "I'll bet they went to the late show. As for Rick making the phone calls, it could have been Greg or even somebody else. The Rick and Denise thing was short-lived, as you may recall."

Vida was quiet for a moment or two. "Denise must've hated Linda. Been jealous, too. Not that Denise could ever have believed she'd be in line to run the bank."

"She might have," I said. "If Larry had taken his father's place, then in some weird way, maybe Denise thought she'd follow in her father's footsteps. But if Linda was the heir apparent, there was Denise looking at Alison Lindahl as a future rival. As I mentioned, Denise had already talked about quitting the bank. Maybe she was hedging her bets." A sudden thought occurred to me. "Oh, my God! I wonder if Denise was pregnant." The possibility appalled me.

Vida looked stunned. "You mean about her being sick before she left work Thursday?"

"Yes. Doc's autopsy will . . ." I stared at Vida. "No. There was a different reason. Denise got sick because she read the paper Thursday."

Vida stared right back. "What are you talking about?"

"Denise didn't know Craig was still alive until she read about it at the end of the workday. She mentioned she hardly ever looked at the paper. I told her she should start ASAP to stay informed about the town's happenings in order to deal with subscribers. When Kip came to work Friday, he had to clean the front office because Denise left in a rush after throwing up. A copy of this week's *Advocate* was under her chair. She hadn't known until then that the man she'd shot had survived. The revelation literally made her sick. Craig was still a threat."

Vida nodded. "A terrible shock to her, I'm sure. Denise lived in a world of her own. And a very twisted world it was. Even if she'd heard any of us talk about Craig Laurentis or an artist, she wouldn't realize who he was and make the connection. In fact, she was so wrapped up in herself that she was the type who probably didn't bother to listen in on other people's conversations. I find that very hard to understand."

"Takes all kinds," Buck remarked, looking not at Vida but at the ceiling.

"Indeed," Vida said, before changing the subject. "I had a chance to speak with Olga Bergstrom at the hospital. Debra Barton had called JoAnne right after my program was over. Naturally, JoAnne was alarmed by what Larry had told Cole on that last prison visit. When I heard JoAnne had decided to come to Alpine sooner than expected, I considered something like that. Of course Olga feels terribly guilty for having those sleeping pills on hand, especially when she began to realize that JoAnne's emotional state was precarious."

"Did JoAnne tell her any specifics?"

Vida shook her head. "But Olga's smart. She'd always sensed there was something wrong about Larry's conviction, but couldn't figure out what it might be. She'd even speculated that somehow JoAnne had been involved in Linda's murder."

"But not Denise?"

"No. Like everyone else, she dismissed Denise as too brainless to do such a thing." Vida sighed. "No one should ever assume anything about other people."

"Brains are one thing," Buck remarked. "Scheming, cunning, conniving—they come from some dark place in the mind. I've seen plenty of that in the military with the enemy. And," he added more quietly, "sometimes with our own."

"Oh, yes," Vida agreed. "Even in Alpine we've had some very odd ducks." She stood up, studying me for a long moment. "Will you be all right if we leave you? Buck has to drive back to Startup."

I assured her I'd be fine. Vida dithered a bit, but Buck finally managed to haul her away. I saw them to the door, trying to act as normal as possible despite the pain I felt after the battle with Denise.

Denise. I still couldn't fathom the depths and intricacies of that poor creature's warped mind. Evil isn't an easy concept to understand, but it exists. I sat back down on the sofa. It was going on eleven. Now that I was alone, the events of the past twenty-four hours came crashing down on me like a sudden spring avalanche. It was too late to call Ben. I couldn't contact Adam except by e-mail, because of the often faulty phone connection between Alpine and St. Mary's Igloo. And Milo was in his own private hell at Harborview Hospital.

Mitch? He was still dealing with the Petersen saga, having returned to the hospital to await Doc Dewey's postmortem results. Leo? I'd have to unload the whole story on him, and I didn't have the strength to do that. Kip? He'd never called back. Maybe he and his wife, Chili, had gone out for the evening. My production manager had earned a night off, especially on a Saturday.

Then there was Spencer Fleetwood. I no longer cared how or if he broke the story. Spence wasn't a bad person. He was a professional who just happened to be in the same business. On top of that, he was about as screwed up in his own way as I was. He'd shown me kindness even as he'd milked every bit of information he could get out of me. "Payback," he'd called his offer of help. I believed him at the time. I still did. After his own tragedy, I'd made that story the centerpiece of the *Advocate*'s front page for two weeks. Now we were even.

It was nearing midnight when I decided I had to get off the sofa and go to bed. I staggered around, putting the mugs Vida had used for tea in the dishwasher and turning off the kitchen light. I went back into the living room to make sure the fire Buck had started was almost out. Looking between the drapes to check on the weather, I realized that the rain seemed to have stopped, but the wind was up, making the trees and shrubs dance in the moonless night.

I was about to close the drapes when I saw headlights turning in to my driveway. Mitch, probably, stopping by to tell me what he'd put on our website. Going to the front door, I cursed myself for not checking my computer earlier. I'd flunked my vocation as badly as Ruth Sharp had flunked hers.

I opened the door before the bell rang. Milo swept me up in his arms as he crossed the threshold.

"Emma." He carried me inside, kicked the door closed behind him, and stood still, holding me tight and not saying anything at all. I was the one to break the silence.

"Tanya?" I asked hoarsely.

"She'll be okay."

"And you?"

He didn't answer. He didn't have to. I already knew.